"It's time to get out your calendar and clear your schedule. Lynette Eason's *Double Take* is sure to cause you to give a second glance at any other commitments until this riveting new story is 100 percent complete. I thoroughly enjoyed the characters, the banter, and the suspense. All the suspense. I bit off every fingernail in hopes that it would help ease the intensity (it didn't), and that is just the way I like it. If you're holding this novel and debating whether it should be your next read, debate no more. Just go. Find a chair. Sit down. Read. It's that simple."

Jaime Jo Wright, ECPA bestselling author of
The Vanishing at Castle Moreau

"Oh. My. Word. Once again Lynette Eason has blown me away with her skills. *Double Take* is phenomenal and had my heart racing from the moment I started reading. I was immediately drenched in Lainie's world by Eason's powerful writing, but I did not want to be in Lainie's shoes! Brilliant plot. Incredible story. Proof again of Lynette Eason's prowess that keeps her at the top!"

Kimberley Woodhouse, bestselling and award-winning author of
26 Below, *The Heart's Choice*, and *A Mark of Grace*

"This book should come with a warning: do not start unless you've got plenty of time to finish! *Double Take* kept me up turning pages and wondering what would happen next. It's a heart-stopping ride from start to finish."

Kathleen Y'Barbo, *Publishers Weekly* bestselling author of *The Black Midnight*, *Dog Days of Summer*, and The Bayou Nouvelle series

"*Double Take* is, without a doubt, the best suspense book I've read in a very long time. The pacing kept me guessing—not to mention a little frustrated—so I couldn't put it down. And the romance . . . perfect. Excellent book!"

Tracey Bateman, Jesus lover, wife, mom, Bubbi, author

"In this psychological thriller, Lainie and her former crush James are determined to get to the truth. In the process, they have to fight to stay alive. This book is a tightly written corkscrew of a race against a twisted mind that is determined to take Lainie on a twisty ride that ends in one destination: her death. Readers who love romantic suspense will love every page of Lynette's latest novel."

Cara Putman, award-winning author of
Lethal Intent and *Flight Risk*

Praise for the Extreme Measures Series

"A pulse-pounding finale to Eason's Extreme Measures series."

Publishers Weekly on *Countdown*

"Eason is a master of edge-of-your-seat inspirational romantic thrillers, combining light faith elements with twisty plots that keep readers guessing."

Booklist starred review of *Critical Threat*

"*Crossfire* is a model for the romantic suspense genre."

Life Is Story on *Crossfire*

"This book is an edge-of-your-seat suspense thriller from start to finish. With great character development and enough excitement to keep readers hooked, this novel is sure to keep patrons talking for months to come."

Library Journal on *Life Flight*

DOUBLE
TAKE

LAKE CITY HEROES • 1

DOUBLE TAKE

LYNETTE EASON

Revell

a division of Baker Publishing Group
Grand Rapids, Michigan

© 2024 by Lynette Eason

Published by Revell
a division of Baker Publishing Group
Grand Rapids, Michigan
www.revellbooks.com

Printed in the United States of America

Library of Congress Cataloging-in-Publication Data
Names: Eason, Lynette, author.
Title: Double take / Lynette Eason.
Description: Grand Rapids, Michigan : Revell, a division of Baker Publishing
     Group, 2024. | Series: Lake City heroes ; 1
Identifiers: LCCN 2023022655 | ISBN 9780800741198 (paperback) | ISBN
     9780800745646 (casebound) | ISBN 9781493444786 (ebook)
Subjects: LCGFT: Christian fiction. | Thrillers (Fiction) | Novels.
Classification: LCC PS3605.A79 D68 2024 | DDC 813/.6—dc23/eng/20230515
LC record available at https://lccn.loc.gov/2023022655

Emojis are from the open-source library OpenMoji (https://openmoji.org/) under the Creative Commons license CC BY-SA 4.0 (https://creativecommons.org/licenses/by-sa/4.0/legalcode)

Baker Publishing Group publications use paper produced from sustainable forestry practices and post-consumer waste whenever possible.

24 25 26 27 28 29 30   7 6 5 4 3 2 1

Dedicated to Jesus. Because.

PROLOGUE

The click next to her ear jerked her out of a deep sleep to roll into a sitting position, a scream on her lips, her eyes on the man with the gun standing next to her. "Adam? What are you doing?"

The man who'd professed to love her only hours before was lining the barrel up for his shot. She dove away from him just as he said, "Cheers, love," in his fake British accent. The bullet meant for her head knocked her backward. She threw herself from the bed to the floor, her survival instincts the only thing moving her.

Vaguely, she wondered why she felt no pain, even as the warmth from the wound in her shoulder soaked her sleep T-shirt.

Slow, measured footsteps worked to close the distance between them as he rounded the bed. "I was trying to make this painless, Lainie," he said. "If you'd just drunk your milk like you usually do, we wouldn't be having this conversation."

She panted, nausea churning, her system in shock. She rolled under the platform bed just as the gun cracked again, chipping out a gash of wood in her newly polished hardwood floor.

"The police will find me, you know," he said, as though he had all the time in the world. "Ask questions. I guess I'll just have to tell them all about the stalker you had. Unfortunately, I won't be able to

9

identify him, but he must have followed you home from work and broke in after you fell asleep."

She couldn't wrap her mind around the fact that he was explaining her death while trying to kill her. Panic, terror, absolute horror—and the desperate desire to live—washed over her in waves.

Move or you're dead.

The fleeting thought spurred her to push aside the storage boxes and aim herself to come out at the foot of the bed, which was right across from the door.

"Where do you think you can go, Lainie?"

Adam's cruel voice taunted her and she expected another bullet to hit her any second. But he was still on the other side of the bed. Thinking she would cower and wait for him to come get her?

Probably.

She scooted out from under the bed and scrambled to her feet. The next bullet hit the doorframe, but she made it out of the room.

"Where do you think you can run that I won't catch you? You want to break up with me? Fine. I can help you with that."

The taunting tone had morphed into a low, throbbing rage that vibrated with each word he spat. She raced toward the front door but heard him closing in behind her. She'd never get the door open in time.

Lainie cut a sharp right into the den and his footsteps followed her. More quickly this time. He was done playing.

Another bullet hit the mantel next to her left ear. With her good hand, she grabbed the poker from the wrought iron tool set and flung it toward him.

The heavy piece caught him in the side of his head. Adam gave a sharp cry and the fifth bullet careened into the ceiling. Lainie ignored the suddenly noticeable fiery pain in her shoulder and launched herself at him, barreling into him while he was already off balance. They both went to the floor, the fire in her shoulder now licking across her chest and down her back. The gun fell from his hand and skittered toward her.

"You're dead, Lainie!"

He rolled toward the weapon, and she grabbed it with a low scream and scrambled backward. He snagged her foot and gave it a hard yank, landing her on her back with a painful thud. Air whooshed from her lungs and dark spots danced in her vision. But she could still see clear enough to note that his cold blue eyes spoke death.

She lifted the weapon and aimed it. "Stop, Adam! Stop now, or I'll shoot you!"

He laughed, those chilly ice-chipped eyes freezing over. "You won't shoot. You don't have the guts." He gave her another tug, his expression promising she had but seconds to live.

The twitch of her finger on the trigger sent the bullet into the base of his throat.

ONE

Lainie Jackson glanced at the clock on the dash and pressed the gas a little harder even though the rain came down in sheets. Her tires spun on the wet road, and she gasped, heart pounding until they clutched the asphalt once more. She lifted her foot. Slow might be the best option after all.

The warm September morning that had been bright and sunny an hour ago was now dark and—she hated to admit it—a little creepy. The gray and black clouds had rolled in and then opened up to release their downpour. And it was still raining. Living in Lake City, North Carolina, brought a variety of weather. Sometimes all in one day. North of Asheville, Lake City had more mountains and cooler weather year-round. Lainie sometimes thought about moving to a warmer location, but she'd grown up in Lake City and had a community of friends she found impossible to leave.

In spite of a lot of bad memories.

Shivering, she flipped the air-conditioning to heat and turned onto the back road that would take her to Señor G's, her favorite local café slash general store slash gas station. It took a little bit of navigating on the mountain roads, but she'd been driving it once, sometimes twice, a week for a year now, so she could basically do it with her eyes shut.

Figuring that would be a bad idea, she wrapped her fingers around the wheel and squinted into the onslaught. "Lord, this was dumb," she whispered. "I should have just gone on to work instead." But this was her routine and she liked routine in certain areas of her life.

Besides, she wanted to check on Julian Gonzales and make sure he was taking his insulin. She finally rounded the curve and pulled into the parking lot, under the protection of the gas station's metal roof.

The front door opened and Mr. Gonzales appeared with an umbrella over his head. He walked toward her. "I figured you would show up in this mess." His near-perfect English sounded musical when combined with his Hispanic accent.

Lainie ducked under and they hurried back to the café entrance. "It's a habit now, Señor G. You know I can't get through my week without my special cup of java from you."

She opened the door and stepped inside, spied her cup on the counter, and made a beeline for it. "You know, if it wasn't so far out of my way on the way to work, I'd come here every day. I think you need to open a location by the hospital."

"You say this every time. And what do I tell you?"

"This was your papa's store and you must carry on the family tradition. I get that, but expanding would be good for you."

"I cannot be in two places at the same time."

"That's why you hire people."

He tsked and shook his head. "You know I pride myself on my personal touch." He waved a finger at her cup. "And I don't give away my recipes."

"*My* recipes, el viejito." Maria Gonzales came from the back to give Lainie a tight squeeze. "Hello, cariña. So good to see you, as always."

"You too, Mama Maria." She turned to Señor G. "What was your blood sugar this morning?"

He shrugged. "Eh."

"Señor G . . ." She raised a brow at him.

"Ah, there's the tone." He sighed. "A little high, but I will work on it."

"How high?"

"Under three hundred."

"Julian . . ."

"Ack"—he pressed his hand to his chest in mock horror—"she brought out the first name."

Lainie sighed and pursed her lips. "This has been going on for a while now, Señor G. I want to add another medication to get that number down."

Lainie saw the concerned glance his wife sent him. She laid a hand on his and lowered her voice. "Mama Maria needs you to be around for a long time. You simply must take care of yourself."

He swallowed, shot a look at his wife, then gave Lainie a look of resignation and a faint nod. "I know, niña, but it's not easy. My body does not like to cooperate anymore."

"I understand." She pulled out her phone and logged into his account at the office of his primary physician. Since it was in the same network as the hospital, she had access as a physician's assistant. She voiced the instruction into the chart, fixed a few typos, and hit send. "There. The meds will be waiting on you to pick up. They're not expensive and I think they'll help. Try them for a week and I'll check on you when I come back."

Mama Maria hugged her. "You are too good to us."

Lainie lifted her cup in a salute. "It's mutual." She spent the next fifteen minutes chatting, catching up on their proud-grandparent news and pictures, then after another exchange of hugs and promises to see them next week, if not before, she hurried to the door, grateful to see the rain had lessened. Before Señor G could offer to walk her out with the umbrella, she said her goodbyes, pulled up the hood of her raincoat, and bolted to her car.

With her coffee in the cupholder, Lainie buckled her seat belt, then wheeled out of the parking lot and onto the road that would take her back down the mountain. She loved the Gonzales family.

They were the kind of parents she wished she'd been born to. Not that she didn't love hers, but growing up with Stan and Louisa Jackson had been hard. To put it mildly. With her father and his "we must prep for the end of the world" mentality and her mother's hoarding tendencies, not to mention the sibling issues, her childhood had been full of uncertainty, fear, and drama.

Which was probably part of the reason she liked her routine.

She sighed, took another sip of the coffee that tasted like none other, and rounded the next curve only to hydroplane.

A gasp slipped from her lips, and she barely refrained from slamming on the brakes. She went with the slide that took her much too close to the edge of the road, but with some careful maneuvering, she stayed on it. The tree-lined two-lane road was slick with standing water, and she slowed even more, creeping along, looking for a place to pull over so she could collect herself and take a look at the tires. How had they lost tread already? They were basically brand new.

Cars passed her from the opposite direction, splashing even more water on her windshield.

A truck approached from behind, lights on and going too fast. Lainie sped up a fraction. On this stretch of road, there was no place for her to safely stop, so she crept along.

The truck behind her revved, came closer, then shot into the oncoming lane, making his intent to pass her clear. She took her foot off the gas. "Fine," she muttered. "Go around me, you lunatic." Which he did—until his back end clipped the left side of her vehicle, sending the wheel spinning under her hands. A scream escaped and her little Subaru hatchback went over the side of the mountain. She bounced once, twice, then crashed sideways into two trees.

The seat belt held her in place. Her coffee cup lay against the passenger window, leaking precious liquid over the glass.

Panting, stunned, heart pounding in a way she'd only felt once before in her life, she sat still for a moment, taking stock.

She was alive. And while she might have a bruise from the seat belt and some sore muscles from the jerking, she didn't think she was seriously hurt. She rotated her neck and nothing felt off. "Thank you, Lord."

But someone had just run her off the road and kept going.

With shaking fingers, she activated her Bluetooth and ordered it to call 911.

"911. What's your emergency?"

Lainie gave the dispatcher the location. "I'm off the road, though, so they won't be able to see me. I'm down the hill and against two trees."

"Can you get out of the vehicle?"

"I'm not sure. I'm not completely sideways, but the seat belt's the only thing holding me in the seat." She glanced out the coffee-covered window. "I'm afraid to do anything that would shift my car. It's a long way down if the car moves."

"Then stay put. I've got people on the way and looking for you. The nearest fire truck is only about a minute from that road, coming from another call. Is there any way you can signal them?"

"Um . . . yeah. I can use my phone's flashlight."

"Do it. They're heading up the mountain now."

Lainie tilted her gaze up and saw a man standing on the edge of the road, looking down at her. She sucked in a hard breath and rolled down her window to get a better look, ignoring the light drizzle that started to plaster her hair to her head. "Adam?" He jerked out of sight. "Adam!" No, it couldn't be. "Hey! Who are you!"

Bracing herself, she reached over into the glove box and removed her gun. She almost thought better of it. She was freezing. Shaking. Slightly nauseous.

Shock.

She looked up again and could see the back of his truck, almost make out the license plate. Then he was back, peering over the edge at her. For several seconds, they stared at each other. He swung a leg over like he planned to try and climb down to her. To help her? Or—

Approaching sirens stilled him. Then he scrambled back up and disappeared, the roar of his engine fading.

It isn't him. It isn't.

Maybe not, but *someone* who looked like her dead fiancé had just run her off the road.

HE RAKED A HAND over his head, then gripped the steering wheel until his knuckles turned white. Almost. So close. He hadn't thought she could survive falling off the side of the mountain, but . . . she had. And he'd looked over to see and found her terrified gaze locked on his.

Her face had gone slack, her lips formed into the *O* shape of shocked recognition.

Oh, she'd recognized him all right. No doubt about it. What would she do now? Tell everyone? The police? Would they be looking for him?

Sweat broke out across his forehead and he pulled in a deep breath. No matter. They might look for him, but they'd never find him. If they even bothered. He wasn't worried about the police, but frustration pounded through him.

Lainie wasn't dead. His plan had failed. All those months of planning, going back and forth, fleshing out one idea only to discard it. Then he'd settled on a foolproof way to get what he wanted and it had failed.

Failed!

Now it was time to regroup, refigure, and recommit to the undertaking. Albeit a new plan, but maybe it wouldn't take too much restructuring to get to the same outcome.

Unfortunately, he'd lost the advantage of a surprise attack, but the more he thought about it, the more he smiled. She'd be looking for him. Okay. Fine. He'd have to work with that. He pressed his palm against his forehead. It would take some scrambling and include working through a lot of little details in a short amount of time, but he could come up with a new plan.

A new plan that would keep her looking in the wrong direction. One that would bring her nightmares, filling her with terror.

And then he'd turn her nightmares into reality.

TWO WEEKS LATER

"Shots fired. 112 Park Lane. All units respond. Officer requests backup."

Detective James Cross tossed his half-eaten breakfast sandwich in the trash and bolted for his Jeep. His partner, Cole Garrison, was two steps behind him.

James threw himself behind the wheel, and Cole slammed the passenger door shut with his right hand while his left snagged the radio. He reported their location. "Three minutes out."

Approximately three minutes later, they pulled to a stop in the Brookfield neighborhood. It was crammed full of new middle-class homes with small yards and wooden fences. James had no trouble locating the home responsible for the call. Uniformed officers had already swarmed the area, evacuating the neighbors and keeping the lookie-loos at a distance.

Three pops sounded. Neighbors screamed. Officers ducked out of reflex. "Answer your phone, Gerald. You're just going to make the situation worse." James recognized Sergeant Luis Sanchez hunched behind a cruiser, megaphone to his mouth.

"This don't concern you!" Gerald's scream came from the front door that was ajar. A small hand wrapped around its edge said he was using one of his kids as a shield. No officer or SWAT member was going to pull the trigger with that situation. "Now get out of here before I start putting bullets in people instead of the wall!"

James and Cole hurried to the officer in charge. "Luis," Cole said, "I assume the hostage negotiator is on the way."

"Ten minutes out."

"Want me to talk to him?" James asked.

Formerly with the Army's Criminal Investigation Division, James had negotiation training that went beyond the average detective's.

"You're welcome to try."

"Tell me what you know. Quick."

"Gerald Henson, forty years old, married, three kids, two of which are in the house, ages nine, five, and two. The oldest one, Trey, got on the school bus about thirty minutes before the call. Apparently, the wife, Patricia, burned Gerald's toast and he hit her. The five-year-old, Katy, called 911, said her daddy was being mean to her mommy, that he got his gun and she and her sister were scared. The two-year-old's name is Gretchen. And here we are."

James took the megaphone and lifted it to his lips. "Mr. Henson? This is Detective James Cross. Is there anything we can do to end this peacefully?"

"Get out of here. This is family business. Nothing for the cops to be sticking their noses in. Everybody always got to know what's going on with me and I'm about sick of it. Stupid wife, stupid cops, stupid family."

"Yes sir, I understand your frustration with all of the attention. Are you mad at the children?"

"What? The kids? No, it's this stupid woman who's always costing me money. She wanted this swanky new house that costs me more money than we have. She needs cooking lessons—which would cost me money, right? Smoked up the whole house with burning breakfast. That was the last of the bread and I don't have the time or the money to get more, and now me and my kids got to be hungry." He muttered a few derogatory comments about his wife that James couldn't hear the whole of, but he caught enough. "And I'm not stupid. I'm the only one around here who's not."

"No sir, I don't think you're stupid at all."

"I know how this ends. And let me just say, it's not with me in cuffs."

He meant to kill his family and himself by the end, and James had no way of knowing when the guy would decide it was the end.

"Hey, Gerald," James said, "what if I send someone to get a loaf of bread so that you can feed your kids? I can tell you love them. I know you don't want them to be hungry."

The man stayed quiet. Was he thinking about the offer? James could only pray he'd say yes. At least then there was hope for a little more time to get the hostages out.

"Can you do better than a loaf of bread?"

"Sure can," James said without hesitation. "What do you want?"

"Li'l Bit here likes them sausage biscuits from the diner down the road."

"Weavers' Café?"

"Yeah."

"Sure, we can get her one of those. What about her sister?"

"Katy-bug likes scrambled eggs and grits."

He was referring to the kids by their nicknames. That was good. And he didn't seem to be upset that the five-year-old had been the one to make the call that set the current situation in progress. Or maybe he didn't know. "And you and your wife?"

"Wife don't get nothing. She lost her chance to eat today, but you can bring me a steak biscuit, grits, and bacon."

James' molars clicked together and he ground them to keep his words in check. "Got it. Might take us about thirty minutes or so."

"Call it in. They'll have it ready faster."

"Right." He nodded to Luis, who passed the assignment to the officer next to him. "No faster than thirty minutes," James told her, his voice low. "As soon as they eat, I have a feeling he's going to end it. We need that time." The woman nodded and took off for her cruiser. James noted the negotiator, Marissa Cook, standing next to Cole.

James held the megaphone toward her, and she shook her head while she walked toward him. "You're doing great," she said. "You've got him working with you. If something changes, we'll trade off, but for now, let's not fix it if it's not broken."

James agreed, then slid his gaze to Luis. "Sniper ready?"

"He's ready, but he can't get a clear shot. Man's got the windows covered up, and even if he didn't, the guy's got the kid attached to him like a leech. Risk is too great if the guy moves unexpectedly."

He needed Gerald to let the little one go. "Hey, Gerald," he said, "got your food ordered and an officer is heading to pick it up."

"Good. Good."

"It would be a lot easier to communicate if you'd pick up the phone." James noted the neighbors gathered as close as they could get to the scene behind the tape. They might not be able to see much, but they were getting an earful. "Not to mention, this conversation would be a lot more private. You got a landline?"

"No." A pause. "What do you mean 'private'?"

"Got some nosy lookie-loo neighbors, if you know what I mean. I can give you a number to call or I can bring you a radio. Your choice. But at least our talk will just be between us while we wait for the food." And if the man wasn't worried about being shot when he opened the door, he might let go of the child.

Silence. The little hand gripping the door disappeared and the door shut.

"What now?" Luis asked, arms crossed, a frown pulling his brows to meet at the bridge of his nose.

"Give him a minute. He doesn't like his dirty laundry aired. I took a little gamble that mentioning the neighbors would get him on the phone."

The door cracked. "Can't find the phone! Bring me a radio!"

TWO

Lainie stood at the nurses' counter in the Emergency Department and shut her eyes for a moment. It had been two weeks since she'd gone over the side of the mountain and she was tired. Her body had mostly recovered from the surprisingly minor cuts and bruises, but today her head pounded. Once she'd been extricated from the vehicle, she'd given her statement to the police and gotten a ride home from one of the nice deputies. And told no one what happened, simply because she couldn't quite believe it herself.

She'd rented a car that was very similar to the one she owned, and so far, no one had questioned her about it. Her phone buzzed and she glanced at it. A text from Sonny at the body shop.

Hope to get to your car soon, Lainie. We're just swamped. I understand if you want to take it elsewhere.

As if. She tapped,

No way. I know and trust you. Insurance is paying for a rental so no hurry. At least not much.

Okay, will let you know when it's ready.

She thanked him, then resumed her position against the nurses' station, closing her eyes once more. Could she sleep standing up? Maybe.

"Hey, you okay?"

She turned to find her coworker, good friend, and brilliant trauma surgeon, Dr. Allison Lambe, walking toward her with her confident, smooth stride. Today, her short, dark, shiny hair sported a finger wave style popular in the 1920s. "Fine. Just tired. Love the hairstyle."

Allison gave her head a light pat. "I'm channeling Josephine Baker."

"Who?"

Allison gasped and clutched at her chest in mock shock. "You did *not* just ask me who."

"Um . . . sorry?"

"I thought I had educated you better than this. Josephine Baker, the famous singer and actress? Among other things, she was the first Black woman to star in a motion picture."

"Oh, wait. I do know who she is. Sorry. I'm a little brain-dead this morning."

Her friend waved her hand and narrowed her thick-lashed eyes. "You pulled a double. What's up with that?"

Lainie shrugged. "Dr. Maloney asked and I said okay."

"It's too much," Allison said, her voice low. "You need to learn to tell him no." The nurses behind her typed up notes, rushed to answer the ringing phones, or hurried to patients' rooms. As the biggest hospital in Lake City, North Carolina, there was never a dull moment.

"I'm fine. I managed to snag a couple of hours in the on-call room." She needed a few more, but for now, she'd manage.

"Lainie . . ." Allison dragged her name out and raised a brow.

"I know, I know, but I don't want to take anything to sleep." Especially not in light of what had happened. The incident had triggered all kinds of nightmares.

Understanding flickered in her friend's eyes. Allison knew how hard Lainie found it to allow herself to fall into a deep sleep. Getting shot in your own bed could do that to a person. "PTSD stinks."

If only that was all it was, but she wasn't ready to talk about it yet. Lainie pulled in a deep breath even as her fingers went to the small key she wore on a chain around her neck. "It's been a year and a half," she said, her voice low enough not to be overheard. "I should be over this by now." She pressed the edge of the key against the pad of her thumb, and Allison eyed her with a knowing look. Lainie dropped her hand.

"*Over this?* Did you really just say that? I don't think there's a time limit on getting over something like that. If you ever can."

"Okay, maybe not *over* it, but . . ." And she found she did want to talk about the accident. With Allison. "Something happened the other day that's caused me to have a setback anyway, so getting over it is probably not going to happen anytime soon."

Allison leaned forward with a frown. "What are you talking about?"

Lainie told her, and although the telling didn't take long, Allison's eyes widened with each word.

"Are you kidding me? Someone actually did that on purpose?"

"I don't know. The more I think about it, the more I don't know. I was going slow, trying to find a place to pull over. I thought he got mad and was going to go around me, but his truck clipped my car and . . ." She bumped her palms, reliving the moment of the impact, and shuddered. "If that had been all, then yeah, I wouldn't think twice about it, but . . ."

"But?"

"The guy came and looked over the edge and I—I swear it was Adam. I mean, I know it wasn't, but it sure looked like him."

Allison blinked, then huffed a short laugh. "Adam? As in the Adam who . . . you . . ."

"Yes."

"But—"

"I know. He's dead. It couldn't have been him, but for a moment..."

"Wow, no wonder you've been so spooked lately."

Leave it to Allison to notice. "I know it was someone else, but..." She shrugged and rubbed her eyes before dropping her hand to curl it around her phone. "That means if it wasn't an accident, then someone tried to kill me. And not just anyone, but someone who looked like Adam."

"Could it have simply been an accident and the guy's resemblance to Adam has you PTSD-ing?"

"I've asked myself that numerous times. I mean, he started to try and come down to me, but when he heard the sirens, he ran."

"Maybe he was scared? After all, he was responsible for you spinning off the road, down an embankment. From what it sounds like, if you hadn't landed against those two trees—"

"I would probably have gone straight to the bottom." A shudder rippled through Lainie. "I keep playing it over and over in my head and I just can't believe it happened." She frowned. "I was doing better with the PTSD, the nightmares, the ... everything. At least I thought I was. But now ..."

"Are you still seeing your therapist?"

"Like clockwork."

"Is it helping?"

Was it? She sighed. "I think so. But you know what? I don't want to talk about this anymore. The cops are looking into it. Change of subject."

"Sure. What do you want to talk about?"

"Camping."

"Lainie..." Allison drew Lainie's name out again and wrinkled her nose. "You're still on that? Let's go back to your therapist."

"This is therapy. I stand by my idea that it would be good for us all to get away." She narrowed her eyes. "And you agreed, but you haven't given your vote."

"And that'd be the first weekend in October, right?"

"Right."

"Well . . ."

Lainie waited. "Allison . . ." Her drawing her friend's name out, mimicking Allison, wasn't lost on the doctor.

"Oh, good grief," Allison said. "You already know what I'm going to vote for."

Lainie scoffed. "Seriously?"

"Glamping." Allison shrugged. "I don't do hikes and bugs and stuff. I want to sit in a hammock wrapped in mosquito netting while under the open skies and read a book."

Lainie rolled her tired eyes.

"Hey"—Allison held up a hand—"I'm not saying you guys can't do your thing. I'm just saying that I want my little slice of nature next door to a comfortable bed and indoor plumbing. Not all of us grew up with a dad who had an end-of-the-world mentality."

True enough. And that had been a good and, a little too often, a bad thing. Knowing how to use a gun had saved her life eighteen months ago, but her father's constant harping on being prepared for the end had probably contributed to her mother's hoarding issues. "Fine. There were about three glamping choices on the list. Which one?"

"What's the budget?"

"As cheap as possible. Not all of us are on Dr. Allison's salary."

"Oh hush. Your salary isn't anything to sneeze at. Now, tell me. Who else is coming again? The usual crew? Even Kenzie?"

"Yep. Kenzie's in. Assuming she doesn't get called out for something." Kenzie King, a SWAT medic who'd come in last month to have a wound caused by the graze of a bullet stitched up. She invited Lainie to lunch, Lainie accepted, and the two had been tight friends ever since. "And Jesslyn, I hope." Jesslyn McCormick had been a longtime friend to Lainie. Almost as close as she and Stephanie Cross, the one she'd considered her BFF. But in fifth grade, Jesslyn and Lainie had bonded when Jesslyn's family died in a house fire. Jesslyn had been spared because she and Lainie had been spending the night with Steph. And now she fought fire on a daily basis as Lake City's fire marshal.

"What about Kristine?" Allison asked.

"I haven't heard from her yet, but I think she's on a flight." As an air marshal, Kristine Duncan flew about fifteen days a month, spending five hours a day protecting those in the air. "I'll text her again to make sure."

"Okay then," Allison said. "I'll go with glamping."

Lainie groaned, but grinned. "Fine, you little diva. Glamping it is. We will even let you pick the place, but I'm bringing the Scrabble game."

Allison laughed. "Well, I'm not playing. You cheat."

"I do not!"

"You've practically memorized the Scrabble dictionary. That's cheating."

"That's just smart." Lainie lifted her nose and pasted a snooty expression on her face. "But if y'all can't handle the competition, then . . ."

"Ugh. Fine. Bring the game." Allison frowned. "Seriously, if you guys want to leave me behind for another time—and a different kind of excursion—I'm fine with that. I don't want to be a spoilsport."

"Hey, I gave you all options with the links. And Jesslyn said if she could make it, she'd choose glamping too."

"Really?" Allison's eyes lit up. "I knew I liked her. What about Kristine?"

"She said as long as it was on the ground, she was fine."

"And Kenzie?"

Lainie groaned. "Glamping," she muttered. "Stephanie too."

Allison laughed, a deep belly laugh that echoed through the area, turning heads and bringing smiles to faces. She clapped her hands. "Oh goody. I can't wait."

Lainie's phone buzzed and she checked the text. Then sighed and dropped her chin to her chest.

"Your mom?" Allison asked with another knowing look. Allison was very *knowing* today.

Lainie grimaced. "Yes."

"When are you going to help her?"

"Maybe next Friday. If she'll let me in." Her parents lived in one of the nicest parts of town in a massive home that her architect father had built before Lainie was born. While her father kept the outside of the home immaculate, the inside was another matter altogether. And her mother wanted Lainie's help in cleaning it because she was too embarrassed to allow someone else to do so. "You know how she is. I may get there and she'll have some reason why we can't clean."

"I'm sorry, Lainie."

"Me too."

"What about your brothers or sister?"

Lainie tilted her head. "You know they don't do much of anything. I mean, my sister has done more, I guess. She did drive Mom to a doctor's appointment two weeks ago, but I had to beg her to do that. Nothing since then, so overall, even she avoids the issue—and our parents—at all costs. What makes you ask?"

"Because I've been praying and I expect God to answer."

"Well, when he does, you'll be the first to know."

"So . . . that's a no."

"Exactly. Mostly."

"I'll just have to keep praying."

"You and me both, my friend." She shrugged. "It is what it is for now."

"Yeah, but—" Allison's phone buzzed and she glanced at it. "Gotta go. I'll be adding fresh prayers for you and the situation with your mom."

"As opposed to stale prayers?" Lainie pressed her lips against a smile.

Allison pursed her lips. "Girl, you better watch yourself."

"Thank you, Ally," Lainie said with all seriousness. Grateful to have the prayer warrior on her side, Lainie hugged her, then watched her disappear down the hall and around the corner.

Which left Lainie alone with her thoughts once more. Since that wasn't a pleasant place to be, she checked her schedule and headed up to Trauma Room 3 to check on the woman who'd found herself on the wrong end of her husband's fist. Lainie shuddered, gripped the little key on her necklace for a brief splash of comfort, and prepared herself to tell her story.

She'd lived through a betrayal of the worst kind. If sharing that with just one other person gave them the courage to walk away, then it was worth the uptick in nightmares she'd be sure to experience.

She hurried to the elevator, skirting the visitors and other hospital workers in the area.

When she glanced down the length of the hallway, she locked gazes with a pair of familiar blue eyes for a fraction of a second. Her heart thundered and she stared. Time slowed down as the person attached to those blue eyes turned and walked to the stairwell exit.

"No," she whispered. "It can't be."

"Lainie? The elevator's here. You coming?" Her coworker's voice came from a distance, barely heard over the whooshing sound ringing in her ears. "Lainie?"

"Uh . . . yeah. Yeah." She took a deep breath and shook her head, pushing aside the dizziness that threatened to overtake her.

"You okay?" the person asked.

She glanced at him. Chris Stanton. One of the radiologists. "Uh-huh."

"Because you don't look like you're okay. Your color's off."

"I'm good." She was anything but good.

He pressed the button on the panel. "Where you going?"

Crazy. "Um, three."

He took care of the floor while she ran the incident over and over in her head. "It can't be."

"Can't be what?" Chris asked.

She'd said that out loud? Clearing her throat, she forced her thoughts in order. "Nothing. I just thought I saw someone I recognized, but there's no way it could be him." And it wasn't him who'd run her off the road last week.

"No? Why not?"

"Because he's dead."

And no one was going to convince her otherwise. Not even a twin that Adam didn't have who was running around the hospital playing peekaboo with her.

TWENTY-FOUR MINUTES HAD PASSED with no real change. That was the good news. That meant no one had died. But no one had been released either, and time was ticking down.

The food had arrived, but James wasn't ready to let it go quite yet. He spoke into the radio. "Hey, Gerald, the food is here."

"Good, send it in."

"Well, I can't just do that. My boss said I need a hostage released. Will you at least send the kids out?"

"No."

James closed his eyes and whispered a prayer. "What would you do if you were in my shoes, Gerald?"

A pause. "What do you mean?"

"I mean, what if you were out here and I was in there? What would you do?"

"I . . . I don't know. Why are you asking this stuff?"

"Would you want to save the kids?"

"I mean . . . yeah. I guess. Everyone wants to save the kids, right?"

There might have been a sneer in the words, but the man wasn't delusional. He was able to see another perspective, which meant, hopefully, James could work with that.

"See, that's where I am right now," he said. "I want you to let the kids go. Can you do that for me? And I'll bring the food myself."

The radio went silent, and James could only pray the guy was thinking about it.

Marissa was frowning at him. "What are you doing? This isn't negotiation protocol."

"I know, but we're running out of time and I need to get those kids out of there." And hopefully, the mom. He'd even take Gerald alive, but that gnawing feeling in his gut said this wasn't going to end exactly the way he wanted.

"And you think this is the—"

"Okay." Gerald's voice sent the radio crackling. "Yeah, okay. Li'l Bit can come out, but Katy-bug stays with me."

"Ger—"

"Take it or leave it."

Marissa nodded and James sighed, then nodded back. "All right. I'm going to come up to the porch with the food. Give me a minute to take the little one's out so one of the officers can feed her, but the rest is in the bag. Plus a little extra just in case anyone is still hungry."

Moments later the door cracked open and James grabbed two bags of food in his left hand. The earpiece in his right ear sat snug in his canal and he'd be able to hear everything Luis or one of the others had to say—especially Buzz Crenshaw, his SWAT team member and sniper. "Buzz? You got a shot?"

"Negative," came the instant response.

"Right." James walked toward the front door. They'd formulated several plans over the last half hour and discarded them. He'd finally settled on one that was risky but would present the least amount of danger to the children. "Gerald? I'm here. Can you hand me L'il Bit and I'll pass you the food?" *Please don't shoot me.*

The door opened a little wider and he stared into the biggest—and oldest—green eyes he'd ever seen in a child. She had a rope around her waist and James knew he wouldn't be grabbing her and running. "Hi," he said, keeping his voice gentle so as not to scare her. "I'm James."

"Hi."

"Are you Katy-bug?"

She nodded.

"You hungry?"

Another nod.

He couldn't see behind her, so he knelt, knowing Buzz was watching all the windows for anyone who might be aiming a weapon in James' direction. "Can you send your sister out?" He set the bags down in front of the open door.

She turned and spoke to someone out of sight. "He wants her."

Soon, Katy pulled another little girl to the door and pushed her out. The child screamed and tried to go back in, but James caught her and turned sideways, protecting her from anything that might come from the house.

Like bullets.

She flailed against him, and it was all he could do not to drop her. For her own safety, he pinned her arms to her sides and held her. She continued her ear-piercing wails while he searched for a way to grab Katy. But with the rope around her, he was at a loss. Katy stepped forward, reaching for the bags. "Go to the bedroom window," she whispered. "Hurry."

"Get away from the door and shut it! Now!" Gerald's voice bellowed from the inside.

The door slammed and James hoisted the furious two-year-old into a better position against his side and kept his back to the house while he carried her to safety. "It's okay, baby. You're going to be just fine."

Once he'd passed her off to the officer with the child's food, Gretchen calmed down and grabbed a french fry.

James walked over to Marissa. "I need you to take over."

"What?"

He handed her the radio. "Katy told me to go to the bedroom window—and to hurry—just before she shut the door."

"Which one?"

"I'm assuming the only one at the back of the house."

"You're going?"

"Yes."

She frowned. "Could be a trap."

"I know."

"But you have to go anyway. Let's get the place scouted to make sure you can get back there without anyone spotting you."

"No time for that." He jogged over to Luis and briefed him in as few words as possible. Luis offered him a frown that matched Marissa's. "The kid told you that?"

"Yes."

"I don't like it."

"I don't either, but I feel like I need to do it."

"What if she was coached?"

"What purpose would it serve? Get me back there and shoot me? Why?" He edged backward, watching the house.

"Beats me. But I'm not sure I'd want to find out."

"I have to."

Luis stared at him a moment, then shrugged. "All right. Chopper's in the air. We'll get them to do some recon."

"Again, no time. She sounded like she needed me to get back there ASAP. She used the word 'hurry.' Just watch my back." He tapped his earpiece. "Buzz, you just yell 'duck' if I need to."

"Copy that," the man answered. "Moving into position now."

James hurried down the street a few houses before cutting between two to make his way back to the Hensons' backyard. His gut kept sending warning signals that time was of the essence. As soon as they were finished with the food, Gerald was going to act.

James made it to the edge of the property next door to the Henson home and scouted the backyard. No fence, just a few signs that small children lived there. Swing set, little beat-up plastic car, shovel and pail, and a bicycle with training wheels.

James inched closer, eyes watching for any sign of movement at the back of the house.

"All clear on my end," Buzz said, his bass voice echoing in James' ear.

Movement at the window in the corner of the home made his decision of direction easy. He'd just taken three steps toward it when the window slid open and a little hand pushed the screen to the ground with a clang.

He froze, but she didn't.

"Katy! Katy! Get back in here! What are you doing, you little brat?"

"Breach now!" James raced toward the window, and Katy looked up at him, then back over her shoulder.

"No! Daddy! No!" She turned back to James, eyes frantic, and held her little arms out toward him. "Get me! I want to be with Gretchie!"

He grabbed her as the first bullet whizzed past his cheek. Wrapping his arms around her, he turned his back as the next bullet slammed into him.

The pain registered, the breath left him, and he went to his knees, his mind still working, his only thought to protect the little girl from the man who was supposed to do the same.

Another crack ripped the air, then a scream echoed from inside the house.

Blackness threatened.

"Suspect's down," Buzz said, and James allowed himself to fall sideways to his hip, careful not to crush the child still wrapped in his arms.

Running footsteps reached him while he struggled to pull in the next breath.

THREE

Lainie shut the door on the patient with the broken nose, two black eyes, three cracked ribs, a broken wrist, and a fractured shin. The woman had refused to speak against the man who'd beaten her, but she'd listened to Lainie recount her own experience without moving.

For one brief moment, Lainie thought the victim might say something, but she'd simply taken a deep breath—as deep as one could take with broken ribs—and closed her eyes. Effectively shutting Lainie out.

Allison hurried toward her. "Tough one?"

"One of the toughest." Lainie let her gaze roam the hall behind Allison, looking for the person she'd seen earlier.

"I'm sorry, Lainie."

Lainie shrugged, not nearly as nonchalant as the gesture indicated. "I can only do what I can do." *He's dead. Stop thinking about him.* Her phone went off and she straightened. "Gunshot victim coming in." Good, a distraction. Not good someone was shot, of course, but she desperately needed to keep busy, keep moving, and stop thinking.

Allison waved her phone. "Got it too. Let's go."

The surge of adrenaline energized her like nothing else could, and she shot toward the elevator with Allison on her heels. Her phone buzzed once more and she glanced at it while she jogged. "It's a cop."

"Oh boy," Allison said. "But he's alive?"

"Yes."

"Let's keep him that way."

When they reached the ER entrance, the paramedics already had the man wheeled into a designated room with other officers trailing behind him.

"I'm fine." His deep voice reached through the open door. "It got my vest and just knocked the breath out of me."

Lainie gasped and pushed into the room. "James Cross?"

His dark brown eyes met hers and widened. "Lainie Jackson?" He blinked away his shock and shook off a nurse. "I'm fine. And don't you dare call Stephanie or my parents."

He didn't want his sister or parents to know he was here? She narrowed her eyes at him, silently conveying her disagreement, but dipped her head acknowledging that she'd honor his wishes.

"Thanks."

Allison stepped forward. "Hey, James, let us take a look, all right?"

Lainie held back. He didn't look in danger of dying at the moment—and he probably didn't want her treating him. "You got this?" she murmured to Allison. "I'm going to—"

"Dr. Lambe! Need you on a code! Room 6!"

So much for escaping. Lainie hurried to James' side while Allison bolted from the room. She smiled at the sweaty, tight-jawed man on the gurney. His rugged good looks struck her as they always did when she was in his presence—which hadn't been in years. He was in his early thirties and frowning ferociously at her while one hand raked through his spiked dark hair. His five o'clock shadow stood out in 3D against his pale face.

"I'm glad you're okay," she said.

The frown eased slightly. "I am, thanks. So no need for all this fuss."

"I'm guessing your supervisor ordered you to come?" She hooked the stethoscope into her ears and lifted it in a silent ask for permission.

He sighed and jerked his head in a short nod.

She took it as an affirmative to both questions. "Then let's get this out of the way so you can get out of here, okay?"

"Right. Yeah. Fine."

"Thanks." She noted his vitals and that his heart rate was slightly elevated, along with his blood pressure. All normal in his current situation, but they'd monitor it. "Can you lie on your stomach, please?"

He hesitated, then closed his eyes. "My back's not pretty."

She raised a brow. "I can handle it."

"Right." He moved slowly, wincing as he settled, resting his head on his arms. The paramedics had gotten him out of his vest, but the bullet had left a very red area that would turn into a nasty bruise right above his left kidney. Lainie bit her lip against a cry at the angry scars crisscrossing his formerly smooth flesh. "Yikes, James," she whispered. Then cleared her throat. "I see what you mean about your back. I'm sorry."

He chuckled, then groaned. "Thank you."

"For?"

"For not dancing around the sight of it."

"Why would I do that?"

"Never mind. It's been a long time, Lainie," he said. "You're looking . . . uh . . . good. Different. All grown up."

She let him get away with the awkward change in topic. "I've been all grown up for a while. And remember, I'm not the one who left town."

"I was deployed. A little different than just leaving town."

"True. How long have you been home?"

"Three months."

She was glad he couldn't see her shocked flinch. She masked it, then glanced at the nurse. "Let's get a urine sample and a complete blood workup. I'd also like X-rays of the area."

"On it." The woman tapped her iPad, entering the information.

"Anything else hurt?" she asked James.

"No. Like I told the paramedics, I've done this once before. I hurt for a while, then the bruise heals up and I'm good."

38

"Hmm." A major oversimplification of being shot. Even if the bullet hit the vest, it could still do damage. Lainie stepped aside while the nurse worked. Once she left, Lainie picked up where they left off. "Three months? Steph never said you were home. Why would she not tell me that? We see or talk to each other just about every week."

He went silent, then sighed. "She doesn't know."

"What?" She walked to his side and crouched so he could see her face. "I thought you just didn't want them to know you'd been injured and were in the hospital, but they don't know you're even on the same continent?"

"It's a long story and I'd appreciate it if you didn't say anything about it." His lips quirked into a small smile. "They're not on my HIPAA list."

"Of course, I won't say anything."

His smile flipped back into a frown. "Um, Lainie?"

"Yes? What is it?"

"I . . . uh . . . I really don't want to admit this, but it kinda hurts when I pull in a breath."

"Show me where."

She stood and he pointed to the area slightly above the kidney, but right at the lower portion of his rib cage.

"One of your ribs might be fractured." Or worse. "The X-rays will tell us."

"Yeah. Great."

"All right, we've got some time until we put everything together. You rest until they wheel you up to X-ray, okay? The pain meds are going to make you sleepy anyway."

"Sure, but nothing too strong." He closed his eyes and Lainie moved to the door, her gaze running over him. She and Stephanie had grown closer in high school when they'd both joined the drama department. On opening night of the end-of-year play, Stephanie's big brothers, James, Keegan, and Dixon, attended the production. That night, James had been the one to capture her attention, but he'd never looked at her as anything other than his sister's friend. If only—

No. She wasn't going down the highway to the past. She was only going forward, but while she was working and seeing other patients, she couldn't help wondering why the man had been home three months and hadn't told his family.

An hour later, Lainie returned to find James in a drug-induced doze. While she stood in the doorway, pondering whether she should let him rest or try to wake him, his eyes fluttered open.

"Hi," he rasped.

"Hey." She stepped into the room and pulled a chair closer to his head. "How are you feeling?"

"Pretty good right now. What's the verdict on the ribs?"

"Bruised. We think."

"Not broken?"

"There's a tiny, almost microscopic, place that could be a hairline fracture, but I'm not entirely sure and neither was the radiologist. I consulted another doctor and she said the same thing. Unless you want to do another X-ray at a different angle—"

"That's okay, I'll pass."

"—you should take it easy for the next few weeks just to make sure."

He frowned. "Few weeks? Not an option."

Why did she know he'd say that? "Well, if it's just a bruise, you'll heal up faster than if it's a fracture, and then you'll know. In other words, time will tell."

"Time. Right." He leaned his head back and closed his eyes. "Thanks."

She patted his shoulder. His very nice, muscular shoulder. She cleared her throat. "Rest for now. We should have the results back from the UA shortly." If his urinalysis came back showing what she thought it might— Her iPad pinged. "Well, speaking of . . ." She read, then looked up. "Hmm."

"What?"

"I'd like to keep you overnight."

His eyes popped open. "No way."

Lainie sighed. "You have blood in your urine. It's very faint, but it's there. I'm sure it's only because your kidney was slightly traumatized, but I don't want to release you until we know for sure—or the blood is gone." She paused. "Actually, I think we'll do a CT scan with contrast just to see how that kidney is functioning."

His hands fisted at his sides. "I can't stay overnight. I only agreed to the drugs because I didn't think I'd have to." He raked a hand over his face.

Lainie frowned and covered his hand with hers. "I'm sure your friends or Stephanie would take care of anything you need at home. Or whatever it is you're worried about."

Her phone buzzed and she ignored it.

He shook his head. "That's not what I'm worried about. I'm staying with Cole while I look for a place."

"Cole Garrison?"

"Yes, we're partners."

Partners and best friends since college. And now James was a cop in the town they'd grown up in. "I haven't seen him in a while either." She'd heard about him over the last month because he and Kenzie worked together, but apparently those two were keeping their distance from each other when they could. She eyed the man in the bed. "So what's keeping you from staying? I mean, no one in their right mind actually *wants* to stay overnight in a hospital, I suppose, but . . ."

His jaw clamped shut and he breathed in through his nose. "Nothing. It's nothing."

"Listen to the doc," a voice said from behind them.

Lainie turned. She'd been so focused on the man in front of her, she hadn't heard the door open.

"Cole, dude," James said. "How long you been standing there?"

"Long enough to know you've got blood where you shouldn't have it and a doc who thinks you should stay here for the night."

"PA," Lainie murmured. No one seemed to hear her.

James glowered. "That's a violation of my HIPAA rights."

The handsome man in the same uniform as her patient smirked and told her, "Don't worry, Lainie, I'm on the list."

Unlike his family. Not even the brothers he was so close to. Or *had been* close to.

Lainie tapped her iPad and found the form—and Cole's name. "Yep, I see you."

"Remind me to rectify that," James muttered.

"All right, boys," she said as she stood. "I'm going to leave you two to hash this out. Cole, I'm pulling for you."

"Hey now," James said. "I'm a hero, remember? Everyone's always on the hero's side, right?" His eyes clouded. "How are the girls?"

Cole turned serious. "They're fine thanks to you. So's the mom."

"The girls? The mom?" Lainie asked.

"That's how he got shot," Cole said. "Pulled a kid out of the bedroom window, turned his back to shelter her, and got hit with the bullet just before our sniper got his shot off." Sorrow flickered briefly in his eyes before it was gone. "If James hadn't insisted on getting that little girl out, she'd be dead right now. The whole family would. The guy had already taunted his wife about killing them all. The fact that James talked the guy into letting the littlest one go was nothing short of amazing. He masterminded the whole plan and was definitely the hero of the day."

"Shut up, dude," James said, his voice mild, even while his face flushed. "You talk too much. A man still lost his life."

Again, that flash of sadness. Then resolve. "He had ample opportunity to choose otherwise."

James' and Cole's gazes connected, a silent message passed between them, and James nodded. "Absolutely."

Lainie's heart slammed into her rib cage. "James," she whispered. Her phone buzzed in her pocket. She ignored it. Again.

He waved a hand. "I was just doing my job. Nothing any person there wouldn't have done. Thankfully, the bullet hit my vest and I'm fine. Something I've repeatedly said in spite of the fact that no one is listening. I'm also ready to go home."

"I think you *are* fine," Lainie said, "but just to be on the safe side, I also think you should stay put so we can run a few more tests."

"Lainie . . ." He drew her name out on a sigh.

"Why is everyone saying my name like that today?" she muttered.

"There must be a reason, trust me."

"James . . ." She mimicked him and the man had the audacity to roll his eyes before he started to protest once more. She shook her head. "Nope, not going to change my mind." And what was with all the eye rolling? Seriously, her friends must have set a record in the last few hours.

"But—"

"Don't make me call your supervisor."

James scowled and Cole crossed his massive arms over his equally huge chest and grinned down at her from his six-foot-plus height. "He's not going anywhere."

She raised a brow at him and let her gaze flip between the two men. "Too bad I'm not a betting woman. I know who I'd put my money on. Then again, I don't suppose a sure thing can really be called a bet."

She slipped out of the room to the sound of Cole's laughter and James' groan. Finally, she could check her buzzing phone.

Multiple texts from different people.

I swear I just saw your ex, Adam Williams.

Lainie, heads up. There is someone who looks just like Adam Williams in the hospital.

I think I'm seeing things. There's a guy who looks like Adam Williams walking around the third floor.

So, she wasn't dreaming.

She glanced up and caught the eye of the man in question standing on the other side of the ER. The meeting of their eyes, just like the one earlier, lasted a fraction of a second before he disappeared through the stairwell exit door. She bolted after him.

JAMES CROSSED HIS ARMS over his chest and glared at his best friend. "You know why I can't stay here. I took the painkillers."

Cole dropped his defensive stance and walked over to stand next to James. "You got to do what the doc says, my friend. Just because it's Lainie doesn't mean she doesn't know what she's talking about."

"She's not a doc."

"Huh?"

"She's a PA."

Cole rolled his eyes. "Oh, right. I knew that. You still need to do what she says."

James shifted and winced. Cole raised a brow.

"I hate this," James muttered.

"I know. I hate it for you."

"Not enough to get me out of here, apparently."

"You're also going to have to speak to your family at some point," Cole said, pointedly disregarding James' irritation.

"I know that too."

"So, you have a plan for when you're going to make that happen?"

"Nope." And he wasn't going to come up with it now.

"Right." Cole crossed his arms again, this time in a much more relaxed stance. "Want me to hang out here with you? In case . . . you know."

As much as he wanted to take Cole up on his offer, James' pride protested. "No. I'll be fine."

"You're not going to sleep a wink, are you?"

"Probably not."

"All right, let me know when Lainie gives you the green light and I'll come get you."

"Thanks." James' phone buzzed with a text. From his sister.

I hear you're back in town. Thanks a lot for letting me know.

44

A low groan slipped from him. "Great. I gotta deal with this." Cole waved then slipped out the door while James tapped a response to Stephanie.

> I've been laying low for a bit. Working with Cole at the police department. I guess Lainie hasn't learned to keep her mouth shut in all these years after all.

> What's Lainie got to do with it? I saw you on the news. They're reporting an officer down. I didn't know you were back and working? How long have you been home? Obviously long enough to get a JOB??? With the local PD??? Thanks so much for letting me know. Really. Thanks SO MUCH.

He was a terrible brother. And son. But he just couldn't deal with . . . well, there was no helping it now. He was going to have to deal. With a silent apology to Lainie, he typed,

> Do Mom and Dad know?

> Not unless they watched the news and got a glimpse of you sitting on the ground holding that little girl. They're calling you a hero, big bro.

He flushed, praying his name would be kept out of the media, but like it or not, someone was bound to let it slip. Heaving a mental sigh, he looked at the screen just as her next text popped up.

> Why haven't you gotten in touch???

> It's kind of a long story. And one question mark will suffice.

> So when are you going to tell me??????????

Never. And leave it to her to add extra question marks simply to aggravate him.

> I'll call you soon. Right now, I'm dealing with something that I can't get away from.

Fine, but why does Lainie know you're back?

Before he could answer, three dots appeared to show she was texting again.

Wait a minute. Lainie's working today. Are you at the hospital??? Sorry, that requires more than one?

Yes, but I'm fine.

He refused to lie, as tempting as it was.

His phone rang and he tapped the green button to answer it.

"Fine?" Stephanie's clipped voice came through the line, her agitation making him wince even before he placed the device against his ear.

"Yes, fine." He was alive. That qualified as fine, didn't it?

"What's going on, James Lee Cross? Do Keegan and Dixon know you're home?"

"No, they don't."

Silence. Then, "But . . . why? I mean, I know you and Dad aren't really speaking, but the rest of us are, so what's—"

"I'm speaking. He's the one who's . . ." He smothered a sigh. "I don't want to have this conversation on the phone." He didn't want to have it at all. "I'll come over soon and we'll talk."

"Why don't I come there?"

"Because I've got paperwork to fill out for a case and I need to get that done." He really did. And he needed sleep. Somehow, some way, he needed to sleep without dreaming.

"The job always comes first, huh?"

"Steph—"

"Never mind. You're going to do what you're going to do, but one day you'll realize you need to stop and smell the roses, dear brother."

"I know." One day. Not today. "Don't tell Mom and Dad, okay? I want them to hear it from me."

"Sure. Now that you're home, you'll be coming this weekend, right?"

He stifled a groan. The family weekend at the lake. "That's this weekend?"

"You know it is! You can't not come. If Mom finds out you were home and didn't come, she'd be shattered."

He thought that might be a bit of an exaggeration. He also noticed she didn't say anything about their father being upset at his absence. "Steph . . ."

"James . . ."

She wasn't going to take no for an answer. "Okay, yeah. I'll see what I can do about being there." He hesitated, then blurted, "Has Dad forgiven me yet?" He grimaced. Why ask when he knew the answer?

Her sigh reached him. "I'm not sure if forgiven is the right word, but he may be in the acceptance phase."

Okay, that kind of surprised him. He and his father had butted heads since James could talk, but when James joined the military police, his father cut him off. All because James' uncle Dean had been killed by a police officer. No matter that it had been his uncle's fault for pulling a gun on the man, now his father hated every cop on the planet—military, local, fed, whatever. After one particularly heated argument when he was twenty-two years old, James had walked out of the house, went straight to the recruiter's office, and joined the Army.

In total, his dad hadn't spoken more than four sentences to him since.

And while James' reasons for joining hadn't been the best, he found he loved the life and the sense of achievement when he'd worked his way up to agent with the Army's CID.

He'd hoped by now that his dad would come around and be proud of him.

So far, that hadn't happened, and he was almost convinced it never would.

James shut his eyes on the pain the thought brought to the surface, determined to keep his sleep in the twilight phase. Deep enough for some rest, but not deep enough to dream.

FOUR

Lainie stood on the sidewalk in the heat of the mid-September afternoon and glanced left, then right. Then left again while her heart pounded, and her fingers pulled at the key on the necklace.

Nothing. And there had been nothing for the ten minutes she'd been standing there. But he hadn't appeared again, and she didn't have all day to wait on him to do so.

If he would.

If he was real.

She stepped back inside, wondering if she was seeing things. After eighteen months of intense therapy—both physical and mental— was she on the verge of losing her mind in the space of a day?

But someone had run her off the road.

And she had texts affirming Adam's appearance in the hospital.

Nevertheless, it wasn't Adam. She'd dated Adam for a little over six months before *the incident*. He'd been charming and fun and attentive, and she'd allowed herself to believe she could be happy with him. No, she hadn't been in love with him, but she figured that would come in time. Boy, had she been wrong.

Lainie raked a hand over her ponytail, tightened it, then made her way back to the ER. She had patients to check on, lives to save. She didn't need to be chasing after a ghost. Not that she believed in ghosts. With the exception of Jesus, she definitely didn't believe that dead men rose from the grave. And that guy sure wasn't Jesus. Jesus didn't play mind games—or run from those chasing him.

"Hey, Lainie?" The voice came from the nurses' station.

"Hey, Maggie, everyone okay?" *Everyone* meaning her patients.

"Yes. Just needed your signature on this." Maggie, the charge nurse, passed the iPad to Lainie, who read through the information, then signed her name with the stylus.

She handed the iPad back. "How's James Cross doing?"

"We're waiting on a room, but don't count on one coming available anytime soon. Be prepared for him to spend the night in the ER."

"Okay." Lainie glanced at the clock on the wall. "And I'm heading to sign out." She planned to go home and sleep for as many hours as her mind would let her get in. As long as she was completely exhausted, she could rest without dreaming.

"Take cover! Take cover!"

Lainie gasped and spun toward the shouts.

"Incoming! Go left! Go left! Ground attacks on the way! Two mikes away!"

Maggie's jaw swung open as she stared at James, who stood holding his IV pole like a weapon. And like it weighed nothing. Lainie rushed toward him, noting the frantic sweeping eyes, the sweat on his forehead, his breath coming in short gasps.

He was going to injure himself further if . . . "Soldier!"

He froze at her shout.

"Stand down!" she said. "Stand down right now!"

He stayed still, eyes wide, and focused on something only he could see. "But . . ."

"I said stand down. You know how to follow an order, don't you, soldier?"

"Copy that, ma'am."

"Put the weapon down."

The pole clanked to the floor and the sound jarred him from whatever place his mind had gone. He blinked, blinked again, then focused on her. "What . . . ? Where . . . ?"

He was back. And mortified. Her heart went out to him.

She waved the onlookers away, took his arm, and tried to turn him back to the bed. "Careful, James. Watch the ribs."

His eyes flicked from one person to the next, then met hers, but he finally made his way to the bed and lay back on the mattress, heat climbing into his cheeks, his jaw clenching, nostrils flaring.

She turned to the others watching from the door. "Give me a few minutes, please? And shut the door."

They backed out, leaving her alone with the man on the bed. He wouldn't look at her, just kept his eyes closed, clenching and un-clenching his fists while drawing breaths in through his nose and releasing them through tight lips.

"I have PTSD too," she said.

He stilled but didn't open his eyes.

"And I hate sleeping," she said. "Which is why I agreed to pull a double and am about to drop. I can only sleep without dreaming when I'm so exhausted, my body has no other options." She paused. "I'm not saying that I understand what you're going through, but I can make an educated guess that the drugs overrode your plan not to fall into a deep sleep."

His eyes opened and jerked to hers. "Yeah. Probably." A slight pause. "I heard what happened to you."

"Well, considering it was splashed across national news, I'm not surprised." No one had been more disturbed than her to see her case used in a domestic violence documentary. It had been just a mention. Less than sixty seconds, but it had brought her more attention than she would have ever wanted.

"I'm sorry," he said.

She sighed. "I am too, but it was a year and a half ago and I've moved on. I think most everyone else has too." The man's face flashed in her mind's eye. "At least I thought I had."

"Nightmares?"

"Oh yes. Definitely those." Another pause. "And seeing my dead fiancé wandering around the hospital today, which makes me wonder if he was the one who ran me off the road almost two weeks ago. That's a new one."

James frowned. "Sorry, what?" He seemed to have forgotten his own embarrassment and was now focused on her. Which had been the goal when she'd started the conversation, but now she squirmed, uncomfortable in trying to explain what her mind had possibly conjured. "I don't know. Guess I'm more tired than I thought."

"Ran you off the road? On purpose?"

"Sure felt that way, but maybe I'm just . . ." She shook her head.

"And you think he's here? At the hospital?"

"Of course not. It has to be someone who looks like him, but it was . . . freaky." She shuddered and cleared her throat. "But never mind that."

"You guys were engaged?"

"Mm-hmm." She clutched the necklace, ran the key through her fingers in an absent motion, then pressed the end of it against the pad of her thumb. Realized what she was doing and let it go.

James' frown deepened, the concern in his eyes laser focused on her. "I can't picture you staying in an abusive relationship. What happened?"

"That's the question of the decade." She sighed and shook her head. "I don't know how to explain it, James. To anyone or myself." A humorless laugh escaped her. "I don't exactly know what happened, but around the time of my twenty-third birthday, I had made up my mind that I wasn't going to let my parents' weird marriage affect me. I was going to meet someone, fall in love, get married, and have a normal life. It became almost an obsession, if I'm honest. Like I had something to prove to someone."

"To who?"

"I have no idea. Maybe just myself. When I met Adam, I had tunnel vision. My goal was to get the ring on my finger. And I did. But once it was there, all I felt was dread. I hadn't even met his family at that point, so it was pretty fast."

"Ouch."

"No kidding. I kept telling myself this was what I wanted." She shrugged. "I know some people won't find it terribly current, but I just wanted to get married and have a family." She looked away. "A normal family."

"Not sure there's such a thing as a normal family."

She laughed. "Well, there is that, of course."

"Regardless, there's absolutely nothing wrong with that as long as it's to the right person."

"Except I knew Adam wasn't the right person. Not right away, of course." She picked imaginary lint from her pants, avoiding his eyes but glad he seemed to have forgotten his own embarrassment.

"How so?"

"The most glaring clue was the spiritual differences. We weren't on the same page when it came to our faith. I could tell that Adam only expressed an interest in God because I was interested in God, and he only came to church because I asked him to. Other than that, nothing."

James grimaced. "Not a good sign."

"No, it wasn't. And there were others too. He was impatient with children. Never mean or deliberately ugly or anything, just no time or patience for them. And then there were the flashes of rage followed by the instant apologies." She sighed. "Thanks to my work, I knew the signs of an unstable person. Not that I wanted to admit they were there. But one night, I sat down with my Bible and had myself a good conversation with the Lord. By the time I went to bed, I knew I was going to break it off with Adam. I couldn't marry him, not with all of the doubts and concerns I had. The next day, when he came over, I told him. He was furious and I finally saw the real him in all its ugliness. It was scary and soul sucking, to say the least. It felt like all my dreams of the fairy-tale wedding and happily ever after were well and truly dead."

He took her hand and squeezed. "I'm sorry. I've heard of that happening more times than I'd like to admit."

She concentrated on the feel of his warm, rough palm wrapped around hers. It gave her strength to continue. "The crazy thing is, I have too. Of course I have. I've patched up those women—and a few men—right here in this hospital. I just never thought it would happen to me." She swiped her free hand down her cheek. "I suppose I should have had a clue when my parents didn't like him at first."

"They didn't?"

"Not really. But they tried. Like, really tried. For them, anyway. I didn't want to introduce him, but he insisted. Strangely enough, he said we couldn't have a relationship and not include my parents. It was true, of course, so I sucked it up and introduced him." She pulled away from him and fiddled with the iPad, loath to admit the next part, but . . . "I thought they didn't like him because they were afraid they were going to lose the one kid they had who was willing to take care of them." She glanced at him. "I suppose that makes me a terrible person."

"Aw, Lainie, of course not."

"In the end, Adam finally had them convinced that while they might not think we were a perfect match, he was at least a good guy."

"But he wasn't."

"He wasn't. When I tried to talk to him about some things like his hair-trigger anger, do you know he actually had the gall to tell me not to worry about anything? That my job was to just be happy and he would take care of everything else and I should be grateful for that."

"Sounds like a 'don't worry your pretty little head about life' kind of thing."

"Exactly." She paused. "Now that I look back on it," she said, her voice low, "I truly think Adam was a psychopath. Or technically, an antisocial personality disorder sufferer."

James nodded. "Excellent actor, manipulative, uses people for their own gain. And so on."

"Exactly." She shook her head, wondering if she should spill an additional reason as to why she hadn't been happy. The one that had a lot to do with James. Like every time she'd pictured being married, he was the one by her side.

She bit her tongue. No way would those words leave her lips. Not only would that be too much for him to process, she'd simply embarrass herself—and him—because there was no doubt in her mind that he didn't have a clue about her feelings. She fought a surge of tears and familiar guilt.

"As much as I tried, I didn't really love him. Not like you're supposed to love someone you're going to marry. I think I loved the idea of love, of what I envisioned my future to be. I loved that in the beginning he made me feel like I was the most important thing in his life. He sent flowers, bought me fancy dinners and expensive jewelry, took me to concerts and left notes on my windshield. He wooed me and won me." And she'd figured he was the next best thing if she couldn't have James. She'd hated herself for comparing the men, but she had. At least the man Adam had presented to her. She cleared her throat. "But as time passed and more and more things came to light, such as Adam's temper, his worrisome family dynamics—perfect on the surface, but a roiling mess of tensions and strain underneath—the more I knew I had to get out. I thought I was going to have my normal with Adam, but the deeper I became embedded in his family, it was quite obvious I wasn't and it . . ." She shook her head. "But I kept telling myself that I wasn't marrying his family, that they would play a minimal role in our lives."

He grunted, but didn't say anything.

"I know." She shot him a sideways look. "Anyway, I knew he was going to be angry when I broke up with him—but not so angry he would try to kill me. It honestly never occurred to me that he was capable of that, and I almost died because of my blindness. And . . . he *did* die. Because I shot him before he could kill me."

"Self-defense, Lainie."

"Yes, but I feel like I set him up in some way. Like maybe I should have approached the whole thing differently or used different words. I don't know, but I *did* know the situation would trigger his anger. I just didn't expect . . ."

"Yeah. I'll say it again. Not your fault." He reached for her hand once more and squeezed. His eyes were drooping. Part adrenaline crash, part painkillers. He roused. "No more drugs, Lainie. Promise me."

"You need them."

"No more. I mean it."

She sighed. "Okay. I promise. No more drugs that make you sleepy. We have other options. For now, go back to sleep as best you can and I'll be close by in case you start dreaming again."

"Thought you were going home."

She met his hooded, hazy gaze. "Not just yet."

WHEN JAMES WOKE, he stayed still, trying to figure out what had died in his mouth and why his head pounded and his lower back burned with each breath. Oh yeah, he desperately needed to brush his teeth and he'd refused any more pain meds.

His stomach rumbled.

Loud.

"Breakfast is on the way," Lainie said from the chair in the corner.

He shifted so he could see her, hoping he covered his low gasp at the movement.

"How about something nondrowsy and nonnarcotic for the pain?" she asked, standing.

"Do you notice everything?" He was sure starting to notice her. How the fiery highlights in her red-gold hair flamed to life under the fluorescent lights and how her gray eyes sparkled with the desire to help him.

"When it comes to my job, I try." She smiled, causing a small dimple to form in her left cheek. He'd never noticed that about her before.

And he shouldn't be noticing it now. She was Steph's friend and had always been like another sister to him.

But she *wasn't* his sister and his interest had nothing to do with sibling feelings. He shook himself. "Fine." He barely managed to suppress a groan. "As long as it won't put me back to sleep."

She popped the cap off a syringe, walked over, and inserted the needle into the IV port. "That should take the edge off."

"You knew I was going to wake up feeling like this, huh?"

Lainie shot him a small smile. "This isn't my first rodeo, cowboy." She stuck the syringe in the biohazard container.

"What time is it?" he asked.

She glanced at her phone. Something he could have done, he supposed, but didn't feel like making the effort. "Early. 6:02." He groaned and she smiled. "I know. But the good news is, the results from your CT scan finally came back, and the kidney seems to be working like it's supposed to. I just need another urine sample. If there's no blood, we can discuss you getting out of here."

"You stayed here all night?"

She tilted her head. "I did. I clocked out and caught a few hours of sleep in the chair."

"That's not healthy."

Her left brow rose. "I'm aware, thanks, but oddly enough, I slept better here than I usually do at home—in spite of your snoring—so, I'll take the win, thanks."

"I don't snore."

"Actually, you do. It's a soft snore, not obnoxious or anything. Kind of comforting."

"Oh." He couldn't tell if she was serious or messing with him. He cut her a sideways look. "Come on, I don't snore."

She shot him a Mona Lisa smile. "You snore."

Now he'd have to record himself sleeping. "Well, glad to hear you could sleep through it." He hesitated. "I . . . uh . . ."

She raised one of her expertly plucked brows once more. "What is it?"

"Um . . . I didn't dream or . . . do . . . say . . . anything else, did I?" He blurted the words, unable to stop himself from asking.

Compassion softened her still-weary eyes. "No. Seriously, you slept mostly well. A little restless at times because of the pain, I'm sure, but no more episodes, if that's what you're concerned about."

How would she know that unless she'd been awake? But relief swept him at her reassurances. "Good. Thanks."

"Sure." She pulled out a sealed cup from her coat pocket and handed it to him, then walked toward the door. "Just let me know when you're done. Bathroom is across the hall. Second door on the left. You okay getting there by yourself?"

Was he? He stood, noting the pain had greatly diminished thanks to the fast-acting shot, and took two test steps toward her, grateful his legs held him. "I can make it."

They exited together, him toward the bathroom and Lainie toward the nurses' station. On his return trip to the room less than two minutes later, he spotted Cole talking to one of the doctors. His partner had a smile on his face, but his eyes were scanning the area. When they landed on Lainie, he excused himself and beelined for her.

The look the woman shot Lainie could have added another layer of ice to the arctic tundra. James just stood there a moment while he caught his breath—how could he be winded?—and watched the interactions. Lainie definitely noticed the woman's look but ignored it and smiled at Cole. The fact that James was tempted to level his own chilly look at his partner took him aback for a moment. Why did he care that Cole might find Lainie attractive? Why did he suddenly find himself looking at Lainie in an entirely different light? She was his sister's best friend. He needed his head examined. The last thing he should be thinking about was a possible romance with her.

Actually, with *anyone*. But certainly not with Lainie.

He moved closer. Neither noticed his approach.

"Good to see you here this morning," Lainie said to Cole.

"How is he?"

"Doing fine, I think. He had no problems during the night, so he's probably good to go."

"No problems at all?"

The tinge of disbelief stung. "None at all, partner," James said.

Cole stilled, then turned with only a hint of a smile that suggested he wasn't bothered a bit by James catching him questioning Lainie. "Glad to hear it. You ready to get out of here?"

James looked at Lainie. "I don't know. Am I?"

"As soon as the results come back, we can make that call. Until then, I recommend you stay put."

"Then I guess that's what I'll do."

"Need some help?" The low throaty voice came from the woman who'd tried to laser Lainie in half with her glare.

"Uh—" How did he say no politely?

"I'm Dr. Bridgette McPherson. Let's get you back in the bed so you can get comfortable."

"Fine." He had no strength to argue at the moment.

He headed for the room, anxious for the bed. If Lainie had said he could leave, he would have had to ask if he could rest first—or request a wheelchair. Never had he been so glad to have to wait on test results.

He rolled onto the bed and closed his eyes. He hurt.

Someone leaned over him, and he opened his eyes to see Dr. McPherson holding her stethoscope. "Let me take a listen, all right?"

"Sure."

She did so, her hands lingering on his chest longer than he was comfortable with. Her flirting with Cole was one thing, but he was a patient, and frankly, he didn't want anything other than her professional attention focused on him. She seemed to pick up whatever vibe he was giving off, because she finished up, her gaze holding nothing but the look a doctor gives a patient. "Everything sounds good. I'll let you get some rest while we wait for the results."

"Great."

She left and he shut his eyes once more, wondering what just happened.

"Sure you don't want something a little stronger?" Lainie's quiet voice reached him from the door.

How did she know? "I'm sure. I'll be fine." He opened his eyes to see her gaze full of compassion, and the look touched something deep inside him that he'd kept locked off for so long he almost didn't recognize it at first.

Longing.

The deep desire to connect with another person other than his partner. The walls he kept around his heart were in danger of cracking with her.

She walked over, allowing him to see behind her in time to watch Dr. McPherson waylay Cole once more. "What's her deal?"

Lainie turned. "The doctor talking to Cole?"

"Uh-huh."

"That's Dr. Bridgette McPherson." She closed the door enough to shut off his view.

"We've met, but why do you say her name like that?"

She turned back, innocence on her face. "Like what?"

He laughed, then regretted it when the area on his back protested. "Like you could do without her presence contaminating your space."

"Ouch, that's kind of harsh, isn't it?"

"But accurate?"

She grimaced. "Okay, you got me. Yes, Bridgette is one of my least favorite surgeons."

"A surgeon." So, she probably had been making a pass at him. At least she'd backed off when he'd indicated his disinterest. "Let me guess. A god complex?"

"Something like that." She paused and shrugged. "Okay, exactly like that. I'm not one to bash a fellow employee, but the truth is, she's too convinced she can do no wrong."

"Can she?"

"It doesn't appear that she can. That's the part that stinks—but is also a huge plus for her patients' welfare . . . for now. If she's ever done anything wrong, I haven't seen it or heard about it." Her jaw tightened, then she shook her head. "But my fear is that she will one day, and I just pray it's not a patient who pays the price with their life. The bad thing is, she's gotten a lot worse since her sister's death." She snapped her lips shut, her expression betraying that she thought she'd said too much.

"What happened?"

She paused, and he figured she was trying to decide whether to continue talking about the subject. Then she sighed. "A freak accident. Something happened with the gas in her house and the carbon monoxide alarm didn't go off. Bridgette is the one who found her."

"That's really sad."

"Very. Which is why, even though I don't care for her attitude, I try to be patient and have compassion for her, because I know she and her sister were really close."

The door opened and a nurse stuck her head in. "Just checking to see if you need anything."

"No, thank you, we're good."

The woman nodded and left, leaving the door open enough that James could see Cole still talking to the pretty doctor. He frowned. "She seems to like Cole."

Lainie followed his gaze. "She likes any handsome man who has the misfortune to cross her path. And besides, I have a feeling most women probably like Cole."

The smirk on her lips intrigued him. She was right. Most women fell all over themselves to get his way-too-good-looking-for-anyone's-good partner to notice them. But not Lainie. Why not? He almost asked her, but said, "What's interesting is that Cole seems to like her as well."

Lainie hesitated. Then bit her lip.

"What?" James asked. "You're dying to say something."

"Well, since I'm on a roll in speaking out of turn, I might as well look out for a friend's friend."

"Might as well."

"Just warn him that as soon as he falls short of her expectations, she'll have no trouble chewing him up and spitting him out like a bad piece of meat. Now, that I *have* seen firsthand and it's not pretty."

"Thanks for the heads-up. I'll make sure to have his back." And he was glad his instincts were still spot-on when it came to dangerous women.

The door opened and a woman stepped inside, her gaze frosty. "Lainie, I need your signature, please." She held out the iPad.

Lainie signed the screen. "Thanks, Helen."

The woman left, and Lainie clamped her mouth shut, then pressed fingers to her temples and peered at James with a worried look. "The door was cracked. I hope she didn't hear any of that."

"She and Bridgette are friends?"

"Yes, but that's really beside the point. Telling you that was a lapse in good judgment. I shouldn't have said anything. Especially not here."

"I'm not going to say anything."

"I know. I wouldn't have said anything if I thought you would." She checked his IV. "You need another bag. I'll just grab one and be right back."

"Thought you were off the clock."

"I am, but I don't mind doing this for you. I have the rest of the day off, tomorrow, and the next day too, so I'm good."

She patted his hand, and he couldn't help turning it to snag her fingers and lock his gaze with hers. "Thank you," he said, his voice an octave lower and a few decibels softer than usual. Her grip tightened around his a fraction, then she pulled away. He cleared his throat, at a loss as to what to do with the emotions running through him. "Um, I'm going to close my eyes for a few minutes while you do that."

"Good idea."

"Then I want to talk to you about the dead guy you say you keep seeing."

FIVE

Lainie headed for the supply closet, her gaze scanning the hallway. She really didn't want to talk about Adam but could tell she'd piqued James' curiosity and was going to have to fill him in. Besides, it might not hurt to get his take on things.

And decide she was losing it?

No, if anyone would understand, he would. And the fact was, she trusted James. She wouldn't spill to a coworker, but she hadn't thought twice about telling him.

Maybe her PTSD was morphing into something new and weird—and horrible. It certainly seemed to be loosening her tongue. No, she couldn't blame it on that. It really was as simple as trusting James to keep a confidence.

Footsteps behind her sent the hairs on the back of her neck spiking. She spun.

Nothing but hospital workers and patients. And visitors. So many unfamiliar faces swarming the halls, but no one to be alarmed about. Except, maybe, the guy in the hoodie? He turned down a connecting hallway. Lainie huffed a sigh and continued her trek to the room on the right.

Her phone buzzed, and she glanced at the screen and tapped the button to answer as she stepped into the supply room. "Hi, Dad."

"Hey, Lainie-girl, how you doing?"

She smiled at the nickname. "I'm at work so can't talk long. What's up?"

"I thought you had the day off."

Her mother posted her work schedule on the refrigerator. "I do, but it's a long . . . story. What do you need?"

"Your mother mentioned you were coming over next Friday to help her clean out some stuff."

Lainie's brow rose. "She told you that?" Her mother never willingly involved her father in that scenario.

"Her counselor said she needed to start sharing that kind of thing with me. I think she's trying."

"Oh. Okay."

"Anyway, I've ordered a dumpster—"

"Dad, whoa, stop. A dumpster will terrify her. She's not going to get rid of that much stuff."

"She said I could order it."

"Of course she did, but you and I both know she's going to change her mind."

He fell silent. "So, I should cancel it?"

"I would." She sighed. "But you do whatever you want."

"I don't know what to do now."

Lainie rubbed her eyes and grabbed the bag she needed. She was so tired. She couldn't deal with this. "Dad, I have some stuff I need to finish up even though I'm technically not here. I'll have to call you later, okay?"

"No, no. Never mind. I'll cancel it." He sounded so defeated. He truly didn't know what to do with his wife and her issue. And frankly, neither did Lainie.

"Wait, Dad. I'm sorry. It's good she told you. That's progress. Why don't you cancel it, then see if you can get her to order the dumpster—or at least be in the room with her when you schedule it. With the phone on speaker. That way she thinks this is her idea too."

"You think?"

"Yeah. I do. And if anytime she freaks out, reassure her. And then give her the number to cancel the dumpster. Giving her the control will help. I think."

"Excellent idea. If she cancels it, she cancels it. I'll prepare myself." He'd gotten some of the hope back in his voice. "Thanks, Lainie. See you next Friday."

"I—"

He hung up. She groaned, then left the closet and hurried back down the hall toward the ER, stopping when a wave of dizziness hit her. She stumbled to the wall and leaned against it until the moment passed. "Dumb, dumb, dumb. You need to stop doing this," she whispered.

She might have overexaggerated the amount of rest she'd gotten in the chair next to James' bed, but she hadn't wanted him to be concerned about it. However, sleep deprivation was a real thing, and she was, at the moment, deprived.

If she didn't get some sleep, some *good* sleep, she was going to be in trouble—or worse, make a mistake that could put a patient at risk. Something she'd judged Bridgette McPherson for and here she was—

"Sorry, God," she whispered. "I shouldn't have said that about her even if I do believe it. Please protect all the patients from human fatigue and error. And keep your hand over my mouth." She never talked about her coworkers. Her motto was, if she didn't have something good to say, she said nothing. Cliché, maybe, but it had held her in good stead for many years. And then she just went and word-vomited all over James Cross.

A patient.

Yes, a guy she'd known almost her entire life, but at the moment, he was a patient.

Which made her an idiot.

No, she was beyond exhausted and her filters were leaking.

"Lainie? You okay?"

She pulled in a steadying breath. "That seems to be up for debate," she muttered. "Hi, Doc." Dr. Nate Maloney was in his midsixties, good-looking in a rugged, older-beach-boy kind of way, with a lot of gray mixed in with the blond, and one of the physicians she worked with on a regular basis. He was a good supervisor, and she appreciated his compassionate heart that hadn't hardened with time.

"Need some help?" He frowned and eyed her with concern.

"No, just some sleep. Which I plan to get as soon as I deliver this." She waved the bag. "And food. Definitely could use some food too. I think I forgot to eat."

"Here. Hold on." He pulled a roll of mints from his coat pocket and dumped three in her hand. "Eat those."

"Thanks." She popped one in her mouth and let the sugar coat her tongue.

"Gotta take better care of yourself, Lainie. I need you around. You're one of the PAs I actually like."

She laughed. "You like everyone."

"Okay, so that might be true, but I like you the most. You don't do dumb stuff—except maybe work too much."

She refrained from reminding him he'd asked her to pull a double shift, and choked back a small laugh. If he only knew all the dumb stuff she did. "Well, you won't see me for the next couple of days, but thanks." The sugar did help. At least she told herself it did. "I've got to go."

He nodded, and she swiped her card to open the doors to the ER. Once back in James' room, she found him with Cole. Their conversation stopped as soon as she stepped through the door, and she couldn't help wondering if James had warned him about getting involved with Bridgette. She hoped so. "Hey, guys, I'm just going to hang this, then check and see if the results are back yet, okay?"

"Thanks, Lainie."

"Sure thing." When she was done, she walked to the nurses' station. "Maggie?"

The woman looked up from her iPad. "Yes?"

"I'm going to eat something from the vending machine, then crash for a couple of hours in the on-call room, but my patient, James Cross, is waiting on test results before being discharged. As long as the results are clear, he can go home. Just wake me to sign the paperwork. If they're not clear, then that's another issue, of course."

"You don't just want to go on home?"

"I would if I thought I wouldn't fall asleep at the wheel."

She raised a brow. "You live like two miles away."

"Exactly."

"All righty then, I've got you covered."

"Thanks." Lainie made her way back into James' room one last time. "As long as you're okay, I'm going to get some rest. Maggie will take care of you from here. You good?"

He frowned, but nodded.

"It was really good to see you, James. I do hope you'll let Steph know you're home. She's really missed you. I'm sure your parents have too."

A flicker of regret crossed his face before he covered it with a tight smile. "I've missed her too. And she knows I'm home. She texted me after the . . . uh . . . incident and I told her."

"Oh, good!" Lainie hesitated, unsure whether she should leave him or not, but the bed was calling. "All right. Take care of yourself, James."

"You too. Thanks. For . . . everything."

"You're welcome."

He looked like he wanted to say more, but instead, shot her a weary smile, took a deep breath, and shut his eyes.

Cole wrapped her in a hug. "Thanks for taking care of my best bud," he whispered.

At first, Lainie wasn't sure what to do, then chuckled and hugged him with a pat on his broad back. "Of course."

He stepped back with a flush. "Sorry. I'm a hugger and I love James like a brother. Seeing him lying there on the ground, knowing he'd been shot, not sure if the bullet hit his vest or—" He looked away, his throat working.

"I understand." She squeezed his hand. "But he's going to be just fine."

"Yeah." He cleared his throat. "I know. See you later."

With one last pat on his bulging bicep, Lainie left him, made her way to the lounge, and swiped her key card. Once inside, she let the door snick shut behind her. To her left were two sets of bunk beds, to the right, a sitting area with a television. Three vending machines that held an assortment of food ranging from healthy to junk graced the wall next to the bathroom.

The area was empty, which meant she had one of the beds instead of the recliner, but if someone else had been in the room, she would have welcomed their presence. She shrugged out of her lab coat and slipped off her shoes. It only took her five minutes to gulp down a surprisingly good turkey sandwich. Then she turned on the television for the background noise she couldn't sleep without, collapsed on one of the beds in the corner, shut her eyes, and dropped into a deep, immediate slumber.

Lainie woke like she always did. Instantly awake, alert and on guard for the threat. And just like always, she lay still, practicing the coping mechanisms taught by her therapist. *Breathe in, breathe out. I'm safe. I have a lot to do today.* She gave herself time to go through the list, but with each task she mentally checked off, unease grew. She glanced at the clock on the wall across the room and noted she'd slept for four hours.

Surely James' test results were back by now, but Maggie hadn't woken her. Lainie sat up and raked a hand over her face as though she could push the weird feelings aside.

She was the only one in the room, which was not unusual, but she'd fallen asleep to the sound of the television, and now it was off. Which was probably why she'd woken up.

Either that or the fact that she was freezing. Shivering, she grabbed her lab coat and shoved her arms through the sleeves, then reached into the pocket to find her phone. Wrong pocket. But she pulled out a piece of paper she didn't remember being in there. A sticky note.

Cheers, love.

JAMES FROZE AT THE SOUND of the crash on the other side of the door. Then he grabbed the handle and twisted.

Locked.

Of course, he'd need a key card to get in.

He pounded on the door. "Lainie! You in there? You okay?" Silence. He knocked again. "Hey, Lainie. Open up."

"I'm coming, I'm coming." The door swung open and Lainie's ashen face and terrified gray eyes greeted him. "James?"

"What happened?" His hands came up to grip her biceps, and he felt the tremors coursing through her. Pain shot through him at all his actions. He ignored it. "I heard something that sounded like someone fell or . . . something."

She waved him inside and motioned to the overturned chair on the floor. "I stumbled over that." She picked it up and shoved it under the table. "What are you doing here?"

"Looking for you. Maggie said you were here sleeping." He followed her inside and led her to the chairs in front of the television. She dropped into one, and he turned his so that he faced her, then settled into it with slow, careful movements. "What happened? Did you . . . have an episode?"

"No. At least not like what you're thinking." She studied him a moment, then sighed and rubbed her eyes. "You know how I said I kept seeing my ex?"

"Yes."

She reached into her pocket and pulled out the sticky note.

"'Cheers, love'?" He looked up, questions in his eyes.

Lainie nodded, blinking at tears. She sniffed and the sound nearly broke his heart. "Adam used to say that all the time," she said. "He was obsessed with all things British and used to say that in a British accent. Whoever left that might as well have written, 'I'm back,' but . . . how can he be back?"

"He can't be."

"I know that!" Her shout echoed around the room and she

clapped a hand over her mouth. "I'm sorry," she whispered through her fingers. "I shot him, James. I shot him in the throat. He was dead at the scene in spite of my attempts at CPR." She swallowed hard. "I got a pulse back for just a moment, then it was gone again. And then the paramedics were there and . . ." Her bewildered gaze connected with his. "I've been to his grave. I . . . just . . . don't understand . . . I . . . just don't."

His own pain escalated at the bewilderment in her words and tone. "There's probably a very good explanation for this."

"Like what?"

"I have no idea. Someone you've made angry and is trying to get back at you? Someone playing a very not-funny practical joke?"

"I can't imagine that, but it's possible, of course." She palmed her eyes, smearing what little was left of the black mascara. Before he could mention it, she stood. "I need to get out of here." She paused, looking at him. "What did your test results say?"

"They came back clear and another doctor signed off on my discharge papers so you wouldn't have to be disturbed."

"Oh. But why are you still here?"

"I got home and realized I . . . uh . . . wanted your phone number."

"You got home and came back? Please tell me you didn't drive."

"Cole brought me."

"He's a good friend."

"Better than I deserve. He said to text him when I was ready to leave."

She paused, then sputtered a shaky laugh. "Wait, your words just registered. You wanted my phone number? For what?"

Was he an idiot? He'd give anything to be able to stop the heat creeping up the back of his neck that, from previous experience, was getting ready to flood into his cheeks. "So I could text you. Keep in touch with you."

"Um, okay. Steph has my number, you know."

"I know." He sighed. "But then I'd have to explain why I wanted it and . . ." Yeah, that wasn't going to happen.

"Ah . . . right. Okay." After a narrow-eyed look, she gave him the number, and he tapped it into his phone, then she slipped her feet into her shoes.

He rose—moving in a way to incite the least amount of pain—and followed her to the door. "Lainie, before you go home, what do you say we head to security and check out the footage of this area? See if we can get the identity of any people who entered while you were sleeping."

She stilled. "I actually thought of that, but . . ."

"But?"

"But was too scared to see what might be there. Or . . ."

"Or?"

"Or what might *not* be there." Her tortured gaze landed on his and she shrugged. "What if nothing—no one—is there? What if it's all in my messed-up head?"

"Well, from one messed-up head to another, I think we need to know for sure. Once you see that it's not really Adam, you'll be able to put this behind you."

"But that's just it. I don't think I will. Before the note? Maybe. The note feels like something else."

He couldn't say he blamed her for that thought. "Then let's find out who."

"What about you? You should be resting, not worrying about my problems."

"You know as well as I do that I don't rest well. Helping you will help me too."

"And your pain level?"

"About a five, but I'll deal."

"James . . ."

"Lainie . . ."

He knew the moment she caved.

"All right, then," she said. "Let's see what we can find on the security footage. I'll call and let them know we're coming." She paused. "Should I talk to the police? I mean, I have the note, of course, but what are they going to do about it? It's not exactly something someone would consider threatening."

"Agreed. They'd take your statement, but yeah, I doubt the note would be considered anything more than a bad joke. Especially since the person just left it when he had the opportunity to hurt you if he wanted."

She shuddered, then nodded. "All right, let's go see what we can see."

Ten minutes later, she knocked on the door of the security room. Jared Beckham opened it and motioned them inside. It was a large, impressive area with monitors on all the walls displaying multiple areas of the hospital on each one. Two other security personnel looked up at their entrance, and Lainie gave them a small wave. "Thanks for letting us do this."

"If there's someone running around the hospital who shouldn't be, we need to know," Jared said. It didn't take long for the man to pull up the footage from the areas she described and the approximate times. "All right," he said, "let's look at this one first. I'll play it and you tell me when to stop."

Lainie watched the footage while James watched her. "Okay," she said, her voice low, "there I am, walking toward the elevator. I look down the hallway and that's when I see him." In the video, James could make out the expression on her face. She definitely saw something that did not sit well with her.

"Who's the guy on the elevator?" he asked.

"Chris Stanton, one of the radiologists. He asked me if I was coming." She stepped into the elevator, her gaze distant, expression troubled. The doors shut and that was it. "Do you have another angle?" she asked. "The guy that I saw was standing by the stairwell door."

"Yes. There are cameras trained on the exits." Jared worked the mouse and tapped a few keys. Then pulled up the man by the exit just as he turned to slip through the door.

"Wait," Lainie said, "go back."

Jared did and finally got the guy's face in the frame. "It's not perfect, but you should be able to say whether or not you know him."

The visible shudder that rippled through her brought a frown to James' face. She looked at him, and her hand went to her throat to grasp the key like she had done each time he'd seen her stressed. "It's absolutely not possible, but I know him."

SIX

Lainie dropped the key and pressed her shaky hands to her thighs, confusion and fear running rampant. "At least, I think I do." She was just glad they saw the guy too and she wasn't hallucinating. "If you see him again, would you try to detain him? I need to talk to him in person."

"Of course." Jared played the footage once more. "He does seem to be looking in your direction."

"He was. Both times that I've seen him, he made sure to catch my eye. He got my attention, then disappeared. Could you show the footage outside the on-call room?" She gave him the approximate time to start the search.

"Sure." He pulled it up and fast-forwarded the video. Workers and visitors and patients sped back and forth past the room, but only one other person entered and Jared paused the playback.

"He's the one who left the note in my pocket," she said. "He had a key card—a badge. Could it be someone who works here?"

"Probably not," James said. "Most likely he lifted it from someone."

"I can tell you who went in that door at that time." Jared's fingers went to work on the keyboard once more. "Alex Carlisle."

"Well, that's not Alex Carlisle who went in the room. I know Alex and that's not him."

"Let's look at the other footage and see if we can get some other views," James said. "Maybe we can run him through facial recognition software and get a name with the face."

Jared leaned back, studying the pictures from the security footage. "That first shot is the best of the bunch. In the others, he keeps his head down a lot or his face turned from the camera. I'm kind of surprised I got that one."

"It's not perfect, but it's better than nothing," James said. "If I give you an email address, can you send it through? The woman's name is Caitlyn Evans."

"Sure thing."

James rattled off an email and Jared sent the picture. "Done."

"Thanks." He looked at Lainie. "Okay if I follow you home?"

"How are you going to do that? You don't have a car and you really shouldn't be driving, so I'll pass, but thanks." She frowned. "But why . . ."

"Well, if not me, then someone. I mean, it can't hurt, right?"

"Right. True." But having him—or someone—follow her home almost felt like admitting the man from the hospital was some kind of danger to her. But he was dead, so . . .

No. *Adam* was dead. The man in the hospital was very much alive. But what did he want? "No," she said, "forget it. He's messing with me, but he hasn't done anything threatening."

"You mean, like leave a note in your lab coat? Not to mention you were asleep at the time."

When he put it like that . . . She sighed. "I mean, like you said, this could all just be some stupid joke. A prank." She rubbed her forehead. "I just want to go home and put this day in the rearview mirror." Adam was dead. She'd watched him breathe his last. If the person wanted to hurt her, he could have while she'd slept.

Great. She'd never sleep again at this point.

She stood. "Thanks again, everyone. I'm going home." She looked at James. "I recommend you do the same."

"Lainie—"

"No." She held up a hand. "I promised myself I'd never be a victim again. First with Adam, then the break-in at my house—"

"Break-in? What break-in?"

"Someone broke into my house shortly after Adam died. Before I was even released from the hospital, I had a storage unit reserved and movers lined up to get everything of Adam's out of my place and moved over there." She paused. "I suppose I should have just asked his family to get his stuff, but I couldn't . . . deal with them. Not at that point in time. And I didn't want any reminders of him in my home."

"Understandable."

"It was mostly just files, since he worked from my house occasionally. And he'd already moved his favorite recliner in. That kind of thing. But I wanted it all gone. Anyway, a couple of days later, I walked in and my place was trashed." She sniffed and swiped a tear. "Whoever it was stole my jewelry, the television, anything and everything of value. The file cabinets and dresser drawers had been turned upside down. It was a hit and grab."

"I'm so sorry, Lainie. That's just awful."

"It was, but you know what I did?"

"I can't even imagine."

"I sat on the floor and laughed."

He huffed a short laugh. "What?"

"And then I called the cops, gave my report, and started cleaning. The anger fueled me. I was furious. Livid. Beyond livid. I don't think a word has been invented for how angry I was at . . . everything."

"Understandable. But weren't you healing from a bullet wound?"

"Yes, but it was the proverbial straw. And I swore I'd never be a victim again. So, if I start acting like one—" She shuddered. "I . . . I just can't."

"Acting like a victim and playing it smart are two different things," James said.

"Maybe, but I just don't understand the point of it all. If the person's goal is to get to me—I'm talking mentally, not necessarily physically—then I'm not going to let him do it. I'm just not."

"Lainie . . ."

She shook her head and bit her lip to keep the tears at bay. Why this? Why now? But more importantly, *who*?

Familiar fury buzzed like bees in a hive, blocking rational thought and sending her heart rate off the charts. She had to get out of there before—

She stormed from the security office, breaths coming in fast pants, eyes sweeping the area and seeing nothing but friendly faces. Definitely not *his*. And that was good, but . . .

Vaguely, she heard James calling her name, but she hurried on down the hallway, her only thought to get to her car and go home where she could fall apart. She couldn't let James see her like this. *No one* could see her like this.

Her chest ached and she pressed a hand to it. "Not now, not now." She honestly couldn't remember the last time she'd done this. Sometime before Adam's death. But his death had seemed to end the attacks. And now, with an Adam look-alike haunting her, her physical symptoms were back.

The stairwell exit was just ahead, and she bolted toward it, hit the bar, and pushed through.

Footsteps echoed behind her, and she picked up her pace, made it to the door that opened into the parking garage. Someone else did too. She reached into her pocket for the mace that was never very far from her fingertips and spun. She lifted the small canister and froze. "James."

What little breath she still had whooshed from her lungs, and she leaned against the nearest pole, fighting the breathless, heart-pounding panic.

He frowned and stepped closer. "It's just me. I was calling your name. Why are you ignoring me?"

"Because I don't want to talk to you!"

He reared back, and instant remorse nearly sent her to her knees. "I'm sorry. I'm sorry. I shouldn't take my issues out on you." She grabbed the key on the chain around her neck, then pulled in a deep breath. The pressure on her chest had eased and she felt almost back to normal. Minus the fact that James had scared her spitless.

He caught her hand, and she let him pull it away from the necklace. "I was just worried," he said. "I didn't want you leaving alone."

A blue four-door sedan backed out at the end of the row of cars and headed toward them and the exit ramp. Only it slowed as it drew closer. The passenger window lowered.

James pulled her behind the safety of another vehicle, but not before she got a look at the driver, who locked eyes with her and smiled.

"That's him." She tugged against James' hold. "That's him!"

The engine roared and the car sped away.

WITHIN SECONDS, James had a 911 operator on the line. He identified himself and his badge number, then spouted the information as well as a partial plate number on the vehicle. Only when he was assured that officers would be looking for the car did he hang up. He clipped the phone to his belt and walked to the parking spot the guy had backed from.

A white piece of paper lay on the concrete. He snapped several pictures of it with his phone, then turned to Lainie and showed her one of the photos. "This looks like it fell out of his car. It's a dry-cleaning receipt dated yesterday. You heard of Hartwell Cleaners?"

She paled. "Yes. Adam used them on a regular basis. I picked up his clothes from there a couple of times on my way home from work. What's going on, James?"

"I don't know. I don't suppose you have a pair of tweezers in your purse?"

She stood beside him, her expression a cross between dazed, confused, and furious. He wasn't sure he'd ever seen that look before. On anyone.

"Lainie?"

"Uh, yes." She let out a shuddering sigh. "Sorry. Yes."

"Really?"

"Really." She slid the bag off her shoulder and rummaged in the side pocket, then pulled out a pair of tweezers that he took from her. He snagged the receipt, his wound protesting the movement, and he made sure to straighten a lot slower than he normally would. "What about tissues? I need two. I'll slide the receipt in between them until I can get to an evidence bag. I want the lab to run this for prints."

"Right. Prints." She pulled two tissues from a small packet and returned the rest to her purse. Then she held the tissues while he arranged the receipt between them.

He tucked all of it into the front pocket of his shirt, then raised a brow at her. "We've covered the fact that I probably shouldn't drive yet. But Cole can. We'll follow you home. Just to be on the safe side."

She ran a shaky hand over her hair, then pressed a forefinger and thumb to her eyelids. In that pose, she nodded. He took her hand in a light grasp and lowered it. She opened her eyes and met his gaze. "I'm sorry. I should have stopped when you were calling my name."

"Why didn't you?"

She bit her lip and looked away. "I just . . . needed some space."

"You had a panic attack, didn't you?"

Her eyes locked back on his. Her cheeks darkened to a deep red, but she nodded once again. "I did."

"And you were embarrassed for me to see it? Even after my episode in the hospital?"

"Yep. Pretty much."

"Aw, Lainie. You need a break."

"No, I need to figure out who this guy is and what he wants, but honestly, I just want to go crawl in a hole and hide."

But she wouldn't. "Let's get you home, okay?"

She sighed. "Fine. Thank you."

"Come on, Cole's probably worn a hole in the tile."

Her gaze swerved to the direction the car had disappeared. "Wonder if the driver will show up on any of the cameras."

"Might get the full plate number. We can check. *Then* Cole and I will follow you home."

Ten minutes later, with a BOLO put out on the plate and make and model of the vehicle, he, Cole, and Lainie headed back to the parking garage, where he climbed into Lainie's car to ride with her.

"Let's stop at the dry-cleaning place," she said.

"I already have that on my list to take care of."

"I'm sure you do, but I want to see for myself what Sophie, the woman who works there most days, has to say. She knew Adam. She and I only talked a few times, but I think she'll remember me."

"All right." He texted Cole and got a thumbs-up emoji in response. The three made their way to the dry cleaners about a mile from the hospital, where James followed her inside, his back molars clamped against the pain.

Cole joined them.

When the little bell above the door announced their arrival, a young woman came from the back. Her eyes widened. "Lainie Jackson? I haven't seen you in forever. Not since . . ." She frowned, her gaze soft with compassion. "Well, since Adam died. I saw what happened on the news and was shocked. I'm so sorry."

"Thank you, it's good to see you again." Lainie cleared her throat. "I found a receipt from here and wanted to see if you could tell me who picked up the clothes."

"What's the date on it?" Sophie's curious gaze flipped back and forth between James and Cole, but James didn't bother to say anything since Lainie was doing a fine job in getting what they came for.

"Yesterday," Lainie said.

"You have the receipt number?"

"47078."

James exchanged a glance with Cole. His partner was just as surprised she'd memorized the number with one look.

"Um . . ." Sophie's fingers flew over the keyboard. "I wasn't here yesterday. It was my day off. So Bobby would have—" She gasped. "What?"

"What is it?" Lainie asked.

"The name on it is Adam Williams."

This time it was Lainie who gasped. "But it can't be."

"I know. But . . . he dropped them off a week ago—also on my day off, so it was Bobby who processed them."

"And Bobby wasn't here two years ago."

"No, he's been here about six months."

"Thank you, Sophie. I appreciate the help."

"Of course." The woman frowned. "What's going on?"

"That's the question for the day, trust me. I don't suppose you have video footage from yesterday?"

James shot Cole a small smile. Lainie had been around cops enough to know what they wanted. "Ugh," Sophie said, "no. I'm so sorry. Our footage resets at midnight every night."

Lainie pursed her lips and sighed. "Okay. Thanks again." They walked outside and paused a moment. "Adam is not alive," Lainie said. "It wasn't him who dropped those clothes off and it wasn't him who picked them up."

"I know." James pressed a hand to his side.

Lainie eyed him. "That's enough for today. I'm ready to get home."

James felt sure she only said that for his benefit, but he wasn't going to argue with her.

Less than two minutes later, Cole pulled to a stop at the curb after Lainie swung into her driveway.

James placed a hand on her arm. "Stay here for a second, okay?"

"What?"

"I want to go inside with you."

"Oh. Okay."

With a pained effort, James climbed out and walked to his partner's vehicle. "I'll just be a few minutes. Do you mind sweeping the perimeter? I'd feel better leaving if you do it while I walk her inside."

"Sure." Cole climbed out and headed for the side of the house while James followed Lainie up the covered front porch to her door, his gaze automatically gauging her security. No garage, just a carport.

"You have an alarm system?"

"No."

"You need one."

"After today, I'm inclined to agree with you."

Once inside, ignoring his wound screaming that it was time for some more pain medicine, he shut the door behind him. Lainie flipped on the lights and he took in the simple floor plan of the small cottage-style home. Nice and open, which made it seem larger than it was. The front door opened into the great room that flowed into the kitchen on the right. To the left of the great room was a hallway he assumed led to the bedrooms. "Cute place."

"Thanks." She set her purse on the table next to the door and headed down the hallway. "I'm going to change. Be right back," she said over her shoulder. "Make yourself at home. The couch is comfy." She disappeared into the bedroom on the right at the end of the hall. He assumed the two rooms on the left were either guest rooms or maybe one an office. He was curious, but too tired to snoop.

He lowered himself with great care onto the sofa cushion, then leaned back with a soft groan. He shut his eyes, willing the pain to go away. To distract himself, he listened to her footsteps.

She exited the bedroom and headed for the kitchen. The refrigerator door opened, then closed, then her bare feet padded toward him.

He opened his eyes to find four little orange pills in one outstretched hand and a bottle of water in the other. He sighed. "You gotta teach me that mind-reading stuff. You're very good at it."

She laughed while he swigged the water and pills. "It's not mind-reading stuff at all. It's simply being observant of a man who's overdone it and is in pain."

"Hmm. I suppose."

A knock on her front door swung her around.

"That's probably Cole," he said, "but be sure to check first before you unlock the door."

"Goodness, how did I ever survive without you?"

He refrained from sticking his tongue out at her droll tone and settled for a scowl. She pursed her lips—hiding a smile, he felt sure—and crossed the room to peek out of the side window. "Yep, that's him. He's a good friend to both of us, being willing to play chauffer and bodyguard."

"He wouldn't have to if he'd let me drive myself." The petulance in his voice made him wince.

Lainie shot him a knowing look, opened the door, and his friend stepped inside.

"All clear out there." Cole wiped his feet on the mat. "How's the patient?"

"In pain. I think you need to take him home."

"Happy to if he'll let me." He looked at her. "Your basement door needs another lock on it. We'll get that taken care of ASAP."

"Guys, come on. I'll be fine. This whole Adam thing is just . . . weird. Creepy."

She shuddered and James frowned. "What?"

"Just thinking about my slide off the mountain. Maybe I do need to consider the idea that the guy really did try to kill me."

"Exactly," Cole said. "Which is why I asked the local uniforms to do extra drive-bys tonight. Told them you'd had some trouble at the hospital, and we just wanted to make sure it hadn't followed you home."

"Whoever came to the hospital to do whatever it was he was doing probably doesn't know where I live, right?"

James glanced at Cole, who frowned. "There's no telling what he knows, Lainie," James said. "He knew a note with two simple words would be enough to send you into a tailspin. I don't want to leave you here alone."

"Well, you have to. I can't have you two playing bodyguard for the rest of my life. I have my gun."

Cole's frown deepened. "I'm going to assume you have a permit for it."

She huffed. "Of course I do."

"Sorry, had to ask."

"Right." She shook her head. "It's fine. I'm just irritated at myself for letting this get to me." She pressed her lips together and narrowed her eyes. "You know, there was this one person who worked with Adam at the law firm. She was a paralegal and didn't care much for me because he turned his attention to me instead of her. It's a shot so long it could wrap around the earth, but her name is Nichelle Zachary. She came to the hospital one day to warn me away from him."

"Warn you how?"

"She said that his obsession with me wasn't healthy, and I needed to stay away from him if I knew what was good for me." She sighed. "I wish I'd listened, but at the time . . ." She paused. "Now that I think back on it, I wonder if she knew something I didn't. Maybe it wasn't a threat, but more of a concern. When she found me, she just irritated me—mostly because by the time she said something, it was just confirmation of what I already knew, but wasn't ready to face yet."

"I can check into it," James said.

"Actually, I'll handle that." Cole nodded to James. "You, my friend, need to rest so you can heal. So, we can do this the easy way or the hard way. It's your choice."

"You're such a bully," James muttered.

Lainie tried to hide her smile, but James caught it. She lifted her chin. "I agree with Cole."

"Why doesn't that surprise me?"

She sobered. "I'm glad Stephanie knows you're home. If I had to keep that a secret from her . . ."

"I know."

"It's going to be bad enough that you were here and I didn't tell her."

"She understands why you couldn't."

"True, but you and I both know she's not going to let me off without some ribbing."

He chuckled. "You can take it."

"Guess we'll find out. Now go," she said, pointing to the door. "I'll be fine. I'm going to fix some lunch and head to the humane society."

James blinked. "The what?"

"The place that takes in stray animals?"

A snicker from Cole earned him a glare from James, who flipped it into a questioning look for Lainie. "You getting a dog or something?"

"I wish, but no. I volunteer there once or twice a month. It's very therapeutic. You should try it sometime."

Cole cleared his throat. "After he heals?"

"Absolutely."

"I love how y'all are planning out my life here," James said. "I can take a hint." He headed for the door.

"James?" Lainie's soft voice turned him and Cole at the same time.

"Yeah."

"Thank you."

His heart turned to mush at her sincere gratitude and he nodded. "You're welcome. Call me if you need anything, promise?"

She hesitated, then tilted her head sideways. "Yes. I will. I promise."

And now he felt like he could leave.

SEVEN

Once the guys were gone, Lainie paced, trying to wrap her mind around everything. Including the receipt. Someone was going to an awful lot of trouble—

Her phone rang and she activated her Bluetooth. "Hello?"

"Hey, girl, this is Annie at the body shop. Got some news for you." Annabelle Franklin and Lainie had grown up together in the same church and hung out some as teens. Then Annie had gone to work at her grandfather's body shop while Lainie went off to college.

"My car's ready?"

"I wish. Seems like every car in Lake City landed in our shop last week. And yours is at the end of the list."

"Well, I'm assuming this call is to let me know you've at least looked at it?"

"Yep. And here's the thing, Lainie. Your front tires were bald. You were very lucky you weren't killed."

Luck had nothing to do with it. "I don't understand. Bald?"

"Like they were freshly shaven."

"I'm still confused." That was an understatement.

"Like someone who just shaved their head?"

"What? No. I mean I'm confused as to how they could be bald.

Never mind." She bit her lip and glanced at the clock. "When do you think y'all will get to it?"

"Probably in the next couple of days. Gramps had to order a couple of parts. I'll keep you updated."

"Right. Okay, thanks."

"Bye."

Lainie hung up, trying to get her brain to process the words.

Bald front tires? No way. She took care of her car like she took care of her patients. Down to the last detail. She'd just put new tires on the Subaru less than six months ago. So . . . why did she have bald tires? It didn't make sense. Then again, not much did right now.

Her phone buzzed. A text from James already.

I feel rotten for leaving. Are you sure you're okay?

Should she tell him about the tires? Yes, but not yet. She'd tell him once she had all the information.

I'm sure. I'm heading out to the shelter. Talk to you later. Oh, and please tell Cole thank you again for offering to put a new lock on my basement door.

I would do it for you, but Cole threatened to report me to my mother if I didn't follow orders and be careful not to stress my ribs.

Knowing how the woman smothered her children when they were sick or hurt, she could understand how James managed to resist doing the work himself. And yet, she couldn't help the small shot of jealousy that stung her. She'd love to have a mother who . . .

But she didn't.

Your mother loves you.

He might not need the reminder, but she sent it anyway.

And I love her.

But you haven't told her you're home yet.

Not yet. Soon. Enjoy your furry friends, but don't
drop your guard and let me know if you see
anything suspicious.

I will. Bye James.

Bye Lainie.

Before heading to the animal shelter, Lainie fixed herself a sandwich, then decided to detour to the body shop. This was something she needed to see for herself. Fingers tight on the rental's steering wheel, she kept an eye on her mirrors for the entire ten-minute drive.

When she arrived without incident, she let out a low breath and climbed out. Sonny Carpenter, the owner of the shop, was as tall as Cole, in his midsixties, built like Santa Claus, and smelled like a chimney. Thanks to her friendship with Annie, Lainie had known the man forever.

He must have seen her pull in, because he stepped outside to greet her, arms outstretched. "What you doing here, baby girl? Annie just went to grab us coffees."

She hugged him, then stepped back. "I'm not here to see her. I came to see you."

"Always happy to see you, but didn't she tell you that your car's not going to be ready for a few days?"

"She told me. She also said that my tires were bald. I just don't understand how that's possible and wanted to come see for myself. You still have them?"

"Sure do. Just took them off about an hour ago when I told Annie to call you. They're in the stack to recycle."

"Will you show me?"

He raised a brow, but motioned for her to follow him through the shop, dodging cars, car parts, and workers. At the back, he pushed through the exit leading into an area that looked like an organized junkyard. The stack of tires to her right drew her. "How am I supposed to find them in this?"

"You're not. I am." He started pulling tires off the top and setting them against the wooden fence. It took him five minutes before he gave a grunt and held a tire up for her to see. "This is one of 'em." He set it on the ground and rolled it to her.

She caught it and pushed it over. It landed with a thwack in the wet mud. For the next several seconds, she studied it, then stood. "That's not my tire."

Sonny frowned at her, then scowled. "You think I don't know what tires come off which cars?"

"Of course you do. And I know what tires I bought and had put on. I bought four at the same time. But that wasn't one of them."

He leaned in and came up with a second tire. "This is the other one."

It was identical to the first. "Again, not one I purchased." She bit her lip and ran her fingers over the almost nonexistent treads. No way would she have worn them down this much in six months. But they *were* the brand she'd bought.

Sonny scratched his bristly chin. "Then what were they doing on your car?"

"That's a very good question. Were the other two like this as well?"

"No, they were practically brand new."

"Exactly." She shook her head. "Can you throw these in the back of my rental?"

"You're gonna *keep* them?" His eyes narrowed. "You in trouble, Lainie?"

"I'm not sure how to explain what's going on, but say prayers for me when you think of it."

"Always do, Lainie girl." He patted his shirt pocket and grunted. "Left my smokes in the office."

"You need to stop that, you know."

"Course I know. I know a lot of things. Doesn't mean I always do what's best for myself."

"You should, Sonny," she said, her voice soft, hoping he could hear the love in her words. "You deserve the very best."

"Aw, girl, you know how to go straight for the heart, dontcha?"

She smiled, gave the man another hug, then climbed back in her car, eyes on her surroundings, nerves twitching. She didn't see anything that alarmed her, so she aimed her vehicle toward the shelter. She'd promised to be there, so that's what she would do. Better late than never. Then she'd ask James to help her figure out how her perfectly good tires could go bad so fast.

Ten minutes later, she pulled into the parking lot of the humane society and climbed out of her vehicle. She headed for the side door she always used, climbed the two steps to the postage-stamp porch, and pulled on the handle.

Locked.

"That's weird," she muttered. Candace usually had the door open by the time Lainie arrived.

A light breeze sent strands from her ponytail whipping around her head and across her eyes. With a hand, she brushed them away and scanned the area behind her.

Goose bumps prickled her skin in spite of the muggy heat, and a ball of anxiety curled in her belly. The facility was set in the middle of four acres surrounded by a chain-link fence that was divided into exercise sections.

She hurried to the back of the building, looking for Candace Freeman's white truck parked next to the door. The empty spot kicked her heart rate up a notch and Lainie glanced at her phone. 1:57. Okay, so technically, Candace wasn't due back from lunch until 2:00, but she was usually early.

Once again, she studied her surroundings, fully expecting to see the man, but she was the only human on the premises. Trees rose in the distance, blocking the sight of the main highway, but she could hear the cars zipping past.

Where was Candace?

The vet's office attached to the shelter usually opened at nine, so someone was probably there even though it wasn't busy. She couldn't see the parking lot from her current vantage point, so she started walking while the stillness surrounded her, making her feel small and exposed.

The breeze seemed to whisper, *Cheers, love*, and it sent shudders rippling up her spine.

The memory of the note in her pocket and the shot of fear it had ignited was fresh and unwelcome. "Stop it. It's not possible."

But the uneasiness wouldn't leave her alone. She'd never felt this way before on the property. So, what did it mean? Was someone really watching her or was she just being paranoid?

She stood still, breathing in and listening.

The hair rose on the back of her neck.

Adam wasn't back, but someone was.

And he was watching her. From somewhere close by.

She knew it like she knew her own name, although there was nothing that should have set off her internal alarms.

So where was he? He'd had to have followed her to the place. The fact that she hadn't noticed although she'd been watching didn't sit well.

With a bad feeling pulsing through her, Lainie rounded the building with the intention of climbing into her car and locking the doors until Candace got there.

Her car was only thirty feet away—and someone was standing not far beyond it.

Him. With a baseball cap and dark sunglasses, wearing a black button-down shirt with the first two buttons undone, revealing the base of his throat.

And the puckered white scar there.

She lurched to a stop, a scream building, spots dancing before her eyes. Passing out was a real possibility and she fought to hold on to consciousness—and her sanity. "Who are you?" Her voice came out breathless and terrified. "Answer me. Who are you?"

"Who do you think I am, Lainie?"

Her weapon was in the glove compartment, and there was no way she'd be able to get to it should he decide to come after her.

But he didn't.

"Now's not the time, but it's coming. Cheers, love." He smiled and walked to the black SUV idling behind him, climbed in, and drove down the drive, leaving her gaping at red taillights.

The plate! Get the plate number!

But he was already rounding the curve and too far away to see the digits.

Instead of wilting into a puddle on the asphalt, Lainie forced her shaky legs to close the distance to her car, climb in, and slam the door. She hit the locks and drew in a ragged breath. "God, what's going on? Who is he? It can't be. I know it's not, but . . ."

But the scar . . .

A white truck pulled around the side of the building, spiking Lainie's pulse once more. Then she huffed a relieved sigh. Candace was here. Lainie leaned her head against the wheel and sucked in several more deep breaths to get herself together.

Less than a minute later, the front door opened, and Candace looked at her, head tilted, questions in her eyes.

Lainie stepped out of her car once more and shut the door. "Hey."

"Hey, I didn't think you were coming in today. Figured you got a call or something."

"No, sorry I didn't let you know. Things have been kind of crazy lately, but I needed some furry hugs." She was relieved her voice didn't betray the turmoil swirling inside her.

"Well, I'm so sorry I'm late. There was a wreck on Highway 9. You been waiting long?"

"No, just a few minutes." A few minutes that had lasted a lifetime. Lainie walked up the steps and into the building, still seeing the man in her mind's eye. "I'm going to take Rex and Tex for some playtime in the back and let them run off some of that morning energy." They were her favorites and she never tired of their antics.

"Perfect. Ricky'll be here in about five minutes. He can start cleaning their area."

Ricky Strickland, one of the kennel techs.

Lainie chewed her lip while she headed to the back area, where the dogs barked their greetings, ears perked, tongues hanging to the side of their mouths while furry hind ends wiggled with their joy at her presence.

A lump rose in her throat against her will. She cleared it away. "Hello, babies, don't worry, you'll all get a turn." She made it to Rex and Tex's cage and slipped inside. The brothers each weighed about twenty pounds and were a mixture of beagle and something she'd yet to figure out. She scratched Tex's ears and he moved in closer. Rex nudged her hand and she laughed. "But you're both cuties, right? You'll find homes soon. I sure wish it could be with me." Maybe one day when she had the time to devote to them. She already had the yard, but the work schedule just wasn't pet-ownership friendly. Of course, the work schedule was her own fault, but . . . one day.

She leashed them and led them out to the run where she released them, picked up two of the tennis balls from the bucket on the table, and tossed them.

Both dogs loved the game of fetch and right now, Lainie was grateful she was able to play it while she looped the incident in her mind. She now had no doubt the man had targeted her, but why?

"It's not Adam," she whispered.

But the scar . . .

But it still wasn't possible.

Regardless, whoever he was, he was toying with her, scaring her on purpose. She took a seat in the chair next to the gate and rolled the key between her fingers. No way. She wasn't going to give him the satisfaction of being scared.

"Lainie? You ready to move on to the others yet?" Lainie looked up to find Candace standing at the door, then glanced at the dogs. Once she'd stopped throwing the balls, Rex and Tex had run their little hearts out, wrestling and playing with one another. They now lay under the shaded area, panting and happily tired.

Lainie lurched to her feet. "Right. Sorry."

"You okay?"

The fact that everyone in her life felt compelled to ask that question spoke volumes. "I've got some personal stuff going on." She rubbed her hands down her jean-covered hips. "And I have a weird request."

"Okay."

"Could I look at footage from the security cameras during your lunch break?"

Candace's brow rose high enough to hide under her bangs. Then she frowned. "Yes, but is there a problem I should know about?"

"I don't know. That's why I want to see the footage. About ten minutes before you got here."

"Do we need to call the police?"

"Not yet."

"All right. Get the dogs back in the kennel and meet me in the office."

"Thanks."

Three minutes later, Lainie watched the black SUV creep up the drive, then park out of sight of the camera. Her vehicle was in plain view. Then the man from the truck walked into range of the camera and stood on the driver's side of her vehicle. The sight she'd been greeted with when she'd rounded the building. They had their confrontation and he turned and left while she tried to keep it together.

"Who was that?" Candace asked. "That was kind of creepy."

"No 'kinda' about it," Lainie muttered. "It was super creepy."

"Who is he?"

"I have no idea." Because it *wasn't* Adam.

"Well, he sure seems to know who you are."

Yes, yes he did.

WHILE RIDING A DESK wasn't exactly his favorite way to spend his working hours, James would be the first to admit it had its advantages. Especially when this particular desk was Cole's couch. He'd just finished getting information on Nichelle Zachary and had moved on to Adam Williams.

A search of the man's family revealed a sibling—not a twin—a variety of cousins, and parents who were alive and still married to one another. He noted they lived in Asheville in the home Adam had been raised in. Their comments to the press about Lainie had not been flattering. In fact, they'd been downright threatening. Talking to them might prove enlightening.

Reading the report and what Adam had done to Lainie made him sick to his stomach, but the man was dead and buried and James was glad of it.

"'I was asleep,'" he read, hearing her voice in his head, "'and a noise woke me up. A loud click . . . or a pop, next to my ear. Like it misfired. It woke me up and I rolled and he fired again. That bullet hit me in the shoulder, but I . . . I don't know. I kept moving and rolled under the bed. Adam went one way, I went the other, and I made it out of the room, down the hall, and into the den. He followed me. I threw a fireplace poker at him and it hit him. I tackled him, he dropped the gun, and we both went after it. We fought and I managed to grab the gun, but he just wouldn't stop. I yelled at him to, but he wouldn't. He was going to kill me, told me he was, so I pulled the trigger.'"

James shuddered and clicked to the investigation notes. All evidence pointed to self-defense and it had been ruled as such. Crime scene photos were never pleasant to look at, but knowing Lainie had lived this grieved him deeply. He clicked off the screen and back to the report. The detective had asked her to go back to the argument. "'I called off our engagement. He was angry. So very angry. We argued and I insisted he leave. He refused, and I didn't really know what to do next. I was afraid if I called the police right then, it would push him over the edge. I just wanted him gone. So I told him if he didn't go, I would, that I didn't want to be around him, and that when I returned, if he was still there, I'd call the cops. He didn't say a word and I left. I was gone for about three hours. When I came back, he was gone and my house key was on the table. I planned to have the locks changed the next day.'"

James stopped reading and rubbed his eyes. As he read, he could hear Lainie's voice in his head, almost see the tears in her eyes, hovering on her lashes, refusing to fall.

Cole walked over to him. "I have some things at the office I need to do. I'm going to make some fresh coffee, then head out. You want some?"

"I'm good." The last thing he needed was more caffeine.

Cole nodded to the screen. "Anything jump out at you?"

"Just that it's a shame some guys give the rest of us a bad name," he muttered.

"True, but that's been the case since the beginning of time."

"I know." He scrubbed a hand over his face. "I know."

Cole headed for the kitchen and James turned back to the report.

"'When I got home,'" he read, "'I poured myself a glass of milk, which I do every night. It was the last of it. I carried it to my bathroom, intending to drink it after I got out of the shower, but ended up knocking it over and onto the floor. Thankfully, it hit the rug next to the sink and not the tile, so it didn't break. But it triggered something inside me. I sat there and cried. Over spilt milk. Cliché, right? But mostly over what my life had become. Over knowing what I needed to do. So, I threw the rug in the washer, cleaned up everything, and crawled into bed. The next thing I knew, Adam was there and trying to kill me.'"

Which would explain why the glass in the bathroom held residue of milk and sleeping pills, but there'd been no drugs in Lainie's system.

Cole waved on his way out and James went back to the screen.

Lainie went on to describe the incident and how she managed to get away from Adam, grab the gun, and pull the trigger. The second telling matched the first.

Once again, James closed his eyes, picturing it all happening and how terrified she would have been.

He rose, needing to move, pace, go for a run, something. He snorted. Yeah, a run would be nice, but probably not until his ribs had healed a bit. He grabbed his phone and headed toward the kitchen, deciding maybe caffeine wasn't a bad idea after all. A knock detoured him, and he opened the front door to find Lainie standing on the porch.

"Lainie?"

With hands clasped in front of her, she peered up at him through thick, dark lashes. "Hi, I hope it's okay I stopped by."

"Of course." He stepped back and she swept past him. He got a whiff of the scent that he always associated with her before following her into the den. "What's going on?"

"First, how are you feeling?"

"Fine. Back to normal." She shot him a knowing look and he shrugged. "Well, maybe not normal, but I'm okay. Now, what brings you here?"

"I wanted to show you something. It's a video of the security footage outside the humane shelter this afternoon."

She held up a thumb drive and he raised a brow. "All right." He took it and plugged it into his computer, then settled on the couch to click his way to the only video file on the drive. "What happened?"

Lainie paced in front of the mantel. "The guy from the hospital was at the animal shelter. I think he followed me there."

James watched the video play out, his heart rate picking up as the seconds ticked past. When the vehicle pulled out of sight of the camera, he started at the beginning and played it again. Lainie joined him this time, sitting beside him.

When the video finished once more, Lainie crossed her arms and tapped her toe, a deep scowl on her face and fear in her eyes. "I'm scared. I don't want to be. I keep telling myself not to be. But . . . I am."

"Of course you are."

She hugged herself, then rubbed her biceps. "He's making me

crazy, James. I know it's not Adam, but he had the scar." She pointed to the base of her throat. "Exactly where I shot him."

James frowned, started the footage again, and tried to zoom in. "I can't see it on here."

"It was there."

"I'm not saying it wasn't, just that this isn't the best quality video." He glanced at her. "If you say you saw it, you saw it."

Her eyes reddened, then she looked away. Cleared her throat. "Thank you."

He stood. "You're not crazy, Lainie, but I'm wondering if someone wants you to *think* you are."

"That thought had occurred to me. But why?"

"I don't know, but I think it has a lot to do with Adam and his death. And the fact that you shot him."

She swallowed. "Like someone has decided to get revenge?"

"Possibly."

"Well, that would explain the bald tires."

"Bald tires?"

She told him about her adventures at Sonny's. "And while those are my brand, there's no way they're the same tires I bought and had put on."

"You're saying someone changed them?"

"It's the only thing I can think of—which kind of discounts the whole accident theory. And it would take some planning to get the timing right. Watching the weather, seeing when it was a better-than-maybe chance of rain, actually changing the tires . . . maybe even knowing that I made a weekly, sometimes twice-a-week trip up the mountain to the Gonzaleses' store." She fell silent, then cleared her throat. "But if someone wants revenge, why not right after Adam died? Why wait eighteen months?"

He shook his head. "I'm just speculating. Could be something else entirely, of course. Any new thoughts on who would want to come after you in that scenario, though?"

She sighed. "A few."

He raised a brow. "Seriously?"

"Well, there's Nichelle."

"Yeah. She lives at the top of the mountain and is still working as a paralegal. I talked to her briefly by phone and asked her why she warned you about Adam, and she said she didn't mean to come across threatening, but he gave her bad vibes and she was worried about you."

"And I took it entirely different." She pressed a palm to her forehead. "Because I didn't want to hear what she was saying. I didn't want to admit she was right."

"Maybe. I don't know that I'd be so quick to believe that. I asked her if she'd be open to me coming by to talk to her, and she said she was."

"When will you do that?"

"She's going to call me when she gets off work. In the meantime, have you thought of anyone else who might have it in for you?"

"Second on the list would be Adam's brother, Nick. He wasn't— isn't—too fond of me. He and Adam were super tight, so he blamed me for Adam's death. Which is understandable, I suppose. After all, I did shoot him."

"And if you hadn't?"

"I would be dead." Her complete assurance behind the statement chilled him to the point of goose bumps. "But, sadly, that doesn't matter to Nick. I'm sure he wishes it had been me who'd been killed and not Adam."

James already didn't like the guy. "Anyone else? Other boyfriends?" *Please say no.*

"I mean . . . before Adam, I dated a few guys. It was never anything serious. But no one since Adam and no one I'd consider dating again."

He hoped he hid his relief. "Names?"

She listed three and he wrote them down. "We'll check them out if only to *rule* them out."

"And then there was a patient at the hospital who hit on me. He reported me for unprofessional conduct when I turned him down. Logan Richards."

Okay, now that could be something. "All right. Definitely will check him out."

"I figured he'd do something like that and went straight to my boss and filled out an incident report. There was also security footage that showed him grabbing my arm and me pulling away, then hurrying out of the room. So while it was annoying, I was cleared of any wrongdoing almost immediately."

And now James wanted to find the guy and punch him. "I'm sorry that happened to you."

She shrugged. "It's all part of the job. Surprisingly, that kind of stuff doesn't rattle me too much. You can almost tell which patient is going to step out of line as soon as you enter the room. A lot of times, I'll swap with a male doctor to avoid the potential for a volatile situation."

But she shouldn't have to.

"And," she said, "every so often, I'd see him in the cafeteria like he was waiting for me. I told security I was uncomfortable, and Jared would often walk me down. Richards finally quit showing up and I haven't seen him since." She rubbed her nose and sighed. "Honestly, if I had to point more fingers, I'd say look at the rest of Adam's family while you're checking out Nick. I think one of the reasons I was drawn to Adam was because of his family. Initially, they looked like wonderful people. They were kind and welcoming and on the surface were the picture of exactly what I was looking for."

"That normal family?"

"Exactly. Only the more I got to know them, the more the image fell apart. His mother is a cold woman, but she's all about appearances and can come across as very caring and warm. She's not. As for his father, he didn't seem to mind me dating Adam, and in the beginning, I liked him. But then one night, he made me uncomfortable."

"Uncomfortable?"

Her jaw tightened and she looked away for a fraction of a second before she met his gaze. "He hit on me one time when Adam wasn't around. He never touched me, but what he said was completely inappropriate. I told him if he ever said anything like that to me again, I'd tell his wife. I think it shocked him."

James curled his fingers into fists, revisiting the idea of punching someone. "Good for you."

"Maybe. I've never been very good at confrontations like that, but I couldn't just let him think that I was okay with his behavior. When I told Adam, he just rolled his eyes and said to ignore it, that his father has always been that way."

"Unbelievable. He made excuses for him?"

"He did. And while it infuriated me, I didn't say anything. I was already on the verge of breaking up with Adam, but that sealed it for me. Adam didn't defend me even when he knew how his father was. And I kept thinking . . ." She rubbed her cheek, red creeping up from her neck.

"What?"

She glanced at him. "I kept thinking that the man I married should defend me."

"Absolutely right." After a short pause, he said, "What did your friends say about him? Steph and the others?"

Lainie groaned. "In the beginning, they were thrilled for me, but the longer we dated, the more controlling Adam became and the less time I spent with my friends. Steph finally asked me about it, and I realized she was right, but I just let it go on. When Allison, Jesslyn, and Kristine decided I needed an intervention . . . well, that definitely didn't sit well, but they did get me to thinking. It wasn't long after that, things went south fast, and I found myself in the car with a man who told me to ignore his father's proposition."

"Aw, Lainie."

She waved a hand. "I should have ended it with Adam right then and there, but I didn't want to make a scene in the car and while my temper was running hot." She shook her head. "I don't know. Maybe if I had, then the whole thing at my house wouldn't have happened."

"It would have happened," he said. "One way or another, he would have come after you."

"Probably." She sucked in a steadying breath and let it out in one slow exhale. "As for anyone else, Adam had a couple of good friends, but I don't see them doing this kind of thing." She palmed her eyes and sighed. "I don't know, James, I'm reaching. The hard truth is, it could be anyone."

"No, it couldn't," James said. "This is personal. This is someone who knows you and knows you well."

EIGHT

Someone who knew her. Someone seriously unstable—and they knew her. The question was, did she know them? Her phone buzzed, and when she saw it was her mother, she sent the call to voice mail with only a small twinge of guilt. She wasn't in the mood to deal with what was waiting for her on the other end of the line.

"What is it?" he asked.

She glanced at him, soaking in the tenderness in his eyes. "My mom. That was her. She's never been a typical mom, and deep down, I've always resented it even while I understood it was because of the trauma of her past. She was better when we were younger, but as we got older, she wanted *us* to take care of *her*." She paused, then finally said, "She has mental health issues."

"I've known there was something going on but have never heard the details. What kind of mental health problems?"

Lainie frowned. She wasn't used to airing her family's dirty laundry, especially to someone who couldn't really understand them. He'd grown up in a completely different environment, as had his sister, of course. "I don't know if Stephanie told you, but my mother is a hoarder." But even Steph didn't know the full extent. Lainie had hidden it from everyone in her life.

He raised a brow. "Like television-worthy hoarder?"

"Yes. Like that."

He winced. "That's tough."

"It is. There are certain rooms that are off-limits because Dad keeps her in line for the most part, but the other areas are getting bad—which is why she was willing for me to come help her clean. Only it looks like I'm going to have to miss this time around if we don't have this whole thing cleared up by next Friday." Maybe she'd call her sister and give her a chance to help. Deep down, she knew Ellen would say no, but maybe if she tried just *one* more time . . .

"Why does she do it?"

"I think it all goes back to her childhood. She grew up poor without anything to call her own, and then her father was murdered. At first, she just clung to those things that belonged to him, saying she couldn't bear to part with anything of his. But now it's morphed into *everything*. She doesn't want to let *anything* go because she 'might need it' at some point." She shrugged. "She knows she has a problem, says she wants to do better, but refuses to follow through on anything that would actually help her. Like counseling and staying on her medication. I keep praying for her and just trying to love her as she is."

"That's admirable."

"Maybe, but I'll also admit it's a daily struggle. It's hard sometimes. Extremely hard."

He swiped a hand over his eyes. "Well, that all kind of puts me to shame."

"What? No. Why would you say that?"

"Because I don't have the patience you do."

"Oh, it's not *my* patience."

"You're saying God gives it to you?"

"Most of the time, anyway, when I take the time to get prayed up."

He smiled. "I like that. Prayed up."

"My youth pastor used to use that phrase. 'You can't face what you have to face if you don't get yourself prayed up.'"

"Good saying."

"That's not to say I don't have my moments where my mom makes me want to scream, especially when I go over to help—at her request—and she refuses to let me in the door. But in general, after I make sure I'm all prayed up, I'm okay and can deal with her moods."

"Your dad doesn't let you in?"

"When he's there and knows I'm coming. Which I try to make sure he does. But when he's off on one of his adventure hikes or guiding people down the river . . ." She tilted her head.

"I had no idea."

She wrinkled her nose. "Most people don't. It's not like I advertise it."

"I can't believe Steph never said anything."

"Steph doesn't *know* everything. I've never told her how bad it was." She shot him a sad smile. "Why do you think we were always at your house and I never invited Steph to mine?"

He stared, remembering. "I guess I never really thought about it." He hesitated, then seemed to make up his mind. "My mother hovers—it can be suffocating. I feel like I can't breathe by the time I have to leave my parents' house. I'm ashamed to say I used to practically yell at her about it. Thankfully, I've matured over the past few years and handle it better, but probably not as well as it sounds like you handle your mom." He shook his head. "I'm not sure what's worse. A mom who pushes us away or a mom who wants to hang on too tight."

"I know which one I'd vote for, but it's probably because I've never had that."

He smiled. "You're not the Lainie I thought you were."

"What's that mean?"

"You've always just been Stephanie's friend." He studied her with an expression in his dark brown eyes that made her feel like a bug under a microscope.

"I'm still Stephanie's friend."

His gaze never wavered. "I'm aware."

The fact that he was seeing her as something other than Stephanie's friend was . . . unnerving. Exciting. Terrifying.

Time to take the focus off her. "Your mother worries about you. Think about it. Your job is dangerous. It's only natural for her to be concerned." His eyes glinted at her change of subject, but he let her get away with it.

"I know. I could handle concerned. She takes it beyond concerned to . . ." He grimaced.

"Suffocating."

"Yeah."

"It was dangerous when you were in the Army and now you've come home to another career that could have deadly consequences."

"Which she doesn't know about yet."

"Oh. Right. You sure about that?"

"Well, I haven't told her or anyone other than Steph, so . . ."

Lainie snickered. "I'm not saying her behavior won't make you want to pull your hair out, but it is understandable." She smiled to soften any sting that might be in her words and hoped he didn't notice she was rambling.

He probably noticed, but his eyes narrowed, and he sighed, then dropped his chin to his chest. "I know that too."

"I'm telling you a lot of things you already know."

"You are."

She reached over and squeezed his fingers, then pulled her hand back, missing the contact but needing the distance. He made her heart do crazy things and she couldn't think when that happened. Clearing her throat, she nodded to the screen. "So, what's the next step?"

James drew in a deep breath and nodded, turning to the computer. "Next, I'm going to go talk to Nick and the rest of Adam's family, get a feel for them, see what's what. Let me give them a call and see if they're home."

Lainie checked her text messages while he looked up the number and dialed. Stephanie, Allison, Kenzie, and Jesslyn had been having an entire conversation about their camping trip while she'd been involved with her crazy morning. Nothing from Kristine, though. She caught up on the thread and responded.

> I'm fine with glamping. Y'all just need to tell me where. Pick one of the places and we'll get a deposit on it. Anyone text Kristine to see if she can make it?

"Hey, Cole."

She looked up to see James on the phone.

"Can you come pick me up? I've got an idea I'd like to follow up on and I'm going to need your help."

Lainie could hear Cole speaking but couldn't make out the words. He must have asked where they were going, because James said, "To ask some questions about a dead man who keeps showing up."

"I don't suppose it would be a good idea for me to come?" Lainie asked.

James' brow quirked upward. "I'm going to say probably not."

She nodded. "Can't I sit in the car?"

"Lainie . . ."

"Okay, okay. I had to try." He clipped his phone to his belt, then paused. Looked at her and pursed his lips. She frowned. "What?"

"Then again, it might not be a bad idea to keep you in my sights."

"Really?"

"As long as you promise to actually stay in the car and keep your head down."

"I'll do my best." She stood. "Now, before Cole gets here, I want to show you something."

He followed her out to her rental, and she lifted the hatch to point at the tires. "Those were on my car."

He leaned in and ran a finger over the rubber. "Wow. I see why you slid off the road."

"I almost didn't need any help, but he bumped me and over I went."

"Where do you think someone would have had the time to change them?"

"While I was at work. Or in my carport, but I seriously doubt it happened there."

"I agree. I'll get Caitlyn Evans to ask about security footage around where you park at the hospital."

"There are cameras, and if it's someone familiar with the hospital, then my guess is he's not going to show his face. And no one is going to remember him, because who's going to really notice someone changing a tire in the parking lot? It happens."

"True, but I still want to try." He studied her. "I know Adam was a lawyer, but how'd you guys meet?"

"He was the lawyer for one of my patients." She smirked, but the look held no humor. "A domestic abuse case. Can you believe it?"

"Ouch."

"Anyway, he was on the floor visiting her quite a bit while she was healing, so our paths crossed a few times and that's how we met."

"So, other people at the hospital would have recognized him if they saw him lurking about?"

"You mean if he wasn't dead and showed up? Yes. A few would. Like I said, he was on the floor off and on for the two months his client was there. And I got a few texts from people saying they saw him yesterday—or at least someone who looked like him—when you wound up in the ER."

"I see. Okay, so help me get this straight. Adam just walked up to you one day and asked you out?"

She gave a humorless laugh. "No, we'd struck up a casual friendship. I was caring for his client. He'd come by to talk to her, then he'd take a break or she'd fall asleep. Sometimes he'd come out to the station to talk to me and some of the others. Then he started getting more interested, and I . . . was flattered, I guess. One day, he asked if I wanted to grab some lunch in the cafeteria and I said sure. After that, we started eating together just about every chance we got. And then one day, he asked me to dinner. We dated for about six months before he asked me to marry him. You know the rest."

"I'm sorry, Lainie. I can't tell you how angry that makes me. On your behalf."

She blinked at the suppressed fury in his tone. "Thank you. Makes me angry too, but I'm trying to put it in my rearview mirror." She nodded to the 4Runner coming their way. "Cole's almost here."

James shut the hatchback, then went to lock the door. As soon as Cole pulled into the drive, she hurried to scramble into the back seat, not wanting to give James any time to change his mind. Cole raised a brow at his partner, but James just nodded. Hopefully, they both knew keeping her close was a good idea.

The drive to Asheville went quickly in spite of the city's traffic and multiple construction projects, and Lainie soon found herself staring at the familiar two-story middle-class home with a well-kept yard and two cars in the driveway. The windows were open to take advantage of the mild weather.

Cole parked on the curb and looked at her in the rearview mirror. "I don't need to remind you why you have to stay in the car, right?"

"I got it, I got it."

"Honk if you need something," James said.

She scowled, crossed her arms, and slouched in the seat. He winked at her.

Winked at her.

Before she could think of an appropriate response to that, he and Cole were out of the vehicle and heading up the walk to the pretty red front door. Cole knocked while James hung back, his head on a swivel. Always watchful, always on guard. No doubt thanks to his time in the Army, not to mention his current occupation.

The door opened and Adam's mother, Carol Williams, a woman in her late fifties, faced the detectives, arms crossed, a frown creasing her brow. Seeing her nearly stopped Lainie's heart. She was an attractive woman who bore a strong resemblance to Adam, and Lainie would know her anywhere. She hadn't aged a bit in the last eighteen months, and when Cole introduced himself and James, her frown morphed into a smile that seemed genuine. She waved the two men in and the door shut.

Lainie hesitated. James had brought her only because he trusted her to stay in the car, but this was Adam's mother. She was as black-hearted as he had been. Now that James and Cole were inside, her nerves kicked in and various scenarios ran through her head. What if she poisoned them? Or just plain shot them?

No, she was being silly. They could take care of themselves.

But . . . could they? If they got into trouble, how would Lainie know to call for help?

Unable to shut off the chilling scenarios, she opened the car door and climbed out, shut the door with a soft click, then hurried to the nearest open window. If she could just make sure everyone was okay, then she'd get back in the car with no one the wiser.

". . . and I told you it's possible someone may have seen him." Adam's mother's voice filtered to Lainie through the window screen. "He's not dead."

JAMES WASN'T SURE what to think. Of course, he didn't tell the woman Lainie was the one who'd seen Adam, just that someone had reported spotting him at the hospital. And now, Adam's mother was simply verifying Lainie's sightings of the man. Which was impossible because *the man was dead*.

Wasn't he?

James was starting to wonder. Faking one's death was rare, but not unheard of. Although, it sounded more like a situation of taking advantage of the opportunity to *stay* dead rather than planning to *be* dead. He had no doubt Adam didn't intend for Lainie to survive his attack.

"But . . . the funeral . . ." James spread his hands. "To go to all that trouble."

"It was a small service. Just family. We didn't want to make a big production of it so if Adam ever decided he could come home . . ." She shrugged. "We didn't even bother with an obituary. We just needed it to be enough so she—Lainie—would believe he was dead"—Mrs. Williams spoke quietly, enunciating each word—"and *that's* what we want her to continue to think."

"So, who was in the coffin?"

"It was empty."

James frowned. "But someone would have discovered that."

"No, they wouldn't," another voice to his left said. A young man in his early thirties stepped into the room. Nick Williams, Adam's brother. They looked very similar, and it was obvious they were brothers, but there were definitely differences, and they wouldn't pass for twins even from a distance. Nick walked over to his mother and rested a hand on her shoulder.

"What do you mean?" Cole asked. "Of course they would have. It would have been too light."

The man shrugged. "I don't know about that. Coffins are heavy. No one's going to notice if it's minus a body."

Maybe. "Well, what about the people at the hospital who worked on him? The paramedics?"

Nick shrugged. "If anyone asked, they would be told he died later. I'm not aware of anyone who asked. Honestly, I would be surprised if anyone remembered him. How many paramedics actually check up on the patients they bring in?"

James exchanged a look with Cole, then swung his gaze back to Nick. "But, why go to all that trouble? Why does he want everyone to believe he is dead?"

"Not everyone, just Lainie. But that results in everyone else needing to believe it too. He said he was afraid that she would hunt him down and finish the job."

It took all of James' self-control not to scoff. This was the biggest bunch of— "What do *you* think? You know her. You think she's capable of something like that?"

"Who knows what people are capable of?" Mrs. Williams answered before Nick could. "She seemed okay when we first met her, but it soon became obvious she wasn't good enough for my Adam."

Again, James kept the professional face mask in place. "I just want to know how he survived. He was pronounced dead at the scene, correct?"

"No, no. They revived him in the ambulance, and he managed to communicate that he was in danger. He was put into protective custody with the marshals, I believe. Like I said, they were afraid she'd come back and finish him off."

James frowned. The woman's narrative was total fabrication. None of that was in the file. Then again, if the marshals were involved, it wouldn't be. He made a note to check with a marshal buddy who would be able to find out for him.

"I'd had heart surgery the morning of the incident," Mrs. Williams said, "then multiple complications after, so I never even got to see him before he went into hiding. Neither did my husband. He was with me, of course."

"Ma'am—"

"Mom," Nick said, "why don't you grab the tea from the fridge and pour us some drinks while I talk with the officers."

"Detectives," Cole said.

"Right. Detectives."

Mrs. Williams crossed her arms and raised her brow at her son. "Are you trying to get rid of me?"

"Of course not. I'm just thirsty. You were getting me some tea when they knocked, remember? And besides, if we're going to have an extended conversation, I'd like to do it seated in the den."

She sighed. "Fine. I'll be there shortly. I'll have to brew more tea."

"We'll wait. Thank you, Mom."

Her gaze softened and she patted her son's arm. "Of course."

Once she was in the kitchen, Nick motioned for them to follow him into the den and they seated themselves. James and Cole on the oversized sofa and Nick in the recliner next to the fireplace. He leaned forward. "Look, leave her alone, okay? She was just starting to accept that she's never going to see Adam again, and we don't need you two stirring her up."

"So, you don't think Adam is alive like she does?"

"Oh, he's alive and he's in hiding just like she said. But he's made it clear that he's never coming home again. Unless Lainie moves or is dead."

"Where's your father, Nick? When I called, I asked for him and your mother to both be here."

"He left. Said he was done talking about Adam, that it was too painful."

James rubbed a hand down the side of his face, his brain scrambling, lower back throbbing. This might not have been a good idea, but he—and Lainie—didn't have time for him to sit around and heal. And while he wished Adam's father were here to talk to, they'd have to work with what they had. "Okay, so Adam was afraid of her. Did he file a police report?" He knew the man hadn't.

And the marshals didn't just hide civilians who were afraid for their lives.

Nick scoffed. "No. He'd already decided to go into hiding and let everyone believe he was dead. Filing a police report would kind of mess that plan up, wouldn't it?"

"Okay, then did Adam have information on a case or a criminal that would come after him if someone discovered he was working with the authorities?"

"No." The man frowned. "At least I don't think so. The only person he was afraid of coming after him was Lainie."

Then the marshals didn't have anything to do with Adam's disappearance. But, he'd still check. "Who told you about the marshals being involved?"

"Adam did."

"You spoke to him?"

"Yes. The day before his funeral. He asked us to go through with it in order to make sure Lainie thought he was dead. He thought she might show up, but I never saw her there." A muscle in his jaw ticked. "Good thing I didn't."

"And you don't mind telling us all this?"

He shrugged. "Why not? The only person we need to keep it from is Lainie. And besides, Adam has to be tired of hiding. He has to want to come home. Maybe you guys can help make that happen if you know the truth."

James wanted to pull his hair out. None of this made a lick of sense based on what he knew about the man stalking Lainie. That guy didn't care if Lainie knew he was alive or not.

Cole sighed. "You know, faking your death is against the law, right?"

"Well, if you can find him, you can arrest him, but good luck with that. And it's not against the law if the marshals help you, right?"

If the marshals were helping. Which James highly doubted. Unless Adam's family just didn't have the whole story. "You don't have any idea where he could be?"

"I don't. He said it was better that way. Once the marshals got him relocated, he texted on a burner, but then dropped off the radar again about a year ago."

And James had a feeling Nick wouldn't share if he did know. "So, you haven't seen him either."

"No."

"Let's circle back to the marshals," Cole said. "Just to be clear, Adam told you the marshals were hiding him."

"Yes."

"But he's showing himself to Lainie now." He didn't see the harm in mentioning that fact now.

Nick's frown deepened. "What are you talking about?"

"She's seen him a couple of times," James said. "He even showed up at a place she volunteers. We have him on the security footage."

Nick scowled. "That's impossible. He was terrified of her. Said she was a psychopath, and if she ever learned he was alive, she'd come after him until he was dead. No way would he come back here."

113

James shook his head. "Okay, let me get this straight. According to the report, Adam and Ms. Jackson—Lainie—argued. Lainie got control of the gun and shot Adam in the base of the throat. She then called 911 and tried to stop the bleeding, but by the time the paramedics got there, he was thought to be dead."

"Yes."

"But then you're saying the paramedics revived him in the ambulance."

"Yes. According to Adam."

"And you're absolutely certain that it was Adam you were talking to."

"Just because you ask me the same question over and over doesn't mean my answer is going to change." Nick laughed. "Yes, it was Adam. I think I would know my own brother. I mean, his voice was a little different, but he *had* been shot in the throat. It was a wonder he could speak at all. So one would expect that, right?"

"Yes, of course."

Nick clasped his hands between his knees. "At first, I'll admit, I was skeptical and I brought up things that only Adam would know." He shrugged. "It was Adam. No doubt about it."

"Do you have a phone number for him?"

"He asked me not to give it out."

"I'd still like it, please. It'd be a big help and save us a lot of trouble finding it. But rest assured, Mr. Williams, we'll find it."

The man sighed. "Fine." He pulled out his phone and rattled off the number. "Honestly, I don't even know if it's still active. He hasn't called and I haven't called him."

"Can you dial it?"

"What? Now?"

"Yes. Now. And put it on speaker."

Nick pressed the number to dial it. It rang four times and went to voice mail. "This is Jason Haywood. Leave me a message and I'll get back to you." The voice was definitely raspy, almost a whisper.

James raised a brow at Nick. "Jason Haywood."

"Well, he's not going to use his real name if he's trying to hide from the woman who wants him dead, is he?"

James shot a look at Cole, who pursed his lips and shook his head. "He would have needed all kinds of special care. The recovery time would have had to be months."

"He was in a private hospital. The marshals arranged it. It was somewhere in New York. That's all I know."

"Okay, just one more thing," James said. He pulled up the footage outside the humane shelter and turned it around for Nick to see. The man's eyes widened, then narrowed, his attention completely focused on the screen.

When the video ended, Nick lifted his gaze to meet James', then Cole's, all the color leeched from his cheeks. "That doesn't make any sense. I don't know why he would show up there, but he must have a reason."

"Doesn't look like a man afraid for his life."

Nick raked a shaky hand over his head. "I don't know. I don't have an explanation for it. All I can tell you is what he told me."

"Will you let us know if he contacts you?"

Nick frowned, his troubled expression saying they'd caught him off guard. "I don't know that either. It will probably depend on what Adam wants."

Carol Williams entered the room with four glasses of tea on a tray. James stood. "Thank you so much for going to the trouble of fixing that, but I think we've gotten what we came for." Not that he had any intention of drinking anything the woman prepared. "We'll just show ourselves out."

NINE

Lainie hurried to slide into the back seat of the sedan and scrunched down so no one could see her from the front door.

Seconds later, Cole settled behind the wheel and James into the passenger seat.

"How much did you hear?" James asked, buckling his seat belt.

"Pretty much all of it, I think."

"What happened to your promise to stay in the car?"

"I didn't exactly promise." He sighed and Lainie bit her lip on a surge of guilt. "Sorry, I was worried about you. My imagination went wild, and if you needed help, I was going to call for backup."

Cole pulled away from the home, and Lainie shifted into a sitting position. She snapped the seat belt into place and met James' eyes.

He raised a brow. "I guess you heard them say why they believe Adam is still alive."

"I did." Anxiety clawed at her throat and she drew in a steadying breath. "For the record, I don't believe a word of it."

"I'm not sure I do either," Cole said, "but I'm not sure they were lying."

"What?" Lainie shot the back of his head a scowl.

"I think *they* believe it."

Lainie shook her head. "I don't care what they believe. Adam's dead. He has to be. Because if he's not, then I'm not sure I'm in touch with reality and that's extremely scary for me."

James frowned but shot her a quick look, and the compassion in his gaze nearly melted all her fears away. Almost. "You're in touch with reality," he said. "There's an explanation for all of this, we just don't have all the pieces to the puzzle. Once we get those, things will make sense."

She could only pray he was right. "How do you plan to get all the pieces to the puzzle?"

"Just like we would if someone was alive. First order of business is, I'm going to call my marshal buddy and see if he can get me some information. At least confirm or deny what Adam's family believes. Then we'll look into Adam's bank statements," James said, "cell phone records, his family's phone records, credit cards, and everything under this new name. We'll look for anything that will lead us to where this guy's staying."

"Well, Adam's not *staying* anywhere except six feet under! He's dead!" The words came out sharper than she intended, so she breathed in through her nose and out through her mouth. "I'm sorry, but you're chasing a dead man," she finally said in a softer tone.

"Well, someone may have assumed—stolen—his identity then," Cole said. "And since that's a crime, we can pursue it." He glanced at Lainie. "Did you hear his voice on the phone call?"

"Yes. I didn't recognize it."

"Right." Cole's gaze flicked to the rearview mirror once more, but he wasn't looking at Lainie.

"What is it?" she asked.

"I see it too," James said. "The truck two cars back. He's been on our tail since we left the neighborhood."

Lainie's fingers curled into fists next to her thighs. "We're being followed."

"We are." The words had just left James' lips when the truck floored it around the two cars and pulled up beside them, in the other lane on the two-way street.

"Lainie, get down!"

James' shout sent her diving onto the empty seat beside her.

But not before she caught a glimpse of the driver.

Adam.

But not Adam.

She jerked back up to get a better look and time slowed. Her eyes met his. He wore a ball cap with a Panther football team logo. His face was in the shadows, but his eyes were Adam's.

Not possible!

Time accelerated again as he roared ahead to swerve in front of them, then around the curve, barely missing the green sedan that zipped past, horn blaring.

Cole pressed the gas and the vehicle surged forward, slamming Lainie back against the seat. "Call it in," he said, steering around the sharp curve.

"On it," James said.

Cole rattled off the plate while James connected to the dispatcher, repeated the letter and number combo, then gave their location and the direction the chase was headed in.

"Four-way stop ahead," James said.

"Yep." Cole slowed. The driver of the truck did not. He blasted through the stop sign, barely missing a guy on a motorcycle. The rider jerked the handlebar to the right, his rear tire skidding out behind him. He came to a wobbly stop and his leg shot out to keep the bike upright.

Cole slammed on the brakes and rolled to a stop. James had his window down. "Are you all right?"

The biker pulled his helmet off, his dark eyes blazing his fury. "Who was that idiot?"

"We're not sure. If you're okay, we're going to try and catch him."

The biker waved them on, and Lainie pressed shaking fingers to her eyes while Cole got them back on track to go after . . . the Adam impersonator.

It didn't take long to figure out the man was gone. "What is he doing?" Lainie whispered. "Why all the cat-and-mouse stuff? Why doesn't he just confront me and tell me what he wants?"

James glanced at his phone. "The vehicle was reported stolen earlier this morning. Hopefully, he'll ditch it, and once we get our hands on it, CSU will go over it and find something that will give us a hint of who this guy is."

Cole's phone buzzed and he snagged it with a grimace. "I've got to go. SWAT is being called up. You mind dropping me? Kenzie can bring me home. You okay to drive?"

"I'm fine. And if I decide it's too painful, Lainie can drive. Let's go."

When they dropped Cole at his location, Lainie spotted Kenzie near the command center truck and waved. Kenzie frowned, her confusion at Lainie's presence clear. Only when Cole hurried out of the vehicle did Kenzie's frown ease. She nodded at Cole, and the two of them walked toward the truck, heads turned toward one another.

James slid behind the wheel, leaving the passenger door open for Lainie. Once she had her belt buckled, he looked at her. "I have some time off before I have to be back at work." He touched his lower back and pulled onto the road. "I haven't had time to build up much leave with the department, but getting shot on the job has earned me some unexpected leave. I'd like to take advantage of that and try to help you figure out why someone seems so determined to get to you."

"Wait a minute. Are you saying you're not going back to work so you can help me?"

"And continue to heal."

Lainie bit her lip and narrowed her eyes. He wasn't lying, but he wasn't being straight with her either. "Are you saying you would be back at work if I didn't give you the impression that I needed help?"

"So, you don't need my help?"

Biting her tongue on prideful words hurt, but she wasn't stupid. She sighed. "Yes, I need your help." She rested her hand on his forearm and squeezed. "Thank you for offering."

With a glance in the rearview and side mirrors, he turned onto the exit that would take them to her house. "You said you're off for the next couple of days, right?"

"Yes."

"What do you think about hiding out while we chase this guy down?"

"Hide out where?"

"With my family. We can drop Cole's truck off at his house, pick up mine, and be there in time for dinner."

THE WORDS LEFT HIS LIPS before he could bite them off, but then he realized it was best. It would work with the plan he had in mind. It was the family weekend, and everyone was at their lake house for the mini family reunion. His brothers, Keegan and Dixon, were there, and both were skilled with their firearms, so if somehow this guy appeared, he'd have help protecting Lainie.

Then again, would taking Lainie there put his family in danger? James' gut said the guy was going to escalate.

"Hello?" She was frowning at him, waiting.

"What?"

"Are you listening?"

"I am."

"You're not. But, I can't stay with your family."

"Why not? You love my family and they love you." More than they loved him. Well, his father did, anyway.

"I mean—"

"They're at the lake. It's the weekend thing we—they—do four times a year. You've been dozens of times and are one of the family, so what's the problem?"

"But—"

"And, truthfully, I'd like to use you as a buffer. There. I said it." And now he wanted to take it back.

"A buffer?"

He groaned. "That kind of came out more blunt than I'd intended, but this is going to be the first time I've seen my family in months, and my dad is . . . difficult." To say the least. "If you're there, maybe he won't be *quite* . . . as . . . difficult."

"What's with you two? He's not like that with Keegan and Dixon or Steph. Why you?"

"Because I went into law enforcement, and he can't forgive what happened to his brother. He hates anyone involved. Including me." He glanced at her, and she turned to gaze out the windshield. Remorse tugged at him. "Never mind. That's the coward in me speaking. I'll take you wherever you want to go, get someone to drive by and check on you on a regular basis, and go deal with my family." Because if he didn't show up for this, and they found out he was home, he would be blackballed by all of them. Not just his father. And they *would* find out, because Steph would let it slip eventually.

"James Lee Cross, the last thing you could be labeled is a coward." Her instant defense did something for his heart, and he suppressed the desire to pull over and hug her. And maybe kiss her. No, no, no. *No* kissing. At least not yet. Not until she let him know that she had similar feelings? "I may not be a coward when it comes to doing my job or defending my country, but when it comes to facing my dad . . . well, coward is the only word that truly fits."

"Hmm. I can come up with a few good arguments against that, but I can tell they'll fall on deaf ears. So . . ."

"So?"

"I'll go."

"Okay." He cringed at how fast he jumped on that.

She laughed. "Is Jess going to be there?"

He wasn't surprised she asked. Jesslyn was a frequent lake weekend crasher. "No, Steph asked her, but she's working."

"Bummer." She paused. "Wait, Steph already asked her, but she didn't ask me?"

"I told her I'd ask you if I wound up coming."

"Oh. So, you weren't planning on going until just now, which is why I got the last-minute invitation?"

"Um . . . sorry?"

"You're forgiven."

"Besides, you know you have a standing invitation. You don't have to wait for one of us to ask you."

"I know."

He smiled—then frowned at the rearview mirror. Was the truck back? It looked similar to the one—

No, it turned off.

His fingers flexed around the wheel. He didn't want to be paranoid, but this guy who seemed to have some kind of score to settle with Lainie was a real concern.

He pulled into her drive. "While I make a few phone calls, why don't you get whatever you need for a couple of days and we'll stop and get my Jeep, then head out to the lake house?"

"I can't believe I'm agreeing to this."

"I'm glad you are. Now, let me just scope the area and then I'll wait inside while you pack."

While Lainie worked in her bedroom, James called Savannah Gleeson. Savannah worked in the Organized Crime Unit and, except for her hair, looked enough like Lainie that his plan might have a chance of working.

"James," she said, "good to hear from you. What's up?"

He paced to Lainie's kitchen and looked in the fridge. Almost empty. He pulled out two water bottles. "I've got a favor to ask."

"Ask."

He explained the situation. "We both know the guy is dead, but someone is working awfully hard to convince her he's still alive. How would you feel about doing some undercover stuff while I get Lainie away from everything?"

"And bring down a bad guy? My pleasure."

"Potential bad guy. We just need him in custody so we can figure out what his end game is, but most importantly, *who* he is. He did some dangerous driving earlier and just about took out a motorcycle rider. It could have ended really bad. I want this guy off the streets, if nothing else. So, if you could basically house sit, wear a wig to make you look like Lainie from a distance, then nab the guy if he comes around . . ."

"I'll need to clear it with the captain, but, yeah. I'll let you know when I know."

"Okay, assuming he says it's fine, here's the plan." He ran what he was thinking by her, and she added her own thoughts until he was happy with the details. "I'll text you as soon as I get the okay from Lainie."

"And I'll be getting clearance from my captain."

The next call was to US Deputy Marshal Art Larson who, in answer to James' inquiry, said, "Never heard of Adam Williams, and there's nothing in the system that I can see. Not to say there couldn't be something going on under the radar, but whoever said we were involved is lying. At least that's my take on it."

"I trust your take. One last question that I already know the answer to but have to ask. The marshals didn't arrange for Adam to be transported to a private hospital in New York, right?"

"Well, since we have no record of him, I'm going to say that's a negative. I can dig a little deeper and see if there was anything going on off the record, but . . ."

"Right. Thanks. Check, if you don't mind."

"Don't mind. I'll shoot you a text with anything I find out."

"Appreciate it."

He hung up, searched his contact list for the lab number, and hit call.

When he reached the lab tech, he was surprised he got a person and didn't have to leave a message. "Any prints on the receipt?" he asked once he clarified what he was calling about.

"Not really. There are a few smudges and an oil stain, probably from the parking garage floor, but no usable prints. Could have been rubbed down to get rid of them, but I can't tell."

."Thanks."

When Lainie returned to the great room, he filled her in on his and Savannah's plan first.

Her eyes widened with each word. "I don't know about that," she finally said when he finished. "I don't want to put anyone in danger."

"She's a trained detective and has been undercover multiple times. She can take care of herself. Plus, she'll have someone watching from a distance in case she needs some backup."

Still, she hesitated.

"What is it?"

"It's not that I don't think your detective friend can take care of herself, I just wonder if whoever this guy is will fall for it."

"He might if she pulls your car into the carport and goes in the side door."

"Assuming he's watching."

He nodded. "True. But I have a plan for that as well. I want you to get in your car and drive toward the hospital. Go inside like it's a normal workday. Savannah will meet you in the ladies' locker room for your keys. She'll be dressed in scrubs and have a wig that matches your hairstyle she'll put on before she exits. I chose to ask her because she's about your size. Maybe an inch or two taller, but from a distance, no one will know she's not you. Once she exits and gets in your car and leaves, her partner will follow her, watching for anyone else who might be following her. Make sense?"

"It makes sense, but what if no one's following?"

"Then she gets to your house and goes inside. She'll turn lights off and on and make it look like someone's home just in case."

She pursed her lips and he was afraid she might refuse the idea, but then she gave a slow nod. "Okay, it sounds like all the bases are covered as far as keeping her safe."

"Great. As soon as she gets the green light, she'll head to the hospital. Also, it doesn't look like the marshals are involved in this, so we're going to run with a full-on investigation."

"Not involved, huh? Shocking."

"And, last, no prints on the receipt."

"I do find that a little odd."

"The tech thinks it was rubbed down."

She blinked. "The receipt? Who does that?"

"I don't know. It's weird. I'm still thinking on it." He smiled. "In the meantime, how about some food?"

"Food?" She pressed a hand to her stomach. "I'm not sure I can eat."

"You need to keep your strength up. Eat this." He pulled one of her protein bars from the basket on the counter.

She took it. "In case I have to fight off a dead man?"

He squeezed her hand. "The goal is to not let it get to that point."

"Right." She walked toward the kitchen door that led out to the carport. He followed her and waited until she was buckled up. "You ready?"

"Ready. I'll be watching my rearview mirror."

"You watch the road," he said, his voice low. "I've got your back."

TEN

Lainie backed the rental out of the carport with James' words ringing in her ears and twisting her heart into a ball of longing. Mulling over the man she'd crushed on for most of her life, she headed toward the hospital, thankful it was a short drive.

James hung back but close enough for her to see him when she looked for him. Which was constantly for the entire 2.2 miles to the hospital. She pulled into her regular spot and hurried into the building. She didn't bother looking over her shoulder to see if *he* was there because, like James said, he had her back.

"Hey, Lainie," Allison called, "thought you had the day off."

Lainie walked over to the doctor. Bridgette stood next to her, and while Lainie wouldn't mind avoiding her, she didn't want to be rude to Allison—or Bridgette, although that would be easier. "I do. Just making a quick stop to grab something from the locker room."

"Have you decided on a place for our glamping trip?" Allison asked.

"Glamping trip?" Bridgette looked up from her laptop for the first time since Lainie's approach.

Allison pressed her lips together, then mouthed, *Sorry*, to Lainie.

"A group of us are going." Lainie hesitated. "Would you want to join us?"

Allison gaped and Lainie kept her gaze fixed on Bridgette.

The woman raised a brow. "I don't think so. I just didn't realize you did that sort of thing."

Because you haven't come down off your high horse long enough to get to know me. Lainie bit her lip on the response. "Well, I do. Only I prefer camping, not glamping."

"Like in a tent with no running water?" Bridgette actually looked intrigued.

"Yes," Lainie said, starting to get amused at the whole conversation. "Exactly."

Bridgette shuddered. "I'll pass, thanks." She went back to her computer and Lainie edged toward the locker room.

Allison cleared her throat. "Dr. Maloney said if I saw you to ask you if you'd be interested in teaching a suicide prevention class to a group of high school kids."

Lainie smothered a sigh and stopped her escape attempt. A very worthy cause, but . . . "When?"

"In a couple of weeks." Allison glanced at the calendar, but it was Bridgette's sudden stiffness that caught Lainie's attention.

"Uh, I'm not sure, to be honest. I have some stuff going on right now and adding anything else to my calendar is probably not a good idea. If he can find someone else to do it this time, I'll take the next one."

"Didn't do my sister any good," Bridgette muttered.

Lainie and Allison exchanged a look. "What do you mean?" Allison asked. "I know your sister passed away, but are you saying—"

"I am. She killed herself. Over a man. Or rather a woman who *stole* her man. Someone who lured him away from her. Elle had her issues, but she seemed to finally be in a good place when all of that happened. And it sent her spiraling. She didn't deserve that." She sniffed. "She turned the gas on in her home and breathed it until she was dead. So preach all you want about suicide prevention, but if someone wants to kill themselves, a stupid program isn't going to stop them." She grabbed her laptop and walked away.

"Oh boy," Allison said. "Now I feel like a jerk."

"I'm sorry about her sister, but don't let her make you feel like a jerk. These programs *do* help people. I'm just sorry she can't see it."

"I agree. She's just hurting."

And hurting people hurt others.

Lainie pushed Bridgette to the back of her mind with effort. "In answer to your question, I'm still waiting on Kenzie to get back to me about what her location vote is. But I think we'll wind up at the place near Looking Glass Mountain." Assuming her life was hers once again. She wasn't going camping—or *glamping*—while trying to dodge someone out to hurt her. She wondered if Nichelle had called James yet. She was tempted to call the woman herself but would refrain. James would handle it.

"Oh, that's a good one. And not too far from here."

"Exactly." She shoved stray strands of hair behind her ear. "I'll catch up with you a little later, okay?"

"Sure."

Lainie hurried down the hall, impatient to get everything in place so she could stop worrying about it. Not that she would.

Once in the locker room, she let her gaze scan the area. "Savannah?" Two nurses she often worked with greeted her, then slipped out the door. "Savannah, you in here?"

The stall door to the end toilet opened and a woman with long reddish-blond hair stepped out. Lainie gaped. "Wow."

"Hi, Lainie, I'll take that reaction as a compliment."

"How did you . . . ?" She waved a hand at the woman's disguise.

"I found your hospital picture online and James sent me a recent one he took."

When had he taken her picture? Lainie hadn't noticed him doing so. Which was kind of freaky. She pushed that to the "unimportant things" corner of her mind and rubbed her hands together while blowing out a slow breath. "All right, what now?"

"You stay here while I walk out the door, get in your car, and drive to your house." She held out a bag. "While I'm doing that, you put this on."

"What is it?" She opened the bag. A wig, an oversized fall sweater, a pair of glasses with clear lenses, and a baseball cap. "I guess you're not the only one leaving here in disguise."

"Exactly." The woman patted Lainie's arm. "I'll see you when we have this creep in custody."

Yes, Lord, please. Let this work. "Thank you for doing this," she said, her voice low.

"Nothing I'd rather be doing."

Lainie placed a hand on the woman's forearm. "Be careful," she said. "I know this guy isn't Adam, but he wants me to think he is. And if he's capable of behaving like Adam, then he's dangerous."

"I got this, I promise. This is what I do on a daily basis, so please don't worry about me."

Lainie nodded, still not completely convinced, but feeling slightly better about the whole thing. "Oh, wait. Our scrubs are different. Allison spoke to me when I walked in. If I—you—walk out in different clothes, she'll wonder."

"Good point. Let's trade."

Once they were done, Lainie rubbed her arms and gulped down her anxiety. "All right, then, out you go while I get myself all fixed up with the rest of this."

Savannah shot her a reassuring smile that did nothing of the sort for Lainie's nerves, turned on her heel, and walked out the door.

Over the next ten minutes, Lainie transformed herself into a completely different person. She slipped a surgical mask over her nose and chin for good measure and headed for the back exit where James should be waiting.

And he was. She slid into the passenger seat of the 4Runner, and he grinned. "Wow. You don't look like you."

She removed the mask and rolled her eyes. "I think that was the point."

"Well, you did a good job."

"Savannah did too." She fisted her hands on her thighs. "I really hope this works, James."

"As soon as they catch him, we'll head to the station so you can hear what he has to say."

"Okay, thank you."

"And, I'll share a little secret with you. We've got cameras set up in your house. Kind of like sophisticated baby monitors. Savannah's in communication with her backup, and I can talk to her through the app on my phone."

Lainie wilted onto the seat. "Okay, you've convinced me."

He shot her a lopsided grin. "Good. We'll get my Jeep, and then I guess it's time for me to pull on my big-boy britches and go say hello to my family."

FOR THE NEXT FORTY-FIVE MINUTES, James took his time navigating the twists and turns that finally led them to the road to Lake City Lake, set high up in the mountains. Dumbest name for a lake that ever was, but he'd grown up on its shores and spent time there whenever possible, and he had to admit, he loved the place.

The fact that Lainie was going to be with him this time made him glad in ways that almost made him laugh. Lainie had been a regular at the lake house from the time they were kids. Granted, she'd been there as Steph's friend, not his, so why would this time be any different?

Because he was different.

Lainie was different.

Everything was different.

But . . . *why* was it different?

He shot a glance at the silent woman beside him. Because of an attraction that hadn't been there before. She'd always been Steph's friend. A cute friend, but that had been it. Now . . . now? Yeah, now, she was still Steph's friend, but . . .

Unfortunately, there was that *but.*

And there shouldn't be one.

But there was.

So what was he going to do about it?

Nothing. Absolutely nothing.

"Are you okay?" she asked. "You have a weird look on your face."

She'd have one too if she could read his thoughts. Either that or she'd rupture something laughing.

He cleared his throat. "Yeah, I'm fine. All good." She wouldn't laugh. Not Lainie. Now, Steph was another story. She'd definitely laugh.

"Why don't I believe that?"

She was entirely too perceptive. "Sorry, I'm processing . . . stuff." Time to move on to another topic. "Just to give you a heads-up, if things get, uh, awkward, feel free to just walk away."

"Awkward?"

"With my dad and me."

"I'm sorry."

He shrugged. "It's been years."

"And he's carried a grudge that long?"

"Well, he hasn't called."

"Have you called him?"

"In the beginning I did, but when he refused to talk—or would only talk through my mom—I finally gave up and told my mom that the ball was in his court."

"Talk through your mom?"

"Yeah, you know. 'Tell James I'm not interested in hearing about his cop work. When he gives up that nonsense, we'll talk.' Then he'd wait for her to repeat it."

"Wow, that's really sad."

He snorted. "No kidding. More than sad. Just stupid." She fell silent, but then he could feel her looking at him. He glanced at her. "What?"

"Years?" she asked.

"Years."

"What about holidays?"

"The ones I've made? They've been painful. It's been easier just to stay away." Easier, true, but it wasn't solving the problem. Why was he spilling all this to her? Between the PTSD and his family situation, she was going to think he was pitiful. "Anyway, I just wanted to give you a heads-up. I figure it's only fair to let you know what you might be walking into."

"Okay. Thanks." She frowned. "How old are you? Thirty-one? Thirty-two?"

"Thirty-two."

"How old were you when you joined the Army?"

"Twenty-two. After college."

"So your father hasn't talked to you in *ten years*? Except through your mother? Steph's never really said anything about this."

"Eh . . . he's *spoken*, or rather grunted might be more accurate, but we've not had what I'd call a conversation. When I was just in the Army, he'd at least speak or answer a direct question, even if it was one or two words here and there, but when he learned I was working with the CID, he went mostly silent—or, again, only speaking through my mother. And, of course, once he finds out I'm with the police department, well, I don't have to describe how that's going to go over."

"That's why you didn't tell your family you were back, isn't it?"

He sighed. "Yes."

She shook her head and turned her gaze back to the window. "That's so wrong. I'm sorry, James."

"Me too." He fell silent, then nodded to her phone. "I've been thinking."

"About?"

"A couple of things. I want to find the death certificate for Adam, and I want to know, who did the autopsy on Adam?"

"Good idea on the death certificate. I'd thought about that too. As for the autopsy? I don't know. One of the MEs at the hospital, for sure, though."

"Why don't you see if you can find out who did it? I'm curious."

"Of course. I should have thought of that. We'll just pull up his autopsy report and end all of this nonsense." Her fingers tightened around the phone hard enough to turn her knuckles white, but she tapped the screen and dialed. She left a message for the person to call her back, then clasped her hands between her knees and fell silent.

His phone rang and he glanced at the screen. "That's Nichelle." He tapped the button to answer, Lainie listening on speaker. "Hello, Nichelle. This is Detective James Cross."

"Hello, Detective. I'm still at work but was able to grab a break. What can I help you with?"

"You stated you warned Lainie away from Adam because you were worried about her. Can you go into a little more detail on that?"

A sigh filtered through the line. "I dated Adam before he dumped me to date another woman. Then he dumped that woman to date Lainie. He never did anything horrible to me, and as far as I know, he never did to any woman, but he was different. Charming, yes. Intense, attentive, funny. But there was a darker side to him that I just couldn't figure out."

"Dark how?"

"I don't know if I can even explain it. He'd have mood swings where he would be fine one moment, then yelling about something the next. He was in too big of a hurry to get engaged and plan the future. I was more into having fun than thinking about marriage. He didn't care for that and finally broke it off. Honestly, if he hadn't, then I was going to."

Lainie had paled, but she was listening, her head cocked toward the phone in the holder.

"Do you mind telling me where you were if I give you a few dates?"

"Sure."

He gave her the first one and she said, "At a fundraiser at church."

"I suppose you have witnesses?"

"Of course."

He gave her the second date. "At the hospital with my sister while she gave birth to my niece."

James shook his head. This was a wild-goose chase. He'd check out the information, of course, but his gut was saying she didn't have anything to do with the threats on Lainie's life. "Thanks so much. If we need anything else, we'll be in touch." He tapped the button to end the call.

"I don't think she's involved," Lainie said.

"You read my mind."

He wheeled onto the road that would take them to the house. To his family. His father. And it took everything in him not to turn around and go back the way he came.

ELEVEN

Lainie wasn't sure what was happening with James and her, but something was going on. A connection that she'd never thought would be possible. And yet, here they were.

Before the incident at the hospital, she would have called James an acquaintance—the brother of one of her best friends. Today, she would call him . . . what? A friend? Yes. At this point, after all they'd shared, he was a friend.

And hopefully something more? She'd always wished James would see her as something more than a "sister." Did she dare hope again? What if she was reading his signals or vibes or . . . whatever . . . wrong?

He pulled to a stop at the gate. The officer on duty had been on the day shift for as long as she could remember. He stepped out of the booth, took a look at James, and did a double take. "Yo, James Cross? That you?"

"Hey, Stan, good to see you're still here."

"Where else would I be? Too many perks come with this job." The residents asked him to house and pet sit when they were going to be on vacation. He never said no. His gaze landed on Lainie. "And I haven't seen you in a while. How are you doing?"

"I'm hanging in there, thanks, Stan."

After a small salute, he waved them through, and James followed the road he could probably drive with his eyes shut. The road she'd ridden with him and Steph too many times to count. And every time she wondered if that would be the weekend James would see her as more than his sister's best friend. He never had. But this time . . .

Uncertainty tugged at her, and she clamped down on her emotions to focus on the home that had just come into sight. "So many memories here," she whispered.

"I know."

She shot him a sideways glance. "Don't worry. I'll be right beside you."

He parked but made no move to get out of the vehicle, so she waited, watching him. "The truth is, Lainie," he said, "I'm angry with him for the way he's treated me. It's been petty and selfish, and I never thought my father was either. I mean, we had our moments when I was growing up where we disagreed and argued, but he never acted like he has the past few years. Granted, joining the Army was done to spite him, but if I hadn't loved the life and my job, I wouldn't have stayed as long as I did. I tried explaining that to him one day on the phone, and he listened for about five minutes, then hung up on me."

She winced. "Why *did* you leave the Army?"

He palmed his eyes and sighed. "The official reason is the injury I sustained when our MRAP rolled over an IED. Three buddies were killed. Two of us—me and a journalist—survived."

She gasped. "Steph didn't tell me."

"Steph didn't know. I didn't tell anyone."

"James!"

"I know. If I had it to do over again, I'd probably make different choices, but it was the decision I felt was right at the time and that's that. I recuperated at the base hospital and went back to work eight weeks later, but . . . it was just different. Being in that environment, it was hard. Very hard."

"I'm sure. The injury you're talking about . . . your back?"

He nodded. "It's hard to admit, but I got out of the Army more for my mental health than physical. They put the physical reason on my discharge papers."

"Oh."

"I'd been talking to a psychiatrist on base, and he recommended I take an extended leave. The PTSD had gotten to the point that I couldn't focus, couldn't really do my job, so I took his advice and came home. I took four weeks off to do nothing but try to decide what I wanted to do with the rest of my life."

"Four weeks? That doesn't seem very long."

"It was about three weeks too long for me. I was climbing the walls. The only thing that kept me sane was Cole telling me about the cases he was working and letting me brainstorm with him on how to work them. After I was discharged, he encouraged me to apply with the department. I did and got hired. Over the past couple of months, things were getting better. I was even sleeping better until that whole thing in the hospital. I hadn't done that in a long time. I'd dreamed, yeah, but not . . . *that*."

"I'm sorry." She frowned. "So you came home and took a job with the police department? How is that different from what you were doing in the Army?"

He smiled. "It's a lot different. I know it seems weird. I think just the whole change of scenery with different people and the counseling, learning coping skills, made a difference." He sighed. "Like I said, I still dream, but I don't do what I did in the hospital. Not since coming home, anyway."

"Getting shot probably triggered it."

"No doubt. I wondered if it would."

"Which is why you didn't want to stay at the hospital. Obviously."

"Yeah."

"I wish you'd told me."

"I wasn't ready to do that."

But he was now. Interesting.

A knock on the window made Lainie jump. She placed a hand

over her racing heart and looked up into Dixon's brown eyes. The same color eyes as James'.

"Lainie?" Dixon held the reins of a horse. The beautiful black-and-white paint shuffled closer.

Lainie opened the door. "Hi, Dix."

His gaze moved past her and settled on his brother. His eyes widened. "James? James! What in the . . . what are you doing here?"

"I decided to come home for a while. Couldn't miss the lake weekend, could I?"

"Dude . . ." He walked around to the driver's side, and James climbed out of his Jeep to be enveloped in a hard hug. When Dixon stepped back, he shook his head. "You should have called or something. Given us a heads-up."

"I wanted it to be a surprise."

His brother shot him a knowing look. "You mean you didn't want to give Dad the opportunity to tell you not to come."

Dix could always be counted on to tell it like it was. "And that."

"The surprise was seeing you on the news and that you're working with the department."

"Oh. You saw that, huh?"

"I did."

"Who else saw it?"

"Everyone. Eventually. Apparently, Steph knew you were here?" The reproach was clear.

"She's only known since yesterday."

"Well, the news has latched on to that story, bragging about their local hero. Dad saw it this morning."

"I see."

"Sorry, bro, he's still being a pain about everything. But Mom's another story. You might very well give *her* a heart attack showing up like this. She was thrilled you were back in town, but she'd never expect you to come today."

James grimaced. "Why don't you go in and give her advance warning?"

"Yeah. Why don't I do that. Hang tight." He handed the horse over to James, who ran his hand over the animal's side while Dixon jogged toward the house.

Lainie walked over to join them, and James shot her a tight smile. "Have you met Jericho?"

"Of course I have. Jericho and I are good friends." She rubbed his nose and the horse nudged her, looking for the treat she usually had with her. "Sorry, boy, I don't have anything today." She shook her head. "It still cracks me up that Dixon brings his horse to the lake like anyone else would bring their dog." He'd even built a barn for the beast.

"That's Dixon for you."

The screen door slammed open. "James!"

His mother's excited cry reached them, and he looked at Lainie. "And so it begins."

"You've got this. Just hug her and assure her all is well."

"Even if it isn't?"

"Even if." Footsteps pounded toward them. "She doesn't know about your ribs. Brace yourself."

He dropped the reins and his foot went back just as his mother threw herself into his arms. Lainie caught the slight wince before he wrapped her in a tight hug.

"Hi, Mom."

Lainie snagged the leather reins. More for something to do with her hands than to keep the well-trained horse from bolting.

"Oh, James!" His mother stepped back and ran her hands over his face, then hugged him once more. "I thought Dixon was messing with me when he said you were out here."

"I wouldn't do that, Mom." Dixon took Jericho from Lainie with pursed lips. "Seriously? She thought I would do that?" he muttered under his breath.

"Of course not," Lainie said. "She was just dealing with her shock."

"Well." Dixon nodded to the front door. "Unfortunately, there's more shock to come."

HIS FATHER STOOD on the porch watching the reunion. He met James' gaze for a moment, looked like he might say something, then turned and went back inside.

"Still mad, huh?" he murmured to his mother.

"I don't even know what to do with him about this situation, James. I keep telling him he needs to move on, but . . ."

"Yeah. I know." He forced a smile. "I'm looking forward to a good visit with the rest of you." At least his father didn't hold it against his mom or siblings that they still spoke to him. His father had tried that, and his brothers and Steph had set him straight. They were speaking to James, and if he didn't like it, he'd lose all three sons and a daughter too.

James appreciated their loyalty but still hated the family division.

His mother swatted his arm. "You've been home a while."

"Yes ma'am."

"And you couldn't share that with us." The sorrow in her voice nearly cut him in two. "That you're working with the police department?"

"I was planning on it, Mom. I just had to get one part of my life settled before dealing with this part. And I didn't want you to have to keep secrets from him."

She nodded. "That was quite the rescue you and your team made. I'm glad those little girls and the mother—and you—are safe."

"Thank you."

She looked like she wanted to say more but, instead, just gave him another hug and waved at Lainie. "Glad you could come too, Lainie."

"Thanks, as always." Lainie smiled, and James raised a brow at the small miracle of his mother's silence. And while his main goal was to keep Lainie safe, everything he'd said was true. Part of the reason he wanted to come to the lake was to see if he could try once again to talk to his father and make things right. And if Lainie would be safe as well, then that was a good thing.

He grabbed his bag, and Lainie shouldered hers and followed him into the house. "Ah," she said, "good to be back."

He squeezed her bicep and she automatically moved toward the room she'd share with Stephanie. Once Lainie disappeared, he turned to his mother. "Thanks, Mom."

"Lainie's always welcome here, you know that."

"I know."

"Stephanie went to the little market up the road. She'll be back any second now and will be thrilled to see you."

"It will be mutual. I'm going to put this stuff in the room, then we can visit for a bit." He really wanted to get on the laptop to do a little more investigating into Adam Williams and find out if there was even a remote possibility the man could be alive, but his mother had missed him. The truth was, he'd missed her too in spite of her helicoptering.

"I'll pull out some drinks and snacks," was all she said, then she headed for the kitchen.

He smiled. One thing was for sure. No matter what else went on during their time at the lake, they wouldn't go hungry. He headed down the hall to the room he'd share with Dixon. Keegan had the garage apartment, and Stephanie had the room nearest the bathroom for her and Lainie.

James set his bag on the twin bed.

"I heard you were here."

James spun to see Keegan. His brother leaned his rifle against the wall.

"Word travels fast."

"Dixon called." He walked over to give James a bro hug, then slapped him on the back. "Good to see you."

"You too." James went back to his bag and Keegan walked to the door. "Hey, Keg . . ." His brother turned. "Mom seems . . . different."

"Different how?"

"I don't know. More mellow or something."

"She is. I think you'll appreciate her new temperament."

"What brought that on?"

Keegan shrugged. "God's really been working on her. Mom said she had to quit being so suffocating and trust that he was going to take care of all of us."

"Interesting."

Stephanie appeared. "I need a hug." She glided over to him and wrapped him in a hug only she could give. He held her, breathing in the lavender scent that had been hers since childhood. "Hey, little sis."

"Hey. I've missed you."

"Missed you too, squirt."

She pushed him away. "Don't start with that squirt stuff or I'll short-sheet your bed."

He laughed and held his hands up in surrender.

She hugged him again. "I'm glad you're home."

"Me too." And he was. He just dreaded walking into the den where his dad was no doubt stretched out in his recliner with a football game on the television.

Lainie walked out of the bathroom and leaned against the door-jamb. "Feels like our teenager days."

Keegan groaned. "Let's not revisit that time in our lives. You and Steph were little terrors."

Lainie sniffed. "I have no idea what you could possibly be referring to." James and Stephanie laughed, while Keegan rolled his eyes. Lainie grinned at Steph. "I'm thirsty."

"Mom's got lemonade."

"That works."

Stephanie linked Lainie's arm in hers and together they left the room, slipping past Dixon, who stepped inside.

James sucked in a breath. "Guess it's time to take the bull by the horns."

"We've tried to tell him he's wrong," Dixon said. "He's stubborn."

"Well, at least we know we come by it honestly."

Dixon patted him on the back as he passed, and James made his way into the den. The room was large, but welcoming, the stone fireplace on the far wall dominating the space. He remembered well many a cold, dark night, with snow on the ground and the power out, when his father had fired up the gas logs to keep them all warm.

So many good memories.

And hard ones too.

Like the time he'd stormed out of the room to enlist in the Army. His phone buzzed and he snuck a quick glance at the text from his deputy marshal buddy.

Nothing pinging with your Adam Williams on this end. No record of him, nothing.

Fabulous. Then who was feeding his family this stuff? Or had they just made it up? And if so, why?

Putting thoughts of work aside, he walked over to his father. "Hey, Dad."

"Refs can't get a call right to save their lives."

James shifted, almost crossed his arms, then dropped them, unsure how to interpret that response, but not wanting his body language to show it. "All right if I watch the game with you?"

"What's going on with Lainie? Heard she was having trouble."

A sentence longer than three words and a direct question. Had hell frozen over?

"We're not sure," he said, keeping his surprise out of his tone. "Trying to figure that out." He walked to the window, glad for the interaction, but on guard at the same time. His father still hadn't looked directly at him. "I thought it best to bring her out here for a little break from the trouble she's having."

"Lainie's always welcome here."

As opposed to him? "I appreciate that." Movement caught his eye. "Dad, should anyone be out near the boathouse?"

"No." This time his father met his gaze. "Why?"

"Because I saw something."

"Could be a deer."

It wasn't. "I'll be right back."

"James?"

143

He froze. It was the first time he'd heard his name on his father's lips in years. He turned, saw the troubled look in the man's eyes, and almost decided to ignore whatever it was by the boathouse.

But he couldn't. "I'll be back." He strode toward the door and thought he heard his father mutter, "Seriously?"

He'd just have to mutter. As much as James wanted to stay and continue the conversation, no way could he ignore his gut screaming at him to go investigate.

"James? You okay?"

He glanced back to see Keegan following him. "Just something I need to check on."

His brother fell into step beside him. "I'll go with you."

James almost protested but figured it wouldn't do any good. "How's the practice going?" He still had a hard time seeing the kid who'd been nothing but trouble as a full-grown adult and a surgeon too.

"Lucrative. It's nice."

"The new partner working out?" James sidestepped an old tree trunk and kept his gaze on the boathouse. Nothing.

"So far. He's still in his probationary period, but he's doing a great job. Really taking some of the load off."

"Glad to hear it." James didn't bother opening the door of the small building. No one could get in without the key code to the pad, and the light was still flashing red. He walked around the side of the building, scanning the ground.

The area was disturbed, the rain from the previous night turning the dirt to damp mud. He walked the length of the wall, then turned the corner and stopped. Again, the ground was messed up, but this time, James spotted something.

"What is it?" Keegan asked. "You just went all tense like a bloodhound on the scent."

"A footprint. Anyone been down here today?"

"Not that I know of. Mom was out here yesterday before it rained."

The print had been made after the rain, and if no one from the family had been down here . . . He pulled out his phone and snapped four pictures from different angles.

"You going to call someone to come make an impression?" Keegan asked with a raised brow.

"Nope. No crime has been committed. Not wasting resources on something like this, but that's not Dad's print. It's too big. He wears a size 9, right?"

"Yeah, think so."

"That's at least an 11, if not a 12."

"Hmm. Right." A pause. "Got some plaster of Paris in the boathouse if you want to do it yourself."

"What in the world would you have that for?"

"Mom had it for one of her craft things. I don't think it's ever been opened."

Because his mother had more ideas than time for her many projects that she ordered materials for. "Well, it's not dental stone, but it should do the trick for what I want."

"I'll get it." Keegan disappeared around the side of the building, and in seconds, James heard the keypad beep. When his brother returned, they got to work, and soon James had the mold forming. It would take twenty to thirty minutes to dry, according to the label.

He stood, his legs protesting the length of time he'd been squatting. When his left knee popped, Keegan snickered. "Need a hand there, old-timer?"

"Shut up."

The mild words sent Keegan into a full-blown chuckle, and James rolled his eyes while smothering a smile. He'd missed the camaraderie of his siblings, the belonging, the community. A pang jabbed him right in the heart. He shouldn't have been such a coward. He should've called them as soon as he'd gotten home. But he hadn't and that was that. Dwelling on it wouldn't change anything. He was here now.

His gaze roamed the area, then settled on the water. A lone figure in a canoe was about a hundred yards out. "Know who that might be?" James asked, tilting his head in the direction of the lake.

Keegan shrugged. "No idea. Why?"

"Someone's been after Lainie."

"Who? And why?"

"Those are the questions of the week." James walked back the way he'd come, then stepped off the dock and made his way down to the edge of the lake where the grass met the sandy beach.

"What are you looking for?"

"That." He pointed to the deep grooves left in the sand and dirt. "If I were a betting man, I'd say that fellow pulled his canoe up here and got nosy with the boathouse."

"You sure?"

"Not positive, but I'm happy with the odds."

"You think he's the one following Lainie?"

"Don't know. Keep an eye on him, will you? I'm going to grab the binoculars."

"Better hurry. He's pulled the paddle out."

James rushed back to the boathouse, grabbed the binoculars from the hook on the wall, and bolted back to the spot next to Keegan. He lifted the glass to his eyes and focused in on the man in the boat.

The man ducked his head and started paddling. Fast.

"Can you tell who it is?" Keegan asked.

"No, but it sure does look like the guy who's been following Lainie. From the back, anyway. Wish I'd gotten a look at his face."

"He didn't want you to see his face."

"No. No he didn't."

TWELVE

Lainie watched from the window of the sunroom off the den that gave her a good view of the lake. Dixon walked toward the barn with Jericho following behind him like a puppy. A barn. At the lake. Why not? She smiled and shook her head. Dixon was his own man and didn't really care what others thought of him. He'd started his own law practice before the ink was dry on his license and had made a name for himself in the legal world. Steph sat on the couch, curled up with a book open in her lap. Every so often she would glance in the direction of the kitchen where the hushed voices of James' parents and the smell of dinner cooking drifted from. Probably Mrs. Cross encouraging James' father to behave himself.

Lainie wasn't quite sure that would happen, but at the moment, she was more interested in the fact that James and Keegan seemed overly interested in the man paddling toward the cove that was just around the bend. It didn't take him long to disappear from sight.

The guys stood at the edge of the lake, talking and pointing. About what? The man in the canoe? Who was he and why had James raced into the boathouse to get a pair of binoculars? A bad feeling grew in the pit of her belly while she watched for a few more minutes. When they walked over to look at something on the ground, her curiosity got the better of her. "Excuse me a sec," she said to Stephanie and strode to the sunroom door.

"Where are you going?"

"To see what's going on."

"There's something going on?"

"I don't know. That's what I'm going to find out."

Steph set her book aside and stood. "Well, I'm coming too."

Together, they walked out the door and down the deck steps to meet James and Keegan heading back toward the house. The look on James' face slowed her footsteps.

"What is it?" she asked.

"He . . . or someone . . . followed us here."

She froze. "That was him on the lake?"

"Possibly. I didn't get a good look at anything but his back." He shook his head, then nodded to the house. "Let's get inside."

She just noticed the object in Keegan's hand. "What's that?"

"A not-quite-dry footprint," he said.

Steph's gaze was going back and forth between her brothers and Lainie. "Why do I feel like I'm missing something?"

Lainie headed back the way she came.

"I'll explain inside," James said.

Once they were in the den, away from the exposure of the sunroom's windows, Lainie planted her hands on her hips, her mind working to process this latest development. After bringing her friend up-to-date, she looked at James. "How did he follow us here? Does he have a tracker or something on your Jeep?" She pressed a hand against her stomach. "Me?"

He shook his head. "I don't think so, but we'll check the car—and your purse?"

"I didn't bring a purse, just my backpack, and I pulled it out of my closet to pack to come here."

"Then it's definitely not on you."

"Do you think it's safe for me to stay?"

"We've got good security here at the lake house as far as where it's located. With the lake at the back, fencing on either side, and the gated entrance to even get into the neighborhood, we really only have to keep an eye on the water. I think we should stay put for now."

"I don't know. I don't want my presence to endanger anyone."

"It's not. And now that we know *he* knows you're here, we can be on guard. I've also got a call in to the local PD. They're going to send some units to canvas the area and see if they spot him. The water police are also on alert, so I think we're well covered."

That did make her feel better. Somewhat. "And the detective at my home?"

"I'll let her know she can leave." He frowned. "I still don't understand why our plan didn't work. It should have."

"You think he has some inside information about me?"

"You tell anyone what you were doing?"

"No." She narrowed her eyes and pulled out her phone. "Could he have tracked this?"

James stilled, then ran a hand over his head. "Yeah. It's possible, but that takes some sophisticated technology if you didn't share your location with him. Which obviously you didn't."

"I only share my location with a few friends." She gave a slight shrug.

"Like me," Steph said. "And on that note, I'm going to help Mom in the kitchen. You can fill me in later on anything I need to know."

She left and James shook his head. "If he had that sophisticated technology, he would have to know how to clone a phone—and then get close enough to do it."

Lainie hesitated, bit her lip, then pressed fingers to her eyes before she looked at him. "You mean like when I was sleeping in the on-call room?"

He nodded, awareness dawning. "Do you connect to the hospital Wi-Fi?"

"Yes."

"Then . . . yeah. It's very possible."

She took her phone out of her pocket and with a little effort removed the SIM card, then powered down the device. "Feels kinda like closing the barn door after the horses have run away, but there you go."

"Guys?" Stephanie stepped into the room. "Dinner's ready."

"We're coming."

She disappeared back into the kitchen just as his phone buzzed. He glanced at the text.

When his breath caught and he swallowed hard, Lainie walked to stand in front of him. His gaze lifted from his screen to lock on hers. "What is it?" she asked.

"There's been an . . . uh . . . incident at your house."

HER EYES WIDENED. "An incident? What does that mean?"

"There's been a small explosion of some kind."

She flinched like he'd struck her, then swayed, gasping. He gripped her bicep and led her to the sofa, where she dropped onto it.

"What?" She finally spoke. "An explosion? Is Savannah okay?"

Flashes from the bomb that had sent shrapnel ripping into his back and killing three of his friends pulled at his consciousness.

"James! Is she okay?"

He shuddered, forced himself to stay in the present, and read the text again. "Uh, yeah." He shrugged away the memories that threatened to drag him under, pulled in a deep breath, and let it out slowly. "She's on her way to the hospital."

"If she's okay, why is she going to the hospital?"

Get it together, dude. "She got hit with some debris, but it's minor. They're taking her in for a few stitches in her arm. I promise, she's not hurt bad at all. She was outside when the blast went off." He shook his head. "But Cole said you're going to need a new front door and probably some work on the front."

"Oh. My house." His heart twisted. Her only concern had been for the agent. Now, the news of her home hit hard. "Well, it's just stuff," she said, her voice low. "Everything in there can be replaced should I even want to do so. All that matters is she's okay." A pause. "When did this happen?"

"About an hour ago."

Her frown deepened. "But if that was him on the lake, then he knew I was here and not at my house. Why would he blow up my . . ." She frowned. "I'm confused."

"If it was him, this guy is doing the complete opposite of what his family believes he's doing," James said. "Their argument for believing he's living under the radar is that he was scared you'd come after him to finish the job should you find out he was alive."

"And yet he showed himself to me when he ran me off the road."

"Maybe you weren't supposed to see him."

Lainie blinked at him. "What are you getting at? He didn't seem to mind me seeing him at the hospital, the shelter, and the parking garage."

"Yeah, true, but—" Laughter spilled from the kitchen, distracting him for a brief second, then he focused back on Lainie. "Maybe when he ran you off the road, he believed you to be dead, looked over the side, saw you looking at him. Realized you'd recognized him . . . and now he's working on another plan."

"Oh. Maybe." She raked a hand over her head. "No one's called me back from the message I left about the autopsy report. Let me try again. Maybe Carina Black will pick up her phone. She's one of the medical examiners at the hospital. She can pull up Adam's autopsy and tell me who did it. That should prove once and for all that he's dead and we can all move on from there."

"Good idea."

He handed her his phone, and in a couple of minutes, she said, "Carina, this is Lainie." James listened while she went on to ask the woman to pull up the autopsy report. "No, I'm not kidding. Please." Pause. "Yes, of course I'll hang on. Thank you."

She chewed on her bottom lip while she waited, and James smiled. He remembered her doing that from the first day he'd met her. She hated waiting but could give the appearance of being at perfect peace in doing so. Except for the lip chewing. When she straightened, he tuned back in.

"What?" She met his gaze with a ferocious frown. "What do you mean you can't find it? It was done at that hospital. It should be in the system. Can you look again?" She waited once more. "Still nothing? That's just . . . Okay, sorry, one more request. Can you check the night he was brought into the hospital." She gave the date. "There should be medical records, and will you check to see if you can find a death certificate with vital records as well? It should be a quick search." Another pause. Less than a minute later, she sighed. "Unbelievable." She fell quiet, then said, "Okay, do you remember him? Adam Williams?" She shook her head at him. "I have a call in to Otis. Is he around? Uh-huh. Okay. Well, when he gets back, will you ask him to call me at this number? Thanks." She hung up and looked at James, disbelief stamped on her pale features. "It's not there. None of it. No autopsy report, no death certificate, no record of him being in the hospital, nothing. It's gone." She was repeating herself, her shock evident in her tone. "And Carina said she doesn't remember Adam or doing an autopsy on him." She frowned at him as though expecting him to make sense of the whole situation.

He had no answers, so he sat beside her and pulled her into a hug. She burrowed against him like she belonged there, her arms encircling his waist.

He tried not to notice the perfect fit and cleared his throat. "How is that possible? Thoughts?"

"I have no idea," she murmured against his chest. "I can't believe I don't know who did his autopsy. I should know that, shouldn't I?"

"Why would you know that?"

"I just . . . think I should. There are only three options of who could have done it. Now I'm down to two since Carina didn't." She stilled. "But one of the MEs passed away about a year ago, so if it was him . . ."

"Right."

"Could that be a coincidence?"

"The death of the ME who did Adam's autopsy?"

"Yeah."

"Well, if it was him, then . . . that would be weird to me in light of everything going on."

"I agree." She glanced at his phone. "Hopefully, Otis will get my message and he'll call me soon."

"What's Otis like?"

"Old." She laughed. A genuine chuckle James let wash over him. He loved her laugh. "He's been at the hospital since about the sixth day of creation. I keep expecting him to retire any day now, but he'll be able to tell me who did the autopsy. Bart Sheffield is the one who died in a car accident last year. If Otis didn't do the autopsy, then Bart did it."

"Guess we'll know when we know."

"I also think there's more behind all of this than someone wanting me to believe Adam is still alive."

"What do you mean?"

"Whoever is doing this wants to wipe out any trace of him ever being dead."

THIRTEEN

But he was dead. *He was.* At the moment, she didn't even care because being wrapped in James' arms was a dream come true and she was never moving for the rest of her life if she could manage it.

She heard Steph's voice calling out. "What's taking you guys so long? We're about ready to eat. You coming?" Steph's eyes went wide as she popped her head out of the kitchen, and while Lainie knew how it looked, she was still relishing the moment. In fact, the words "go away" were on the tip of her tongue.

She bit them back and forced herself to pull out of the security of James' embrace, instantly missing the brief, lovely moment of feeling perfectly safe, like nothing could touch her as long as his arms were around her. "Yes, of course. Thanks." She'd better not ever let that happen again. Getting involved with a man was not in her future. Allowing herself to get close to James was nothing but a recipe for heartbreak. She was too messed up emotionally, carried too much baggage to place on another person. Her fingers crept to the necklace and she latched on to the little key. Her reminder.

Rats. Now the whole situation just felt awkward. "So—do I run over and see my house? What do I do now?"

He touched her cheek and sighed. "I know you're concerned about your home. Firefighters are there, law enforcement, the works. Why don't we eat and wait to hear what's going on. But for now, let them do their jobs."

And just like that, the awkwardness was gone. "Okay. Fine." She wasn't sure she could eat a bite, but she'd sit with them and do her best. "More importantly, will you let me know when you hear something about Savannah?"

"Of course, but I promise you, she's fine."

"Well, let's keep this between us for now. No sense in telling everyone about this when we won't have answers to all the questions they're sure to have."

"Good idea."

She followed him into the kitchen where everyone was gathered around the huge table in the middle of the room. Steph eyed them with questions in her gaze but, thankfully, refrained from commenting. Lainie had no answers for her anyway. Mr. Cross sat at the far end of the table. As soon as James entered, his gaze dropped to his plate. James' mom shook her head and sighed.

In spite of that, James' siblings made the meal a lively affair, and Lainie could honestly say she enjoyed it when she wasn't thinking about her house or Savannah.

After dinner, Dixon left to take care of Jericho and Lainie helped with cleanup. She glanced at the kitchen clock, anxious to get it over with.

Steph sidled up to her. "What was that in the den with James?"

Steph was rarely good at waiting for an appropriate time to talk, although she'd done an admirable job of it earlier. "Nothing. He gave me some bad news, I was upset, and he hugged me. That was it." It really was. Wasn't it?

"Oh." Steph stepped back and frowned. "I'm sorry. What kind of bad news?"

"Someone vandalized my house." Blew it up was more accurate, but she'd settle for the less severe sounding description.

"Oh no!" Steph hugged her, then released her. "I'm so sorry. You're really having a tough time right now, aren't you?"

"I am, but James is helping me and I really need him to do that. So, please, don't read anything more into that scene in the den. It wasn't what you're thinking." Or was it? She didn't know what it was. Well, she knew what it was on her part, but James'? She didn't want to project feelings onto him that weren't there.

"Okay. Fine. But I can't say I'm not disappointed. Keep me updated?"

Disappointed? "Um . . . sure." An easy promise to make since she doubted there'd be much—if anything—to update. The thought depressed her.

"Great. Now, I'm going to go see if Dixon needs help with Jericho. One day, I'm going to run away with that horse."

"Better not. If Dixon catches you, he'd have you arrested and thrown in jail."

"I'm worried." Her expression said otherwise. "And I'm praying that there's something between you and James. Nothing would thrill me more." Steph's laugh echoed behind her, and she waved before shutting the kitchen door. Mrs. Cross bustled into the kitchen and checked the oven. Lainie just noticed the delicious aroma of cookies baking.

Before Lainie had a chance to process that last comment from Steph, James stepped into view, caught her eye. "I think we should stay here for the night. It's late and there's nothing we can do before tomorrow."

Heat found its way into her neck once more, and she couldn't help wondering if he'd heard Steph's parting comment. Then again, did it matter? Right now, she had other stuff to deal with. Not a crush on her best friend's brother. "Are you sure? I mean, the whole reason for bringing me out here was in hopes he wouldn't know where I am. But he does, so . . ." She honestly had no idea where she should sleep tonight. Stay here where she was the safest she was going to be and possibly bring danger down on a family she loved? Or go home and walk into danger all the same, and at least James' family would be safe?

"Not the whole reason," he murmured with a glance toward the den where his father had settled into the recliner, the remote in his hand and football on the screen. He sighed, then cleared his throat. "In the meantime, why don't we have a distraction?"

"Such as?"

"Scrabble," Steph said, walking up with a gleam in her eye.

Mrs. Cross chuckled from behind her.

He flinched and held his hands up. "No way. Why would you even suggest that? I thought you were helping Dixon with Jericho."

"He didn't need me, so . . . Scrabble?"

James' jaw jutted and he crossed his arms. "No. I feel quite sure she still studies the dictionary for fun."

Lainie huffed. "You're as bad as Allison, and I only started doing that so I could beat you."

Steph laughed. "I'm game. I'll see if Keegan and Dixon are in." She slipped out the door once more.

James' father stepped into the kitchen and his eyes locked on the three of them. He seemed about to say something, then shook his head, hooked a right, and walked down the hall.

"Dad? Hold up." James hurried after the man.

Mrs. Cross cleared her throat and set a tray of cookies on the table. "If there's going to be Scrabble, I imagine you could use some of these."

"They look amazing," Lainie said. James rejoined them, his face tense, jaw tight. His father must have rebuffed him. Lainie placed a hand on his, her heart hurting for him. "Just have fun, James."

"Yeah." He nodded. "Yeah, let's have some fun."

Mrs. Cross frowned, firmed her jaw, and headed after her husband as Steph, Keegan, and Dixon entered with grins.

"I hear we're playing Scrabble," Keegan said, rubbing his hands together and looking at Lainie with narrowed eyes. "I'm going to beat you this time."

Lainie smiled. "Right. You keep that positive attitude and we'll see how that works out for you."

For the next three hours, they let the cares of the past few days roll off. Lainie threw herself into the fun of catching up with friends and eating cookies, and in the end, she remained the champion. But just barely. James had been stiff competition with Dixon also winning one of the games. Then again, he *was* a lawyer. Keegan conceded he'd been too confident and declared he wanted a rematch. After he studied the dictionary over the next couple of months.

Lainie helped collect the tiles and return them to the bag, while Steph and the others filtered out of the room ready to call it a night.

Lainie carried the game into the den and noted that James followed her. She set the box on the shelf and turned to find him watching her with a strange look on his face. She paused. "What?"

"You're very competitive, aren't you?"

A flush started at the base of her neck and worked its way up. "Um . . . yes? I would think my studying the dictionary to beat you would be your first clue."

He laughed. "True. I find it admirable and . . . cute."

She raised a brow. "Cute?"

"Is that the wrong word?"

"Admirable is good. Cute? I guess that depends on what you mean."

"It's . . ." He shrugged. "I don't know what I meant. I guess I just never noticed that about you before and I'm not sure why. You've changed."

Never noticed? But he'd noticed now? And had she changed that much? "I've discovered I like to win."

"No kidding. You're brutal. I refuse to play Scrabble with you anymore."

She laughed at his teasing. "Don't refuse to play, just do what it takes to get better."

He paused. "That's what you've done your entire life, isn't it?"

Lainie frowned at him. "What do you mean?"

"I mean, you don't quit. You might take a hit on the chin, but you pick yourself up and keep going, doing whatever it takes to come out ahead."

His words resonated, vibrating within her brain, and she wasn't sure how to respond. But was he right? "I wouldn't say that's true about my *whole* life, but in the last eighteen months? Maybe."

"Maybe? I'd say definitely to all your life after everything you've shared about growing up in your family. The last eighteen months have probably just solidified that."

"I suppose."

A silence descended and James shoved his hands into the front pockets of his jeans. "We'll leave first thing in the morning to go to your house, okay?"

"Sure. Thank you."

He nodded. "I've asked a couple of officers to ride by here tonight on a regular basis. The house alarm is set. I've filled Mom in on the situation and she's filled Dad in, so tonight we can rest. Okay?"

"Okay."

"So . . . you good?"

"For now." Before the conversation could turn awkward, she pointed down the hall. "I'm beat. I'll see you in the morning."

"Yeah. Night, Lainie."

His simple good night held more emotion than the words called for, and she had a feeling he wanted to say more. She wasn't sure she could handle it, so she backed away and hurried toward the bedroom, where Steph was already curled under the covers. "Night, Lainie," her sleepy voice said.

"Night, Steph."

Lainie headed for the en suite bath. When she returned to the room ten minutes later and crawled under the covers, Steph shifted. "Still want you and James to get together."

Lainie laughed. "Shut up and go to sleep." But silently, she was saying, *Me too, Steph. Me too.*

WHEN LAINIE WOKE the next morning, she realized she hadn't dreamed. She couldn't explain it when those peaceful nights happened, she just held on to them with both hands and was grateful.

Breakfast was quick, with bagels, cream cheese, eggs, and bacon, and then she was itching to get on their way to her home. James stepped out of the den, his face tight, nostrils flared. He must have tried to say goodbye to his father. Lainie's temper ignited. This wasn't right. Someone needed to verbally knock some sense into the man. But was she the one to do that?

"You ready?" James asked.

"Yes, I just need to grab my bag from the room."

"James, son, do you have a moment?" Mrs. Cross asked, wiping her hands on a towel.

"Sure, Mom." He looked at Lainie. "Let me talk to Mom, then I'll get your bag and meet you in the de—uh—at the front door."

Because his father was in the den.

"Okay."

Lainie left the two of them in the kitchen and, after only a moment's hesitation and a quick prayer for the right words, headed into the den to find James' father. He looked up when she walked in and smiled. He'd always liked her. She hoped that would help him listen to what she had to say. "Hi, Mr. Cross. You have a minute?"

"Always for you. How's your family? Sorry I haven't asked before now." He hadn't asked because she'd been in James' company since their arrival.

"They're doing mostly well. Dad is teaching survival skills to some group for the next few weeks, so that's getting him out of the house. And . . . well, Mom is . . . okay."

"What's on your mind?"

"Something that's probably none of my business."

His right brow rose, but he held her gaze. "Let me guess. James."

"Yes, sir."

"Nothing to say there."

"I have something to say." Could she do it? Could she say the words she'd said to many patients? This was James' father.

"Say it, then."

"What you're doing to him is abuse." There. She said it.

He gasped. Then gaped while anger built in his eyes. She hadn't meant to blurt it out quite like that, but she wasn't sure how much time she had before James would be back. "I'm sorry. I know that sounds terrible and I know you don't hit him or anything like that, but your actions, the way you treat him, can be considered emotional abuse. I've lived it, Mr. Cross. And I survived it. I don't have to tell you the story, you know what happened. But I recognize abuse for what it is."

He started to speak, but she rushed on. "And I know it's not my place, but I can't help it. I care about James and I care about you and Mrs. Cross, Keegan, Dixon, and Steph." She paused, then decided to put everything out there. "I haven't shared a lot about my family. I'm sure you and Mrs. Cross suspected things weren't always great at my house, but you never judged. My family is not 'normal.' I won't go into all of the reasons why, but growing up, you showed me what a 'normal' family could look like—a marriage strong in love, and how a mother is supposed to behave. How a father supports and loves his wife and kids." She waved a hand. "This isn't you. This isn't the family I grew up with. I know you love James, but your refusal to speak to him or have a conversation with him is killing him and it's tearing your family apart. Steph can't talk about it or she cries."

Was that a small flinch? She wasn't sure, but he wasn't stopping her, so she continued. "Truthfully, I don't want to see you go the rest of your life with you and James at odds, only to find you on your deathbed wishing you could do it all over again. Wishing you had this time back. And trust me, I've had patients there. I've seen the regret and the tears. So, please, find a way to fix this before it's too late. Find it in your heart to forgive and move on."

She drew in a shuddering breath and noted his granite features, flat eyes, and tight jaw. Dread pooled in her belly, and she backed away. "I'm sorry. I shouldn't have said anything. It's not my business. I just care about you and this whole family so much . . ." Tears clogged the rest of her words. And truly, that was most likely a good thing as she'd probably already said way too many anyway. "I'll just go wait for James in the foyer." She turned to go.

"He knew how I felt about cops and he went and became one. That's spite. That's disrespect."

Lainie paused at the edge of the den, just steps from the foyer. She turned. "It may have started that way, but he wouldn't have stayed in his profession this long if he hated it. He told me so on the way here. Nor would he do it just to spite you. He wouldn't do that because he's grown and matured and come to love what he does." She paused. "I know you're a believer. I know you love the Lord. And I know he's convicting you about all this." Definitely a wince. "When James was a baby, you dedicated him before the church and prayed he'd become a man of God. Well, your prayer has been answered and this is how God is using him. He's saving lives, Mr. Cross. And in the end, because of what he does, he may very well end up saving mine."

JAMES STOOD THERE, his heart hurting and full all at the same time. And humbled that Lainie would go to bat for him like that. Would she get through to the man when no one else in the family could? Hope sprouted for a brief second until his father aimed the remote at the television and upped the volume.

Lainie bit her lip, murmured another apology, and walked toward the front door. James stepped into the half bath before she could see him, not wanting her to know he'd overheard a lot of what she'd said. And the truth was, he needed a minute to compose himself. His heart thundered and tears burned behind his eyes. How he longed for his father to show him forgiveness and grace.

He counted to ten, then walked out to see Lainie by the door, hugging his mother. ". . . be back. Thank you for a wonderful time."

"I'm praying for you, my dear." She turned from Lainie and walked over to hug James. "And you, my son. I'll admit it hurts my heart to let you walk out that door."

"I know, Mom." He braced himself for the coming verbal onslaught.

"Be careful and keep our Lainie safe" was all she said, and James frowned. That was it? No begging him to stay? Warning him of the dangers of his job? She smiled, patted his cheek, and walked into the den. One day soon, he was going to have to ask her to explain the change.

"James? You okay?" Lainie asked.

He shook his head. "Okay. Confused, but okay."

He opened the door to usher her out. Dixon stepped out of the barn and waved, his gaze concerned, but he didn't try to stop them.

Once Lainie was buckled into her seat, she leaned her head back and closed her eyes, her hand going to her necklace.

"What are you thinking?" he asked.

As was her habit, her fingers rolled the key back and forth, like if she did it long enough, she'd have the answers to the universe. "That someone deliberately bombed my home, not caring if he hurt the person staying there. Because I believe he knew Savannah was there."

"Yeah." James settled behind the wheel, and she opened her eyes just in time to catch the wince he tried to hide but, judging from her expression, failed.

"I'm sorry about all this, James."

"I don't know why you're apologizing. None of this is your fault." He cranked the Jeep and aimed it down the long drive.

"Not directly, no, but I've sure done something to cause all this drama. You should be at home resting and healing. And Savannah could have been killed for what? All of our planning and subterfuge was for nothing because we didn't know that he would—or even could—actually track my phone."

"That's on me. I should have considered this guy was more skilled, more savvy than I did. He's escalating."

"Why didn't he kill me in the hospital?" she asked, her voice low. "He certainly had the opportunity. He could have smothered me or injected me with something or . . . whatever."

James shuddered at the images her words evoked.

"But he didn't," she said. "He left me a stupid, cryptic message and walked away."

"Maybe he was interrupted before he had the chance."

She continued to twist the key between her fingers and her frown deepened the lines in her forehead. "Maybe, but he still left the note. 'Cheers, love,'" she whispered. "He said that, then pulled the trigger that night. Who would know that but Adam?" A shudder rippled through her, and James was tempted to pull over and just hold her.

Anyone who had access to her statement in the police file would know that. The thought left him mighty uncomfortable. No need to mention that to Lainie just yet, but it was something he and Cole needed to think about. He cleared his throat, made a left onto the road that would take them to her neighborhood, and checked the mirrors. So far, no one had followed them. "You said he used that phrase a lot?"

"Fairly regularly. Usually when he was in a good mood. Which says a lot about his frame of mind when he was trying to kill me. Don't think *that* escaped me."

James almost wished the man was still alive so he could have the pleasure of pounding on him a few times before throwing him in prison. "I'm sorry."

"I am too."

James' phone rang and he answered it via Bluetooth. "Cross here."

"Uh, yeah, this is Otis Wheeler. Lainie Jackson left this number?"

"Hold on a second, she's right here."

He nodded to Lainie, who leaned forward. "Hey, Otis, I'm here. What did you find out?"

"I checked my records and I never did an autopsy on an Adam Williams." He verified the birthdate and said, "I checked with Lydia, the part-timer, and he's not one of hers either."

"Okay, Otis, thanks for checking. I'd forgotten about Lydia."

"Sure thing."

She hung up and sighed, glanced at him, and frowned. "What are you thinking?"

"I think we have to consider the possibility that Adam is actually alive and what the Williamses believe is real."

"But . . . he's . . . and *it's* . . . not."

"Just track with me here for a moment. Going on the assumption that Adam is alive and believes you will come after him, what if he thinks he has to strike first? You said he was unstable, and angry. What if he's still out there, planning to finish what he started?"

Lainie sighed. "Well, if Adam were still alive, then, yes, your theory would be a valid one. But he's not alive, so . . ."

"Or . . . this person seems to want you to *believe* he is."

"But *why*? What does he gain by making me believe Adam is alive?"

"I keep coming back to some kind of revenge."

"Maybe. Makes my head hurt thinking about it. In the meantime, I'm still tracking down who did Adam's autopsy. Otis said it wasn't Lydia, so I'll call—" She gasped as James turned onto her street, her fingers going back to the key at her throat. "Oh my—oh, James. That looks bad. Worse than what you said." The tears in her voice cut him.

"It's okay, Lainie. I mean, it's not, but it will be. Just keep telling yourself it'll be okay. We'll get you through this." He squeezed the fingers of her free hand, and she clutched him as she stared with unblinking eyes at the destruction.

Emergency crews were still there, having stayed through the night to make sure the fire was truly out. Neighbors whispered and pointed.

Cole broke away from the group he'd been chatting with and approached. James climbed out—carefully. His wound throbbed with a renewed intensity, but he was going to be there for Lainie if it killed him. She slipped out of the passenger seat and walked over to stand beside him and Cole.

Cole nodded to her. "I'm so sorry, Lainie."

"That's what everyone keeps saying." She murmured the words, never taking her eyes from the sight. "But thank you."

"We're going to catch this person."

"I know."

She sounded odd. Distant. In shock? "Lainie?"

"I'm okay."

She didn't sound okay.

"There's more, Lainie," Cole said. "We found something in your mailbox. The door was open. One of the officers went to close it and saw this."

She shuddered and looked at his partner. "Okay. What?"

"Another message."

"A message?"

James studied her. Her voice still had an odd hollow ring to it, like she was responding on autopilot.

Cole glanced at him and James nodded. Cole cleared his throat and read, "'I knew you'd come. Hiding only delays the inevitable. A bullet couldn't stop me and neither will cops in disguise. I waited until she came out of the house before setting off the device. It was just a warning. Hide from me again and there will be no more warnings. Cheers, love. See you soon.'"

James shook his head. "Well, now we know *why* he blew up your house."

"We do? Why?"

"To draw you out." He moved closer and looked around. "He's out there, watching." James had no doubt the man had his eyes on her, and he didn't like that. Not at all. He slid an arm around her shoulders and pulled her closer, putting himself between her and a bullet if necessary.

"Can I go inside?"

"Yeah. The crew said the fire's out with no chance of sparking again. You need to go in through the back. The front needs repair before it's safe to walk on."

The blackened front exterior filled her with dread about what she was going to find inside, but she pushed through and walked with heavy steps to the back entrance of her home. Once inside, she headed toward the front of the house, and James followed her. "After seeing the outside, it's really not as bad as I expected," she said.

James was right behind her while Cole kept an eye on the street. "He set the device off outside the front door, so that took the brunt of the hit." He looked around the great room. "You'll have to replace the flooring in there along with the curtains and maybe a few other water-damaged furnishings, but there are companies who can help you with the smoke damage on pieces that are salvageable."

"Right." She let her gaze roam over her home. She wrinkled her nose. "I'll never get the smell out, will I?"

"Not you, but a professional can. You want to grab whatever you need for at least a week?" He wanted to get her away as quick as possible.

"Yes. I guess I should do that, huh?"

"The floor to your bedroom should be stable enough," James said, "but let me go first."

Lainie did as requested and followed him to her bedroom. "This doesn't smell nearly as bad as the front, but I can tell the smoke reached here as well. It's going to be a while before I can return, isn't it?"

"Yeah, I'm afraid so."

Her breathing quickened and anger flashed in her narrowed gaze. "Well, guess I'd better get busy." With jerky movements, she packed her medium-sized rolling suitcase and an overnight bag. It didn't take her long, and she turned to James, who'd leaned against her doorframe to watch. "I'm ready."

He took the handle of her suitcase and led the way out of the house.

Once they were back at his Jeep, he stowed her luggage in the rear, then opened the passenger door and Lainie slid in. As he was closing the door, she let out a low sob. And another.

"Aw, Lainie." In seconds, he had the passenger door open and pulled her into his arms. James held her while she cried on his shoulder and the whole time the tears flowed, he could feel her working to stop them. "Just cry, Lainie. It's okay."

So she did.

Finally, she sniffed. "Sorry."

"Don't apologize. If someone did that to my house, I'd cry too."

She huffed a choked laugh. "You wouldn't. You'd just start fixing it because that's what you do. You fix things." She swiped a stray tear. "I know it's just a house, I *know*. And I also know everything can be replaced, but it's just . . . the hate behind it is what bothers me more than anything. And I have absolutely no idea why someone would do this—besides Adam, I mean." She paused, drew in a ragged breath, and looked up. "I know what we need to do next."

"What?"

"Dig him up."

FOURTEEN

James gaped. "I'm sorry? What?"

"We need to get permission to exhume the body," she said. "To prove once and for all that the person after me is not Adam."

"Prove to whom?"

"To . . . me," she whispered. Tears threatened and she held them back with sheer force of will. "I *know* he's dead, but . . ."

"But?"

"But I don't know. I can't believe I'm saying this, but what if I'm wrong? What if somehow, some way . . ." She pressed a hand to her throbbing temple. "I need to find the two paramedics who responded that night. I can simply ask them about Adam. Get them to confirm he was dead when they dropped him at the hospital. I have no doubt they'll remember."

"Do you know the names of the paramedics?"

"Of course. I see them at the hospital occasionally. Olivia Buchanan and Ivy Talbot." She looked away, ignoring the heat climbing into her cheeks. "I . . . uh . . . thanked them for their help at the scene, but haven't spoken to them since." Because she avoided them. If she saw them coming, she went the other way. They were a reminder of that horrific night and triggered a shame that she couldn't shake.

Shame that they'd had to show up, shame that she allowed herself to be in that situation, shame—

"Okay, let's go find them. I can put in the request for the exhumation on the way." He glanced at her, his gaze admiring.

She hesitated, not sure what to do with that. Had any man ever looked at her like . . . like she was *special?* A woman a few feet away turned toward them and Lainie gasped. "Jesslyn!" Her friend hurried over and hugged her. Lainie clung to her for a few seconds, then stepped back. "What are you doing here? Fire marshals don't do routine calls like this."

"I heard the address over the radio and had to come, silly. And I was glad to find you *not* here yesterday. I didn't know if you were here or not, and it scared me." Jesslyn shuddered. "I'm so glad you weren't hurt."

"Thank you," Lainie whispered. "I wasn't hurt, but Savannah was."

"The woman who was here?" Lainie nodded and Jesslyn smiled. "She's fine. Was absolutely furious that she didn't catch the guy."

Lainie was very glad she hadn't—at least as long as it meant she wasn't hurt any worse.

"I'm so sorry about this," Jesslyn said, "but the good news is, it's not as bad as it looks. I mean, it's not great, but I think most of the damage is to the outside. Don't even think the water got in much past the foyer. You probably have a couple of weeks' worth of repairs to have done, but you should be able to get back in soon."

"Oh." Hope stirred. "That *is* good news. I appreciate that."

"Sure thing."

Someone shouted Jesslyn's name and she gave Lainie another squeeze. "I need to go see what they want. You have a key to my place if you need it. We already know you can wear my clothes—assuming you can find any you like."

They had different styles, but . . . "Beggars can't be choosers. You have jeans and T-shirts. I'll be fine. Thank you." Lainie clamped her lips on the sobs that wanted to escape. She managed to choke them back as Jesslyn hurried away. Lainie pulled in a steadying breath and looked at James. "I'm ready to go find Olivia and Ivy if you are."

"Cole can follow us just to keep an eye on things."

Meaning make sure they weren't followed.

"Wanna call first?" he asked. "To make sure they're there?"

Not really. "Yes. Of course."

"I'll do it while you get back in the Jeep. I don't like you being out in the open like this." While James took that task from her hands, Lainie slid in the passenger seat and continued to survey the area she called home. Her house, a ranch-style three-bedroom, two-bathroom, sat in a small and older middle-class neighborhood. The yards were large, the homes spread out, with giant trees in the front. When she'd moved in, she'd had to remove three of them for fear they'd land on her roof in a bad storm. But honestly, it felt like living in a forest with the convenience of the big city nearby.

Normally, she loved the area. Now it just felt like the man who was causing all the chaos in her life could be hiding behind any of the trees, ready to pick her off. She shivered and hunched down in the passenger seat.

The driver's door opened. "They're there," James said, climbing in. He moved carefully, and it hurt her heart to know he was suffering because of her. No, not because of her. Because of the person out there twisting her life into a hot mess. But still . . .

Leaving her home in the hands of the fire department, she shoved aside her reluctance to see the two paramedics. With Cole following behind, they made their way to the fire station where Ambulance 82 docked.

Part of her wished they'd arrive to find the paramedics had been called out, but when they swung into the parking area, the ambulance was in the open bay, ready for its next run.

James parked and eased out of the driver's side. Cole stopped on the curb, out of the way of the fire trucks but able to keep an eye on the road. To make sure no one followed them there, no doubt.

For now, she was going to let the men worry about whether her stalker was out there and focus on getting through the next few minutes. She made her way inside the firehouse and spotted a fireman she recognized walking toward her, his gaze on his screen. "Hey, Daniel."

He looked up from his phone. "Lainie? What brings you here?"

"Looking for Olivia and Ivy. Any idea where to find them?"

"Yeah, sure. In the kitchen area. They were scarfing down some birthday cake. Olivia's."

"Ah, good to know. Thanks."

"Sure thing."

Lainie headed for the kitchen with a silent James on her heels. Olivia, Ivy, and three others she knew were at the table, and all looked up at Lainie's and James' entrance. Olivia's eyes went wide and she stood. "Hi. That was fast."

"Hi," Lainie said, hating the weak wobble in her voice. She cleared her throat. "Hi," she said again with more strength. "Happy birthday."

"Oh, thanks. Want some cake?"

"No thank you." She introduced James. "He's the one you talked to on the phone. Do you mind if we talk to you and Ivy privately for a moment?"

Olivia's gaze went to her partner, and the woman in her early forties rose. "Let's step into the conference room off the hall. This way."

Once they were in the conference room, Olivia frowned. "What's going on?"

Lainie pressed her hands together and glanced at James. He shot her an encouraging smile, and she blew out a low breath. "I need to know about that night that you came to my house. The night Adam shot me and I . . . um . . . shot him."

Ivy nodded, compassion in her blue eyes. "Of course. What do you need to know?"

"He was dead when you got there, right?"

"Well, he didn't have a heartbeat when we got there," Olivia said, "but we managed to get one in the ambulance."

Lainie gasped, then gaped. "What? B-but I tried to find a pulse and—and he wasn't breathing." She was stuttering and couldn't seem to help it. "I checked."

"You were in shock, Lainie," Ivy said.

"Maybe, but I know when a pulse is there and when it's not. And it wasn't."

"No, when you checked he didn't. You didn't miss that. But we shocked him," Olivia said, "several times. And got a heartbeat. He was still alive when we dropped him at the hospital. I don't know how, but he was."

Lainie had never actually fainted in her life. She'd passed out from loss of blood. Once. Eighteen months ago. But she'd never fainted from shock. Today might be the day that happened.

"Lainie?"

James' voice came from a distance, echoing in her ears.

"Lainie?" A hard hand gripped her bicep and gave her a soft shake.

She pulled in a breath, and he led her to one of the black cushioned chairs at the table. She sat. *"He was still alive when we dropped him at the hospital. He was still alive—"*

"Lainie!"

She jerked her chin at Olivia and Ivy. "Alive?" The two women nodded. "But . . . he was dead. He . . ." What could she say? Olivia and Ivy wouldn't lie to her. If they said Adam had a heartbeat at the hospital, then he had one. But . . . how? "So, he died on the table? In the ER? In surgery?" She didn't know. She'd never looked at his records and now they'd disappeared.

Ivy shook her head. "I don't know. We never heard."

"There's no record of him ever arriving at the hospital."

"Well, I can assure you, he did," Ivy said.

Lainie pressed a hand to her forehead, willing herself to think. "I don't know who his doctor was." But someone at the hospital would know. All she had to do was look up the schedule for that day, see who was working, and ask. Surely they'd remember working on him. Right? No, not right. They worked so many traumas, Adam would have just been one more in the lineup. She glanced at James. "Do you have any other questions?"

"Not right now."

Lainie looked at the women. "Thank you."

"Any time," Olivia said. "We're so glad you survived that night. I've looked for you a few times at the hospital, but I guess our paths just haven't crossed."

Because Lainie had made sure of that. Shame pushed heat into her cheeks. "I'll look for you and be sure to say hey if I see you."

They said their goodbyes, and James led Lainie back to the car. She grabbed the key at the base of her throat and twisted it, rubbing her thumb over the rough edge. Exhaustion threaded through her. A mental exhaustion to go with the physical. "I want to go home."

"Lainie . . ."

"But that's not an option. Right. I can stay at Jesslyn's or the hospital." She smiled. "Jesslyn has a really good alarm system."

"Or we can go back to the lake house," he said. "I like the security there in spite of the incident on the water yesterday. I turned one of the cameras on the area. If there's movement there, I'll get a notification."

She shrugged. "Okay, the lake house is fine." As long as she had something resembling a bed, she didn't care where it was. "In the meantime, I need to go to Bill's Storage on Carmichael."

"Why's that?"

"Because after Adam died, I locked everything up in storage."

His eyes narrowed on the key in her hand. "And that goes to the lock?"

She nodded. "I haven't been there since I had it all hauled away. It's not a whole lot, but there was a file cabinet, some boxes of papers, probably some pictures, and some furniture. Maybe something there that can tell us about Adam and who he was hanging out with, if he was doing anything on the side that I didn't know about." She raked a hand over her hair and tucked a few strands behind her ear. "He could have had a whole other life and I'd never have known. I wasn't thinking about that when I put the stuff in storage, I just wanted anything that reminded me about Adam out of my line of sight."

James nodded. "Understandable. All right. I'll ask Cole to meet us there. And on the way to the lake house, we need to stop and get you a phone. I don't like you being without one."

"That would be good. I need to text the number to my parents in case they need me."

"Then let's get to it."

Lainie noted his pained expression even though he was doing his best to hide it. It had been a long morning for her, but with his injury, he had to be feeling particularly worn out. "When's the last time you took some pain meds?"

"Just before we left the house."

She nodded. "Good. Tonight, you need to forget about me and rest."

His gaze locked on hers. "I could never forget about you, Lainie."

Once again warmth crept into her cheeks, and she had to wonder if there was anything more than just kindness behind his words. And if so, what was she going to do about it? Nothing. She twisted the key once more. She would do absolutely nothing.

ON A STRAIGHT STRETCH of the highway, James took his eyes off the road long enough to glance at Lainie. She had finished setting up her new phone and now her faraway expression and pinched lips said her thoughts were spinning. He couldn't blame her.

"You okay?" he asked her.

"I don't know. I mean, I'm prepared, I guess." She snaked her fingers around the necklace. "Got the key, got water bottles for all of us, got some snacks from the pantry that weren't damaged." She huffed a short, humorless laugh. "I mean, what does a girl take to go sift through the leftovers of the guy who tried to kill her?"

At least she was being honest. He reached over to grasp her hand

and give it a squeeze. "You'll be okay. One way or another, you'll be okay. I'm going to see to it." He only hoped he could live up to his promise, but if he didn't, it wouldn't be for lack of trying. He let go of her hand with reluctance and wrapped his fingers back around the wheel.

Lainie glanced at her phone again and sighed.

"Everything okay?" he asked.

"I almost prefer having no phone."

"Why's that?"

"I'm supposed to go over next Friday to help my mom do some cleaning, but she's decided I need to come tomorrow and is blowing up my phone with texts."

"And you're off tomorrow, right?"

"Of course. She knows my schedule because I share it with her. Might be time to stop doing that," she muttered.

"Do we need to go by there?"

"No."

The instant response lifted his brow. "Okay."

"I'll text my dad and let him know some details so he can intervene. I think I need to stay away from them for now. At least until we get my situation figured out."

"Might be a wise idea."

She looked at him from the corner of her eye. "But it's safe to be around your family?"

"With the gated community, and a cop at your side?" He jabbed a thumb in his chest. "Not to mention others who are well-versed in using guns against predators? Yes, it's safe. He couldn't get to you there, which is why he went after your house. My guess is, it was to prove you couldn't 'beat' him."

"At least he waited until she was out of the house." She shuddered and her free hand gripped the key. "I still can't believe he went to that extreme."

They fell silent and he drove, watching the mirrors, the side roads, and the air—no need to assume the man didn't have access to drones—just in case.

"Is your mom still texting you?" James asked. "Wondering where you are?"

"Of course."

"We can do whatever you need to do, Lainie. If you need to go see your parents, we'll figure something out."

"No. I'm worried about her. Them. But I'm more worried about leading a killer to them." She paused. "I just want my mom to be happy, James, but she's not. Never really has been, that I can remember. She can't grieve her father's death and move on. It's like she's stuck in the grieving mode with only a few spurts of happiness sprinkled in when the depression lifts."

"Meaning when she takes her meds?"

"Yes, but she's pretty typical of a lot of people. She takes the medicine, gets her life back the way she wants it, then goes off the pills. I mean, I get it. I know they can have unpleasant side effects, but it seems like those are the lesser of the two evils." She paused. "Then again, I'm not the one dealing with it, so I can't say. I pray for her every day, but . . ."

"But?"

"Some days it just feels hopeless."

"It's not hopeless. At least, I have to believe it's not. I pray for my dad and our relationship too. Seems like maybe I should just give up and let him wallow in his misery, but I don't want that. With your mom, I don't know. Maybe it's a mental illness. In the beginning, I believe my dad was just acting from a place of hurt, but now, I think it's pride, and I have to believe God is still working even if I can't see it."

She reached out and gripped his fingers. "I'm going to choose to believe that too."

"And keep praying."

"Absolutely." She twisted the key between her fingers and stared out the window. "I need to call my brother. He's a contractor and can take care of the repairs on my house."

"That's convenient."

"Very. If he'll agree to do them."

"Why would he not?"

She shrugged. "If he thinks I'll try to talk to him about our parents, he'll avoid me."

A sorrowful sigh slipped from her and he wanted to call the guy himself. Or shake him until some sense rattled into his head. "I'm sorry, Lainie."

"Me too."

They fell silent for a moment before he checked the mirrors and glanced at her. "Tell me about that key. Why do you wear it on a chain when it's got to be a reminder of a really bad time in your life?"

She pulled her hand from his, but it was an emotional withdrawal too. She fell silent, fingers fisting on her thighs, and he wanted to take the words back, but then she gave a tiny shrug. "It *is* a reminder. A reminder that I have lousy judgment and that mistakes can be fatal. It's a reminder not to be too proud to listen to people who may know more than I do."

"You're the bravest person I know."

She huffed a short laugh. "Adam wasn't the only one who knew how to wear a mask." She pressed against the key again.

"Lainie—"

"And it's a reminder that getting involved with a man is something to think real hard about, because if I ever fall for someone again, he's going to have a lot of baggage to deal with. I have to decide if I can trust him. And if it's even worth it." She cut him a sideways glance. "We're just friends and I can't help but wonder when you'll get tired of my 'issues' and decide . . ."

"Decide what?" James kept his roiling emotions in check. He wasn't sure whether to be mad or insulted. Maybe both.

"Decide that I'm not worth it. Adam . . ." She bit her lip. "Never mind. It's hard to put what's in my head into words."

"Thanks a lot, Lainie." The words came out sharper than he'd intended. Okay, mad it was.

She whipped her head to face him. "What? Why are you mad?"

He barked a short laugh. "Because you're using *Adam* as the measuring tool for other men and that's not fair. *Adam* is the exception, not the rule. So, excuse me if being compared to him is insulting. I'm made of better stuff than that." Her eyes widened and tears formed. *Way to go, jerk.* He meant what he said, but he could have said it better. And in a different tone. "I'm sorry, Lainie, I—"

"No, don't apologize." She blinked the tears back. "You're right. I didn't really see it that way. That I was comparing you to him." She gave a tiny shrug and looked out the window. "You're *nothing* like him." After several seconds of silence, she turned back to him and caught his gaze. "Nothing."

"Thank you for that, but I shouldn't have jumped down your throat. As you can see, I'm not like him, but I'm not perfect either."

She laughed. A low, throaty chuckle that twisted his gut into a knot. "Well, rest assured, I was under no illusions that you were perfect. I did grow up with you, remember?"

"Cute."

But her shoulders relaxed a fraction, and he breathed a little easier, even while he berated himself for letting his anger get the best of him. Before he could stick his foot in his mouth again, they arrived at the storage facility.

FIFTEEN

Cole was already there, sitting in his 4Runner. James cut the engine and Lainie sat still, her gaze on the unit, dreading what was to come. But first things first. She threw James a sideways look. "I'm going to try calling Grant. He's the contractor brother."

"Gotcha. Go ahead."

Did she want to do this in front of him? Why not? She hit speed dial and was totally not surprised that it went to voice mail on the fourth ring. "Hi, Grant, it's Lainie. Can you please call me? Someone blew up part of my house and I need a contractor. Thanks." She hung up, caught the look on James' face, and shrugged. "I'm at the point I'm not above using the circumstances to pique his curiosity to the point that he has to call me back. Otherwise, he'll just ignore me."

"Well, that's just . . ."

"Rude? Yes, yes it is." She rubbed her temple. "But I understand too. Which means I feel guilty when I call."

"That's terrible, Lainie. I'm sorry."

"Yeah. Told you I had baggage," she muttered.

"Trust me. We all have baggage."

His low voice soothed her frazzled nerves, and she closed her eyes, trying to focus on something else. Anything else. For a moment, she just wanted to run away from it all. *God, give me strength.* She hesitated. *No, be my strength. Please.*

She stepped out of the vehicle and unhooked the necklace—the first time she'd taken it off since she'd had the stuff stored. She inserted the key in the lock and twisted.

Only it didn't turn. She frowned. "What?"

"What is it?" James asked from over her right shoulder.

She tried again and got the same result. She pulled the key out and looked closer. "Wait a minute. That's not my lock. It's similar, but it's not the one I put on there." Her hands shook and she took a step back. "Someone changed the lock."

"All right," Cole said from behind her, "I can take care of that. Be right back." He jogged toward his car and popped the hatch. In seconds he was back with a bolt cutter and snapped the lock off.

He raised the door, and Lainie stepped inside and gaped. "Um . . . this isn't what it looked like when the movers left it here." Boxes had been opened and their contents scattered, furniture overturned and shoved to the side, the two filing cabinets empty of drawers that had been dumped and tossed aside. "It looks like someone beat us here," she whispered.

"And put a lock back on so no one would notice from the outside," James said. He ran a hand over his head. "No telling when this happened."

Lainie knelt and picked up a piece of paper. She blew on the top of it and dust billowed in the air. "I'd say it's been a while."

"Not sure a crime scene unit would help at this point, but I can call one."

She shook her head. "That'll take time, won't it?"

"Yeah, but if he didn't wear gloves, there could be some prints here."

Lainie bit her lip and nodded. "If there's a chance he left a print, I think we should try, but can we look through the stuff first? Maybe wear gloves and be careful not to compromise anything?"

James and Cole exchanged a glance. "I've got gloves in the car," Cole said.

James nodded and Cole pulled his keys from his pocket once more.

When they were all gloved, James pointed to the floor. "Don't step on the paper, just push it aside. If there are prints, they'll be on the boxes or the furniture most likely." He met her gaze. "Got it?"

"Got it."

Memories swept over her. Good ones from the beginning of her relationship with Adam, then the bad ones. So many bad ones. So much anxiety. So many tears. So much . . . everything.

A hand on her back spun her to find James looking at her with such compassion she wanted to hurl herself into his arms and weep on his chest, trusting he'd make all the bad stuff go away. How could she want that so much and be so terrified at the thought of opening herself up to pain once more?

She straightened her shoulders and motioned to the mess. "Well, where do we start?"

"We'll figure it out," Cole said, moving to the far wall. "You might want to designate a couple of boxes as 'trash' and 'keep,' though."

"Right." She couldn't imagine what she'd put in the "keep" box.

For the next hour, Lainie held it together while she sorted through papers, files, and pictures. The pictures were the worst part. Seeing Adam's face next to hers made her want to vomit. She'd been so blind. She ripped the one she held right down the middle of Adam's face and tossed it into the box she'd labeled "trash." So far, the "keep" box was still empty.

"How you doing?" James' quiet voice broke into her forced focus. He handed her a water bottle he'd snitched from the side pocket of her purse.

She twisted the cap, took a swig, then shot him a tight smile. "Thanks, I needed that. And I'll be all right. You find anything?"

He shook his head. "Nothing that—"

"Got something," Cole said.

"What?" James headed toward his partner, when something rolled into the storage area and hit her foot.

Lainie looked down and gasped. "James!"

The door began to close and James rushed toward it as smoke billowed from the device. Then flames. "Get out!"

But the door slammed shut.

Flames continued to spurt, grabbing papers and anything else they could reach, spreading too fast to even think about stomping them out. But it was the smoke that terrified her.

"Whatever that thing is," James said, "it's burning hot! See if you can find something to smother it with while we try to get the door open."

Lainie ran back to the area where she'd seen a stack of blankets, grabbed one, and threw it over the flames. Her nose burned and the smoke choked her.

Cole shook his head. "The door won't move!"

Lainie shot to James' side as the smoke continued to thicken. "Guys, we have to get out of here!" She ran to the door and pounded on it. "Hey! Anyone out there! We need help!" She glanced back. The flames were already burning through the blanket. "Tools," she muttered, abandoning her useless screaming. "There's a tool kit around here somewhere," she said louder. "Did either of you see it?"

"In the far-right corner," Cole said. Then coughed. "Under some papers!"

Lainie raced to the corner and shoved aside a stack of files, no longer worried about fingerprints—she just wanted to get out alive. She grabbed the heavy box with a grunt and lugged it to the front, gasping, craving a breath of fresh air. "What are we going to do? The fire's growing!" Sweat rolled down her temple and she swiped it away while a ragged cough ripped at her lungs.

James looked up. "Find something to cover your nose and mouth, then call 911. I'm going to try and bend the rails or pull them down, knock the door off, and bend the panels. Then we can kick them out."

Lainie dialed 911, then looked down at the silent phone. No cell signal inside this metal box. Stuffing the phone into her pocket, she grabbed the razor blade from the toolbox and cut the bottom of her T-shirt into one long strip. She doused it with water, then passed the bottle to James, who did the same, and then to Cole, who beat at the flames. James had dragged one of the chairs over, and he stood to reach the rails. He grabbed them and pulled. Then stepped off the chair to put his full weight on them. Still nothing.

Fear pounded through Lainie as she pressed the rag tighter over her face. It didn't help when James dropped beside her, hand pressed to his wound and a tinge of panic in his eyes. It wasn't hard to read his thoughts. The fire wasn't going to kill them, the smoke was.

Cole backed toward them, coughing, eyes squinted through the thick, swirling haze. "Anyone got another idea?" His muffled words reached her.

James grabbed her hand. "On the floor! Get low, get a breath, and *think*."

They dropped and the smoke was lighter there, but still made her throat burn. James spun, belly on the concrete floor, and pounded on the door with his feet. Prayers slipped from Lainie's lips while her eyes teared and fear swelled.

Then the door rolled up.

JAMES DIDN'T QUESTION the divine intervention. Instead, he grabbed Lainie's hand and pulled her to her feet. He saw Cole rise, and they darted out into the fresh air while the smoke chased after them.

Lainie gagged and coughed while he did the same. Cole leaned on the unit opposite them, bending over with his hands on his knees, dragging in deep breaths.

Then James looked up to see the stunned face of a young man who couldn't be more than eighteen years old. "Thank you," James rasped.

"I . . . I saw the smoke and called 911, then came out here to see where the smoke was coming from and heard you guys yelling in the unit. Then the pounding on the door."

"You saved our lives, kid."

"Someone locked you in there on purpose." He held up a metal rod. "This was wedged in where the lock goes."

"We can't thank you enough," Lainie said, her voice low and rough.

Sirens reached them and James nodded. "We're going to have to file a police report, I guess."

Lainie shot a look at the unit. "Well, I guess that takes care of having to figure out what to do with the stuff, but unfortunately, it means we won't ever know if anything was in there that would help us discover what's going on."

"Maybe not," Cole said. He still leaned against the unit, but swiped a hand across his face and pulled a folded stack of papers from his waistband.

Lainie walked over and James followed. "What is that?" she asked.

"About four months' worth of bank statements. In Adam Williams's name."

Lainie nodded. "I'm sure there were a lot of old records and statements, bills, that kind of thing, in those boxes."

"But this is interesting—"

The fire trucks and police arrived, cutting him off, and he indicated he'd continue after they finished what they needed to do at the scene.

James knew the officers, explained the situation, and while the firemen and women got to work putting the blaze out, they gave their statements, refused medical care, and were finally free to go.

Lainie looked at the storage unit one last time. "I guess we won't be finding any fingerprints in there."

James slid an arm around her shoulders, wishing he could take the burden from them. "No, probably not, but they're pulling security footage, so maybe we'll get something from that."

"I'm not holding my breath." She coughed. "Literally couldn't if I wanted to anyway."

"Yeah."

Cole rubbed a hand over his head. "Wanna find someplace to grab some food and look at this stuff? I want to show you what I found, but I'm also hungry."

Lainie shuddered. "We smell like smokestacks."

"Eh, I don't care if you don't," Cole said.

"I care, but I can ignore it for a while." She shook her head. "I can't believe it was only five minutes from when the fire started to our rescuer opening the door. It seemed like a lifetime."

"Or two," James muttered.

Finally, they were on the way to a local diner where the server wrinkled her nose before leading them to a booth. She set the menus in front of them. "This place is no smoking. If you need to light one up, feel free to step outside and around the corner. That's the employees' area, but you can use it."

James noticed Lainie barely covered a snort, but Cole just smiled. "Thanks, but I think we've had enough of smoke for today. I'll take the Cobb salad, a double cheeseburger, and a large, sweet tea."

James and Lainie put their orders in and soon had their drinks. Cole shifted and pulled the papers out to spread them on the table. "Okay, these were mixed in with a pile of other papers shoved up under the desk in the back. Like they'd been dropped, then just pushed aside. But anyway, look at this." He pointed to a deposit made three years ago. "That's two thousand dollars there. Then down here"—he ran his finger down a few lines—"it's withdrawn."

He flipped the page. "This is the next month. Same thing. Same deposit date and same withdrawal date give or take a day or two, depending on how the weekend or holidays fall." He went to the next month. "Again, the same." He stacked the papers. "There are five months here. I'm guessing the other statements would have the same thing, but we could check with the bank to make sure."

"Can we get a warrant for the bank records?" Lainie asked. "To see when the payments started and ended?"

"Well, they probably ended with Adam's death," James said, "but it would be helpful to know when they started. So, while we wait to get a decision on the exhumation—I'm assuming the family would say no if we asked—we can ask for the bank records, see if we can figure out where the money came from and where it went, and—"

"Hold up," Cole said. "I just realized this one was a check written off the account. They usually attach a picture of the check, right?" He flipped to the last page of the statement and sighed. "Well, that would have been too easy, but if we can find out who the check was made out to, that might help answer quite a few questions." He ran a finger down the list of transactions. "There are a couple of drafts on here I'd like to know what they're for. I can't tell what a couple of the abbreviations stand for."

"Google it," Lainie said.

Cole shot her a quick nod, then pulled out his phone. After a few seconds, he raised a brow. "Looks like it's a company that sells insurance."

"Does it say what kind?"

"All kinds. Car, home, life, accident, et cetera."

"Any more monthly drafts?"

"Um . . . just one to some charity." He clicked his tongue. "My biggest interest are these two-thousand-dollar deposits and withdrawals. I really want to know about those."

"So, our next step is to visit the bank," Lainie said.

James nodded. "After we get a warrant, I think that's a reasonable next step."

"Actually," Cole said, "our next step is to clean up and make ourselves presentable so we don't get kicked out of where we wind up next."

James nodded. "Good point. Lainie's going to need a change of clothes too."

"I have some clothes in the bag I got from my house. I could always shower and change at the hospital, but I'd rather not have to explain this whole situation. If you can take me by Jesslyn's house, I can clean up there."

"Perfect."

After they finished eating, Lainie rubbed her forehead. "I need to make some phone calls. Most specifically to my insurance company. They can get in my house at this point. And I'm going to try Grant again."

"Just stay where we can see you, if you don't mind," James said.

"I don't mind at all."

With the phone pressed to her ear, she walked into the small alcove where the bathrooms were, and James looked at Cole. "How fast do you think we can get a warrant?"

"Well, after we draft it, considering all three of us could have died today, I'm thinking the boss might put a rush on it."

"You want to call him?"

"Sure." Cole hit the number they both had on speed dial for Commander Judson Hill, and James took another dose of ibuprofen. His back was not happy with the gymnastics he'd tried in the storage unit.

He closed his eyes and tilted his head back against the booth while he listened to Cole explain why they needed the warrant for the records. When he hung up, James opened his eyes, glanced at Lainie still on the phone, then at Cole's self-satisfied smile. "You got it."

"Well, he did. Said it would be on our phones within a couple of hours and we could head to the bank when we see it."

SIXTEEN

Two hours later, after stops at Cole's home, then Jesslyn's for a shower and change of clothes, Lainie was once again in the car with James and replaying the conversation with her insurance company. She frowned. While she appreciated the sympathetic agent and the promise to get someone out to her home for an assessment as soon as possible, she was annoyed she even had to deal with the whole thing.

And she was still getting Grant's voice mail.

She was so tired of it. All the ways her family expected her to keep the plates spinning, but didn't bother to show up for her when she needed them. And yet she kept trying, kept hoping, and kept praying. Why did caring for her parents feel like such a chore?

Serve them out of love. The thought speared her, and she froze for a brief second.

"Lainie?"

She blinked. The Jeep was parked in front of the bank, and James was standing next to her open door, waiting for her to get out. "Oh. Sorry."

"Deep thoughts?"

"Very." If he pushed, she'd tell him, but it was better to wait for a different time when they wouldn't be interrupted. He didn't push but eyed her with curiosity as she got out of the car. She'd probably be answering questions about those thoughts later.

Cole had driven separately and parked next to them. He climbed out and checked his phone. "You get it yet?"

James looked. "Yep. There it is."

"That didn't take as long as he—or I—thought it would."

"That's why he's the boss."

Cole chuckled. They made their way inside, Lainie lagging behind, and James turned back toward her. "Coming?"

Still battling her thoughts, Lainie let her gaze hold James'. He was looking at her with . . . something in his eyes. Not pity, exactly. But definitely some concern mixed in with . . . what? Curiosity? "Sorry. Let's go."

Once they were all seated with the bank manager, James presented the warrant and the bank statements. "We'd like all of the records related to this account. But can you tell us when these payments started and ended?"

"All right, let's see what we have here." He tapped a few keys and nodded. "Adam Williams. Here we are. And his father is on the account as well."

Cole raised a brow. "His name isn't on the statements."

"No, Adam is the primary account holder, so his name is on the statement, but his father, Myles, has full access to the account."

"You're talking in the present tense," Lainie said. "Wasn't the account closed when Adam died?"

He shook his head. "No, no one closed it. We don't have a record of his death." He leaned in, narrowing his eyes at the screen. "And it's still in use. A withdrawal was made just yesterday."

Lainie leaned forward. "Seriously?"

"Yes. A check was cashed."

"And it was made out to . . . ?"

"Victoria Irwin."

"Well, who's she?"

The man chuckled. "She's been coming in for quite a while. Lovely woman, if a bit reserved. But once a month, like clockwork, she cashes her check."

James rubbed his chin. "All right. So you know her fairly well?"

"Sure. I mean, we're not best friends or anything, but when I see her, we exchange pleasantries."

Cole blew out a low breath. "I'm so confused."

Lainie nodded. "So, let me get this straight. Adam Williams and Myles Williams are the joint owners of this account. Is anyone else on it?"

"No, just the two of them. Adam Williams and Myles."

"But Victoria Irwin cashes a check each month."

He nodded. "She used to just make cash withdrawals. Or rather Adam did. He'd take out the cash, then walk outside and give it to Ms. Irwin. But she cashes the checks now."

"Who's putting money in the account?"

"Myles Williams is still making the deposits as far as I know." He frowned at the computer screen. "Those are the only transactions for the month. And have been for . . ." His voice trailed off as he scrolled. ". . . for about eighteen months now. She started cashing checks instead of Adam coming in to get the cash."

Lainie clasped her hands between her knees. "Because he couldn't since he's dead."

"I'd heard rumors, but the last time I saw the senior Mr. Williams, he assured me Adam wasn't dead, he was in hiding from the person who tried to kill him."

Lainie sat back, staring. "If everyone is so worried about him being found by the person out to kill him, why is everyone telling everyone else that he's alive?"

The man flushed. "I suppose you're right, but in my defense, his father didn't seem too worried about it."

Because he knew Adam was already dead?

"Where is the money coming from that gets deposited into the account before the withdrawal?" Cole asked.

"It's always a cash deposit."

"That Mr. Williams, Adam's father, makes."

"Well, I assume it's him."

"Can you see if it's coming out of his account?" Lainie asked.

"Ah—" James shook his head, but the man was already typing, apparently wanting to get them what they wanted and out of his hair. "Sir, that's not part of the warra—"

"Well, I can tell you Mr. Williams cashes a check here every month," the man said. "And the same day a cash deposit goes into this account."

"Thank you," Lainie said with a shrug at James and Cole. She knew the warrant didn't extend to Myles Williams's account, but it didn't hurt to ask, did it? Since they got the information, she was going to answer that, no, this time it hadn't hurt to ask.

Once they had paper copies of everything the bank manager had shown them, Cole walked away to call in the request for additional records in Victoria Irwin's name. When he nodded, James and Lainie stood. "Thank you so much," James said. "We appreciate your help."

They left and climbed into James' vehicle. Lainie sat in the front passenger seat while Cole took the back for the few minutes he'd be there.

"So, now what?" she asked. "We go see Adam's father?" The thought made her shudder.

"*We* don't," James said, "Cole and I do." Then he shook his head. "No, I think we go see Victoria Irwin first. I want to ask her about the money and why Adam was paying her."

"And why his father felt the need to continue the payments," Lainie murmured.

"Hmm," Cole said, "you think Adam had a child with another woman and was paying child support? And that his father is keeping up the payments?"

"Maybe?"

"Honestly," James said, "it was the first thing that popped in my head. And I'd say he was doing it secretly. There was no mention of Myles's wife's name on any of the accounts, so she'd never know about the money. Cash deposits are a red flag too."

"It just gets better and better, doesn't it?" She frowned. "But why would his father be on the account?"

"Some people do that," Cole said. "Just in case something happens to them and the money isn't tied up forever waiting on the legal stuff."

"Right. Of course."

"In this case, it seems to have worked out for Adam's father to just continue the payments without upsetting anyone's apple cart. Convenient."

Cole opened the door. "All right, I've got the address. It's about twenty minutes away. I'll follow you, keeping an eye on your rear, and meet you there."

James pressed a hand to his back, and Lainie touched his forearm. "Do you want me to drive?"

"You have defensive driving training?"

"Um . . . no."

"Then I think I'd better stay behind the wheel, but thanks for the offer."

"Sure."

James gave her a steady look. "You ready for this?"

"Absolutely not."

SHE WASN'T READY, but she'd endure and see it through to the end with a strength and dignity James couldn't help but admire. The more time he spent with her, the more time he *wanted* to spend with her. But with a potential killer after her, it probably wasn't the best time to express his interest in starting a romance. Assuming *she* was interested.

He glanced in the rearview mirror and spotted his partner about a car length back.

Lainie's phone buzzed, and she slid it out of her pocket, glanced at the screen, and groaned.

"What is it?"

"It's my brother Brent."

"You don't want to talk to him?"

"It's not that I don't want—" She broke off. "Okay, I don't want to."

"Why not?"

"Because he wants to tell me how to deal with my parents from three hundred miles away."

"Ah."

The phone buzzed until it went to voice mail. "The last time he saw them was two Christmases ago, but because he calls like clockwork once or twice a month, he thinks he has a good idea of what I need to do for Mom and Dad. And honestly, I'm getting pretty sick of it."

The rush of anger at her family caught him off guard, and he cleared his throat. "What about Grant and your sister, Ellen? I know you called him about the contracting stuff. I'm assuming he hasn't called you back?"

"No, not yet. If he's on a job, he might not check his messages until he gets home. I'll be patient. With that. And, Ellen's okay. We chat, but she flat-out tells me she's not helping, that our parents made their bed and can sleep in it. She has real anger issues toward our mother—which is understandable because Mom has always been pretty nasty to her. Honestly, if she treated me the way she treats Ellen, I'd probably keep my distance too."

He winced. "Ouch."

"Exactly. Ellen talks to Dad, though. I think she feels sorry for him. She's just mad at Mom."

"That's hard. I'm so sorry."

"I keep praying she'll see Mom's issues for what they are, but right now, she's not budging." She shrugged. "I get it. I think all three of them have some anger toward me because I want to help Mom and Dad."

"Anger because you want to help? How does that work?"

She hesitated, bit her lip, and looked down at her hands.

"Lainie?"

"They call me 'The Enabler.'" He shot her a look just as she glanced up and caught the sheen of tears in her eyes. "And I suppose I am, but I'm their daughter. It's my duty to do whatever I can to help them, isn't it? I struggle with that, though. Am I an enabler? Or do I keep trying and praying with the belief—and hope—that by doing so, one day I'll see change. That because I didn't quit, I'll make a difference in their lives. Because that's all I really want. I want to love them enough to influence change in them." She flushed and swiped a tear from her cheek. "I guess that sounds stupid, huh?"

"Never, Lainie." Never. "I'm in awe of you."

"Awe?" She sniffled and gave a watery laugh. "I hope that's a good thing."

"It's a great thing. But while I understand the wanting to love them to influence change—I'm in the same situation myself even though it's a different scenario—we also have to have boundaries."

"Boundaries. Right."

"Boundaries are a good thing, Lainie. They protect us. If we don't have boundaries, then yeah, some people will take advantage of that and use us." He shot her a side glance. "Boundaries can be very helpful."

"I know you're right. I'm just not very good at them when it comes to my family."

He smiled. "Well, now that you've acknowledged that, think about what that would look like."

She went still and he wondered if he'd offended her. Then she let out a low sigh. "I'll do that. Thanks, James."

He spun the wheel and they pulled to the curb of the address on the GPS. Cole stopped behind them.

Lainie climbed out and shot him a pleading look. "Don't make me stay in the car."

"What if she recognizes you?"

She frowned at him. "Why would she?"

"What if Adam or someone showed her a picture?"

Lainie sighed. "Can we just see?" She crossed her arms. "I don't want to stay out here by myself."

James suppressed a groan. "Fine. But no talking."

"Not a word." She glanced at the empty drive. "Is anyone even here?"

"Guess we'll find out."

James knocked on the door and shortly, footfalls on the foyer hardwoods sounded.

A woman in her midsixties opened it with a raised brow. "Yes?"

James held up his badge and introduced himself and Cole. When he turned to Lainie, she smiled. "I'm Elaine Jackson," she said before he could speak, then snapped her lips shut. She didn't want him to call her by her nickname. He gave a faint nod of approval.

"I see," the woman said. "What can I help you with?"

"Are you Victoria Irwin?" Cole asked.

"I am."

A small gasp escaped Lainie, but James didn't think anyone else heard it. He glanced at her and she swallowed hard. He had a feeling she'd been expecting someone a lot younger. Frankly, he had too. So much for the idea that she had a child with Adam. She was more the age of Adam's mother. "Do you mind if we come in? We'd like to ask you a few questions about some banking transactions."

Confusion flickered in her eyes, but she stepped back. "All right. Let's go into the sunroom."

They followed her through the foyer, past the den, and into a bright room filled with greenery and comfortable furniture. "Nice," Cole said.

She smiled. "It's my favorite room."

Once they were all settled, she clasped her hands in her lap. "Now, what can I do for you?"

"We'd like to know your relationship to Myles and Adam Williams?"

She stilled for a fraction of a second, and James thought she lost a shade of color in her face. "May I ask why you need to know that?"

"According to a reliable source, Adam died about eighteen months ago. Recently, some questions about his death have come up and we're looking into it. During the course of our investigation, we came across some bank statements. They show a number of deposits and withdrawals in the same amounts. And those withdrawals—and checks—were made out to you."

"From Adam's account?"

"Yes."

"Well, I can't explain that, but I do get monthly support from . . . a friend."

"Myles Williams," James said.

She laughed. "Now, darling, I can't say. He's a married man and I won't go spreading tales."

Or risk jeopardizing her golden goose? "That's fine. He's left a paper trail. Not much of one, I'll grant you, but it's there. So, we know Myles is paying you on a monthly basis, which means, to us, that you're still involved with him in some way. I don't need the details, I just have a question. Do you have any reason to believe Adam is alive?"

Her nostrils flared. "I won't talk about Adam or Myles. So, if there's nothing else . . ." She rose. "I think I've used up just about all of my hospitality. Y'all can leave now."

James and the others stood as well. Obviously, they'd hit a sore spot, but they weren't going to get anything else out of the woman. "Well, thank you for your time."

She swept out of the sunroom and made a beeline to her front door. Only when they got there, Lainie was missing. He frowned. "Lain—er—Elaine?"

She was trailing behind. Far behind. Victoria stomped to the den. "I asked you to leave."

"Of course. So sorry. I was just admiring your beautiful painting over the mantel."

The woman's expression softened. "Thank you. Now, please. Go."

Once they were out on the porch, Victoria Irwin didn't waste any time shutting the door behind them.

Lainie looked at James and Cole. "You need to go see Adam's father and ask him why Victoria Irwin has a picture of her, Adam's father, and Adam on the end table in her den."

SEVENTEEN

"What? Let's talk about this in the car. I don't want you out in the open." James ushered her to the vehicle, and just like before, Cole climbed in the back to hear. "Now," James said, "what are you talking about?"

"I wasn't sure whether to confront her or not, but I noticed a picture on her end table. It was of her and Adam and Adam's father. I was trying to get a better look when she came back."

"Well, that kind of confirms our theory that she's involved, but she's not the mother of Adam's child. She's Mr. Williams senior's lover."

"And he's paying her to keep her quiet?" Cole asked. "Or just paying to keep her?"

"Why don't we ask Myles Williams?" James glanced at Lainie. "But you can't go."

She sighed. "I know. Drop me at the hospital. I should be safe enough there." She paused. "As long as I don't fall asleep in the on-call room. I can look into some old cases. Maybe I'll find a clue in there." She'd start with the M&M committee. Morbidity and Mortality. If the person after her was someone with a grudge, a family member of a patient who'd died was a good place to start. Otherwise, she'd have to ask James to get a court order. Every keystroke was monitored, and if she went looking through old cases, someone would notice and ask why. So unless she went through proper channels . . . that would definitely not be a good career move. She paused. Which meant there should be a record of anyone who erased any information about Adam. In order to find that, though, she had to know who would have done such a thing. Who had Adam been close to at the hospital?

"Lainie?"

"Sorry. Just thinking."

"I was saying, I'm okay with that as long as you let security know you're there and that this guy might show up in the hospital."

"I'll tell them. And James? I had a thought." She explained about the keystroke monitoring. "Adam was friendly to a lot of people at the hospital. He was a regular. He was charming and thoughtful and . . ." She waved a hand. "You get the idea. If someone thought they were helping him in some way, they'd probably do it."

"So, if he were to ask a friend to wipe all evidence of his death . . ."

"Yes. But that doesn't explain the lack of a death certificate. That's a whole different database."

James sighed. "Lainie, I know you don't want to hear this, but I think we need to consider that, against all odds, he's still alive."

She shook her head and was still shaking it when James pulled up to the entrance of the hospital. "I'm not going to argue with you. Any sane person would have to consider it after everything that's come up, but I promise there's something else going on here. As soon as we figure out who's after me, everything will fall into place. So, that's the goal, right? Not just prove Adam is dead, but to find the person targeting me."

"That's the goal." He gripped her hand. "We'll get him, Lainie. We will."

"I know." She climbed out, put on her best pleading expression, and met his gaze. "Please let me know what happens as soon as you know?"

He rubbed his chin. "I've been thinking about something. I'd like you to hear the conversation."

Her ears perked up. "Okay."

"I'm going to call you and let you listen in while we talk to the man. You take note of everything he says. I want your thoughts on the conversation."

"Of course."

Lainie made sure she had her phone ringer on, then walked into the hospital, her home away from home. She made her way to security and found Jared in the office.

"Hey," he said, looking up at her entrance. "What's up?"

"You got a minute?"

"Sure." He pulled a chair over for her and she sank into it. "You ever figure out who left you that note in the on-call room?"

"No, not yet, but the person has escalated. He likes to play with fire." She told him about the bomb at her house and the incident at the storage unit. "I'm hanging out here until James, one of the detectives you met, can come back and get me."

"Holy cow, Lainie, that's crazy."

"Tell me about it. So, anyway, you mind if I stay close to this area?"

"Not at all. In fact, put my personal phone on speed dial. I'll come running if you need something."

"Well, hopefully, I won't, but thanks." She got his number programmed and hesitated. Then stood. "On second thought, since this office is so close to my workstation, I'm going to see if there's anything I can do while I'm here, but would you pay attention to the cameras in my area and give me a heads-up if you see the guy anywhere?"

"Absolutely. I'll take another look at his picture to get his face fresh in my head."

"Thanks."

She left the office and walked to her station, where she found Allison going over a chart. The doctor looked up at her entrance and frowned. "Hey, what's up with you coming in on your days off?"

"I just can't stay away, I guess."

Allison narrowed her eyes. "What's going on, Lainie?"

"Adam."

"Adam again?"

"Well, not Adam, but . . . someone who looks like him is still try-ing to . . ." She shrugged. "He's terrorizing me . . . and occasionally anyone who happens to be around me." She explained once more, and Allison's brows rose higher and higher.

"Lainie, my friend, you need a bodyguard."

"I've got one, in a sense. He's just a little busy right now, so that's why I'm hanging around here with people I know. I'm going to check my M&M cases and see if any of them set off alarms for me."

"I recommend taking the laptop into the security office."

"Think I'll do that. Thanks."

"Our glamping trip still on?"

"Of course. Stay tuned for details." By then she had a feeling she'd either be dead or whoever was after her would be behind bars. "See you later."

With the laptop tucked up under her arm and her eye on the people she passed in the hall, she was almost back to the security office when someone called her name. She turned to see Bridgette walking toward her. "Do you have a moment?"

The ice in the doctor's eyes sent a shaft of wariness darting through her. "Okay."

"I hear you like to warn men away from me."

Lainie stilled. "What?" She hugged the laptop to her chest like a shield.

"Helen overheard a conversation you had in the ER with a pa-tient." Bridgette's nostrils flared. "Very unprofessional."

Lainie sighed even as heat crept up from her neck and her stom-ach churned with shame, but she'd own it. "You're right. I shouldn't have said what I did, and I owe you an apology. I'm truly sorry and it won't happen again."

For a moment, the doctor simply stared at her like she wasn't sure what to say. "My personal life is none of your business. It better *not* happen again, or you won't like the consequences." With that parting shot, she was gone, striding down the hallway, heels clicking, shoulder-length hair swaying with each step.

Lainie let out a low breath and shook her head. She was racking up so many enemies lately, she'd have a hard time picking out the one most likely to want her dead. She stopped in front of the security office. James should be calling soon, and she'd need a private place to listen in to the conversation.

She pulled her headphones from her pocket and plugged them into the phone. Well, she'd be ready. She knocked and Jared opened the door for her, pointed to the empty workstation beside him, and turned back to the screens on the wall. "I followed you on the monitor to where you spoke to Dr. Lambe, then Dr. McPherson, and then you came back here. As far as I can tell, no one else followed you."

"Thanks." That was good to know, but she was under no illusions that "Adam" had given up. He was just lying low, waiting for the "right" moment to strike.

For the next fifteen minutes, she worked, scanning the notes from the M&M committee files, but had trouble focusing as she expected the phone to ring at any minute. She tapped a text to James.

Did I miss your call?

No, discussing strategy. Stay tuned.

That helped, but she still wasn't in the mood to read clinical notes. When Steph's text came through, she didn't hesitate to set aside her current material.

What's going on with you and James?

Nothing. I told you that.

I know what you told me, so what's the truth?

Unfortunately, that IS the truth.

Unfortunately??

Of course, Steph would latch on to that little slip.

> Steph, you know I've had a crush on James since the time I came home with you from school and he made us cups of hot chocolate, but—

BUT?? Don't leave me hanging. That's mean.

> BUT, we're adults now. We're different people who've lived through some tough stuff.

CONSENTING adults.

> That's all you got from that?

Look, James likes you. He always said you were his favorite out of all of my friends.

> Wait, what? He did?

NOW I have your attention?

Lainie rolled her eyes, tempted to not answer.

> As much as I love this conversation, I'm working. I've got to go.

Xoxoxo.

Just as Lainie returned to her tedious search for someone who either wanted her dead or to think she was losing her mind, her phone rang.

JAMES WAITED IN THE CAR until he heard Lainie pick up. "You there?"

"I'm here."

"Sorry it took so long. We did a little background checking on him"—which had been interesting—"and then had to chase him down at work. I'm going to drop my phone in my pocket. Text Cole if you have any trouble hearing."

"Okay." James dropped the phone into his pocket and nodded toward the BMW sedan turning in to the parking lot of the real estate office. Myles Williams parked. "There he is. Ready?"

"Yep."

They climbed out of the Jeep just as Myles stepped out of his vehicle. "Hey, Myles? Myles Williams?"

The man slammed the car door and turned. "Yes. Who wants to know?"

James and Cole flashed their badges and introduced themselves.

"You the two who showed up at my house and talked to my wife and son?"

"We are."

"Then why are you harassing me here?"

"I don't believe we can call this harassing, sir," James said, keeping a smile on his face, even while Lainie's words about the guy ran through his mind. "But we would like to ask you a few questions if that's all right."

The man sighed. "Sure, come on inside." He led them to a corner office at the back of the building and motioned for them to have seats in the two maroon wingback chairs facing his desk. He leaned against the desk and crossed his arms. "What is it you need to ask me?"

"Do you believe Adam is still alive?" Cole asked.

Mr. Williams hesitated. "Why are you asking me that?"

"Because that seems to be the consensus of your wife and son."

He sighed. "Yes. I believe Adam is alive."

"You've talked to him?" Cole pressed.

"I have."

James leaned forward. "What was your impression of Lainie Jackson?"

A snort escaped him. "I liked Lainie in the beginning. She seemed a little quiet, but was nice enough and treated Adam well. I don't know when things changed, but in the end . . . well, you know what happened in the end. She tried to kill him and, thankfully, failed."

James made a mental note to check on the warrant to exhume the body. Those things took time—mostly when there was no time to waste—but they had no choice but to go through the proper channels. Digging up the body would give them an answer once and for all.

"We went to see a woman by the name of Victoria Irwin. Could you tell us the nature of your relationship?"

The man paled, then shoved out a laugh. "I really don't see how that's your business."

"Look, there have been reports that Adam is still alive. Your wife and son, Nick, told us the marshals were involved in hiding him. I checked. They're not."

He leaned forward, a frown on his face. "Wait, what? Of course they were involved."

"No. They weren't."

"Well, if they weren't involved, where is he?"

True concern reflected in the man's eyes and James frowned. "That's what we're trying to figure out. We were at the bank today, and the manager there said you told him Adam was alive. If Adam faked his death, then that's a crime. We're just trying to put it all together."

"So what does Victoria have to do with this?"

"That's what we'd like to know. We found bank statements with Adam's name on them and the money from his account is going to her. She admitted it."

The man huffed a hard sigh. "She's a mistress, okay? Yes, I'm a terrible husband, but I love her."

Cole frowned. "But you won't divorce your wife?"

His face reddened. "Of course I *want* to!" He slammed a fist on the table, then gulped a breath, taking a moment to pull himself together. "I can't stand being at home. Why do you think I work all the time? But if I left her, I'd lose everything," he finally said in a lowered voice. He lifted a hand, then dropped it. "The money is all hers. Except for the little bit I manage to bring home after I pay

Victoria. If I divorce, everything is gone, and the truth is, I've gotten used to the good life. I can't afford to divorce her."

James suppressed a sigh. He had no problem with wealth—or with people who had it. But the verse about the love of money being the root of all evil resonated. Only, his interpretation was that money wasn't evil, it was those who had it and chose to do wrong with it— or chased it to the exclusion of all else. In other words, those who worshiped money instead of their Creator. "But you still use Adam's account," James said.

"Well, my name is on it, so technically it's mine too."

True. "And it's one that your wife doesn't know about."

"Yep, and I'd like to keep it that way."

"There's a draft on the account for an insurance policy. I just want to verify that?" He gave him the amount.

"It's a life insurance policy for Victoria. Adam convinced me that I owed that to her at the very least. He didn't approve of my having a mistress, but mostly because of the lack of security for her. He really liked her a lot."

Adam concerned about someone other than himself? That sounded out of character. "So, Adam knew about her and he kept your secret from his mother?"

"He did."

"What about Nick? Does he know too?"

The man made a pained face. "No. And I'd appreciate it if he didn't find out. He's close to his mother and this would just turn him against me. I've already lost one son—in a sense. I'd really rather not lose my remaining one."

James had a few things he could suggest the man do to that end, but kept his mouth shut about that. "Mr. Williams, we have a court order in the works that's going to allow us to exhume Adam's body. Do you have any objections to that?"

Mr. Williams raised a brow. "Wow, that's kind of taking things to the extreme, isn't it?"

"Maybe, but we're still doing it. For whatever reason, there's someone who wants the world to believe he's your son. We need to prove your son is the one in that coffin."

"Help yourself. It's not him."

James had to admit the certainty in the man's tone and words stopped him for a moment. "Then why isn't he contacting his own family? The family who believes he's alive."

Mr. Williams swallowed and shook his head. "I don't have an answer for that, but I'm sure he has a good reason."

And Mr. Williams had an answer for everything. "All right. Then you'll give us permission to exhume the body?"

He shrugged. "Sure."

They didn't need permission, but the fact that he gave it without hesitation made James pause. And once again, doubt crept in. Could Lainie be wrong after all? Could Adam Williams truly be alive?

EIGHTEEN

Lainie bit her lip and pressed her palms to her eyes while she listened. Myles Williams sounded exactly the same. Arrogant. Cocky. Completely convinced he could do exactly as he pleased without consequence. She should have told his wife when he'd assaulted her with his suggestive words.

Regrets swirled. She should have done a lot of things differently back then, but dwelling on her lousy choices wasn't going to do her—or anyone else—a bit of good.

"You okay, Lainie?" Jared asked.

The question almost made her smile. Everyone in her life, at some point over the past couple of days, had asked her that. At least they cared enough to ask. She looked up and nodded.

Jared shot her a doubtful look but returned to his monitors, then nudged her. "Hey, isn't that the guy?"

She whipped her head up and stared at the screen. "That's him." James' voice fell to the background, but she thought he was saying goodbye.

"He's hanging around your workstation." Jared stood. "Stay here."

"No way."

She stood too, but he scowled at her and slid a radio over to her. "I need you to watch the monitor and let me know which way he goes."

"I don't know how to work this!"

"Click on the arrows with the mouse to move to the next screen. It's not rocket science." And then he was out the door.

Lainie picked up the radio and listened while she watched the screens. Adam leaned against the wall near the nurses' station outside a patient room while he appeared to scroll his phone's screen. She picked up the radio. "He's just standing there." The words had no sooner left her lips than he looked up and started to move. "No, wait, Yasmine just stepped off the elevator and he spotted her. It spooked him and he's heading for the exit." Which was about ten steps from the room he was near. He'd chosen that spot very strategically. Near the exit, a view of the nurses' station, and in sight of the elevator.

"Got it."

Lainie clicked to the camera where she thought he might exit, but the door never opened. She started scanning the other floors, but it was like looking for a needle in a haystack. He knew the hospital and was dodging the cameras, but . . . she thumbed the button on the radio. "He may still be in the stairwell. I can't find him on the cameras."

For the next ten minutes, they went back and forth until Jared finally returned to the office with a disgusted curl to his lips. "Lost him."

She nodded. "I know."

Her phone rang and she glanced at the screen. *James!* "Hello?"

"What's going on there? All I could hear was your end of the conversation." She explained and he huffed a long sigh. "But you're all right?"

"I'm fine. I'm still in the security office."

"Stay there, will you?"

"Yes, but when you get back here, I want to get my bag out of my locker."

"I'll be there in about thirty minutes and we can take care of all of that."

"Fine. I'm still going through the M&M patients."

"Anything ring a bell?"

"Not really. I mean, I could probably come up with a few who weren't happy with some aspect of their loved ones' care, but for the most part, I don't see anything." Yet. She still had files to go through.

"Make note of them anyway," he said.

"I am."

"See you in a bit."

She hung up and went back to her cases, and lo and behold, she found one. Julie Darwin. She called James. "Hey, I found something."

"What?"

"A woman by the name of Julie Darwin." She read through the case even though she remembered it clearly. "Julie was twenty-seven years old and had an ectopic pregnancy. She'd waited too late to get help and her tube had ruptured. I diagnosed the issue and sent her to surgery where they removed it—and saved the woman's life. Unfortunately, the other tube had been completely damaged with scarring, and when Julie woke up from the surgery, she was faced with the knowledge that even with surgery on the remaining tube, she'd probably never be able to have children."

"Heartbreaking," he said, his voice soft.

"It shattered her and she blamed the entire surgical team, but focused most of her bitterness toward me. I guess because I'd reassured her that she'd still be able to have children with just one tube."

"You couldn't have known."

"I know, but she accused me of lying to her."

"She was hurting."

"And hurting people often hurt others," she murmured. "What if . . ."

"Yeah. How long ago was this?"

"About six months." She paused. "Why wait this long to do something? But get this. She worked at the hospital for a while. After her surgery, she never came back. Her reasoning was that it was too painful to be in the same building where she lost her child. I can't believe I didn't think of her until now, but her name never crossed my mind until I saw it."

"It's okay. It's not like you haven't been under some stress. But that's a good lead. We'll chase it down. I'm getting close to the hospital. Stay put and I'll come to you."

"All right." She hung up and went back to work, looking for anything else she could find. Time passed as she lost herself in the files.

"Lainie?"

She looked up to find James and Cole standing in the doorway. Her pulse did that funny little rhythm thing it had decided to do every time James showed up. James. Not Cole or any other man. Just James. *Stop it.* She cleared her throat. "Hey. Any luck with Mr. Williams?"

"Not really," he said. "He just managed to confuse us even more."

"And I didn't hear anything that I thought needed attention."

"Ready to head to your locker?"

"Ready."

She said goodbye to Jared and led the way to her locker. Cole and James stood guard at the door while she spun the combination lock, then lifted the little metal piece to pull open the door. She reached for her bag, then stumbled back, a small scream escaping.

James raced over. "What?"

She pointed and he sucked in a swift breath.

A small black coffin lay on top of her bag, and a dead mouse rested on the satin lining. A small black rose lay beside it and a note pinned to the raised coffin lid glared back at her. "You can't hide where I won't find you. I'm back. Like a cat with nine lives. I have eight left. How many do you have?"

JAMES PULLED HER AWAY from the locker, feeling the shudders rippling through her. Tears glittered in her eyes, but something else did too. A new look that said she was close to being done. At the end of her rope. And yet . . . determined too. He led her to a bench positioned between the two rows of lockers. It reminded him of his high school track days.

She sat on the bench, placed her elbows on her knees, and leaned forward, dropping her chin to her chest. "It's not him," she said, her voice low. "It's not."

"Lainie . . ." James didn't know what to say because he wasn't sure of anything at this point.

Footsteps sounded and a man in his midsixties rounded the end of the lockers. "Lainie?"

She sighed and closed her eyes for a brief second before she stood and turned. "Hi, Dr. Maloney."

"Are you all right?" Genuine concern glinted in his green eyes.

Lainie shrugged. "I'm okay. Dr. Maloney, this is Detective James Cross and Detective Cole Garrison. Guys, this is my supervisor, Dr. Maloney."

The men shook hands, then Maloney turned to Lainie. "I hear you've been having some trouble."

"Yes. And now it's followed me here in a very terrible way. I'm sorry."

"I'm sorry *for you*. I know this isn't your fault, but I'm going to recommend you take a few more days off and see if the police can catch this person. Don't worry, your job is safe. Now it's time to make sure *you're* safe."

She nodded, and James had a hard time controlling his urge to reach for her and wrap her in his arms.

The man patted her on the shoulder. "This too will pass, Lainie," he said.

"I know. Thank you."

James' phone buzzed and he read the text from Caitlyn Evans, the analyst.

Got that video footage you wanted of the tires
being switched in the hospital parking garage.
Looks like the guy is about six feet tall, slender

build. He's got on sunglasses and a baseball hat, black sweatpants, and solid colored T-shirt. Never got a good look at his face. I'm sure that was intentional. Don't know what you might find on it, but here you go if you want to try.

Seconds later, the video came through. He'd watch it with Lainie as soon as they had a spare minute. Leaving the locker with the CSU team, they made their way through the hospital, heading for the exit, when someone called Lainie's name. She turned and James recognized Kenzie King. The woman, dressed in her SWAT gear and carrying a backpack, approached. "Lainie? I thought that was you."

"Hey, Kenz, what's going on with you? Why are you here?"

"Had a call and one of the guys got grazed by a bullet. He's fine, though." Her eyes slid past them to Cole, who'd been standing there in silence. "Cole."

"Kenzie."

The coolness in his friend's tone surprised him.

Kenzie turned her attention to Lainie. "I wanted to ask about the glamping trip."

"The wha— Oh. That."

Kenzie's brow rose. "You okay?"

"Not really. Can we talk about this another time? I'm not even sure what to tell you about that right now."

Kenzie drew back, her frown deepening as her gaze went to Cole, then James. "What's going on? This have anything to do with what happened to your house?"

"Yes, it does. We haven't had a chance to talk, sorry. I guess Jesslyn told you about my house?"

"She mentioned it. I've been meaning to call you and ask you about that, but it's been one thing after another. Jess said you were fine, so I put that at the bottom of the list." She bit her lip. "I'm a bad friend, I'm sorry."

"You're not a bad friend. We've all got stuff going on right now."

"Lainie's having some trouble with a guy trying to make her think Adam's still alive," James said. "We're working on finding him."

Kenzie's eyes widened. "Adam? Still alive? Not a chance."

"That's what I keep telling everyone," Lainie said, the words spitting from her with force. She seemed to snap out of whatever daze had held her captive since she'd found the dead mouse, and she dragged in a ragged breath. "That's why we're going to dig him up. As soon as we get permission—which is taking forever, of course."

"I don't know what to say." Kenzie looked slightly shell-shocked at the influx of information. "Dang, that's a lot."

"You don't have to say—or do—anything. You have enough going on, and James and Cole are helping me." She hugged her friend. "I'll get back to you on the trip. Forget what I just said. We're still going. I'm not letting this guy do this to me. But for now, we need to go do something—we'll talk later, all right?"

Kenzie stepped back and nodded. "Keep me updated? Let me know you're okay?"

"Sure."

Kenzie's gaze slid to Cole. "See you tomorrow?"

"No, I traded with Joe. I'm doing my best to help Lainie and James, so I won't be there."

She nodded. "Let me know if I can do anything?"

"Will do."

Kenzie waved at Lainie and James, stepped past them, and headed down the hallway.

James made a mental note to ask Cole about the awkward situation. Weird. If he didn't know better, he'd think Cole was trying to hide feelings for Kenzie, but since Cole wasn't about to get serious with anyone, most especially not someone he worked with, James shrugged it off. "You and Kenzie are close," he said to Lainie. "Why haven't you told her everything?"

"Kenzie has enough on her plate trying to fit in with the SWAT team." She eyed Cole. "I find it interesting you haven't said anything about that in all the time we've been together."

Cole raised a brow. "Work is work. From what I can tell, Kenzie's doing a great job."

"Oh. Okay. Well, good. Regardless, I haven't wanted to bother her. Steph and Jesslyn know some, obviously. Allison knows a little bit. Kristine's been flying so much this past week that her texts are super sporadic, so I haven't bothered her with this mess and that's the way I want to keep it. Now what?" She rubbed her arms.

"I still want to take you to the lake house, but Cole and I want to pay Julie Darwin a little visit. So, let's get you to Jesslyn's, then he and I will do that. Think Cole's working on getting you bodyguard coverage."

"I'm not even going to ask to go to that one."

"Appreciate that."

Lainie stayed beside him on their way out of the hospital, and thankfully, they got in his Jeep without any trouble. He aimed the vehicle toward Jesslyn's, watching the mirrors. The only person he saw was Cole, right behind them. Watching out for them. He called his partner. "You find anyone?"

"Buzz Crenshaw's off today. He's going to play bodyguard for a while."

With thanks, he hung up.

After a moment of silence, Lainie said, "I don't want to be a victim anymore, James, I just don't know how to make that happen."

Her soft statement held more than just words and struck him right in the heart. He glanced at her. "You're not a victim. Bad stuff has happened to you, but I wouldn't call you a victim. At least not in the sense that I think you mean."

"I would. I've been a victim all my life." She paused. "Or door-mat might actually be a more accurate description." He laughed. He couldn't help it. She shot him a disgruntled look. "Well, thank you. I appreciate that you find this so funny."

"I'm not laughing at *you*, I'm laughing because I'm kind of shocked you could ever consider yourself a doormat. You've never had a vic-tim mentality, so I guess that's why I don't consider you a victim—or a doormat. Didn't we have this conversation already? You don't have quit or doormat in you."

"But I am."

He frowned, wondering if and how he could convince her. "Tell me why you see yourself that way, and I guarantee I can refute every single thing you come up with and convince you you're wrong about yourself."

"You really think you can convince me, huh?"

"I know I can."

"All right, then. Challenge accepted. I was born to dysfunctional parents who thought the end of the world was just around the corner. My dad finally wised up and quit that nonsense, but for a few years it was . . . rough. We were yanked out of our schools where we had friends and were involved in activities we loved. My lessons consisted of wilderness survival and being paranoid of any government entity or church. My dad was so skeptical of anything related to church or God, I only found Jesus because I went look-ing for him."

"How'd you find him?"

She smiled. "I had a sixth-grade teacher who was the kindest, most gentle man I ever met. One day, I walked out of the woods after a lesson on how to skin a deer—during which I puked, by the way—and hitchhiked into town. I knew the school schedule and waited until Mr. Flanders walked out to the parking lot. He was surprised and happy to see me, and I just flat-out asked him why he was the way he was. What made him care so much about his students."

"What'd he say?"

"He told me teaching was his calling. His ministry. He pulled an old, worn Bible out of his backpack and handed it to me. Told me to start with John. Then he gave me his phone number and said if I had any questions I could call him or his wife."

"Wow."

"I know. I still talk to them occasionally."

"And now your parents and sister are believers. Once your dad came to know the Lord, he stopped with all the end-of-the-world mentality, right?"

"He did. He still loves the outdoors, of course, but he's channeling it in a better way. My mother, however, still has a long way to go. As I mentioned before, Ellen is still dealing with her anger issues, and she, Brent, and Grant still dump on me because I let them. They're angry at our parents. So very angry. They expect me to be the one to take care of whatever our parents need and to leave them alone. As a result, I never ask them for anything."

"Never?"

"Well, after being told no over and over, I quit asking. Mostly. So, I guess I do have some quit in me despite what you think."

"Hmm. What about holidays? Don't you get together?"

"No, not usually. I mean, I go see Mom and Dad, and Ellen comes in. I'll give her props for trying, but it doesn't usually end well. She knows how much time I've spent working to clean a path from the foyer to the dining room to the kitchen, and she can't stand all the stuff she knows is behind the closed doors. My brothers are busy with their own families, and they've said they don't want their kids knowing how sick their grandparents are. So they stay away. Even Grant, who only lives about fifteen minutes from them."

Wow. He had no idea she was living—and dealing—with so much. "What if you didn't give them a choice?"

"I tried that. Not exactly on purpose, but . . . Dad was out of town on one of his outdoor leadership camping trips, I had two days of training I had to do, so I asked Grant to check on Mom. He said he would, then at the last minute said he couldn't. I told him he had to because I wasn't even in town. He refused to go by, and Mom wound up running her credit card up to the limit because she saw something—a lot of somethings—on the shopping channel that she had to have. All of the items reminded her of her father. When my dad saw the bill, he blew a fuse. I was there when he saw it. He checks the card every day because of her. I thought he was going to pack his bags and walk away right then and there."

He winced and tried to find the right words. "I'm very sorry. That's hard, on everyone. But how is that your responsibility?"

"I just feel like it is, I guess. Isn't that honoring my mother and father?"

"Honoring them?" He paused. "I'm honestly not sure of the answer to that. At what point is it not honoring but enabling?"

"But if I can stop her from doing that? Shouldn't I at least try?"

He didn't know. He'd always been a big proponent of "natural consequences," but where did that fall in the realm of mental illness? He was starting to see why she felt like she was such a doormat, though. "You love your family. It's only natural that you want to help." But again, where did she draw the line?

"Of course I do, but I convinced myself that I loved Adam too. And I let him walk all over me. So, is that it? If I love someone, I'm bound to become their doormat? I let myself just be . . . controlled? Sure seems that way."

"You really believe that?"

She hesitated. "I don't know. If I were listening to someone who was saying the things I am, I'd think they were blowing the situation out of proportion, but . . ." She shrugged and sighed, looking away. "Whatever the truth is, I won't be a victim anymore." She paused, then cut her eyes at him. "Nice effort, but you still haven't convinced me I'm not a doormat."

He grinned and gave her a wink. "Day's not over yet."

NINETEEN

On the way to Jesslyn's, James made a call to nail down the exhumation while Cole worked to contact Julie Darwin. Ten minutes later, he pulled into Jesslyn's drive and cut the engine, thankful the call to Commander Hill had been productive. The man was going to fight to get the exhumation scheduled ASAP. "I'm really curious about this myself," his supervisor said. "This case is about the wonkiest I've ever heard of and I've heard of wonky."

Wonky was one word for it. James shook his head, glanced back at Cole, who had to be getting tired of his bodyguard role, and waved.

Cole waved back, a signal that all was well and Lainie could exit the car.

He hurried her into the house and she stopped just inside the door, pulling her phone from her back pocket. "It's work. I need to take this."

"Go ahead. I'm just going to crash on the couch for a few minutes." He was loath to admit his back was hurting, but the knowing look she shot him said she was aware.

She tapped the screen and stepped into the kitchen while Cole shut the door behind them.

"Buzz will be here in a few minutes," Cole said. "I talked to Julie Darwin and she said to come by her office first thing tomorrow morning and she'll be happy to see us. Apparently, she's on a business trip and won't be home until late."

"First thing tomorrow? On a Sunday?"

"She's making a special trip to the office just for us."

"You tell her what we wanted to talk to her about?"

"No, just that we had some questions for her." He lowered himself in the chair opposite the couch and rubbed his chin. James knew that look. "What?"

"Just thinking."

"I can tell. Spill."

"I can't decide if Adam is alive or not. We haven't had a chance to discuss this, but are you not having a single doubt that Lainie's wrong?"

James sighed and leaned his head back against the sofa. "I don't know, Cole. In spite of a few moments of doubt that she pushes away as soon as they happen, she still insists it couldn't be him, but frankly, all the evidence points to the opposite. And I've always been one to follow the evidence."

"Yeah. Same here. You think she's just in some kind of denial thing?"

"Maybe. But Lainie was there that night. She lived it. She saw Adam after she shot him. Heck, she tried to save him."

"Maybe she succeeded."

James' eyes locked on Cole's. "Maybe. But if she didn't, who benefits by making her and the rest of the world think she did?"

A sound at the entrance to the room pulled his gaze to see Lainie there, holding her phone, betrayal in her eyes. "I'm not in denial, thank you very much. But I *am* going to take a shower, so y'all can go on home." She did a one-eighty and headed down the hall.

James stirred to go after her and Cole waved him back onto the sofa. "Let her stew about it. She's smart. Even she has to realize why we'd consider the fact that Adam might be alive."

She stepped back into the room. "I'm not stewing, nor am I really in denial. I've admitted the thought has occurred to me that he could be alive, but I keep going back to that night."

"Thought you were gonna take a shower," Cole said.

"I am, but something's bothering me. Aside from your doubts, Cole is right. Even I can see how you would have to consider every possibility."

Cole raised a brow. "Well, thank you for that."

James waved her over to the couch. "I want to show you some security footage before I leave. You were right. Someone changed your tires in the parking lot of the hospital."

"Seriously?" She sat beside him, her gaze on his phone.

"Yeah." He tapped the screen and she studied the video.

"Unbelievable."

"Does he remind you of anyone?"

"Yeah, kind of. His build, the way he's holding his head . . ."

"Adam?"

She nodded and let out a low breath. "It's not him. I don't care what anyone says, it's not him."

"You don't have any doubts whatsoever?"

"No," she said. "No doubts. Not at the moment, anyway." She bit her lip and narrowed her eyes at him. "But you still do."

"Yeah, I do, but that doesn't mean we stop doing what we're doing."

"Thank you." She paused. "Okay, there might be some doubts and I keep ignoring them. It would help to see that he's actually in that grave. If it's really not Adam, then I think I could accept he's still alive." She gave a little laugh. "I guess I would have to." A sigh slipped from her. "I'm sorry for causing so much trouble."

He took her hand. "Once again. The trouble is not yours to shoulder. Got it?"

"Right." She hesitated. "Before you go to Julie Darwin's, will you swing by Bayview Cemetery?"

"What for?"

"Go by Adam's grave. Everything else has been wiped away. I'm just curious about his grave. The marker on it clearly states his name and date of death."

James wiped a hand down his cheek. "Well, that's a brilliant idea. I should have thought of that earlier. Yes, we can do that."

"Good. Thank you." She stood and paced the small area in front of the sofa. "I think we need to revisit Victoria Irwin. That picture on her end table bothered me. I want to see it more clearly."

Cole rubbed his hands together. "Let me take care of that. Buzz is here, and there are two cruisers outside and they plan to stay there as long as we need them, so you should be able to relax a little."

James wasn't sure about relaxing much, but he appreciated his friends being willing to spend their off-duty time watching out for Lainie. And him. Cole got on the phone and dialed Victoria Irwin's number. When he hung up, he shook his head. "She's not answering. I'll give it thirty minutes and try again."

"You want to watch some of the game?" James asked him.

Cole hesitated, glanced at his phone, and shrugged. "Sure, why not?" He dropped on the other end of the couch, and Lainie headed for the shower. "How're things with your dad?"

James tensed at the question, but his friend was well aware of the issues. "I'm not exactly sure. It seemed like we were making some headway at the lake yesterday, but then I had to leave to help Lainie, so . . ." He rubbed a hand over his face and sighed. "I hope once this is all over, we can try again." He clasped his hands on his belly and looked at the ceiling. "I'm such a loser."

"Come again?"

"I told Lainie she had to keep trying with her parents, her family. I told her she wasn't a quitter, that she never gave up—even when she wanted to."

"Ah." Yeah, his partner could see where this was going.

"I'm thinking I kind of need to take my own advice."

"I'm thinking you might be right."

His phone buzzed. A message from one of the officers watching the house.

Homeowner is here and said more people coming.

The door swung open and Jesslyn walked in. "Hey, guys," she said, then settled onto the loveseat and nodded toward the back of the house. "I hear the shower. She okay?"

"For now," he said.

A knock on the door sent James and Cole reaching for their weapons, and Jesslyn held up a hand. "Hold on there, cowboys. That's Kenzie with pizza."

James' stomach rumbled at the word, and she laughed on her way to the door. Kenzie walked in, followed by Kristine. Moments later Lainie stepped into the room, dressed in sweats, damp hair hanging around her shoulders. When she saw her friends, she burst into tears.

KENZIE RUSHED TO HER side to wrap her in an awkward one-armed hug. "Lainie?"

Lainie sniffed and laughed. "Sorry, it's just been a minute since we've all gotten together, not to mention all the crazy that's been going on in my life, and I've missed you all desperately." But she'd been too afraid of putting them at risk by spending time with them.

And yet, here they were. With pizza. Instead of dwelling on the fact that it might not be safe for them to be with her, she decided to appreciate the moments they were there. And besides, she had a veritable army outside Jesslyn's home. She was safe and so were they. For now.

Kenzie bypassed the den and carried the food into the kitchen while Kristine lugged a bag of drinks and, no doubt, some kind of chocolate confection she'd baked. Jesslyn rushed past them. "I'm starving."

Lainie and the others followed more slowly. "What are you guys doing here? And Kris? Thought you were in the air?"

Kris, standing at the refrigerator, looked back over her shoulder, her black hair swinging in a shiny wave against her back. Her dark eyes and white teeth flashed with a smile. "My two flights today were canceled, so I hopped in the car and came here. The airline has a lot of unhappy passengers, but I'm happy for me, so . . ." She lifted her hands in a "what can you do" gesture.

Kenzie reached for plates in the cabinet next to the sink. "We invited Steph and Allison too, but Steph is still with"—she shot a look at James, who'd stepped up behind Lainie—"*most* of her family at the lake and Allison is working."

"Allison is always working," Lainie said. She noticed how Kenzie's eyes fell on Cole, who now stood next to James.

Kenzie cleared her throat. "Oh. Cole. Didn't realize you'd still be here."

"I am."

"So I see." She tilted her head. "You ever plan on coming back to work?"

"When I'm sure my friends are safe. I have plenty of vacation time built up. How's it going?"

Kenzie narrowed her eyes while Lainie's gaze flipped back and forth between the two. "I'm quite sure you know exactly how it's going, but as far as I can tell, it's going well."

"Guys giving you a hard time?"

"Of course."

A faint smile curved his lips. "You can handle them."

She stared at him for a brief second. "Yes, I can."

While she was grateful for the distraction from herself, Lainie wasn't sure she should let the weird interaction between her two friends continue. "Who wants pizza?"

Kenzie spun toward the open boxes. "Grabbing mine now." She paused and motioned for them all to stop. "Lord, bless this food and please continue to keep our friends safe. In your name, amen."

"Amen," came the echoes around the kitchen, then the pizzas disappeared from their cardboard homes, and everyone found a seat back in Jesslyn's den.

Lainie caught the look between Cole and James just before Cole waved his phone. "We've got some time. Victoria Irwin's still not answering."

James nodded. "I'll be ready to go when you are."

"And while we hadn't really planned on this being a co-ed thing," Lainie said, "you and the guys are welcome to come with us next weekend. We're going glamping."

Cole laughed and looked at James. "You in?"

"Works for me."

"Then I'll be there as long as I'm not needed at work."

Cole turned away, and Kenzie's shoulders slumped like she'd only been holding them straight for Cole's benefit. Lainie made a mental note to ask her friend about that, but for now, she picked up a few dishes and carried them to the sink.

James followed her. "We have some really amazing friends."

"We really do."

It didn't take long to get the dishes in the washer and start the machine. When she turned, he was close. Very close. She breathed in, noting the scent that she'd loved since her teen years. A mix of sandalwood, fabric softener—and man. He reached forward and pushed a dried curl behind her ear. "Lainie, I—"

A burst of laughter from the den snapped his lips closed, and Lainie's heart thundered in her chest. "What?"

He shook his head. "Nothing. This isn't the time."

"Time for what, James?" *Please, please, please, give me a hint of what you're thinking.* Because that look in his eyes . . .

"Steph said you had a crush on me when we were younger."

"I'm going to kill Steph."

He laughed, then sobered. "Don't. It gave me the courage to ask you if you'd be interested—"

"Hey, you two," Jesslyn said from the doorway, "forget the dishes. We can do that later. We want to play a card game. You guys in?"

James closed his eyes for a brief second, and Lainie absolutely wanted to slug her friend, but she forced a smile and threw the rag in the sink. "Sure. Let's forget the dishes. Easy to do since they're done. Sounds fun."

"Great." Jesslyn disappeared back into the den, and James stepped away from her.

She caught his hand. "Whatever you were about to ask, I'd probably say yes."

He swooped in and caught her lips in a way-too-short breath-stealing kiss. "Good," he whispered when he lifted his head. "That's good." And then he was gone, leaving Lainie alone to replace the air in her lungs and do her best to wipe the grin off her face.

Then old wounds and past memories came crashing in and the smile slid into a frown while panic pounded at her heart. Her fingers went to her throat, searching for her necklace and the key she'd put back on after the fire.

And the odd look in James' eyes when he watched her do it.

She bit her lip. *God . . . I don't even know what to pray. You know my trust issues and all my hangups. But this is James, right? He's done nothing but protect me and—*

"Lainie! Come on!" Jesslyn's voice rang out from the den.

"And you know the rest, Lord," Lainie murmured. *Do I dare to give love one more chance? James keeps telling me I'm not a quitter, but Adam really messed me up. Help me figure this one out, okay?*

"Lainie! Sometime this year would be good! We're waiting!"

She laughed and shook her head, shooting a glance at the ceiling. *Sorry, later, okay? Gotta go hang out with the friends who interrupt my prayers. But you gave them to me, so . . .* She walked into the den, took her spot around the coffee table, and picked up her cards. *And I thank you very much for them, God. So very much.* Her eyes landed on James, who winked at her. She smiled back, but her insides trembled. Should she shut it down now? Whatever *it* was? Or trust that God had ordained this from the very beginning? And therein lay the problem. She wasn't good at trusting when it came to men and romance. But James . . .

Maybe not even James.

HE SAT AROUND THE CORNER, well out of the line of sight of the officers stationed at the curb, and watched the shadows through the blinds. They were having a party. A party? After everything he'd done and still planned to do? His gloved hands twisted around the handlebars of the bike. No doubt she wouldn't be alone the rest of the night. Her friends were on high alert at this point, and he was going to have to get creative.

He sighed. "Time to come up with a new plan," he muttered. He was getting beyond tired of having to come up with a new plan. Why couldn't the first plan just have worked—bald tires on a rainy day and help over the side of the mountain? All of this would've been over by now.

For the next twenty minutes, he sat there, thinking, flipping through ways to get her alone. Finally, he had a rough sketch of a plan, but he needed some help.

He cranked the motorcycle and sped away, his mind already working through the details of the new plan, aka the *last* plan.

Because this time, he wouldn't fail.

TWENTY

Early the next morning, James and Cole pulled into the cemetery parking lot while James continued to process the evening before—the fun with the friends, of course, but mostly that kiss. Wow. He'd never in a million years expected a kiss with Lainie Jackson would spin his world right off its axis. Then again, never in a million years had he ever expected to actually kiss her. Lainie Jackson. One of his sister's best friends. But he smiled. The fact that she'd lost two straight games of Scrabble made him believe she felt the same way. And that was a relief.

Eventually, he and Cole had gone home while the ladies had a sleepover, derailing his plan to take her back to the lake house. He snorted. More like a stay-up-all-night lock-in than a sleepover. Nevertheless, with all the company and the cops watching Jesslyn's home, James had been glad to crawl in his bed with his phone clutched in his hand in case Lainie needed him. But Buzz Crenshaw was as good as they came, and he knew the man would take care of Lainie and everyone else in the house. The officers in the two cruisers would do the same. With her well and truly covered protection-wise, he slept hard—a desperately needed deep and healing sleep—without any nightmares.

When he woke, Cole was standing over him with a cup of steaming coffee. "Get up, you slug. Time to rock and roll. Julie Darwin moved our appointment to eleven o'clock, so we're going to hit the cemetery first if that's all right with you, RVW."

"RVW?" James rubbed the sleep out of his eyes.

"Rip Van Winkle, of course."

James threw a pillow at him. Cole's laughter had lingered while he showered and dressed. Now James dialed Lainie's phone, thankful when she answered on the first ring. Her face appeared on the screen and she smiled at him. "Morning."

"It is definitely morning."

"I hope you got some rest."

"I did. You?"

"Not much. But at least it was a good kind of not sleeping. We talked into the wee hours of the morning." Her smile widened. "I needed that time with them so much. It was . . . healing."

"I'm glad." He paused. "You ready for this?"

Her smile faded and he wanted to bring it back, but the safest way for her to be there was to do that via FaceTime. "Yes."

He climbed out of Cole's 4Runner and looked at the cemetery. Lainie had described Adam's resting place in detail, and he let her "walk with him" as he headed in that direction.

"It's just over that hill in front of you," she said.

The cemetery was really stunning year-round. Butterflies winged their way from flower to flower, then flitted to gravestones, as though to check in on the occupants under them. Adam's parents had spared no expense, that was for sure, and in the fall it was particularly beautiful. Beautiful and peaceful with the small pond and the trees lining the walking trail. Too beautiful for such a hate-filled soul. Cole followed behind.

"You're getting close," she said.

They crested the hill and came to a stop.

"Not a bad place to be buried," Cole said, echoing James' thoughts. "Bet that cost a pretty penny."

She smiled. "What's the point, though? It's not like you can enjoy it after you're gone."

Cole nodded. "True. All of this is just for those who're left behind."

"I guess."

James aimed the camera at the area in front of him.

"Keep going," she said. "It should be right around there."

He walked slowly, panning the graves and the markers. "You sure this is it? There's an empty plot between these two, then behind that, there's a pretty fresh grave and then—"

She drew in a harsh breath. "Stop. Go back to that spot between the two others." He did. A breathless laugh came over the speaker. "You have *got* to be kidding me."

"What is it?"

"It's gone. And before you ask, yes, it was right in front of you."

"When did you come to his gravesite?"

"I visited after I got out of the hospital. It was for closure. I was having nightmares, and my therapist suggested visiting the grave to help convince my head he was really dead. And when I was there, so was the headstone." She paced, her phone bouncing with each hard step. "I don't believe this. I really don't. Where is his marker?"

"You're sure we're at the right place?"

"Is there a grave with an angel headstone to the left?"

"Yes."

Cole snapped pictures of the area. The markerless grave and everything around it.

"Then you're at the right place." Tears welled and dripped down her cheeks. "I shouldn't be surprised," she whispered. "Not after everything. But I am. I'm actually shocked that the headstone isn't there. Why is this happening?" She disappeared from view, and James could hear her sobs. His heart hurt for her.

"Lainie? Lainie, come back to the screen."

She appeared, her eyes red rimmed and glistening, but her jaw set. "What now?" she asked.

"Now, Cole and I figure out what happened to the headstone."

She frowned, her gaze on something behind her phone screen.

"What is it?" he asked.

"Something's going on outside."

"What?"

Her eyes widened. "Buzz is chasing someone!"

"Who?"

"I don't know, but he tackled him." The camera spun, and James could see Buzz on the ground with a man's arms behind his back.

"We're ten minutes away, Lainie. Keep me on the phone as we head that way." He and Cole climbed back in the car and Cole floored the gas.

"James?" Lainie's voice echoed over the speaker. "You're not going to believe this. Or maybe you will. I think it's Nick Williams."

"Adam's brother?"

"Yes."

"He say what he was doing?"

"They're not actually having a conversation at the moment. Buzz is still trying to get him to settle down. Should I go out there and try to help?"

"No!"

Cole's and James' voices blended as one, and Lainie looked at the screen with a frown. "Well, fine. But once he realizes he's not getting away, I want someone to ask him why there's no headstone on Adam's grave."

"We'll get to that. Just sit tight until we get there."

FRANKLY, LAINIE WASN'T VERY GOOD at sitting tight, but she managed. It seemed like an eternity passed until Cole and James arrived, but in reality, it was closer to eight minutes. Buzz had put Nick in the back of one of the cruisers, and while she could see them talking, it bugged her to no end that she couldn't hear what they were talking *about*.

As soon as James was out of the 4Runner, she opened the front door and noticed the motorcycle parked down the street in front of Jesslyn's neighbor's home.

Nick looked up and caught her gaze. "So where is he?" Nick said. "Huh? Where?"

Lainie frowned. "What are you talking about?"

"He's clean," one of the officers told James and Cole. They parted and let James, Cole, and Lainie approach. She ignored them all and kept her gaze on Nick.

"They said Adam was here in town, that he's showing himself to you. That you're seeing him."

There was something about his tone that lowered Lainie's blood pressure. A desperation that she never would have associated with Nick. "Yes. Why?"

"Then if he's here and you're seeing him, I want to see him too. If he feels safe enough to reappear in your life, why not mine? Or our mother's? Of all people, why you?"

She let his scathing last two words filled with disgust roll off her. "You really believe he's still alive, don't you?"

"You don't?"

"No. I don't."

"But you're seeing him!" He jabbed a finger at James and Cole. "They said so. He's showing up at the hospital and on security footage."

"Someone is, but it's not Adam, just someone who looks like him."

He grabbed his head. "I don't understand. Who is it? If it's not Adam, why are they doing this?"

James waved one of the officers back who'd moved forward, hand on his weapon. "We don't know, Nick, that's what we're trying to find out." He paused, his gaze dropping to the man's feet. "What size shoe do you wear?"

Nick blinked. "What? Um . . . a twelve. Why?"

"Was that you at the lake? In the canoe?"

The man flushed and Lainie curled her fingers into fists.

Nick nodded. "I—I've been watching you."

"Following me? Spying on me?"

"Yeah, but only because I thought I might get a glimpse of Adam."

He ducked his head with a sigh, then met her gaze once more. "At the lake house, I thought maybe Adam would follow you and I'd see him. I climbed a fence, spotted the car in the drive, but that was all I could see. So, I found a canoe that had been pulled up in one of your neighbors' yards and took it out. I was just sitting there, watching. I wasn't going to do anything."

"And here?"

"Dad said you wanted to exhume the grave you thought belonged to Adam. I called the cemetery office and got the details. I came out here because, again, I thought I might see Adam."

Lainie ground her molars together to keep from blasting the man and tried to find some compassion. He just wanted a glimpse of the brother he believed to be in hiding for the past eighteen months.

She hesitated. "Did you put bald tires on my car?"

Nick frowned at the out-of-the-blue question. "What?" She repeated the question and he shook his head. "No. Why would I do that?"

"Never mind. Just stop following me and stay away from the house, okay? Go home. Adam's dead."

James leaned over to the nearest officer. "You said he was clean. Any weapons hidden on his bike anywhere?"

"No. And the bike came back registered to him. The only thing he's guilty of is trespassing."

James looked at Lainie. "Do you think Jesslyn would want to press charges?"

She shook her head. "She would give it back to me and ask what I want. I'm fine with letting it go."

James nodded to Buzz. "Cut him loose."

Nick climbed out of the back of the car but kept his gaze on Lainie. "Why hasn't he shown himself to me?"

"Because he's not Adam and this guy knows you'd see through him."

His mouth worked, but no sound came out. Finally, without another word, he hurried to his bike and roared off.

Lainie rubbed her hands together. "Well, that was a bust."

"Yeah, but at least we know who was on the lake. And it wasn't the Adam impersonator."

"There is that, but he's still out there." She drew in a ragged breath and stomped back into Jesslyn's house. With each step, her rage rose. Unsure what to do with the anger, she went to the fireplace, then spun and paced. On the fourth spin, she slammed into James. His hands came up to grip her arms, and she swallowed hard on the tears that threatened to fall.

"What are you thinking?" he asked and guided her to the couch.

"That I'm sick of this!" She spat the words. "He's got me jumping at my own shadow. I . . . I'm afraid to do anything because I'm terrified I'll do something wrong and there he'll be. I'm afraid he's going to hurt someone I love. I . . ." She swallowed. "I'm afraid I'm going to be a victim once more and this time I'll just . . . stay one." She finally voiced the biggest fear hanging over her head.

"You're not a victim, Lainie." The words were spoken with such conviction that for a brief moment she looked up to catch his gaze. If she'd seen pity there, she would have truly lost it, but instead, he almost looked—angry?

She frowned. "Why do you keep saying that when it's so obvious?" She managed the whisper around her tight throat.

"Obvious to whom? If you don't believe anything I've ever said or will say in the future, believe this now. You don't have the victim mentality. I've watched you over the last few days and you fight back. Every single time. You are a fighter. Can't you see that?"

"No! No, I can't! I can't see past this stupid person who's flipped my life upside down. I need to help my parents, but I'm too scared to go to their house because I might lead this person to them. I . . . I . . . Everyone believes the man I shot and killed is now walking the earth again and I don't believe it. I won't!" She picked up the nearest pillow and flung it across the room. Tears she hadn't planned on crying dripped from her chin, and she swiped them away. James wrapped his arms around her and gently pulled her to sit on the couch, where she leaned against him and—ugh—sobbed.

And there they sat.

On *Jesslyn's* couch because she couldn't sit on hers.

Because someone had blown up part of her house. Because . . . why?

And her tears didn't seem to have an off switch. She finally sniffed, and he kissed the top of her head. "I'm sorry," she said.

"Don't apologize. You needed that. Now, are you listening?" he asked.

"Maybe."

"You fight back when fighting is called for. But not only that, you win. You're amazing!"

She frowned, her heart rate dropping even while embarrassment warmed her skin. "Win? Amazing? Are you crazy? I just had a meltdown while my best friend's brother holds me and lets me cry and snot all over his nice shirt. That is so not amazing. It's mortifying." A rumble started under her ear and she looked up. "And gross."

He laughed. Like full-on guffawed.

"I'm so glad you find my mental break so amusing."

"And that's why I say you're a winner, Lainie. You might falter, stumble, get knocked down, have a moment of self-pity, but you don't quit."

"Well, you're wrong." She snagged a tissue from the box on the coffee table and swiped her nose. "I'd quit if I could. I feel like it's a game to this guy. Like . . . like Scrabble or something," she whispered. "Every time he draws more tiles, his have the better point value. Which allows him to make moves that are worth more."

"So what if he does? Winning isn't necessarily about the most points. There are winners and there are *winners*. In this game, it's about not quitting. And you don't have quit in you, so I don't believe you when you say you quit. You know as well as I do, in Scrabble, it's the next turn that may give you the upper hand. But if you quit, you'll never know. That's you, Lainie. You always find a way to gain the upper hand. You're always one move ahead of everyone else in the game of Scrabble and against this sick guy. We'll beat him, but you can't give up, so no quitting."

"You're a bully. I can quit if I want to." Her petulant words held no sting, and they both knew she didn't mean them. She'd just needed to let off steam and have a good cry. She drew in a shuddering breath and finally tuned into how he held her. Tenderly, carefully, but with strength. Like he knew a good, strong hold wouldn't break her.

He was right.

And whoever her tormentor was wouldn't either. "Thank you," she mumbled.

"You're welcome." He shoved more tissues into her left hand.

"James?"

"Yeah?"

"What if we're so focused on finding Adam that we're missing something really important?"

He nodded. "That's a thought. It's certainly possible."

"What could we be missing?"

He sighed and rubbed his chin. "I hope talking to Julie Darwin's going to shed some light on that." He paused. "Let's get you cleaned up, then I'm going to make some calls, see if we can't get a move on with this exhumation. Maybe that will provide some answers too."

"They won't do it if we can't prove it's his grave, right?"

"They'll have records and security footage." He pulled his phone from his pocket and brought up the pictures Cole had taken at the cemetery.

"That marker isn't there, but the ground says it hasn't been gone long."

She leaned in. "Do you have other pictures?"

"Yes." He swiped, showing her all the pictures Cole had snapped.

Lainie let him pull her to her feet. "All we have to do is ask someone to look back far enough to see when the marker was removed, right?"

"Maybe. Depends on how long they keep their footage."

"Right."

"So, Cole and I are going to have to go back to the cemetery and talk about that plot to whoever's in charge."

"I know."

"And I think you need to come with us."

"Really?" She raised a brow at him. "I figured you'd say I need to stay put."

"That would be ideal, but the officers have been here for a long time and they need to go recharge, see their families. I asked Kenzie about coming, but she's working. She said she could be here in a couple of hours. I have two uniformed officer friends who can take over around the same time, but at the moment, there's no one to stay here with you, so you're safest with us."

She nodded. "All right, give me a few minutes to put myself together."

Ten minutes later, she walked out of Jesslyn's house and climbed into the 4Runner. "We'll hit the cemetery, then Kenzie can hang out with you a bit while Cole and I talk to Julie Darwin."

"Well, at least Kenzie has a gun and knows how to defend herself should this guy decide to show up."

"But most importantly, she knows how to protect you."

TWENTY-ONE

"What if they don't have footage?" Lainie asked, pushing the 4Runner's rear passenger door open.

James climbed out of the front passenger side. "Then we'll figure something out."

"Will they approve the exhumation if we can't prove it's his grave?"

He sighed. "Let's cross that bridge when we come to it. Besides, they'll have documentation in their files."

"No, they won't," she muttered and slammed the door.

He was half afraid she was right. Someone was working really hard to wipe Adam Williams's death—or fake burial—from existence.

The door to the office was open, and James held it while Lainie stepped inside, with Cole following them. The foyer was more like something one would find in a grand home than a mortuary office, but he supposed that was part of the draw. James never heard any noise that indicated they'd entered, but footsteps hurried in their direction from the hallway to his left. A man dressed in a white shirt, black jeans, and denim blazer came into his line of sight. James raised a brow. The man did not look like he would have expected. Interesting.

"Hi there, I'm Chad." His blue eyes crinkled at the corners and

James guessed him to be in his late thirties. "What can I do for you folks?" Chad's sandy-blond hair was cut into a military style that spiked slightly from his scalp.

Cole introduced them and showed his badge. "We have an odd request," he said, "but first, is there a reason the headstone for Adam Williams's grave is missing?"

Chad frowned. "Missing?"

James nodded.

"Uh, no. Not unless it was broken or something and the family is having it replaced."

"Would that be in your records?"

"Of course. Let's take a look."

Chad led them down the opposite hallway into an office with an oversized desk and sample grave markers hanging on the wall. He pulled his keyboard around and tapped it while the three of them settled into the cushioned chairs opposite the desk. "Okay. First, I have three Adam Williamses in my system. Birth date?"

Lainie gave it to him.

"Um . . . no, I'm sorry, I don't have anyone with that birthday here."

Lainie's body actually vibrated. James laid a hand on her forearm. She shot him an "I told you so" look, clasping her hands beneath her chin. "Then where's the headstone that was on the grave? I believe it's 12R2." James raised a brow at her and she shrugged. "I came to visit the grave and had to know where it was. I asked the other guy that works here."

"You must be talking about Vernon Rosen. Older guy in his seventies?"

"Yes, that was him."

"Sadly, he was attacked coming out of here two weeks ago. He was in a medically induced coma, but just yesterday they brought him out of it and he's talking. But he has a head wound and doesn't remember anything from that night. Honestly, no one expected him to live. The police chalked it up to a junkie looking for something to finance his next fix."

James' internal radar blipped. "Was anything stolen?"

"The petty cash from Vernon's desk. It had about three hundred dollars in it. Guess he was happy with the cash because he left all the computers alone."

"Too bulky to carry," Cole muttered.

"I guess. The security footage was less than helpful in identifying the person, as he wore a ski mask, gloves, and was dressed in black."

"I see." James looked back at Cole, who was looking at him.

Chad cleared his throat. "All right. Plot 12R2. I can find that." He tapped more keys and frowned. "We have that as an available plot for sale. No one is buried there."

Lainie stared at the man and James wished he could read her thoughts. She turned her gaze to him. "I may scream." The flat calm of her tone belied her words. "Can I scream? Because I think I need to scream."

"Not just yet," James said, hoping his compassion came through. He turned back to Chad. "Okay, we kind of expected that. What about security footage out there. We noticed the cameras around the place."

"Sure. I just need to know at what point to pull it up."

"The night of the attack," Lainie said.

James nodded. That would have been his first guess.

With a few more clicks, Chad pulled up the footage from that night. "The attack happened after dark around nine o'clock. And this is the camera aimed at that section of the cemetery." He ran the footage forward. Then leaned in with a frown. "Wait. That's weird."

"What is it?"

"The footage stops. And doesn't pick up until the next morning."

"He scrubbed it," Lainie said. "He's always one step ahead. What in the world?"

Cole rubbed his chin, his eyes narrowed, forehead pinched. "I have a feeling we're just following the trail and watching his plan unfold."

"What plan?" Lainie nearly shouted. She shot out of the chair and pressed her palms to her eyes. "What plan? And what does it have to do with me? Why *me*?"

James stood and slid an arm around her shoulders. "I don't know, but I think we're closing in." He sighed. "We don't have all the pieces yet, but we're getting there." He turned his attention back to Chad. "So, how do we prove that Adam's grave is Adam's grave?"

The man seemed to be at a loss for words. "I really don't know what to tell you. According to our records, no one is buried there."

Lainie stiffened and James dropped his arm. "Who's buried in the new grave behind Adam's?" she asked.

Chad clicked the keyboard again. "A teenager by the name of Joshua Clark. His funeral was three weeks ago."

She winced and nodded. "Okay, teenagers have friends. We need to find those friends and see if any of them took pictures. If they did—"

"They might have gotten a shot of Adam's gravestone." James kissed her forehead. "You're a genius."

LAINIE THOUGHT GENIUS might be stretching it, but she *was* desperate. She hated to question the grieving teen's friends and family, but they had no choice.

"Can you give me their number?" James asked.

He did.

James dialed it while Lainie and Cole watched. Just when she thought it would roll to voice mail, a woman answered. "Hello?"

James introduced himself. "I need to ask you a couple of questions about a case I'm working. Would you be free in about an hour to talk?"

"Um. Sure. You're coming to the house?"

"If that's all right."

"I guess. It's kind of a wreck. I haven't been much of a house-keeper, since . . ."

"I understand. We just need to ask you a few questions."

"All right, then. I'll be here."

It didn't take long for them to thank Chad and leave with plans to return once they discovered something. Of course, this put the exhumation plans on hold. A fact that crawled all over Lainie's nerves.

They retrieved James' Jeep, and Cole followed behind them once more. She'd noticed James had taken more pain medicine on the way out of the office, but not once did he complain. "You okay?"

"You see everything, don't you?"

"Obviously not everything."

He shot her a compassionate look and squeezed her fingers. Not wanting to think about how blind she'd been when it came to Adam, she turned her thoughts in a different direction. "Adam's family thinks there's a grave with his name on it, but that he's not in it," she murmured. "They believe it's all a fabrication, designed to make *me* believe he's dead, ensuring he's safe from my murderous intentions. That's their theory, right?"

"Exactly."

"Only everything that's going on would lead one to believe the exact opposite. That he wants me to believe he's alive."

"Yes."

She sighed. "So, they're really not involved in all of this, are they?"

"If they know something, they're not sure exactly what they know. They just know what someone told them, and they're not talking."

"What's the best way to find out if someone has a picture or video of the funeral and gravesite?" Lainie asked.

"We start with the family."

Lainie checked the mirrors constantly, noting how fast the action had become a habit. Just one more reason to find the guy messing with her life. She scowled and stayed lost in her thoughts the entire ride. It wasn't until James was pulling to the curb of the Clark home that she pulled herself back to the present.

"Welcome back," James said.

"Sorry. Just trying to work through some things."

"Let me know if you want to bounce them off me."

"Thank you. I will." She glanced at her phone to hide her growing attraction for her best friend's brother. His tenderness and care were like magnets. But would she feel the same if she didn't have all the crazy in her life at the moment? Once she was out of the car, she looked at James from the corner of her eye. Like the gentleman he was, he waited for her to step in front of him and then followed her up the porch steps to the front door.

Yeah, she'd still feel the same.

And that was just a little scary.

And exciting.

And—

The door opened before he could knock. Cole joined them and they made their way inside after a round of introductions.

Mrs. Clark crossed her arms and frowned. "What kind of help do you think I can be with this investigation?"

"First," James said, "let me just offer my condolences on your loss. I can't imagine what you're going through."

"Thank you. And you're right, unless you've lost a child, you'd never understand. But I do thank you for the sincere compassion. Would you like to have a seat?"

The living room was large with two sofas, so plenty of space to sit.

James leaned forward while Lainie bit her tongue on the words that wanted to spill from it. James and Cole knew what they were doing, and she needed to let them do it.

"Mrs. Clark, this is going to be a very odd request, but did you—or any of Joshua's friends—take pictures of your son's service and interment?"

She blinked. Rapidly.

"I'm sorry," James said, "I know it's an unusual question. You see why I didn't want to ask over the phone."

"Um. Yes. You're quite right. I'm going to assume you have your reasons for asking, and yes, we did. And his friends did. He would have wanted that. It was a beautiful service on a beautiful cool day for this time of year. Like the Lord picked it just for him. A nod to Joshua's love of the fall season."

While Lainie's compassion was great for the woman's grief, her excitement over the pictures was there too. "Do you mind if we look at them? Just the graveside ones."

Her brow furrowed in confusion, Mrs. Clark nevertheless moved to the rolltop desk in the corner of the room and pulled a small photo album from the middle drawer. "They're in here." She swallowed. "I haven't looked at them. My sister did the album for me. She even had his friends send her some to put in there. I don't know if there are any of the graveside or not, but I would assume there would be."

James took it. "Thank you so much for this—and your patience."

"Of course."

James opened the book and Lainie leaned in while Cole stood by the front door, his attention on the front of the house.

HE SAT ON THE MOTORCYCLE, his attention on the house they'd just entered. No matter how hard he tried, he couldn't seem to catch Lainie by herself. Because someone was always with her. Always.

His gloved hands twisted around the handlebars, and he let out a low sigh. But he'd figure that out. This, however, was another story. Who lived here and why were Lainie and the others interested in the occupants?

For a moment, panic flared. What had he missed? Before the panic could blind him, he forced himself to breathe. To think. No. He'd covered all his bases. The plan was impenetrable. Perfect. No holes. No mistakes. Nothing. It had taken some fancy footwork and sleepless nights, but it was done and nowhere they looked would prove Adam was dead.

All the evidence would point to him being alive.

All of it.

JAMES FLIPPED THROUGH THE PICTURES, taking note of the care Joshua's aunt had used in putting together the book. She'd started at birth and highlighted the achievements of his short life. He arrived at the funeral pictures, and there were many teary-eyed friends who'd taken selfies and then typed messages across them. "You'll be in our hearts forever, Josh." "I can't believe you're gone, J-man." "The world will never be the same." And so on. He looked up to see Mrs. Clark swiping tears from her cheeks. "This book is a very special gift," he said. "I hope you're able to look at it soon."

She sniffed. "Thank you. I hope so too."

He flipped the page and came to the gravesite, examining each photo with care. And there it was in the third one. Slightly out of focus, but still legible. "Found it," he said with a glance at Lainie, then Cole. He turned the book around and pointed to the stone in the background. "Adam Williams. Beloved brother and son. Forever in our hearts." And the dates below that. Lainie's breath whooshed from her and brushed across his cheek. He looked up to meet her gaze. "This is it." He turned to Mrs. Clark. "This is exactly what we were looking for and you can tell the location of the grave in relation to the other headstones around it. Do you mind if I take a picture of it?"

"Of course I don't mind. Go right ahead."

James snapped the photos, sent the picture to his supervisor, requesting a rush on the exhumation, and tucked his phone into the clip on his belt. He stood. "Thank you again. I know it's hard right now, but I can tell you're a believer. I'm praying the Lord gifts you with a supernatural peace."

"Thank you," she whispered with tears in her eyes. "He's still good even in this tragic season."

"And, I don't know if this helps or not, but if everything goes the way I think it's going to, we can credit Josh for helping us solve this case."

Mrs. Clark pressed a hand to her chest. "That would thrill him to pieces."

They said their goodbyes and made their way out of the home, with Cole leading the way and James flanking Lainie. He'd gotten the impression that Cole had seen something that had set his nerves twitching.

"What is it?" James asked while Lainie slid into the passenger seat.

"Guy on a motorcycle was across the street near the stop sign. He seemed to be watching the house before he took off."

"Great." James sighed. "Was it Nick again?"

"No, different bike."

"Huh. Then let's have a couple of officers watch the Clarks' house for a while and make sure he doesn't try anything."

"I'll call," Cole said.

James glanced at his phone. "Kenzie's free now and said she'd meet us back at Jesslyn's house and hang out with Lainie while we visit this Julie Darwin person."

"Sounds like a plan. I'll follow you there."

James nodded, grateful to have a partner he could communicate with by just meeting his gaze. "Thanks." He climbed behind the wheel and soon they were headed toward Jesslyn's home.

TWENTY-TWO

While Lainie had given James and Cole every last detail she could think of regarding Julie Darwin, she could only pray it was enough. No doubt, the woman would hate Lainie even more for putting her in the role of suspect, but it couldn't be helped.

Now, sitting back in Jesslyn's den trying to focus on the latest Lynn H. Blackburn book, she kept thinking she should be doing something. The book was fabulous and deserved her full attention, and right now that just wasn't happening. She set the story aside and stood to look out the window. When Nick had been spotted by Buzz, he'd been standing across the street, leaning against a tree. Buzz had caught his eye and Nick had run. Which had been stupid, because that had fueled Buzz's protective instincts.

The whole incident had been fast and scary, and Lainie hadn't had a chance to really think about—or process—everything.

"Hey, you okay?" Kenzie asked. She set aside her own book and leaned forward, her gaze intent. Purposeful.

"I'm struggling, to be honest."

"I didn't realize how bad things were for you, Lainie. I'm sorry."

Lainie turned and crossed her arms. "It's not your fault. You've had a lot going on with the whole SWAT thing, and you never met

Adam, so . . ." She shrugged and walked to the sofa to sit. "How's that going anyway?"

Kenzie snorted. "It's going. I keep telling myself it's only been a few months, that it'll get better and being the only woman on this team will be fine. Key words, 'will be.'" She shrugged. "I have to prove myself—probably over and over—and I will."

"You're amazing. They'll come around."

Her friend laughed. "I don't know about amazing, but determined? Yes. So that probably counts for something."

"Definitely." She hesitated. "Do you mind telling me what's going on with you and Cole?"

Kenzie stiffened and her dark eyes darkened even more. "I'm not going to insult you and pretend I don't know what you mean, but the truth is, I'm not exactly sure myself. I think he feels like I've invaded his space—his bro team."

"Did you know Cole before SWAT?"

She nodded. "My grandmother lived next door to Cole's parents."

"What?"

"My three brothers and I used to spend summers here with her. Cole and my youngest brother hung out quite a bit."

"And then you and I meet at the hospital. It's a small world, isn't it?"

"Very."

Lainie rubbed a hand down her face. "I can't stand this."

"Waiting?"

"Exactly." Her phone rang. "It's James." She tapped the screen. "Hello?"

"We just finished talking to Julie Darwin, and I think we can safely rule her out. She and her husband are in the process of adopting twins who are now nine months old and she seems to be very happy. She said once she recovered from the trauma of the surgery, she realized what happened wasn't your fault. You had no way of knowing that her other tube was damaged. She said to tell you she's sorry for blowing up at you. We're getting closer, Lainie. See you in a few."

She hung up and Kenzie raised a brow at her. "Interesting news?"

Lainie filled her in. "I want to find this person—and the person at the hospital who's been helping him raise Adam from the dead."

FINALLY. SEATED IN JESSLYN'S DEN on Tuesday morning while Lainie and Jesslyn fixed breakfast, James breathed in the stomach-rumbling smell of bacon, eggs, and cinnamon toast while he read the message from Commander Hill.

> Since there's no record of anyone being buried there, there aren't any hoops to jump through when it comes to digging. The equipment will be there and digging will commence at one o'clock.

Yesterday had been filled with tension, but at least there'd been no more "Adam sightings" or attempts on Lainie's life.

He didn't believe for one moment it was because the guy had given up. He had a sinking feeling it was because he was working on another plan.

He dialed his supervisor, and the man answered with a gruff "How you feeling, Cross?"

"Better, sir. Ready to get this thing resolved for Lainie's sake and get back to life as we know it."

"We're ready when you're cleared. But you're doing a lot of good work for someone who's supposed to be taking it easy. I'm going to have to give you your sick days back."

"Thank you, sir, I appreciate that, but I would have taken the time off if I hadn't had the sick leave. This is personal. She's a friend."

"Understood."

"Sir, I know this may seem odd, but I think it would be best to have a hearse on standby."

"You think there's a body in that spot?"

"I do. Especially with that picture as proof."

"Body could have been moved."

"It could have."

"But you don't think so." The man sighed. "All right. We'll have one there."

"Thank you again, sir."

James hung up and texted Cole, who'd returned to work, leaving him and two patrol officers to watch out for Lainie.

Any word on the picture at Victoria Irwin's house?

Still no one answering the phone and I've gone by twice. She's not at home. I'm going to try one more time. I'll keep you posted.

Sounds good.

James stuck his phone in his pocket and let his nose lead him into the kitchen to find Jesslyn hovering over bubbling eggs and frying bacon. Lainie was setting the table.

She looked up and smiled. "Welcome to the Jesslyn and Lainie café. Grab a plate and help yourself."

"Smells amazing."

Once they were all seated at the table, Lainie said a short blessing. When she looked up, he caught her eye. "They're digging up the site at one o'clock today. If they find anything such as a coffin, it will be transported to the morgue, where the medical examiner will extract DNA for comparison to Adam Williams's."

She pursed her lips, then nodded. And took a bite of eggs.

Okay, that was way less reaction than he'd expected. She cleaned her plate in silence while Jesslyn took a phone call. When Lainie finished, she set her fork down. "Good. I don't suppose I should go."

"Definitely not. But once we get word, assuming they found a coffin, and that they're on the way, we can head to the morgue to wait for the results if that will help."

"It'll help."

"Want to play a game of Scrabble while we wait?"

She shot him a ghost of a smile. "Sure." Her phone buzzed and she glanced at the screen and raised a brow at him. "But this is Grant, so let me take this first."

"I'll get the board while you do that."

Jesslyn returned to the kitchen to finish her breakfast and James heard Lainie greet her brother. He sent up a quick prayer that Grant would have some good news for her.

When she walked into the den a few moments later, she smiled. "Worked it out with your brother?"

"Yes. He was horrified to hear why I was calling and promised to get started right away now that the insurance company is done."

"That's great!"

"It is. It really is. Now, distract me." She waved to the game on the coffee table and dropped onto the floor cushion.

James grinned. "By beating you? My pleasure."

Jesslyn snorted from the doorway. "Yeah, right. I'm out of here." She waved her phone. "Got a call. See you two later. Loser buys take-out."

"Why not loser cooks?" James asked.

"Because you can't cook." She shut the door behind her, the parting shot left ringing in the air.

Lainie snorted on a laugh, and James ducked his head to hide his own smile even while his heart thumped at the sight of Lainie's face free of stress and worry. Unfortunately, that lasted only a short time and she once again frowned, her thoughts beyond his reach.

James scooted closer to Lainie and cupped her chin. "We're getting closer," he said.

She scowled. "Not close enough." Then her eyes cleared and she studied him. "Thank you, James."

"For what?"

"For being you." A small mysterious smile curved her lips. "Steph was right. I've always liked you."

"Liked me?"

She nodded.

"As in . . ."

"As in I thought you were the most amazing person on earth, and I thought Steph was incredibly lucky to have you as her brother."

He raised his brow. "Well, I'm glad I'm not your brother."

She giggled, the rare sound pumping his blood a little faster. "Trust me, James, I'm very glad you're not my brother too."

He lowered his head and captured her lips, his head asking him what he thought he was doing, but his heart cheering him on. A small gasp escaped her, and he stopped, lifted his head, and peered down at her wide eyes. "Was that a mistake?"

"You tell me."

He thought about it. "No, it wasn't. I've been wanting to do that again ever since the kiss in the kitchen. The truth is, I like you too, Lainie, but I can't let my feelings take control or I'll be so distracted that I might miss something. Might not be able to focus on keeping you safe."

"That wouldn't be a good thing."

"It absolutely would be a very bad thing." He pulled in a deep breath and let it out slowly before pressing a kiss to her forehead. "So, no more kissing. It messes my head up."

"Really? I thought it was just me."

He laughed. "Trust me, it's not just you." He cleared his throat and pulled himself back to the other side of the board. "Now, you ready for a trouncing?"

"In your dreams."

At 1:45, James' phone pinged and he glanced at it. "They found a coffin."

She sucked in a breath. "Okay then."

"They're on the way. You ready?"

She nodded and they put the game away, with Lainie the clear victor in spite of James' grumbles that someone with a dictionary in her head was cheating. James suggested lunch, but Lainie shook her head. "I couldn't eat a thing. Can we just go? After you eat something, of course."

"I'm not really hungry either. Let's go. We'll get something after?"

"Please." She grabbed her purse and headed for the door while James called to let his boss know they were on the way. Two police cars fell into place behind them, and Lainie reached over to clasp his hand.

James held it all the way to the hospital.

TWENTY-THREE

Once in the hospital, in the waiting room of the morgue, James looked at her. "How are you doing?"

"I feel like I'm going to throw up but could dance for joy that this is finally happening, all at the same time."

"That's a wide range of emotions."

"Tell me about it. I don't want to question an answer to prayer, but I'm so beyond confused that I don't even know what to think. Half of the people who know him believe he's dead. The other half are convinced he's alive. Someone stole his gravestone, went to a lot of trouble to erase him from the system, and now Adam's father says that his son is buried there, but insists there's no body in the coffin because his son really isn't dead. My brain is ready to self-combust."

"Well, we'll know in just a little while what's what."

The door opened and Victoria Irwin stepped inside. Lainie sucked in a ragged breath while James stiffened. "Hello," he said. "I'm a little surprised to see you here."

"Myles asked me to come," she said, "to witness this farce."

"My partner's been trying to get in touch with you," James said, ignoring her statement.

"Yes, I've got a voice mailbox full of his messages. I'll call him after this invasion is finished."

Invasion? Lainie raised a brow and bit her tongue while James tapped out a text message. Probably to Cole letting him know Victoria was at the morgue with them.

What was Lainie going to do if the body in that coffin wasn't Adam? Because she seemed to be the only person who still believed it was.

Unfortunately, she was having trouble truly hanging on to that belief she'd been so sure about just a couple of days ago. Then again, someone was going to an awful lot of trouble to make it look like Adam was alive. If it took that much effort to do so, wasn't he really dead? Again, the thought occurred to her that this was all just a smokescreen. Who would benefit from her believing that Adam was alive? Who would benefit from her being dead?

Lainie released a long sigh and realized she'd been squeezing James' hand so tight her own fingers were numb. She let go and leaned her head against him. "You haven't said much about your back. How is it?" She kept her voice low. Victoria had seated herself across from them, her nose in her phone.

"Better." He kept his voice just as soft while his fingers tapped the screen of his phone. "I'm texting Cole. He's tied up at the moment but plans to bolt over here to see if she'll meet him at her house."

"Why don't you just ask her?"

"Because I don't want to give her the opportunity to say no. Cole can just follow her home and bug her until she lets him in."

"Ha."

When he finished, he looked at her and slid an arm around her shoulder. "As for my back, today is the first day it's not painful to move, so that's progress."

"I'm glad. That was some bruise." She glanced up at him. "Do you ever wonder what happens to the people you help?"

"Of course I do."

"Do you ever get to find out about them?"

"Sometimes. If I'm really curious, I give the victim a call."

"What about the little girl you saved? And her family?"

His jaw worked for a split second before he shrugged. "I haven't really followed up with that one. Those little girls got to me, and if I were to find out that they were in a bad situation, I'd have to do something about it." He rubbed his jaw. "And I can't save everyone. It sounds harsh, I know, but all I can do is the job I've been assigned—and called to do—in that given moment and pray that God takes care of the rest."

"I can understand that." She hesitated. "I even find it admirable. You couldn't do what you do if you spent your time worrying about the after."

"Exactly. I make a difference in that moment of time. What happens after that is really out of my hands. Even if I were to try and help every person after the fact, it's physically impossible. It's like if you were to follow up on every patient who left your care. You simply couldn't keep up."

"I have some patients that I do that with, but you're right, definitely not all. There's a family that I've grown really close to over the last couple of years. They live up the mountain, not too far from the hospital. Mr. and Mrs. Gonzales. I make house calls for him because I know if I don't, he won't get the medicine he needs. Like he hates going to doctors, and I could tell right off that if I didn't create that relationship, he was going to die a lot sooner than he had to."

He shot her a warm look. "So you did."

"I did. I felt like I was supposed to. Like God was pushing me to do so."

"And you obeyed."

"Yes." She cut him a sideways look. "At least that time."

He chuckled. "They sound like good people."

"So good. They have a little store with a café and they make the best donuts, cinnamon rolls, bagels, croissants . . . well, you get the idea. Mama Maria is the best cook, and their coffee . . . oh my, it's divine. I'll have to take you there sometime."

"Is it Señor G's? I'd love that. I've always meant to stop in there."

Victoria rose, phone pressed to her ear. "Can this wait? I'm at the morgue . . ." She stepped outside, her voice fading.

"What do you think about all that?" she asked with a nod to the door Victoria had just walked out of.

"I don't know. Since Myles asked her to come, he apparently didn't have the guts to do so. He might not have even told his wife about it. So he sent Victoria to get information."

Lainie frowned. "I guess."

James lifted her hand to his lips and pressed a kiss against her knuckles.

And just like that, the air whooshed from her lungs. "James—"

The door opened and Carina Black came into the waiting room. Lainie shot to her feet. "Well?"

"It's not him."

Victoria had just opened the door when Carina made her announcement. At the words, Victoria laughed and shot them a triumphant look.

Lainie's jaw dropped and she wilted back onto the seat. "You're kidding."

"I wish I was," Carina said. "I'm sorry. I rushed the DNA results, of course, but I don't even need those to tell you this isn't Adam Williams. For one, there's no evidence he was shot—not in the base of his throat or anywhere else—and he's of Asian descent. The DNA will confirm everything, of course, but I wanted you to know ASAP."

"Well, who is he?" James asked.

"No idea. I'll leave that up to you to figure out. Sorry, but I've got to get to my other cases today."

"I know you're swamped, Carina," Lainie said. "So, thank you for making this a priority." Because this was a law enforcement issue, their request had been bumped to the front of the line.

Carina returned to her morgue, and Victoria lifted her nose and swept out the door once more. Lainie looked at James. "You going to stop her?"

"No, I'll let Cole know to intercept her."

"What now?"

He blew out a low breath. "Now, we regroup. Someone was prepared for us to dig up that grave." He paused. "That may be one reason someone removed the headstone and went to all the trouble to erase Adam from the records. If you don't need an exhumation order, you can dig up a plot a lot faster. As we just proved. I'm not saying he's for sure alive, but if he's not, the trouble someone is going to in order to make it look like he is . . . well, it's pretty astounding."

"Are we just playing into this person's hands?" Lainie asked. "Being his puppets?"

"I'm starting to wonder."

"Then that means someone has been planning all of this for over eighteen months." She pressed a hand to her head. "I'm so confused."

James paced. "I think someone was planning something. Something to do with you. But then somehow, the plan got derailed. Postponed. And it was just recently set back on track."

"Postponed? Derailed? But . . ."

"I have an idea."

"What's that?"

"I want to take you back to the lake house."

"For security reasons?"

"Yes. I keep coming back to this whole thing with Adam being some kind of smoke and mirrors thing. Keegan and Dixon are still there, and you'll have plenty of protection while we focus on finding the person after you."

She nodded. "I'm okay with that."

"We can stop and get some of that coffee from your friends' place. We'll go right past it."

"That works for me."

She followed him out of the morgue to his Jeep, climbed in, and buckled up.

A police cruiser pulled next to them, and James rolled his window down when the officer lowered his. "Cole called. Said you needed an escort."

"Thanks, guys. We're going to make a quick stop first, then head to Lake City Lake."

"We're right behind you." He pointed to another cruiser. "They're going to be right in front of you."

Ten minutes later, they were winding up the side of the mountain, their coffee in the cupholders, Lainie feeling smug at James' agreement that it was the best he'd ever tasted.

He looked at her. "Do you—"

Gunfire peppered the air in front of them and the police cruiser went off the road, bounced off a tree, and flipped over the side of the mountain, disappearing from sight. And where was the second cruiser?

"James!"

"Hang on!"

The gun continued to spit bullets and everything seemed to happen in slow motion.

"Lainie! Get down!"

But she was frozen to the seat, her heart in her throat, pulse out of control and lungs locked on the last breath she'd inhaled.

Then a delivery van spun until the front of the vehicle was facing them for a brief second before it, too, went off the side of the road, the driver's wide-eyed look of terror catching her gaze before it vanished.

The bullets pelted the Jeep and James slammed on the brakes, skidded to the edge of the road, then tipped over the embankment. Lainie's screams echoed, and from the corner of her eye, as they slid past the delivery van, she noted it had become wedged against a tree, keeping it from tumbling farther down.

The Jeep slammed to a stop, jerking her sideways, the seat belt cutting into her. And for a moment, time hung suspended before sound reached her once more.

"Lainie! Answer me! Are you hit?"

"No," she whispered. "No," a little louder. "Are you?"

"No. Can you get out?"

This whole scenario was hauntingly familiar. Hadn't she just done this two weeks ago? Even though the landing had been a hard one and she'd have multiple bumps and bruises, thankfully the Jeep had stopped nose down against the side of a ditch—and she didn't seem to have any broken bones. She shoved open the passenger door and released her belt. When she stepped out, she lost her footing on the damp leaves and went down, her shoulder bouncing off the ground and gravity rolling her fully down the next hill. When she came to a stop, she stayed still, absorbing the aftershocks rippling through her, taking inventory once more.

A quick glance over her shoulder spurred her to move as the delivery van's contents bounced out of the back, scattering around her. "James!"

LAINIE'S CRY ECHOED. James was trying to get to her, but his leg was jammed between the steering wheel and the front seat, which had slid all the way forward upon impact. He was trapped and working furiously to free himself. "Lainie! I'm coming! Hold on!"

But the seat wouldn't budge. He checked his phone, thankful he'd stuck it in his pocket rather than the cupholder. No service.

"Ahhh!" His frustrated cry ricocheted around him. Panting, he replaced the phone in his pocket and fought the memories of his past. Of being trapped in a burning MRAP in the middle of the desert, hearing the cries of the men he worked with—his friends, his brothers.

And being absolutely helpless while his own pain threatened to send him into unconsciousness.

"Lainie!" He had to stay in the present. Had to help Lainie.

Her sobs reached him, keeping him anchored, refusing to allow him to slide into the past. He pulled the lever on the side of the seat again, and using his good leg, he pushed as hard as he could to move the seat. It finally slid back, and he let go of the lever to lock it in place. Pain sliced through his leg, but James gritted his teeth, released the seatback, and slid up toward to the headrest, pulling his legs as he went. Pain sucked the breath from him, and he noted the blood-soaked tear in his pants, the fiery burning in his back where his recent wound protested all the rough stuff.

But Lainie—

Somehow, James finally managed to roll himself out of the Jeep and to the ground. With a worried glance at his leg, he pushed himself to his feet, grateful that he could stand. The leg wasn't broken. He just had a huge gash that needed stitches and hurt like someone had used a blowtorch on it.

He could deal with that.

He shoved himself to the front of the Jeep and looked down the short embankment to see Lainie, who had her back against a tree, trying to stand while pressing a hand to a bleeding wound on her head. "Lainie!"

She snapped her head up, winced, then her eyes found his. "James!"

He worked his way down and leaned against the tree next to her. She hurtled herself against him, shivering. "Are you okay?"

"Yeah."

She ran her hands over his chest. "You're not hit?"

"No. I'm good. I promise." Except for his leg that felt like it was on fire.

Her breath hitched again. Panic attack? James pulled her into a hug, his gaze scanning the place they'd gone off the road. Where was the shooter? It took a minute, but her breathing finally slowed from full-on hyperventilating to a practiced in and out. "You okay now?"

"I will be."

A low moan to his right pulled his attention from Lainie. "Hold on." He stumbled to find the driver of the delivery van lying on his back, his right leg twisted at an odd angle and his head bleeding from a large gash.

Lainie had followed him and dropped next to the driver, switching to professional mode. "He needs help. Now. Did you call 911?"

"No signal. I have a first aid kit in the Jeep, but I don't think I can climb back up there with this leg." Not with any kind of speed.

She focused on the gash in his leg for the first time and gasped. "Oh, James."

"It's fine. Just a cut. Can you get the kit?"

She swallowed, looked up to his Jeep, then nodded. "You need pressure on that leg. If you keep bleeding like that . . ."

She was right. He pulled off his belt, and working quickly, Lainie helped him secure a tourniquet just above the gash while he told her where to find the first aid kit. Then she met his gaze. "That should be okay for the moment. Try not to move too much. Make sure he doesn't have any bullet holes in him. If he does, put pressure on it. I'll be right back."

James pulled his weapon, moved so he could keep Lainie in view, and aimed it at the top of the embankment. If the man who'd caused this showed his face, he was going to lose it. But a choking sound behind him had him scurrying back to the driver. The guy's eyes were open and fixed on James, fear glinting in their hazel depths.

"Hey, buddy." James took his hand. "You're going to be all right. My friend is every bit as skilled as a doctor and will be right back with the first aid kit."

"Th-thank you," he whispered.

"What's your name?" James asked as he did as Lainie said. A quick examination showed one bullet hole in the man's left shoulder.

"Tate Olsen."

"Well, Tate, you're going to be just fine." He would have told him that even if it was a lie, but the wound shouldn't be fatal. Then again, he wasn't the one with medical experience. No telling what other injuries he'd sustained when he was thrown from the vehicle. He'd fallen a long way. He glanced up the incline and Lainie had disappeared. No doubt in the Jeep getting the kit.

When he turned his attention back to the driver, the man's eyes were closed. "Hey, hey, man, wake up."

Nothing.

James checked his pulse.

Nothing.

"Aw, dude, don't do this." He rolled to his knees, wincing as his leg protested with a stab of pain, and started compressions.

TWENTY-FOUR

Lainie climbed, ignoring the throbbing in her head, the ache in every muscle, the sting of the seat belt burn, all of it. A man needed help and she was going to help him. Finally, she reached the Jeep and worked her way around to the back of it, breathing hard. She pulled the back gate open and leaned in, looking for the box James had described.

Something hard jammed into her left kidney and she froze.

"Hello, Lainie. I have to say, you may just be the hardest person on the planet to kill." She took a deep breath. "Don't do it," the voice warned and she cut off the scream. "Call out to him and he dies. I have the perfect shot from here and you can see that for yourself. He'll never know what hit him."

James was bent over the delivery driver, and she had no idea what had happened to the police officers who'd gone over the side of the mountain. And the cruiser behind, what had happened to them?

"Why?" She whispered. "Why?"

"Money. Why else? Now, climb when I say climb and I'll let him live. Fight me and I'll shoot him now."

Money?

She looked back at James to see him doing CPR on the man. He was completely and fully occupied. A fact which her abductor was aware of. He lifted the gun, placed it alongside her ear, and aimed it at James.

"Fine," she said, "I'll go."

"You first. I'm right behind you."

She still hadn't seen the face of the man. "You're not Adam. Your voice is wrong."

"Oh, I'm Adam all right."

But he wasn't. She knew it with every fiber of her being, so who was he?

With her heart in her throat and a prayer on her lips, she forced herself to head for the road. Where were the cops who'd gone over the side? Where was the other cruiser? *Please let them be alive.* She placed one foot in front of the other while her mind spun. Maybe there would be a passing car, or James had miraculously gotten ahold of the police—or something. But when she pulled herself up and onto the side of the road, all was quiet. Except for the waiting van parked on the side. And the second cruiser was crunched up against a large tree with no movement in sight. She searched for an escape, a weapon, anything.

But there was nothing, and panic set in.

"Get in the van." He shoved her toward the back, and she contemplated a run toward the woods.

"If you don't cooperate, I'll shoot you, then go back and shoot them. Your choice."

She climbed in, noted a figure in the driver's seat. The person turned and something glinted. A flash. Almost like a spark. "Who—" Something wet hit her in the face, and within seconds the world wobbled. "What did you . . ."

"Just go with it, Lainie. When you wake up, we'll have a nice chat before you die."

She passed out.

WHERE WAS LAINIE? He glanced up but saw nothing. Tate had not awakened after James had gotten his pulse back and was still hovering between this world and eternity. James checked his phone again. Wonder of wonders, he had a signal. *Thank you, Jesus.*

He dialed 911 and got dispatch, gave their location, and told them to be aware of a possible shooter still in the area.

And then the call dropped. But he'd gotten what he needed. Now, he just needed Lainie to get back. He glanced at the Jeep once more.

No Lainie.

What was taking her so long?

A cold feeling started to build in his gut. "Lainie? You find it?"

No answer.

"Lainie!"

Where was she?

Take care of her—please, God. He checked Tate once more and his pulse was steady for the moment, but that didn't mean it would stay that way. Did he dare leave him to go after Lainie?

Did he dare stay?

James stood, gasped, and went back to his knees. His leg screamed its protest and blood from the thigh wound dripped to the ground. With gritted teeth, he tried one more time, keeping most of his weight on his good leg, and managed to hobble to the bottom of the incline to look up. "Lainie! Answer me!"

The sirens in the distance reached him and he looked back at his phone. Still no signal. He vowed to get a SAT phone as soon as he and Lainie got out of this situation.

"Lainie!"

His voice hoarse from calls and his throat raw, he contained the scream battling for release and scrambled back to Tate.

The sirens pulled closer, and within seconds he heard his name on his partner's lips. "James!"

"Down here. He's got Lainie and I've got a seriously wounded guy here and need a basket. Check on the officers who went over the side a few yards back from where we went over."

"Hold on!"

Paramedics appeared and began their descent.

"Get a rope and drop it over. Then pull me up!" He was climbing up on his own no matter how much his leg wanted to remind him that it was probably a bad idea.

A rope dropped over the side and slapped the ground next to him. He glanced up and saw Cole. Thanking God for a partner who knew when to argue and when to keep his mouth shut, James grabbed the rope, and just like when he'd been injured in the IED blast a few months earlier, he shut his mind to the pain, ignored the swimming in his head, and climbed. Cole was waiting on him and, as soon as his partner could reach him, grabbed him around his wrist and pulled him the rest of the way up and onto the side of the road. James lay on his back, trying to stop the sky from spinning. Lainie . . .

He struggled to sit up and Cole dropped next to him. "Dude, are you okay?"

"Yeah. We've got to find Lainie."

"As soon as you said he's got Lainie, I had an officer start calling, looking for anyone who has security cameras trained on this road. When we figure out which way he went, we can do more."

"Good. Good."

James pulled himself up to a seated position as he worked to catch his breath and fought the throbbing in his thigh.

"You need that looked at. I know you want to go off after her, but you're losing blood in some concerning amounts there." He waved to a paramedic, and James realized there were three ambulances on scene.

"How are the officers who went over?"

"Hurt. One of them bad. But alive. The other cruiser hit a tree. Knocked out both officers, but they'll be okay too."

The young woman with the big trauma kit sank to her knees next to him. "Let me take a look."

"Fine, but no painkillers."

"Can I numb the area?"

"Absolutely." He lay back on the gravel and let her work while his brain scrambled to figure out a plan to find Lainie.

Cole's phone rang. "I'm going to get this while they work on you." He snagged it. "Garrison here." He stood and walked to the edge of the road and looked down. James tried to hear his partner's side of the conversation but couldn't make out the words. However, concentrating on trying kept his mind off the fact that he was getting stitched up on the scene.

Cole talked for thirty seconds, then hung up and returned to squat next to him again. "That was Myles Williams. When I missed Victoria at the morgue, I called him. He said Victoria still wasn't home—and wasn't sure when she'd be back—but he'd meet me there and let me see whatever it is I wanted to see."

"Smart thinking."

Cole shrugged. "When you can't get the one you need, go with the one next in line. Hang in there. We'll find her."

An officer ran up to them. "There's a gas station about half a mile up the road. The owner said he saw everything go down and tried to call 911. When he didn't have a signal, he hightailed it to his station to use the landline. Anyway, he said there was a van that drove up and stopped just as he was backing up to do a U-turn. I got the license plate on the van heading north."

"And it's registered to?" James spat the words through his pain.

"Adam Williams."

TWENTY-FIVE

Lainie had no idea how long she'd been asleep, but right now, she was cold and wanted some hot coffee and a sherpa blanket. And where had the headache come from? And why was her neck so *stiff*? She groaned and tried to move, only to freeze.

She was sitting in a chair, her hands tied to each arm, feet bound. *Wait . . . what?*

Nausea churned and she dry-heaved before gaining control of her stomach. Once everything finally settled, she focused on the details—dragging through her spotty memories until she came to the part of the wreck. Someone shooting at them. Sending them over the side of the road and down the embankment. Now she remembered.

James. "Oh, James," she whispered. "I'm sorry." She was in a home in the main room, with the kitchen to her left and bedrooms to her right. She sat in front of a stone fireplace she would have admired under other circumstances. Instead, she tugged at the zip ties binding her to the chair.

No go, of course.

Could she stand and walk to the kitchen with the chair on her back to get a knife?

She had no idea who'd taken her, nor where he was at the moment, but she had no doubt he'd be back. All she could do was try. She pressed her feet to the floor and hunched forward, wobbled like she was going to fall over, and slammed back to the floor with a thud. Breaths now coming in pants, she started to try again when the door opposite her swung open.

And Adam stepped inside, a gun in his right hand, held at his side. "Hello, Lainie. Glad to see you're awake."

He walked closer, and while her heart beat a thunderous rhythm in her chest, she held her tongue and simply watched him, taking in every detail of his appearance, and finally laughed.

He froze. Frowned. Scowled. And stepped back. "What's so funny?"

"I'm not crazy. You're not Adam."

"No, I'm not. I'm Adam's half brother, Michael."

"The resemblance is uncanny, but I'm sure you worked to make it so."

He shrugged. "At a distance it worked for me. Of course, if you'd just had the decency to die in the car wreck, none of this would have been necessary."

"So you put the bald tires on my car."

"I did."

"Why are you doing all of this?"

"I'll tell you, but don't think the whole 'if I keep him talking I can escape' thing is going to work. This is the day you're going to die, but I figure I can give you a few answers before we make that happen."

Lainie wanted to scream, to cry, to struggle to get away. All of it. Instead, she stayed frozen, keeping her gaze locked on his. "Do you really have a scar there?"

"No." He pulled his shirt down, and flawless skin stared back at her. "But it was a good representation, wasn't it?"

"You said this was about money. What money? I don't have any money."

"Actually, you do. You just have to be dead for me to collect it."

"A life insurance policy," she whispered. It hit her. "That draft from Myles and Adam's account. It's not for your mother, it's on me, isn't it?"

"Wow, you got that on the first try. That's impressive. You're smart."

"But . . . why now?"

"Because being in prison threw my timeline off."

"Prison."

"Yeah. About three weeks after you killed Adam, I, with my usual luck, got arrested." He blew a raspberry and shook his head. "I used to deal in drugs, but it's just too risky once you go to jail and have a record. And I never want to wind up back there again."

"Tell me. From the beginning. I want . . . need . . . to understand."

He held up the gun, looked at it, then her. Then shrugged. "Why not? I've never minded telling someone how brilliant I am. Too bad you're the only one I can tell." He grabbed a chair and pulled it around to sit in front of her. "Adam and I used to hang out on a regular basis. It was our little secret. Our dad and my mother never did know that Adam and I knew each other. But when I was seventeen, I overheard an argument that my mother and father had one night. She was begging him to leave his wife. He was saying he couldn't pay her if he did. She told him she didn't care about the money, that she just wanted the three of us to be a family. And he responded with, 'What about my other kids, huh? Adam and Nick? I'm supposed to just leave them?' And she ran out of the room crying. But it wasn't hard to find Adam Williams. I called him and we started hanging out."

"Adam, but not Nick?"

"Adam said Nick was very protective of their mother, and if he learned of our father's affair with my mother, he'd tell. Ruin everything. So, we kept our mouths shut and got to know one another. We'd meet at a little bar downtown, drink and talk for hours while we flirted with the ladies." He held up an imaginary glass and tilted it toward her. "Cheers, love." His grin looked eerily like Adam's, and chills skittered up her spine while nausea swirled. "People thought we were twins," he said. "Since I didn't have any siblings, I thought it was pretty cool. One night Adam told me about this girl he'd met. Her name was Lainie Jackson. He laughed and said he had you wrapped, that you'd do anything for him."

Lainie grimaced. He wasn't wrong.

"Then not long after you were engaged, he told me that he'd convinced you that it was the responsible thing to get life insurance policies."

"He was a lawyer," she whispered. "I thought that was just his way of making sure he was taking care of me in the event of his death."

"Because that's what he wanted you to think. He said you were worth more dead than alive. Then laughed and wondered if he'd overpriced you. At that moment, I knew that I was going to get my hands on that money. All my life, I've watched my mother take money from my father. Adam's father. I've watched him have the perfect life while my mother had to scrounge for every penny. Adam was okay to hang out with, but when he told me this, I started planning. I had it all worked out and then you killed him."

"I can't say I've missed him." She spoke the words absently while her mind spun.

He looked almost amused. "No, I can't really say I have either. But you did throw a kink in the plans by shooting him. I was there, you know."

"What?" She blinked. "The night I shot him?"

"Yes. He and I had been talking and he said you broke up with him. He was furious and I could tell he was going to do something drastic, and I wondered if I'd be able to use that."

"Sorry?"

"I had planned for him to die—an accident with his poor fiancée—but decided this might be even better. I thought I would see if I could arrange for an intruder at that point. Once Adam killed Lainie—and I fully expected that he would—I'd simply walk in and finish him off with the gun he used on her. Then walk away and wait for my payday. Families would grieve his loss, of course, paperwork would be filed, the money deposited into Adam and my father's joint account, and I, using Adam's information, would have the money transferred to a different offshore account and I would be home free. But by the time I got there, paramedics were—unfortunately—working on him."

"And Adam died, and I was the beneficiary."

"Exactly, but I didn't care about that paltry sum, I needed the money from *your* death."

"But our amounts were exactly the same." She bit her lip. "All of this for a quarter of a million dollars?"

He laughed. "Not hardly. More like two million, my dear."

Lainie gasped. "What? How?"

"Once he had all of your information and you were approved, Adam simply changed the amount, inserted your signature, and hit send. Everything went to his email."

Because he'd been "in charge" of the whole idea. They'd done all the paperwork on his laptop. Everything would have been stored there. She hadn't thought a bit about it, because she still trusted him at that point. She was going to be sick. "I'm such an idiot."

"No, not really. Just an easy mark. And Adam was a very, very good con man."

She refused to take comfort in her kidnapper's—and possibly killer's—words.

She'd forgotten all about those stupid policies. Had never even thought to try and collect on it after Adam died. And now, *this* is what everything came down to? It was so obvious now, she laughed.

Which startled Michael. "What's so funny?"

"All this time, we were chasing after Adam, doing your work for you. Turning over every stone to prove he was dead and finding nothing but proof that he was alive. All because of an insurance policy that I'd completely forgotten about. Unbelievable."

"My main goal was to make sure my father believed that Adam was still alive. I couldn't take a chance he would close the bank account with his and Adam's name on it. He had deposited enough for the payments to be drafted for three years. Adam thought it would look good in case someone decided they needed to investigate your death. After all, why would someone set up three years' worth of payments if he was going to kill off the person."

"But Adam *did* get to the hospital. They worked on him, but there's no death certificate."

"Friends in high places come in handy. I could only hope I was in time, but I called my friend at the hospital. I had them make sure the death certificate disappeared along with every record that had Adam's name on it."

"The paramedics who came to the house dropped him at the hospital."

"Yeah, true, but I wasn't worried about them. They could say that, but if there's no record, there's no record. That night, outside the hospital, I called Adam's family and pretended to be him. I talked real raspy and low and said I wasn't hurt as bad as everyone was saying and that I was alive but had to disappear while I healed. They were to go through with the funeral and not to have an open casket for obvious reasons."

All Lainie could do was shake her head, but her ears perked up. "And they bought it," she whispered.

"It wasn't a hard sell. They didn't want him to be dead. So, he was in hiding from the woman who tried to kill him. I also knew, when the time came for Adam to put in an appearance, if it came down to exhuming his body for final proof, he couldn't be in that grave." He laughed without humor. "It really should be a lot harder to steal a lab coat, walk down to the morgue, and switch bodies, but while it took some maneuvering, it wasn't all that difficult."

Especially since he looked like he belonged there. "Wait a minute. The morgue would have noticed a missing body."

He shrugged. "I found a homeless guy, fed him a meal spiked with some rat poison, and had me a body to put in place of Adam's."

She shuddered and gaped at him. "What about the cameras? The alarm system? All of that?"

He smiled. "That's where friends in high places come in handy."

"Who?"

"Someone who lost a beloved family member thanks to you."

"What?"

"It doesn't really matter now, does it? She got her revenge and I'm going to get my money."

"Adam's money," she muttered.

He scowled and she let it go, not wanting to anger him by pushing. "Where is he now? What did you do with his body?"

"It's buried in my mother's backyard." He laughed. "Whew, you should have seen me trying to do that in the dead of night without any nosy neighbors poking around."

His complete lack of remorse chilled her, and it was all she could do to keep the terror from choking her. *Keep him talking. Keep him talking.* "Where am I?"

"Just a little temporary place. A family place. Thankfully, I know where the key is hidden."

"How did you know we'd be on this road? How did you know where to wait to ambush us?"

"I have my ways."

Lainie couldn't think how anyone would have known. She and James had made the plan seated in the morgue. Alone. She pondered that while she continued her questions. "You broke into my home after Adam's death, didn't you?"

"Had to find the insurance policy."

It clicked. "And when it wasn't there, you went to the storage facility." She frowned. "But how did you know about that?"

"Found the receipt on your kitchen counter. Noticed indentations in the carpet like you'd moved some things and figured I'd try there. And what do you know? Gold."

"Why am I still alive? You could have killed me when I was unconscious."

"Well, if the bald tires on the car had worked, it would have looked like an accident and I'd be well on my way to collecting my two mil. But once you saw my face—and thought I was Adam—I figured you'd be telling everyone that, so . . . I had to tweak the plan. Convince you—and everyone else—that Adam was alive. I already had a head start on that since his family believed he was just hiding from you, but now that you'd seen me and I realized you thought I was my brother . . . well, the rest of it kind of fell in place. I already had his ID, his birth certificate, all that. I just had to stay one step ahead of everyone. As to why you're alive now? Because I had a question I want answered too."

"What question?" She might as well give him what he wanted.

He frowned. "What were you doing at that address after you left the cemetery office?"

She told him about the pictures and the teen who'd been buried there.

He raised a brow. "So that's what you were doing there. Clever. I didn't even think of that. That's kind of disappointing for me, but whatever. It all worked out in the end. The grave was dug up and the body wasn't Adam's." He shifted the weapon and Lainie tensed.

"How did you know about the dry cleaning?" she asked.

"Adam told me, of course. It was such a simple thing to take in a few shirts and pick them up in Adam's name. The guy was new, he had no idea. And since no ID is ever required, it was just one of those things that was so random that it had to be believed."

"You let the receipt fall out of the car on purpose."

"Of course. And you did exactly as you were supposed to with it. And everything else I'd set up. I thought I did really well in the measly two weeks I had to put everything together. Removing the headstone so you didn't have to get an exhumation order was pretty brilliant, don't you think? All of it was, if you think about it."

She didn't want to think about it. Her mind circled back to his friend at the hospital. Someone who'd lost a loved one because of— *"She killed herself. Over a man. Or rather a woman who stole her man. Someone who lured him away from her."*

"Bridgette," she said.

Michael paused. "What?"

"It was Bridgette's sister, wasn't it?"

"How did you put that together?"

"She said something about her sister at work one day and was so bitter about her suicide and the fact that a man dumped her. She was in love with Adam, wasn't she? And that's why Bridgette helped you. To get back at me for stealing Adam from Elle." Even though she hadn't known Adam had been dating someone when they met.

"You're definitely smart."

Lainie bit her lip, trying to keep her voice from wobbling. "Why me?" she asked. "Out of all the people in the world, why did Adam pick me?"

He studied her a moment, glanced at the clock on the mantel, then back at her. "I asked Adam that and he said it was because you were an easy mark. Very trusting and needy. You let your family run all over you, and you never complained about getting stuck with the dirty jobs at work. He called you the perfect victim without an interfering family to keep him from his goals."

He was right. Her family wasn't nosy about her business. They pretty much ignored her and anything she did. Except when it interfered with what *they* wanted.

The perfect victim.

His words pelted like sharp arrows. They were nothing she hadn't said about herself, of course, but this was different.

This was . . . she didn't know what it was, but . . . *Why* was it different?

Because she no longer believed it.

Because of James.

And now she had to live so she could tell him.

But Michael lifted the weapon and aimed it at her.

"Wait! Please!"

JAMES PACED THE HOSPITAL FLOOR just far enough away from the exit to avoid setting off the doors' motion sensors. His leg cried out for him to stop, but sitting still wasn't an option. Since his Jeep was toast, he'd ridden to the hospital in the ambulance against his wishes since it seemed like he was going in the opposite direction of Lainie. But he'd been checked and rechecked—thanks to his supervisor's orders once again—and now was ready to climb the walls, but Cole had told him to stay put, that he'd discovered something from Mr. Williams and was on his way to pick up James.

"Drive faster, man," he muttered.

Finally, Cole pulled up to the door and James slid into the passenger seat, his leg throbbing, his back hurting, but relieved to be on the way to doing something. Whatever that something was.

"What'd you learn?"

"How's the leg?" Cole glanced at the blood-soaked area of his pants.

"I'll live." The stitches would need to come out in a few weeks. Until then . . . "Tell me."

"So, you know that picture Lainie said had Adam and Myles and Victoria in it?"

"Yeah?"

"That isn't Adam."

"So, who is it?"

"Adam's half brother, Michael Irwin."

"Half brother?"

"They look enough like twins that, from a distance, it's conceivable that even Lainie would think he was Adam."

"And he always made sure to keep his distance," James muttered.

"He has a place not too far from where he attacked you. It's a miracle no one was killed, to be honest. That was a semiautomatic rifle he was shooting with."

"And that's where we're headed now?"

"Along with an entire army of SWAT and other law enforcement."

"What about Myles Williams? Does he know what his son is doing?"

"No. I really don't think he does. He's the one who told us about the family place. I'm guessing he took Michael and Adam there occasionally."

"He cooperating?"

"Yes."

James leaned his head back and closed his eyes, sending silent pleas for Lainie's safety winging heavenward. "What else did you find out?" he asked.

"A lot. In my conversation with Adam's father, he muttered something about how Adam should have stuck with the McPherson girl and he would still be alive."

James jolted. "McPherson?"

"Yeah. I asked what about her. He said her name was Isabelle McPherson, and she and Adam dated for a while, but Adam moved on to Lainie, dumping Isabelle, who killed herself."

"What!"

"Yeah."

"McPherson," James said. "Does she have a sister that works—"

"At the hospital?" Cole said. "She sure does."

"What you wanna bet Bridgette was the one who took care of all of the medical records that went missing? No doubt Michael had something to do with that. Maybe because she thinks Lainie stole Adam from her sister and this is her form of revenge?"

"That's my guess."

"Unbelievable. Hurry!"

TWENTY-SIX

Lainie's words hadn't stopped him, but his buzzing phone had. Michael had lowered the weapon and looked at the screen while sweat broke across her brow and panic threatened to consume her.

A curse ruptured from him and he swiped the screen. "Mom? What do you want? I'm a little busy right now." He shot a furious glance at Lainie, then he raced out the door, leaving her alone. His mother had just saved her life. She'd tell the woman thank you when she had a chance. *If* she had a chance.

And now she was going to have to do something if she wanted to stay alive. Once again, she pressed her feet to the floor, and while she wobbled with the chair on her back, she managed to shuffle into the kitchen, ears tuned to the front door. She scanned the countertop, but there was no knife block in sight.

Thankfully, he'd put her hands on the outer sides of the chair arms, and she was able to slip her fingers around the drawer knobs and pull.

Her breaths came in pants, her adrenaline chugged like a runaway locomotive, and all she could think was that if he came back before she was loose, she was dead.

Finally, on the last pull, she found a junk drawer with a pair of scissors on top. She grabbed them and set the chair down with a hard thud.

She didn't bother glancing at the door, just worked to maneuver the scissors, praying she wouldn't drop them. If they hit the floor . . .

She tried again. Missed. Tried again, missed. A sob slipped out. *Don't give up. Don't give up. What if it's the next try that makes the difference?* It took her way longer than she would have liked, but on the sixth try, the edge of one blade slipped under the zip tie. She twisted it so the inside blade was against the plastic, then using her middle finger and thumb, she pinched the handles together. She got most of the way through the tie when the strength in her hand quit and a cramp set in. The scissors fell to the floor.

"Ah! Please, God!" With a desperate cry and a hard tug, she jerked her wrist and the tie broke. Panting, crying, with hope springing from within, she grabbed the scissors once more and cut herself free, only to hear footsteps on the porch as the last tie fell from her ankle.

She hurtled herself out the kitchen door and beelined toward the woods. It took her a moment to realize she knew exactly where she was and where she needed to run.

The harsh cry behind her crossed the distance between her and her captor, spurring her on. She crashed through the trees, looking for the trail that would lead her to the Gonzaleses' store. But did she dare go there?

Did she dare not? She needed a phone and help. The store had locks and security. And landline phones.

She pushed on, the undergrowth doing its best to trip her up, but she stayed on her feet, the sound of Michael somewhere behind her giving her the incentive to keep going.

Finally, heart ready to rupture through her chest, she burst from the trees into the parking lot. A quick glance behind her showed Michael way closer than she thought he was. She hit the rear door of the store and twisted the handle.

Locked.

"Oh, please," she whispered and ran around the side of the building to the front and slipped through the double glass doors.

She twisted the deadbolt and spun to find Mama Maria gaping at her from behind the register. "Lainie?"

"Is anyone else here?"

"No, just me. I was getting ready to lock up." She nodded at the glass doors. "That was my last lock."

"Call 911. A killer just chased me through the woods. Where's Señor G?"

Fear bloomed on her face. "He ran an errand. He'll be back soon. A killer? What you mean, a killer?"

"No time to explain, just call him first and tell him to call 911, but to stay away from the store. And you stay behind the counter. Do you have a gun somewhere?"

"In the safe in the office. Should I get it?"

"No time. Make the call." She'd have to find another weapon.

The woman bustled to the phone on the wall, pulled the receiver, and hunkered down as instructed. While she made the call, Lainie hurried to the back of the store, looked out the storage room window to see Michael burst through the tree line. Then he disappeared around the side of the store and Lainie raced back to the front. Michael appeared at the glass doors, caught her gaze, and raised the gun.

And fired.

JAMES STOOD OUTSIDE the empty building, evidence of Lainie's presence—and escape—vivid in his head. The loud crack of a gunshot snapped his gaze to his partner. "Where'd that come from?"

"Through the woods."

"He found her."

Another crack reached them and James curled his hands into fists. "Which way?"

An officer hurried over. "Sounds like that could have come from the Gonzaleses' store."

James snapped his attention to the man. "Lainie's friends with them. She'd know where it is and she'd go there." He looked at the officer. "Lead the way." He gave Cole a shove toward his vehicle. "Let's go, let's go!"

TWENTY-SEVEN

Lainie had grabbed Mama Maria at the first gunshot that hit the glass on the front door, spider-webbing it. They'd made it to the storage room before the glass shattered.

Now, she huddled with her in the small space, trying to figure out the next move. Should they have gone out the back door? But that would put them out in the open with a man who had a gun. "What did Señor G say?"

"He didn't answer the phone and we had to run back here when the bad man shot the door."

"Oh no," Lainie whispered.

Mama Maria's frightened gaze met Lainie's, and she wanted to crawl in a hole. She'd brought this on her friends. She went to the window. "Does this open?"

"No. It's nailed shut."

"Okay." *Think, Lainie, think. Don't give up. Keep trying.* It was like James was in her head or whispering in her ear.

A spatter of Spanish came from beyond the storage room door, and Mama Maria grasped her rosary and whispered prayers.

Señor G.

"I know you're back there, Lainie!" Michael's voice cut through the woman's words. "Come out and maybe I won't kill this nice man."

Mama Maria wailed and Lainie opened the door. "Lock it," she whispered.

Her friend grasped her hand and shook her head. "No. No. He would not want this."

"This is my fault. The man's name is Michael Irwin. He's a killer. If I don't do this, your husband dies, understand?"

"Lainie!" Michael's shout echoed. "I'm not kidding!"

More rapid-fire Spanish from Señor G.

Tears ran down Mama Maria's age-weathered cheeks and she nodded.

Lainie pulled her fingers from the woman's hand and shut the door behind her. She crept to the end of the hallway and peered around the corner into the main area of the store. Michael stood in the midst of the shattered glass, his weapon held to her friend's head. Señor G's eyes blazed his fear and fury, and Lainie held up a hand. "Let him go. You can have me."

"Just like Adam said," he sneered. "Bleeding Heart Lainie. Door-mat Lainie. Get over here."

Lainie took two steps toward him, just out of reach, and to the side so he had to turn slightly, his left shoulder at a ninety-degree angle to the entrance. Blue lights pulled into the parking lot. "Let him go."

Michael shoved Señor G, and the man stumbled, then whirled to put himself between Lainie and Michael. Michael aimed the weapon and Lainie slammed into the older man, sending him to the floor. The bullet whipped past her cheek as she dove over Señor G.

"Put the weapon down!"

The order came over the bullhorn and Michael paused.

All went quiet for a split second, and she looked up to see Michael take aim at her head, his decision made. He was willing to die, but he planned to take her with him.

Time did that thing again where it slowed. She registered the crazed hate in Michael's eyes, the horde of officers outside, and blue lights bouncing off the walls and inventory.

One pop sounded. A bloom of red erupted from Michael's temple, then his eyes went wide, the gun dropped from his hand, and he went to the floor.

Then time sped up once more. Officers rushed in and Lainie rolled to her feet. Hands reached for her and Señor G.

"Lainie!"

James' voice came from behind her and she whirled. "James?"

"Lainie!"

She scanned the sea of law enforcement faces and found the one she wanted. For now and for all time. "James." She rushed to him and he enveloped her in a crushing hug. "James, it's over. It's over, right?"

"It's over. Mostly. We have a few unanswered questions, but yeah, it's over."

"How did you know?"

"Cole figured it out for the most part. Thanks to you. Adam wasn't the one in the picture, it was Michael."

"I should have known. I should have guessed."

"How could you?"

"I guess I couldn't have, but he got all the hospital records erased and made everyone believe that Adam was still alive, and he probably killed Bart Sheffield who did Adam's autopsy and—"

James settled a finger on her lips. "Sheffield's death was ruled an accident. He had a heart attack behind the wheel of his car and crashed. That's it. But Michael had a friend at the hospital who helped him. We think it was Bridgette McPherson."

She nodded. "I guessed it was her. He said he had friends in high places."

"Bridgette's sister dated Adam for a while. I can explain the details later, but yeah."

"I got some of the details. Maybe you can fill in any blanks," she muttered. She rubbed the wrist she'd bruised getting out of the zip tie. It hurt, but she'd done it. "I didn't give up, James," she said, her voice low. "I didn't give up."

"I never thought you would." He squeezed her tight. "You ready to get out of here?"

"You mean after I give my statement and check on Señor G and Mama Maria?"

"Yes. Exactly."

"More than ready."

WEDNESDAY NIGHT, A FIRE CRACKLED in Jesslyn's fireplace, and James sat on the end of the couch with Lainie's bare feet in his lap. She lay sleeping, her breathing deep and even. He waited for it to change, for the nightmares to surface, but for the past hour, she'd been peaceful.

His phone buzzed with a text from his captain.

> Found the body and it's been identified as Adam
> Williams. Tell your girl she can rest easy.

He glanced at Lainie and smiled. She was definitely resting easy. He had something he wanted to talk to her about but didn't want to disturb her. Not yet. There'd be plenty of time for that after she recovered from her ordeal with a killer. Frankly, he could use a little recovering himself.

The front door opened and Cole stepped inside, followed by Kenzie, Stephanie, Allison, and Kristine. Each person held a food item of some sort. They all headed for the kitchen, except his sister, who passed her bag to Kristine.

"Well, this is rather cozy," Steph said, stepping into the room, a small smile playing on her lips.

"Shut up." His mild tone made her laugh, but she didn't say anything else, just dropped into the chair next to the fireplace.

Lainie sat up with a gasp and James frowned. "What is it?"

"Did they find the woman driving the van?"

James exchanged a look with his sister, who shrugged. "What are you talking about, Lainie?"

"I told the police about her. The driver who was with Michael when he kidnapped me. It was a woman. I just figured it out." She

287

touched her ear. "There was this weird spark or something when she turned her head. It was a dangly earring."

"We picked the van up. There wasn't any evidence of anyone else in there."

"She drove."

How had he missed this? "I didn't hear you tell that part."

"We were separated during that part of the interview, I guess." She frowned. "Who could it have been?"

James shook his head. "Could have been Bridgette. She was helping Michael with some of the other stuff. The police already have her in custody, and according to Cole, she's singing like a canary, so you're safe."

Lainie relaxed back against the sofa. "Maybe. Yeah. It had to have been her." She sat up again. "But no one ever figured out how Michael knew where to lay in wait to ambush us. How did he know we'd be driving that route?"

James shook his head. "I don't know. We may never know."

"There has to be a reasonable explanation." She chewed her lower lip. "Victoria was the only other person in that room besides us, but she'd left before we talked about going to the lake house." She sighed and shrugged. "Beats me."

"Food's ready if you're hungry!" Kristine called from the kitchen. "We have a glamping trip to plan."

Lainie grinned at James, and he put his talk with her on hold. Maybe he could sneak a moment with her at the campsite. It wasn't a conversation he wanted to rush or "fit in." He wanted to take his time and make sure he did it right. He held out a hand and she took it. The sight of the bruise on her wrist sucker punched him, and he wished he could do the same to Michael Irwin, but the man was dead and that was that. And James was looking forward to hanging out with Lainie without having to look over their shoulders. "Let's go plan our trip."

And while they planned, his mind went back to her observation that someone had tipped off Michael. But who? And how?

TWENTY-EIGHT

TWO WEEKS LATER

They had to postpone the trip a week due to work schedules, but that was probably a good thing. When the weekend rolled around, Lainie was more than ready to head higher up the mountains for some fun and fellowship. There was nothing like campfire s'mores, music, bad jokes, and hours of laughter. Even if she did have to sleep in a cabin instead of pitching a tent under the stars.

The best thing about living in a city near the mountains was that it didn't take long to reach the Rocking Porch campground. She snuck a glance at James and noted he was moving easier, his wounds healing.

Her own wounds—internal and external—had healed some as well. Despite everything, since the death of Michael Irwin, Lainie had started sleeping through the night without nightmares. She couldn't explain it and didn't plan to question it. She'd just enjoy it for as long as it lasted.

Maybe it was all about concluding that it was okay to believe in herself. To understand that when she loved, she loved deeply and with her whole heart and wanted to help those in her life. There was nothing wrong with that. It was when she couldn't establish boundaries with those people that the relationship became unhealthy.

With her therapist's help and James' wise input, she'd set up boundaries for her siblings, her parents, and even a few people she worked with—including her supervisor.

All in all, it had been a mentally productive time, and while she knew nothing would be miraculously perfect overnight—or ever—she was excited to see how the future played out. In other words, it was a start.

Once they had their gear stashed in the cabins—guys in one and girls in the other—James stepped up to her and slid an arm around her shoulders. "You got a minute?" His satellite phone buzzed with a text.

"I've got all weekend, so if you need to get that, it's fine."

"No. I can ignore the thing for the next fifteen minutes."

Lainie caught Steph watching with a smirk on her face. Behind James' back, Lainie stuck out her tongue, and Steph's laughter followed them to the campfire area that would be a roaring blaze later that evening. He settled on one of the benches and pulled her next to him. She snuggled up under his arm and waited for him to speak.

"I just wanted to talk to you," he finally said. "We've danced around the topic, but now there's nothing stopping us if you're interested . . . or want to . . . um . . ." He blew out a low sigh. "Wow, I didn't think I'd be this nervous." He touched the key on the chain around her neck. "I know you have reservations about trusting or allowing yourself to have a relationship again, but I . . . I just wanted to ask if maybe you'd feel like you could give us a chance. There. I said it."

She sat up and turned to face him. "Can I tell you a story?"

He tilted his head, curiosity gleaming in his eyes. "Uh, sure."

"When we were younger, I used to watch for you at school. I came to every football game I could because I'd get to see you on the field. When Steph invited me over, I would eagerly wait to catch glimpses of you in the house or the backyard where you guys all played pickup games of football."

"Really?"

She let out a groaning laugh. "Yes, really. James, I guess what I'm trying to say is I've had a crush on you for a very long time, and if you want to ask me out, well . . ." She reached up, released the clasp on the necklace, and held the chain and key out to him. "I know you. You saved my life. You've done everything you could to encourage me and build me up." He took the necklace and she caught the sheen of tears in his eyes. "I don't need that anymore. I trust you, James, I always have, even though I tried to tell myself I shouldn't."

His head swooped in and captured her lips in a kiss so sweet she'd be on a sugar high for the next month. She leaned in and wrapped her arms around his neck, reveling in the moment, cherishing it and holding nothing back.

After several very long moments, he pulled away and cleared his throat. "Okay then, Lainie Jackson, would you do the honor of going out with me when we get home?"

She giggled. "Absolutely.'"

A gunshot sounded, the bullet landing in the firepit, kicking up ash and wood. Cries came from the cabins.

Before it could even register, James had her on the ground behind the bench.

"James!"

"Someone's down by the lake shooting at us!" James' shout echoed and she could only pray someone heard it.

"You killed him!" came a shout, followed by another crack, and the bullet pinged off the bench.

Lainie shook. "What's happening? Why is this happening?"

"Stay put!" he said.

"You killed him!" The crazed voice carried across the campground. "It's all because of you! You were supposed to die and we were supposed to get the money and get away from this evil place, but no, you had to"—more shots that zipped over their heads—"get my baby killed!"

"That's Victoria Irwin," James said.

"You were driving the van!" Lainie's cry echoed through the trees.

"And you were supposed to die—"

Another crack from a different weapon sounded. The woman dropped. Kenzie stepped from the cabin and raced past them, down the path to the edge of the lake. "Subject contained! She's still alive! Call an ambulance!"

Cole got on his phone, muttering under his breath about something Lainie couldn't hear, but James had such a tight grip on her that she also couldn't breathe. She shook her arm. "James. I'm fine. You can let go."

He pulled her into a hug and dropped a relieved kiss on the top of her head. "I'm never letting you go."

"I'm okay with that. And now it's over."

"Yeah. Now it's over." He glanced at his phone. "Guess I shouldn't have ignored that text after all."

"Why's that?"

"Because I couldn't get your words out of my head. So, I finally decided to do something about it. Before we left, I called Carina Black and asked her to look around the area where Victoria Irwin had been sitting. She found a small listening device under the chair."

"And that's how Michael knew where to ambush us. Not only was he working with Bridgette, his mother was helping him with everything else. They were working together the whole time."

"Speaking of Bridgette, how did she get rid of all of the medical records without getting caught? The hospital monitors every keystroke. I was being so careful even when I was doing the M&M reviews. I went through all the proper channels. If I hadn't, I'm sure it would have been noted."

"Oh, I asked about that. Once the hospital knew what to look for, they were able to follow the keystrokes. She logged in under about five different people's names and went to work."

"How did she get access to their passwords?"

"She was very clever. Waited for people to walk away from their computers, then sat down. She's tech savvy—it didn't take her long."

"Wow. I can see how they almost got away with it."

"But they didn't."

"Thank God."

Yes, thank God. For everything.

NERVES HAD JAMES READY to make a U-turn and head home, but Lainie's hand in his gave him the courage to walk up the porch to his parents' home. It had been two weeks since the episode with Victoria Irwin, who'd sustained a flesh wound, thanks to Kenzie's shot. She'd hit the woman's hand holding the gun. Lainie's case was well and truly wrapped.

Just like his heart. He planned to ask her to marry him on Thanksgiving Day, but today, his father had asked to see them both.

They entered the front door. "Dad? Mom?"

"James, Lainie." His mother came from the kitchen and hugged them both. "So good to see you. Your father's in the den."

James nodded and refrained from letting Lainie go in first. He could do this. Take it on the chin like a man. So to speak.

He walked into the room, head held high. He stood while Lainie went to his father and hugged him.

The man patted her on the back.

"I'm all forgiven for speaking my mind then?" she asked him.

"All forgiven."

James' heart lurched. Why couldn't his father say those words to him?

Lainie looked at him. "I could go help your mom in the kitchen?"

"I'd like you to stay if you don't mind," his father said.

"Oh, okay. Sure." She sank onto the couch, hands clasped between her knees.

James leaned against the doorjamb and crossed his arms, fully aware of what his body language was saying. Then he sighed and dropped his hands to shove them in his pockets. "What's up, Dad?"

His father rubbed his chin and cleared his throat. "I . . . uh . . . owe you an apology."

James stilled. "Go on."

"I just want you to know I've been full of regret but wasn't sure how to repair the rift between us. I know it was my doing, but my pride was a fierce force to reckon with. I guess after Lainie lit into me about how I was treating you, calling it abuse . . . well, it made me stop and think. And . . . the short version is, I've been an idiot and need to ask you to forgive me. I understand if you need to think about—"

James walked across the floor to his dad's chair, grasped his hands, and pulled him to his feet. Then wrapped him in a hug so tight his father gasped. James loosened his grip and fought to get words past the lump in his throat. "I've missed you, Dad. I know we haven't always seen eye to eye, and we've always argued more than talked, but I've still missed you. I love you and I forgive you. Please forgive me for giving up on us. For making choices out of spite. That was wrong and I've regretted it, even though it led to my current career, which I can also say is my calling. I'm just sorry for the way it all came about." The words tumbled from him, finally free after being locked inside him for so long.

Sobs shook his father's shoulders and his arms clung to James' waist. James looked up to see his mother swiping tears with her hand towel and Lainie had grabbed tissues from the end table.

Finally, his father pulled himself together and leaned back to clasp James' face in two hands. "You're a good man, Son. A godly man. The kind of man I prayed you'd grow up to be. The kind of man I want to be. And while I'm ashamed I haven't been that for you, I thank you for the reminder that I want to be one."

James flushed, his heart so full of peace that he thought he might explode from it. Instead, he patted his father on the back and nodded to his mother. Her face radiated her sheer joy, and James wanted to hold on to the moment forever.

Slender arms slipped around his waist and Lainie hugged him. "You did good," she whispered.

"All right, you two," his dad said, "I'm going to go wash my face. Will you stay and eat with us?"

"Of course."

Once he was gone and James' mom had returned to the kitchen, James kissed Lainie. He needed her like a drowning man needed a life raft. "Thank you," he said. "I don't know that this would have happened without you."

"I'm glad speaking my mind worked out this time."

He laughed. "Always speak your mind with me."

"Same."

"Thank you for never quitting. For always trying and never giving up. You inspire me."

"Well, not giving up definitely got me one thing I've wanted for a very long time."

James grinned. "Oh yes? What's that?"

"The Scrabble Champion title," she whispered.

He blinked, then threw his head back and laughed. "You're a brat, you know that?"

"What? You thought I was going to say you?"

"You know I did."

"Well . . ." She threaded her hands through his hair, then lifted her arms to lock them around his neck. "There's that too."

"I know things have happened fast, but I'm pretty sure I love you, Lainie," he whispered.

She smiled. "I'm pretty sure I love you too."

He hugged her to him and kissed her. When they came up for air, she sighed. "Are you sure you can handle my family's baggage?"

"If you can handle mine."

"I think you might be getting the short end of the stick on that, but it's a deal."

"Excellent. And now I have a surprise for you."

She raised a brow. "What's that?"

"Come on." He pulled her out the kitchen door and down into the backyard that led to the lake.

"James?"

"You'll see." He placed two fingers in his mouth and gave a piercing whistle.

"What in the world?"

Seconds later, two dogs with trailing leashes whipped around the side of the house. Lainie gasped. "Rex and Tex?" She gaped up at him, even as she dropped to her knees and held her arms out. "How did you know?"

"I have my ways."

The dogs leaped on her, and Lainie spent the next few minutes giving ear scratches and belly rubs.

"This is the perfect place for them," James said, "with a fence on three sides and water on the fourth."

"But . . ." She frowned. "I'm confused."

"I adopted them. For you. And me. I've also bought the lake house and plan to move out here permanently."

She gaped. "B-but what about your job?"

"I'll bunk with Cole when I need to, but this place is home to me, and Mom and Dad were ready to let it go. Steph, Dixon, and Keegan didn't have any objections, so . . ." He shrugged. "I bought it." He shot her a small smile. "The fact that Dad was willing to sell it to me said a whole lot about where he was in his journey to forgive me. And Mom can be very persuasive."

"You bought the lake house on Lake City Lake."

"I did."

"And you adopted my very favorite pups."

"I did."

"I'm not just pretty sure I love you. I think I absolutely adore you."

He kissed her again, thanking God for his protection, provision, and promises. Life might not always be easy, but with Lainie—and the two dogs trying to get in between them—it would never be boring.

Dear fabulous readers,

I do hope you've enjoyed the first book in the Lake City Heroes series. *Double Take* was an interesting story to write. It gave me fits and I almost pulled out every hair on my head in the process. The ones that are left have more gray than not, but in the end, thanks to amazing editors and beta readers, I absolutely love the story all over again and pray it will stay on your keeper shelf indefinitely.

I actually came up with the idea for this book about three years ago, but I could never figure out how I wanted it to go. Or how to get it to make sense on paper. But when it came time to submit another proposal to my publisher, I knew I wanted it to be the first book in the series. And even when I put it in the proposal, I still wasn't clear on how everything was going to work out—I just knew I'd make it work somehow. After a lot of brainstorming with buddies, writing, rewriting, cutting, and pasting, *Double Take* was born and has now landed in your hands. Thank you so much for reading it.

Just in case you're wondering what's next, I've got a little teaser for you. Next up is Cole and Kenzie's story in *Target Acquired*. As of the writing of this letter, I'm just over the halfway mark. I always get excited when I hit this point because the words just seem to flow from now to the end. I really think Cole and Kenzie's story will resonate with you.

Kenzie has grown up and been in competition with her three brothers all her life—and it was a pretty toxic environment for her.

Thanks to her maternal grandmother, she was left a home that she was able to move into and start renovating. Now serving on the SWAT team as a TAC medic, she's finally come into her own and has started to get to know who she is and what she wants from life. Cole has been burned by a previous romantic encounter and has no intention of dating the sister of one of his good friends—regardless of the fact that it worked out well for James and Lainie—and he's keeping his distance. But when someone comes after Kenzie, he's all in for helping keep her safe. And vice versa.

So this is just a teaser for what's to come. I hope you, like me, can't wait to see *Target Acquired* in print! In the meantime, if you'd like to keep up with news regarding my writing and new releases, feel free to head to my website and sign up for my newsletter, www.Lynette Eason.com. You can also find me on Facebook at www.Facebook.com/Lynette.Eason and Instagram @lynetteeason.

Thank you again for being such amazing readers. I appreciate you so much!

Lynette

Can't wait for the next
Lake City Heroes installment?

TURN THE PAGE
FOR AN EXCLUSIVE
SNEAK PEEK!

COMING SOON

ONE

SWAT medic Kenzie King grabbed the Remington 700BDL rifle and her medical kit, then aimed her steps toward Dolly, the TK-4 tactical vehicle. With Commander Judson Hill's quick briefing still playing in their heads, she and the other unit members moved with focused precision.

Outside, snowflakes dusted her and she blinked. Lake City, North Carolina, didn't see tons of the white stuff this early in the year, but the mid-October temps had dropped last night, and the weatherman's predictions had come true. Thankfully, it wasn't supposed to freeze, and the snow should be gone almost before it touched the ground. Next week would find the temperatures in the midsixties.

She'd only been on the job five months, so this was her first fall with SWAT, but she'd lived in Lake City long enough to learn the weather patterns—and the fact that they could be as unpredictable as her schedule. Or non-schedule, as the case was most of the time. Which was fine. Growing up in a military family that had moved twelve times the first eighteen years of her life, she was used to rolling with change. Didn't mean she liked it, but she could do it without thinking twice about it. It helped that the majority of their missions were planned right down to the very last detail as opposed to the hurry-up-and-save-lives missions like this one.

Kenzie climbed into the vehicle, and Sampson Greene eyed her with that flat look she could never read, then turned his gaze to his phone. No doubt checking to see if there were any new or developing details to the situation they were walking into. His K-9, a seventy-five-pound Belgian Malinois named Otis, settled at his feet even while his ears flicked back and forth, tension running through his sleek, well-muscled frame.

Buzz Crenshaw climbed behind the wheel while Sergeant Cowboy "Mac" McEntire—no one knew his given name—checked his weapon in the passenger seat. He shot her a glance when she dropped onto the bench that lined the vehicle's wall. "You good, King?" he asked her.

She bit her lip on her initial response, hating that snarky was her "go-to" these days. Cowboy was also the SWAT team leader when Cole Garrison wasn't there, and she knew he didn't mean anything by the question. And yet he hadn't asked any of the others if *they* were good. *"You catch more flies with honey, sweetheart. Remember that."* "I'm good." Her grandmother was right as usual. Kenzie was just getting worn down by all of the hazing that had been going on since she'd joined the unit. But that was her secret. No way would she let it show.

Kenzie shifted her medical kit out of the way of her feet and checked her weapon before sliding it into her holster. She might be the medic, but she'd been through all the training required to be a part of the SWAT team.

"All right, people," Buzz called out, "we're headed to West Hampton. Update just came in. Three hostages instead of two, still just one gunman. No known fatalities as of this moment. Garrison's meeting us there."

And just the mention of his name tightened her gut and slicked her palms with sweat. A reaction that made her want to bang her head against a wall because of the confusion it ignited. Instead, she clamped her hands together and ran through the plan once more. As the team medic, she'd wait in a safe zone and pray her services weren't needed. Nine times out of ten, the incident resolved peacefully, but there was always the chance this call would be the *one*.

Officer Scott Butler climbed in and slammed the door. His gaze met Kenzie's and his lip curled just before he took the seat next to her. She refused to cringe as his hip butted against hers, rationalizing that it was a tight fit and couldn't be helped. She just wished he didn't hate her simply because she was a woman on the team.

"Rolling!" Buzz cranked Dolly, pressed the gas, and spun the wheel.

Butler rolled with the sharp turn and slammed into her, shoving her against Greene, who shot her a hard look but shifted, creating a fraction more space for her. James Cross sat across from her and frowned, started to say something, then stopped when Kenzie narrowed her eyes at him, daring him to voice his thoughts.

Determined to ignore them all, she righted herself and refused to let Butler get to her. No one had come right out and said it, but she had a feeling he was jealous of her position and acting out his frustrations like a three-year-old. He'd get over it. Hopefully soon. *Please, God, soon.*

Of course, it didn't help that he had medical training and felt like he could do the job as medic just as well as—if not better than—she could.

He couldn't. She had MD after her name. He didn't. Which, she suspected, played into his need to prove something to his other teammates. Some ego thing.

Or it could be something entirely different. Who knew?

She was clueless and wasn't sure whether she should ask him or not. She just kept hoping that when he didn't get a response out of her, he'd eventually let it go.

Five months in and she was still hoping.

Her gear was hot despite the cold weather, and Dolly's air conditioning hadn't reached into the back yet, so sweat slid down the groove next to her spine.

"All right," Buzz said. "Get ready."

Finally, they rolled through the police barricade and to a stop at

303

the edge of the convenience store parking lot. Kenzie checked the pistol at her hip and grabbed her medical kit, maneuvering it to the middle of the vehicle where she could snap it open at a moment's notice.

The men stood behind the protection of the SWAT vehicle, and Cole—she only referred to him as Garrison in front of the unit— exited his 4Runner, dressed in his gear, to join them. Kenzie couldn't help but wonder where he'd been. Probably working one of the many cases he juggled in addition to his duties with SWAT.

And then it was time to focus. She listened as they ran through the plan once more if the negotiator on scene couldn't talk the armed man down.

Two gunshots sounded. Glass shattered. Screams from inside the store echoed. Kenzie jumped out of the vehicle, her feet hitting the asphalt as the men swarmed toward the store, each heading for their Area of Responsibility or AOR. Kenzie hung back, but positioned herself so she could watch everything go down, listening for calls for help. The comms in her ear spit information nonstop as the members stayed in touch, giving by-the-second updates.

Cole's orders came through, and she visualized their movements through the store.

"Stay safe," she whispered. "Please stay safe."

SERGEANT COLE GARRISON relished his role on SWAT when he wasn't working as a detective with the Lake City Police Department. And right now, he was trying to stop a shooter who seemed content to put bullets through windows and inventory before he escalated to people.

Cole and the team had entered through the back of the store in silence and stood next to the candy aisle, out of sight of the round mirror above the checkout counter ten yards ahead. A woman and young child huddled next to the freezer in the corner. Cole raised a finger to his lips in the universal sign for silence. The woman—probably the kid's mother—nodded and pulled the child closer.

If he waved them out the back door, the noise could cause the shooter to turn, and then they'd all be up the proverbial creek. They'd managed to stay out of sight of the worker, but if he took his eyes off the gun pointed at him, he might spot them. They needed to act before that happened.

The man with the weapon stood at the counter, his back to Cole and the team, gun held at arm's length on the quivering teen at the cash register. "I said get him out here! Tell him to come face me like a man!"

"I tried, Kev! You heard me. He won't come out of the office!"

The shooter and the worker knew each other. Good. Maybe. Especially if they were friends once upon a time. Might make it less easy to shoot the worker.

"He fired me and he won't even face me?" Kev scoffed. "Typical. What a coward!" He paused and rubbed his free hand down his face while the hand with the gun never wavered. Then he gave his head a slight shake and flicked the weapon toward the exit. "You've always been nice to me. I got no beef with you. Get out of here."

The teen behind the counter darted around the side and bolted toward the door that led to the parking lot.

James had his weapon up and ready to fire. He nodded to Cole that he had a shot, but Cole balled his fist and held it up— the signal for everyone to freeze. If the shooter was going to let people go, he wasn't going to interfere with the process. "Let's see how this is going to play out," he said, his voice one decibel above silent.

Greene signaled Otis to the floor. The dog lay on his stomach, but was ready to spring with the force of a catapult should the moment come. He kept his eyes on his handler while his ears twitched.

The guy with the gun aimed himself and his weapon toward the office. "Leo! You're dead, man! Stacy left me and it's all your fault!"

Cole signaled Greene, who gestured to Otis.

The dog launched toward the suspect. The guy turned just as Otis clamped his jaws around the forearm attached to the hand holding the weapon.

A scream ripped from Kev's throat, and he pivoted, weapon still clutched in his hand, barrel aimed at the team.

"Everyone down!" Cole's shout echoed as the weapon barked and the team dropped.

Sampson slammed the shooter to the ground with a command for Otis to release. Within seconds, he had the man in cuffs. "Clear!"

As one, the unit rose to their feet and moved in—all except Cowboy. He lay on the tile, gloved hand clutching his cheek while blood flowed between his fingers.

"Cowboy!" Cole darted to his teammate, hand reaching for his radio. "Kenzie, get in here! Officer down!"

Almost before he'd finished the order, she was through the door and at Cowboy's side. "Cowboy, let me see it," she said, her voice low, calm, the eye in the middle of the storm.

Even Cole thought his blood pressure might have lowered a fraction. He nodded when she gently tugged Cowboy's hand from his face.

"How bad is it?" The man's voice sounded like he had gravel in his throat.

"Well, you're conscious, so that's a good sign."

Cole glanced at the others, who'd cleared the rest of the store. The suspect had already been led outside where he would enjoy the view from the back seat of a patrol car. The manager stepped out of the back with Butler at his side. Had to be the man named Leo. "He was going to kill me! You heard him, right? You're going to put him away for life, right?"

"The justice system will take care of him," Butler said. He rolled his eyes at Cole.

Cole frowned. The manager had just lived through a pretty terrifying ordeal. Granted, some might consider him a coward, but not everyone reacted well when they were afraid. He could have compassion for the guy. He stepped forward and placed a hand on

Leo's shoulder. "Take some time to regroup, all right? See a counselor if you need to. Even though it ended without anyone seriously hurt"—including Cowboy, he prayed—"it's going to have a lasting effect on you."

Leo met his gaze and nodded. "Right. You're right. Thank you. I . . ." He swallowed. "I'm sorry I wasn't more brave, I just . . . I didn't know how or what— I knew he hated me because I fired him, but he was late all the time, didn't show up and never called to let me know, and I just— Never mind." He dropped his chin to his chest and headed out the door.

"Coward," Butler muttered.

"Hey, he was scared. You and I wouldn't have reacted that way, but we've had training. Don't judge him."

Butler raised a brow. "Whatever you say, Sarge." He trotted away and Cole shook his head. The guy was young, true, but he had a hardness about him that Cole didn't much care for. Only the fact that he did his job and did it well allowed Cole to let some things slide.

He hurried to find Kenzie and Cowboy and spotted them still on the floor, although Cowboy was sitting up, leaning against a display of chips. Kenzie had her back to Cole and was working around Cowboy's head.

"How is he?" Cole asked.

She glanced up at him, her brow furrowed. "It's just a graze, but I think he should be monitored for a concussion. He was out for a few seconds. If I was his doctor, I'd order a CT scan and keep him overnight."

"Shouldn't have told you I lost consciousness for a fraction of a second," Cowboy said. "I'm fine."

"Ambulance is outside," Cole said. "Go get checked out."

"Aw, man, I—"

"That's an order."

Cowboy snapped his lips shut and nodded. Then winced.

"You'd make me do the same if the roles were reversed," Cole said, his voice softer.

"No I wouldn't. I'd never treat you like that." The whine in his voice was unmistakable, and Cole smothered a laugh.

"Liar. Get out of here. You're done until the doctor releases you." He helped the man to his feet and noticed he swayed before catching his balance.

"Dizzy?" Kenzie asked.

"Uh, yeah, maybe. A little."

She stepped up and gripped his arm. Cole caught the look she shot him and nodded. They weren't going to let him walk out under his own power without some assistance.

Once Cowboy was safely in the ambulance with two paramedics hovering over him, Cole looked at Kenzie. Beautiful Kenzie King who took his breath away and pulled all his protective instincts to the surface. Instincts he had to stuff down into the deepest corners of his heart. "Good work."

She flashed him a tight smile. "Thanks. I just gotta grab my stuff, then I'll be ready to roll."

She hurried back inside the store, and Cole turned to find James watching him. James Cross, his best friend and partner. A man who knew him better than just about anyone. "What?"

"Didn't say anything."

"Didn't have to. What are you thinking?"

"What do you think I'm thinking?"

Cole scowled. "I don't know, but you're wrong."

"If you don't know what I'm thinking, how do you know I'm wrong?"

"Shut up."

James' low chuckles followed him all the way to Dolly.

ACKNOWLEDGMENTS

BIG THANKS to Jennifer Huggins, ANP-BC, who gave me lots of information on how hospitals track keystrokes on computers. Who knew?? So, if I got anything wrong there, it's all my fault, not hers! Thank you tons, Jennifer, I really appreciate the time you took to write me that LONG email. ☺

Thank you to Dr. Jan Kneeland for ALWAYS being just a text away with fabulous medical advice and expertise on how to take care of gunshot wounds, ruptured appendices, strep throat, or just plain old what meds can knock someone out really fast so they can be kidnapped! You're amazing, and I thank God for putting you in my life so we can share the gift of laughter whenever we're together.

Thank you, Barb Barnes, my incredibly detail-oriented editor, for still working on my stories even though you're retired and taking care of grandbabies! Don't stop now!

Thank you to Tamela Hancock Murray for being the best agent EVER. I love you, my friend, and appreciate you to infinity and beyond. ☺

Thank you to all my readers. I really can't say thank you enough for those of you who love the stories and purchase the books, allowing me to do what I love.

Thank you to Jesus, my Lord and Savior. "Thank you" never seems to be enough, but you know my heart. Thank you for loving me anyway and blessing me beyond anything I could ever hope to deserve.

Thank you to my amazing family. I love you more than chocolate.

Lynette Eason is the *USA Today* bestselling author of *Life Flight*, *Crossfire*, and *Critical Threat*, as well as the Danger Never Sleeps, Blue Justice, Women of Justice, Deadly Reunions, Hidden Identity, and Elite Guardians series. She is the winner of three ACFW Carol Awards, the Selah Award, and the Inspirational Reader's Choice Award, among others. She is a graduate of the University of South Carolina and has a master's degree in education from Converse College. Eason lives in South Carolina with her husband. They have two adult children. Learn more at www.LynetteEason.com.

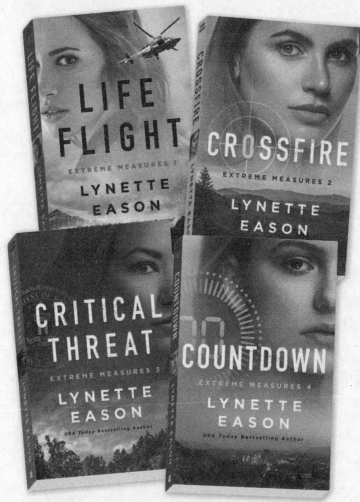

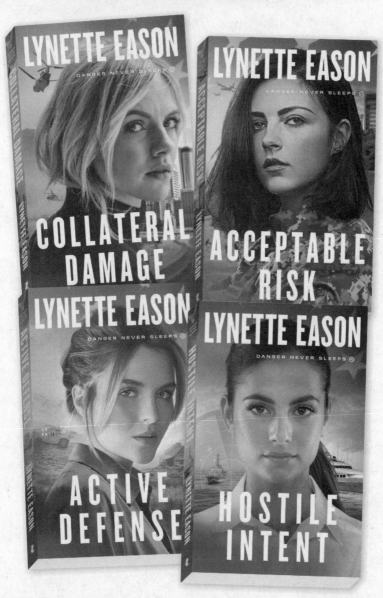